DATING GAMES

"Des, I feel like such an idiot. He has a girlfriend."

"Who?"

Kahlila gave a vigorous chin nod toward Darius's booth and Desiree half stood up to get a better look. "Figures. They love to date those model chicks," Desiree said matter-of-factly. "It's probably not serious. They'll be broken up in a few weeks."

Kahlila stared at the exotic beauty now sitting in Darius's lap, successfully taking his mind off the stresses of the day. Even if Desiree were right, Kahlila knew that she'd been crazy to think that she had a chance with him.

Kahlila reached inside her purse to reapply her lip gloss and saw that the screen of her cell phone was lit up. She flipped open the phone and felt her heart beat faster at the sight of a text message from a New York number that she didn't recognize: I'm going to keep you to that promise. Will call you tomorrow to hear your feedback on the album. Something tells me to trust your opinion. —D

She smiled and returned the cell to her bag. This time, when she looked over at Darius, he was grinning back at her. *Game back on.*

Books by Rachel Skerritt

NO MORE LIES

WHEN THE LIGHTS GO DOWN

Published by Kensington Publishing Corporation

WHEN THE LIGHTS GO DOWN

Rachel Skerritt

Kensington Publishing Corp.

http://www.kensingtonbooks.com

Acknowledgments

Thank you to my friends and family who have gone above and beyond to support me in my efforts as a full-time writer at heart, but part-time writer by trade. From selling *No More Lies* at the beauty salon, to e-mailing everyone you know to pick up the book, to simply reading the novel and giving me valuable feedback, I counted on you to be my promoters, and you did not disappoint. Well, some of you were actually quite disappointing, but you have a chance to redeem yourself now that *When the Lights Go Down* is on the shelves!

I couldn't have written a book about the entertainment industry without the help of several folks who answered my endless questions about music, models, and managers. I'm especially grateful to John Legend and Hassan Smith for making sure my imagination synched with what was plausible.

Much appreciation to my agent, Claudia Menza, and my editor, John Scognamiglio. Thank you for believing in me as a writer and trusting me to get this book finished even as I took on the leadership of a high school. Your input was critical.

Lastly, to the readers who contacted me with comments about my previous novels, those e-mails kept me going whenever I wanted to throw my laptop across the room. Check out my Web site, www.rachelskerritt.com, and keep those messages coming!

Chapter 1

*He must be sensitive enough
to handle my mood swings.*

Contentment for Bree Roberts was lounging on Keith's living room futon with a remote control in her left hand and an oversized spoon in her right. The large bowl of Cinnamon Toast Crunch resting in her lap felt cool against her bare legs. Wearing an oversized Celtics T-shirt and fuzzy slippers that were way too wintry for a weekend in June, she settled into her Saturday late morning routine. Last night, she and Keith had rented movies and eaten a meal that he'd spent an hour preparing. "You should be the one making this food!" he'd teased as he stirred a pot of greens.

"You're older. It's your job to see that I'm fed," she had tossed back. Now, as the sun spilled onto the hard-wood floor, she smiled, remembering their exchange. Smiles were rare for Bree, and happy moments such as this one were few and far between.

At seventeen years old, Bree was an old soul. She rarely

had friends her own age, preferring the company of those students in the grades above her, or of people who were done with school altogether. Even her hobbies were old: sitting in a rocking chair with a book, taking long walks. Her singular youthful activity was watching reality shows about kids her age who lived lives beyond what she had ever known. Laguna Beach was a far cry from New Haven, where she spent most of her life, and from Roxbury, the gritty section of Boston where she'd lived for the past year. It wasn't the wealth of the golden-haired, bikini-clad teenagers that fascinated her. It was the way they took their ease for granted. Their lack of tragedy wasn't a blessing to them. It was a given, like the first step of a proof in geometry class. Tragedy in their world was failing to find the perfect dress for winter formal. Bree's life, on the other hand, was no fairy tale, and the best way she'd found to forget her sorrow was to live someone else's fantasy through Keith's flat-screen TV.

She reached MTV in search of a show about a rich girl's sweet sixteen party, but instead found a repeat of *Total Request Live*. She sucked her teeth in true teenaged fashion, ready to flip to Lifetime television for women, when she saw that Vanessa Manillo was interviewing her favorite singer. Darius Wilson had released an R&B album last year that was a huge hit with a lot of girls her age. The mix of dance tunes and sappy ballads combined to make his debut CD a top seller, and generated comparisons to artists such as Usher and Genuwine. The fact that he was so mainstream would usually have turned her off completely. She hated following the crowd in deciding who was hot (or cool) in popular culture. Though his entire physical package was more than pleasant to look at, there was something about his smile that made her feel like she knew him. Whenever she saw him smiling at her from the cover of his record, or from the stage of a televised performance, she couldn't help but smile back.

Though the volume was up, Bree didn't bother paying attention to the words of the interview. Instead, she observed the easiness with which he sat, slightly slouched back on the edge of the stage, as if there were something supporting his back. A boulder of invisible confidence. She wondered how old he was, and then wondered if he would think she was pretty. He was older, yes, but she liked older guys. They didn't mind that she wasn't perky and bubbly like the other girls at school.

Finally tuning her ears into the conversation, she learned that Darius was premiering a song from a new movie that was coming out next week, starring actors she didn't really respect. In another lifetime, which was really just thirteen months ago, Bree had been an actress. She did community theater (which she always felt to be an inaccurate name, since she had to drive forty-five minutes to get there), and revitalized the drama department at her own urban high school. Since she left Connecticut, she'd stopped acting onstage, but continued her craft in her day-to-day interactions, where she tried to play off her lack of affect as nonchalance. In reality, she was simply numb.

Her eyes were glued to the TV as the video began. In the opening scene, a beautiful woman paints on an easel in her apartment, wearing a man's dress shirt and nothing else. The action moves to Darius on a motorcycle wearing only a pair of jeans, and the woman is clinging to his waist. A car comes out of nowhere. Suddenly she is being wheeled to the hospital, her life hanging in the balance. The chorus swells just as Darius walks into the empty apartment, staring at the unfinished painting. "*If you don't make it through, my heart will die with you.*" Cheesy words. Even in Bree's growing despair, she could recog-

nize that. But the empty room. The sight of it struck a
chord underneath her ribs. Sobs began to shake her
body before she knew what was happening. Milk from
her bowl of cereal ran down her legs as she struggled to
gain control of the bowl and of her emotions, unsuccess-
ful on both counts.

Keith walked into the living room, holding a bagel
and butter on a saucer, wearing shorts and no shirt, the
complement to Bree's Saturday uniform. He had no visible reaction to her hysterical crying. Walking closer and
staring her straight in the eye, he said in an even voice,
"You know I love you, right?" She nodded through her
tears, as Keith took the now soggy cereal from her lap
and brought it into the kitchen. She wondered whether
he really wanted to do these small things for her, or if he
felt that he had to because of everything they'd been
through together. Bree didn't want someone to love her
out of guilt. But she didn't have the guts to have that
conversation. So she sank farther into the couch and
let her mind travel to places where people didn't hurt,
instead spending endless hours finding the perfect dress
to match their eyes.

Chapter 2

He cannot be condescending.

By the time they actually sat down to dinner, Kahlila Bradford's date had a cumulative score of negative one. They'd met one week before at a "Friendly Takeover" in downtown Boston. Friendly Takeovers were events organized by a group of black professionals who sent out e-mails telling other black professionals where to go for an after-work cocktail. Since the upwardly mobile set of color really had no establishment to call its own, promoters would choose various restaurants and bars to patronize as a group. Large numbers of brown-skinned, impeccably dressed individuals would come for Happy Hour and watch amusedly as the regular patrons stared at them, confused. Had they missed the memo? Had the bar changed to a hip-hop club without notice?

Friday evening of the previous week, Kahlila had attended one of these gatherings with her closest friend, Robyn. As soon as they got there, they began to wonder why they had even bothered. The women, as usual, outnumbered the men about four to one. And the guys were the same guys who were always there. Kahlila either knew someone who dated them in the past, dated them already herself, or knew from prior meetings that she would never want to date them . . . ever. Robyn, meanwhile, was in a long-distance, long-term relationship, and only came for the potential of interesting conversation and a couple of laughs. But Boston wasn't one of those places where a stranger might approach you, buy you a drink, and make small talk. The people were cold, like the weather, and the black men were such a hot commodity that they expected to be approached and pursued. Meanwhile, all of the women felt as if they were in competition with one another; therefore, they *never* spoke to other women they didn't know. So the night became what most of these nights ended up being: Kahli and Robyn sitting and talking to each other, something they could have done just as easily in the comfort of their own homes.

About forty-five minutes into their conversation, a tall, well-built man in his late twenties walked up to them and introduced himself. His name was Derek Anderson, and he had just moved from the D.C. area to Cambridge to begin business school at Harvard in the fall. Robyn and Kahlila exchanged high fives with their eyes. "New imports," as they termed them, were the best prospects for viable romantic relationships in Boston. They hadn't yet had an opportunity to become part of the incestuous circle of like-minded twenty- and thirty-somethings in the city. To put it bluntly, they were fresh meat.

Kahlila wasn't proud of the fact that she'd reached the point where meeting the right man was such an urgent priority. Everything else in her life came so easily: she enjoyed her job, she adored her friends, she loved her family. The only missing piece was a romantic relationship. Finding peace in that department had always been a struggle. Her twenties had thus far been a series of missteps and fumbles. Now, at twenty-eight, as she spent hundreds of dollars each year attending other people's weddings (usually by herself), she had admittedly become a bit obsessed with putting an end to her single status. She wasn't in a hurry to get married. But she was definitely in a rush to end that excited feeling in her stomach every time she met a new potential suitor, only to be disappointed down the line when he turned out to be married, unemployed, elitist, corny, too serious, a player, a liar, or simply boring.

So Kahlila couldn't control the nervousness in her belly as Derek, whom she already knew in the back of her mind would turn out to be a disappointment, stood before her. Early on in the conversation, Robyn had managed to insert some random fact about her boyfriend, Lloyd, so that Derek could freely focus on Kahlila. Robyn was a great wing woman that way, as she was totally content with her man, but still loved to go out and meet new people. A lot of Kahli's other friends in relationships seemed surgically attached to their sofas, never feeling the urge to leave the company of their significant others.

"Kahli and I were college roommates. We have to be best friends, because we know all of each other's secrets," Robyn said with a sly smile.

"Oh, I see," replied Derek with a smirk. "So you're too invested to be enemies."

Kahlila liked him immediately. A witty response, a great bio, and a handsome face.

"Where did you two go to college?" Derek asked, setting his Grey Goose and tonic on the bar and leaning against it, clearly getting comfortable.

"Franklin University," said Kahlila, noting the mother-of-pearl cuff link in the sleeve of his crisp white shirt.

"Great school. I went to Yale." Another eye high five between Kahlila and Robyn. "Hey, do folks in Boston ever have events just for the people of color who went to schools like ours? Like a black Ivy kind of thing?"

Strike one for Derek. "I think the black professional community is small enough without breaking it down further by the type of college we went to, don't you?" Kahlila tried her best not to sound critical, and her best wasn't very good at all.

"It's your city. You would know better than me."

Better than I. Kahlila resisted the urge to correct his grammar. She knew that was an awful habit of hers, noticing the most minute slips of language. Her friends always joked that Kahlila's biggest turn-on was a mastery of pronouns. A consequence of her job as an English teacher.

"So, Cali . . . your name suggests that you have roots in California or something. That's a pretty bad joke, I know, but I'm not quite ready for this conversation to be over."

Derek is back in the game. Men in Boston never admitted to actually being interested, even after you'd been dating them for months. This guy was definitely refreshing in his honesty. "No, it's spelled K-A-H-L-I. It's short for Kahlila. I was named after the poet Kahlil Gibran. Heard of him?"

"Can't say that I have. I'm not much of a reader."

Strike two.

Robyn could tell that it was already happening: Kahlila was finding fault in a perfectly good man. For the past several years, Kahlila had been compiling a list of qualities that were absolute necessities in a partner. With every first-date disappointment, second-date letdown, and tragically failed relationship, she added more requirements. She had never shared the actual written content with anyone (it remained stored on her laptop in a Word document innocuously titled The List), but some of the traits would come up in conversation: spiritual but not too churchy, intelligent but not condescending, confident but not pompous, tall but not too tall, lean but not too skinny, politically conscious but not militant. At last count, The List was in the hundreds.

Kahlila felt a swift kick under the table, and she knew that her friend was warning her not to jump to a negative conclusion. "That's cool," she cheerily responded.

Derek glanced at his watch. It was a Movado, and Kahlila was starting to get the feeling that he was a bit flashy for her taste. Her preference was for men to be stylish, but not showy. She tried to rein in her judgment, but halting her thoughts was a lot more difficult than biting her tongue. "I actually need to get going. Kahli, do you have a card so we can be in touch?"

"High school teachers don't have business cards," she said with a laugh.

Derek smiled good-naturedly, and his absolutely flawless rows of teeth earned him a few extra points. Removing his Palm Pilot from the suit jacket slung over his arm, he took her phone number as Robyn looked on excitedly. He walked away and headed out the door, and Kahlila turned to face her friend for the debriefing, catching the evil stares of a few random women as she turned. She felt their eyes piercing her exterior, assessing why this new man on the scene chose to get *her* number and not theirs. They couldn't say that Kahlila wasn't pretty. Her flawless skin looked as if she bathed in bronzer, and people often could not believe that she didn't wear some type of makeup to achieve her natural glow. Her shiny black hair was gathered at the nape of her neck, and her outfit consisted of a barely there tank top, designer jeans, and sequined ballet slippers. She had a funky blazer resting on her lap, just in case the air-conditioning was on too high. Bostonians tended to fight early June humidity by blasting cold air into public establishments with reckless abandon.

If women were evaluating Kahlila beyond the physical, they might mention, if they'd heard of her through the grapevine, that she'd dated many of the "desirables" in the city. However, most of them never even got a second date. The few who made it past the initial round of "screening" had since moved out of Boston, leaving no evidence of her minor indiscretions. Therefore, she was still technically considered "untouched," as opposed to being used goods. Kahlila wasn't at all bothered by the dirty looks she was receiving; she knew that she would have been feeling the same resentment had Derek gotten some other woman's number this evening.

She leaned in closer to Robyn, so no one could read her lips. "He came by himself. That's pretty bold."

"Kahli, stop tallying up his score and just hope that his fine ass calls you."

Derek did call, three days later (the average waiting time after acquiring a phone number), politely asking about her weekend and suggesting that they get together the following Saturday. Since he was new to the city, she didn't hold it against him that he asked her to choose the restaurant. It was easier to fault him for having no car. Kahlila hated being the chauffeur on dates. How was a woman supposed to feel like she was being taken out when she had to do the picking up, navigating, and dropping off? Still, Kahlila was still somewhat excited as she drove to Cambridge on Friday evening. Usually, by the time she embarked on a first outing with a guy, she'd already written him off completely. Either he'd monopolized their phone conversations, or his e-mail messages had too many spelling errors. But this evening, she was still feeling hopeful. As she drove down a surprisingly uncongested Mass Avenue, playing Corinne Bailey Rae's CD at full volume, she thought that this moment, before he even got in the car, was the most promising part of a date. Everything was still possible.

She called him once she pulled up to his apartment, and it took him a full six minutes to come outside. Maybe it was the fact that her job was guided by a series of bells that rang every forty-five minutes, but Kahlila was a stickler about time. When he got in the car, he didn't even apologize for keeping her waiting. But he looked fantastic, wearing a faintly striped button-up shirt and a well-creased pair of jeans. He'd gotten a haircut since she met him the week before, and the almost bald look was working well for him. She assessed all of this in one brisk glance before she pulled off from the curb and drove into Harvard Square. They lucked out with parking and she couldn't help but think that it was a good omen.

But as soon as they stepped outside, it began to drizzle. Foreshadowing? It was difficult for her literary mind to think otherwise. "Damn. I forgot my umbrella," she mumbled as she tried to walk as briskly as possible in her pointy-toed mules.

"Why are you running?" Derek asked with a smile. "It's not like your hair is going to get all messed up. I mean, it's naturally curly, right?"

"Yeah, but sitting at dinner in wet clothes doesn't sound like much fun."

Ignoring her comment, he kept staring at her hair. "I

noticed that about you right away last week. How did
you get hair like that?"

"My dad is half Indian."

"Really? What tribe?"

"Not Native American. South Asian." She would have
added "Dot, not feathers," as a politically incorrect joke,
had she not been so frustrated by his line of questioning.

"That explains it. I love exotic-looking women," he
said, looking at her like she was a glistening piece of
fried chicken.

Kahlila willed herself to continue walking toward
Border Café. She hated men who searched for the non-
black aspects of black women (number 117 on The List:
he can't say ignorant things like "good hair"). She often
attracted those types, as her copper skin and jet-black
curls served as a calling card. Any points that Derek had
earned up to then were revoked, and he was now in the
danger zone as they sat down to dinner.

Derek took control of the questions as soon as the
chips and salsa arrived at the table. *At least he's not mo-
nopolizing the conversation.* "Tell me about your family,"
he said, brushing his hand against hers as they both
dipped at the same time.

Kahlila detested broad inquiries such as that one, but
she acquiesced. "Only child, raised by my mom. I see my
dad every once in a while. He lives in England. My
mother recently got married, and she and her husband
moved to Trinidad. So I'm on my own in Boston."

"What's keeping you in this town, then? From our
phone conversation, it didn't sound like you're a huge
fan of the place."

Kahlila had to admit that this was a good question.

She asked herself the same one all the time. "I think it's my job. I absolutely love it."

He smiled knowingly from across the table. "I know why you love it. Because all those high school boys have crushes on you, don't they?"

Now he's gone and done it. He has busted out the most over-used line ever by men on dates with teachers. "Actually, my students take me very seriously."

"So you're a tough cookie, huh?"

"I'm tough, but I'm fun. I adore those kids. They're my whole life." If she had thought a little more before she answered, she would not have admitted that her students were so important to her. She thought it made her sound a little bit pathetic. But she was being honest, partially due to the tequila in her drink, and partially because she thought she might actually like this guy.

"So you went to Franklin, right? You got your master's there as well?"

Kahlila nodded as she took a big gulp of her frozen mango margarita.

"What was your GPA?"

Is he serious? "Why do you ask?"

"Well, I'm guessing you might have struggled in school, why you chose to go into education."

"Excuse me?"

"Obviously if you were going to Franklin and you were kicking ass academically, there would have been so many other doors open to you—law, business—"

"I *wanted* to teach." She felt her eyes narrowing.

"Sure, fine. Why not do it for a couple years? Give something back to the community and all that. But you graduated school in what, '99? What's next for you?"

Kahlila felt the heat starting to rise in her chest, and it wasn't the mango-rita. "I'm happy where I am."

"Hey, not a problem. I just see women in the b-school,

and you are as savvy and articulate as they are. Why not compete?"

Kahlila hadn't even ordered her entrée yet, but suddenly her appetite was gone. She thought back to her time alone in the car, when the date still held so much promise. *I would have been better off if at that precise moment, I made a U-turn on Mass Ave. and went the hell home.*

Chapter 3

He must be extremely successful
in whatever field he is pursuing.

Darius Wilson stood on the soft leather of the VIP booth, pumping his fist in the air to a Junior Mafia classic. He shook his head to himself with a smile, in disbelief that the song was already ten years old. Though he was knocking on the door of his thirtieth birthday, he could still remember the first time he danced to the song at a college party. The smirk on his face was also due to his memory of the guilt he used to feel for putting his feet on couches where people sat. That was two years ago, when he had first started spending late nights in roped-off sections of clubs with people he used to watch on television. His mentor and one of the hottest rapper/producers in the industry, Flow Steddie, had thrown his head back and laughed when Darius asked if they should be standing on people's furniture. "Do you know how much money we're making this place just by being here?" Flow had asked him that night. At that point, Darius still couldn't grasp the concept of his being a product, an image that could be sold in a variety of contexts. But today, he got it. And as he reached for the hand of a girl in stilettos eager to dance beside him, he couldn't care less that her heels might dent the leather.

The ladies looked great and a music master worked the turntables, but Darius couldn't help but pull out his Treo and review what he had on his schedule for tomorrow. Realizing that there was nothing on the agenda, he was able to fully concentrate on the sights and sounds around him. It was strange to have such a large amount of free time stretching in front of him. His album had dropped eleven months before, and he hadn't had a vacation since. Between tour dates, promotional events, press interviews, video shoots, business meetings, and doing guest spots on other people's records, there wasn't a spare moment to exhale. And Darius was fine with holding his breath. Finally, things were slowing down. Flow Steddie was in L.A. working on albums for other artists, and Darius had completed the international and national end of his tour. Aside from a couple of award shows and benefits this summer, he was off until August, when everyone would get back into the studio to work on his sophomore project. He had many concerns about the follow-up to his hit debut, but he resolved not to think about them until Flow returned from touring overseas. His doubts about the future of his music career were also put on the back burner when he visited the set of *Total Request Live* the previous day and got such a strong reaction from his fans. For his next album, there were a lot of changes he needed to make, but he couldn't forget how lucky he was to even have that opportunity.

The deejay's voice penetrated his thoughts: "Big shout to Darius Wilson in the building tonight." All the females around him gave a collective "Wooo!" and suddenly his breakout song, "Party Till You See the Sun," came through the speakers. Darius smiled good-naturedly and eased his way into a seated position, as he was never quite comfortable dancing to his own music. The high-heeled girl who had been standing next to Darius immediately crawled down to his level and asked to take a picture with him. "Sure," he responded, not quite sure where she was going to get a camera. But before he knew it, she was wrapped around his torso and he was being temporarily blinded by an aggressive flashbulb. "Thank you!" she squealed, and went off with her friend to examine the photo. *Guess that's all she wanted.* It was funny to him that most girls were satisfied with just a picture, as if all they needed in life was evidence that they once stood next to him at a club.

Suddenly he felt like he needed another drink. Darius looked at the small square table in front of the booth, complete with humongous bottles of Grey Goose and carafes of cranberry and orange juices. He tried not to laugh at the timid women who had just made their way inside his circle, unsure whether they should partake of the drinks. "Go ahead," he called to them. *It's not like I paid for it.* The girls looked at him gratefully before concocting their beverage. Again, Darius thought back to the days when he first started hanging with industry folks. Suddenly he was spending way less money when he went out than when he had worked on Wall Street. Promoters went out of their way to make celebrities and models comfortable in their establishments, because it made the spot *that* much hotter. Clubs and lounges were a dime a dozen in New York, and the only way to distinguish one from the other was the clientele.

Though there were about ten bodies between him and his bodyguard, Darius had no problem locating him in the crowd. Standing six-five and weighing almost

three hundred pounds, Rasheed always stood at least a
head taller than everyone else. His primary duty in social
situations such as this one was crowd control. This trans-
lated into screening the women who tried to get near
Darius. Though he couldn't see the person to whom
Rasheed was speaking at the moment, he could tell it was
a woman. Rasheed was wearing his charmer's smile,
bending his head down lower so he could hear her over
the music. He then stepped back and made a path for
her as she entered the inner circle. Darius didn't lay eyes
on the woman until she was standing directly in front of
him. He immediately understood why Darius let her
though. Her face was gorgeous, and her body boasted a
tiny waist, flat stomach, and thick thighs. Something
about her looked familiar to him, but studying her for a
moment longer, he decided that she simply looked like
a younger Nia Long, which was all right with him. She
stood almost expectantly before him, her eyes eager.

"How ya doin'?" he asked, holding out his hand.

"I'm doing well," she answered, taking his hand and
pulling him out of his seat.

Darius had only intended her to shake her hand, but
he appreciated being taken by surprise. Suddenly he was
standing eye to eye with her. She was tall before she even
put on her high heels, and he was just average height for
a guy. "I'm Yvonne."

"It's nice to meet you, Yvonne." He always repeated
girls' names when they introduced themselves. It helped
the name stick in his head, and women always seemed to
enjoy the sound of their names rolling off his tongue.
However, she looked somewhat disappointed when he
said hers, which made him think he might have mispro-
nounced it. "You did say Yvonne, right?"

"Oh. Yeah, I did," she said quickly, snapping on a daz-
zling smile. "Hey, I really like your new song."

He was tempted to tell her that his "new song" was a throwaway track that he was all too happy to give to the producer of the new young black Hollywood flick. "Thanks. What do you like about it?" He often asked this as a follow-up question to assess whether girls even knew his music, and whether they could engage in an actual conversation.

"The words were really touching. And you did a really nice job acting in the video. Maybe *you* should've been in the movie!"

He laughed. Though he personally thought the song was cheesy, her answer was sweet. She continued. "It's good timing for you to release a new song. You know, between albums. Just to stay fresh in people's minds."

Now he was impressed. She'd hit the exact reason that he agreed to sell the song in the first place. The insight of her comment made him look her up and down another time. She looked even better during this assessment, as he took in her designer denim miniskirt, silver sandals, and perfectly painted bright red toenails. "Hey, do you want to grab lunch tomorrow?" He surprised himself by his own words.

"I'm actually only in town tonight. I don't live in New York."

Darius felt himself being disappointed, and was again surprised.

"But what are you doing after this?" she asked, looking him directly in his eyes.

Darius looked at his watch. It was already 2:30 a.m. "I was planning on going to sleep. But I can put that off."

"So, how much longer do we have to stay here?" She looked around impatiently.

Darius was shocked by her boldness. Maybe she thought that she had to act this way because he was famous. But R&B singers didn't live like rappers. Or at least *he* didn't. While he met girls in clubs all the time, he never expected to take them home that night. He'd usually get their phone numbers and follow up with them at a later date. But at the same time, he wasn't mad at Yvonne's approach. "We can leave right now," he replied, touching her waist lightly. Right on cue, Rasheed looked over and caught his eye. Darius gave him a head nod, and suddenly a path was being cleared for Darius and Yvonne to make their way out of the corner booth they'd occupied. He didn't even say good-bye to his manager, Lamont, who was partying with some of his friends at the booth right next to theirs. But he knew that Lamont would understand:

The night air was still warm as they reached the sidewalk. Rasheed motioned to a parked car and it quickly started its engine and pulled up in front of them. Rasheed got in the front seat, and Darius and Yvonne slid into the back. Darius noticed that she sat looking out of the window instead of getting cozy with him. *Yeah, she's definitely never done this before.* Harry, their driver, asked Rasheed where they were going. Darius couldn't hear his answer, but he figured that his boy knew better than to go back to Darius's apartment.

"So, you're headed back to Chicago tomorrow, Yvonne?" Rasheed asked over his massive shoulder as he typed into his Treo.

"Yup. I was just here on business, and now my work is done." Darius was embarrassed that Rasheed knew Yvonne's hometown, when he hadn't even thought to ask. He also realized that he had no idea what her job actually was. It seemed too late to inquire about it now.

Harry pulled up in front of the Hotel Gansevoort. "I'm gonna park and rest in the lobby, if that's okay with you guys." Harry was always their driver when they used a car service in New York, and he'd seen a lot of interesting endings to various evenings. He, Rasheed, and Darius would often talk football and women when the three of them rode to events, but in mixed company, Harry was always the consummate professional.

When they entered the lobby, Rasheed went to the concierge and returned with a key card. "I called ahead. Room 714." He, Darius, and Yvonne left Harry sprawled on a love seat in the lobby and boarded the elevator. Yvonne was still quiet. Darius guessed that she probably felt awkward walking to a hotel room with two guys. He wanted to assure her that Rasheed wasn't going into the room with them, but he didn't know how to phrase that sentence. The evening was becoming more and more awkward.

The elevator opened on the seventh floor and Rasheed led the way down the hall. When they reached the door of their suite, Darius opened it and motioned for Yvonne to enter. "I'll be there in a second," he said. She nodded and closed the door behind her.

"Good look on the hotel," Darius said softly.

"Yo, what's the deal, though? Are y'all gonna be here all night? If you are, I'll have Harry take me home and you can call the service in the morning.'"

Darius hesitated. "I'm not sure. Shit, you know I don't do this every day. And she seems really nervous. Just hang for a minute. I'll text you with an answer."

"Don't have me waiting out here forever, dawg."

"Chill."

Darius opened the door to find Yvonne sitting in a chair by the window of the suite. *Still has her shoes on. Not even sitting on the bed. Both bad signs.*

He walked over to her, taking her hand and pulling her out of the seat. Again they stood eye to eye, this time wrapped in silence. He gently put his hand on her waist, finding a strip of skin between her tank top and her skirt.

Just as he was about to bring her closer to him, he felt a sharp sting on his cheek. After he stepped back, it took a full five seconds to realize that she had just slapped him across the face.

"I can't believe you don't remember me."

"What the hell are you talking about?" Darius asked, stepping back farther, his hand still on his cheek.

"Bahamas. Last August." She glared at him, daring him not to recall.

All at once, he *did* recall. His album had just dropped a few weeks before, and he was performing at an island music festival. He arrived there a day early, and was sitting on the beach when he saw a beautiful woman running along the shore in a bikini top and Adidas shorts, her thick, muscular thighs working overtime. He got off his beach chair and ran to catch up with her (something he wouldn't do anymore, but he wasn't as much of a big name then, especially overseas). Her name was Yvonne, and she was on vacation with a group of her girlfriends. He and Yvonne spent the day lounging on the beach, eating at the resort, and gambling that evening. The next day, she even went to sound check with him, and he got tickets for her and her friends to attend the concert that evening. Afterward, he took her back to his hotel room. The next morning, he had an early flight, and he left her sleeping naked in his bed.

"Your hair was different." It was the only thing he could think of to say. She had indeed changed her formerly shoulder-length mane into a pixie cut, but he knew that the new hairstyle was no excuse for not recognizing a past lover.

She tried to laugh at the weak explanation, but the sound got caught in her throat. "You promised you'd call when you got back to the States. I was a fool for thinking I'd ever hear from you again." Her eyes moistened as she spoke. "I can tell from your behavior tonight that this is just your routine."

"Yvonne, I'm sorry. Let's just sit down and talk for a second." He reached for her arm to guide her to the foot of the bed, but she yanked away.

"Don't touch me." She returned to the window and stood with her back to him. "I heard some people at my conference saying that you were going to be at Lotus tonight, so I thought, 'Maybe I should go. He'll see me, and he'll apologize for breaking a promise, and I'll forgive him.' But I walked up to you, and you didn't even know who I was."

"But I do remember now. I remember what you were wearing on the beach, and that you whupped the dealer's ass that night on the blackjack table. We had a lot of fun."

She whipped around, cheeks tearstained and arms folded. "And I'm sure you've had plenty of fun with plenty of women since then. I hope you find that kind of lifestyle fulfilling, because there's no doubt that you hurt quite a few people in the process."

Yvonne stormed to the door, brushing past him as she went. She swung open the door and slammed it behind her. He debated whether or not to go after her, but the muffled voices outside told him that Rasheed was handling the situation. He sank down onto the bed, lying on his back and staring at the ceiling. She was right. He'd had a very good time over the past year. But he never thought that he would forget a woman he'd been with. A woman he'd liked and respected. He'd had every intention of calling her when he got back home. But after the Bahamas was Europe, and then he was touring the U.S., and meeting people on every stop. Yvonne just kept getting pushed further and further back in his mind, until one day he didn't even remember her anymore.

An aggressive knock made him bolt out of the hotel

bed, and he anxiously opened the door. Rasheed stood in front of him, shaking his head in pity. Darius stepped aside to let him in. "Good thing I didn't tell Harry to go home, huh? I had him drive her back to where she's staying."

Darius nodded, still somewhat dazed by the sequence of events.

"Dude, I can't believe you didn't remember her."

"What! *You* did?" If Rasheed weren't a hundred pounds heavier than he was, he might have thrown him to the floor.

"Of course I did! I thought you did too."

"Well, I see that now." Darius realized that Yvonne got through the crowd at the club not because she was pretty, but because she was recognized.

Rasheed yawned and stretched, his arms extending like the sturdy limbs of a redwood tree. "Go to bed. I got a room down the hall. Your stupid ass has had us running around enough for one night." He felt absolutely comfortable insulting his boss this way, because they'd been friends long before their professional relationship began.

Alone in his hotel room, Darius went to the bathroom and washed his face. Staring at himself in the mirror, he tried to recreate the facial expression he'd had once he remembered Yvonne. *Idiot. You're such an idiot.* Stripping down to his boxer briefs, he climbed into bed, glancing at the digital clock at the bedside: 3:30 a.m. Just one hour ago, he'd felt like he was on top of the world. Now he was second-guessing every decision he'd ever made about women.

Chapter 4

*He should not want to
control me or my choices.*

Bree tried to cross her legs in the cramped passenger seat of Keith's 2005 red Mustang. She managed it, her long, deep brown limbs stretching so far that the toe of her wedge-heeled sandal touched the front of the car. Keith braked at a red light, giving her a quick once-over. "Who you wearing that short skirt for?"

"It's not that short. It just looks that way because I'm sitting down," Bree answered, staring straight ahead.

"And you're not going to be sitting down at school?"

Bree didn't bother to reply, knowing that she wouldn't win in the long run. They were almost at school anyway. She looked over at his right hand as it gripped the steering wheel. His chocolate skin was the exact same color as hers. They often marveled at this, putting their hands next to each other and struggling to find even half a shade's difference. She moved her gaze to his face, where his sternly set jawline and five o'clock shadow shared space with almond-shaped eyes and thick lashes. Bree always thought that his long eyelashes looked out of place on such a masculine face. When she had told him that, he laughed and said, "My eyelashes get me much love from the ladies," at which point Bree playfully punched him in the stomach. Those were better times, before Keith got so serious and so controlling. She knew she shouldn't put up with his orders, but she did. She loved him, after all.

Keith pulled up to the corner of the street where Pierce High School stood. He always dropped her off here, although they'd never spoken out loud about her not wanting him to drive any farther. It was a silent understanding.

"Call me when you get out," he said, looking at her as she adjusted her skirt before climbing out of the car. It was a command, not a request.

"I might be hanging out with friends after school." She didn't know why she said it, because it wasn't true.

He rolled his eyes, knowing better. "Just call me." His expression softened when she looked back in the car, and he shot her a quick smile. She decided not to return the kindness and slammed the door shut, quickly walking down the street toward the school building.

Sometimes Bree felt the need to revolt against Keith's grip on her. Whether their age difference was the source of their problems, she couldn't say for sure. Some days, like the past weekend that they had spent eating and being couch potatoes, it seemed as if they got along great. But other times, it felt as if all they had in their favor were love and loyalty.

There were hundreds of teenagers hanging outside Pierce, buying breakfast from the food truck, sipping iced coffee from the Dunkin' Donuts down the street, squeezing in their last few opportunities to holler and laugh before the school day began. It was as if Bree didn't see them at all as she walked through the crowd, looking neither left nor right. To further block out the distraction of her peers, she unraveled the earphones of her iPod and stuffed them in her ears. It was an antisocial move, but way too common to be deemed as so. Soon her testy good-bye with Keith was a distant memory as the deep, raspy voice of Darius Wilson took her to another place. When Keith gave her the iPod for her birthday, she had been pretty excited. But when she saw that he had programmed her favorite artists into the device already, she was blown away. She hadn't known that he paid as much attention to her likes and dislikes as he had. And as quickly as Keith had left the forefront of her mind, he returned, just as Darius got to the part to the song's chorus: "I got a complex/About our love so complex . . ."

Because it was so early in the morning, students weren't yet allowed to be in the hallways. The cafeteria was the only available place to go. Once she reached the fluorescently lit dining hall, she sat at an unoccupied table, unplugged her ears, and pulled a book from her shoulder bag. While most of the other kids in the caf were rushing to finish last-minute assignments, Bree's homework was all done. These few minutes in the morning were her treasured moments to herself, where she could actually read for pleasure. She hadn't even turned a single page before she heard a friendly voice above her.

"*Raisin in the Sun?* Great book. Which teacher assigned it?" Ms. Bradford held a grade book in one hand and a paper cup of coffee in the other. Her hair was pulled back, but she wore a pouf on the top, allowing her curls to rise off her head a little bit before she reined them in.

"No teacher. It's just my favorite play," responded Bree softly, looking down at her book.

"Great piece of drama. I actually saw it on Broadway when Puffy was starring in it. Or Diddy, or whatever," Ms. Bradford said with a grin.

"I was supposed to play Beneatha at my old high school, but I had to move." Bree surprised herself by this admission. She hadn't talked about her love of acting, or her old school, to anyone at Pierce.

"So that's why we haven't met yet. You're new here. I'm Ms. Bradford." She put down her coffee to shake Bree's hand. Every movement she made seemed so deliberate, so confident. Bree wondered if Ms. Bradford ever second-guessed anything she ever said or did.

Bree knew exactly who Ms. Bradford was. Everybody did. She was Pierce's "cool teacher"—not the way teachers were usually cool, in that they were easy and let students get away with stuff. No, Ms. Bradford was hard; everybody who took English with her said that. But her class was fun, and she always made sure that what kids learned related to their real lives. Guys also liked her because she was hot, although they were way too intimidated by her to actually try to flirt, the way they did with some of the other young teachers. Girls loved her because she was an amazing dresser, and she watched all of the things on TV that they did, like *America's Next Top Model* and *Project Runway*. Bree had noticed her on the first day of school last September. Ms. Bradford was talking to a teacher in the hallway and Bree overheard her say, "I was a young mother. By the time I was twenty-three, I had a hundred fifty kids." As depressed as Bree was on that day, she had to smile at that one.

"I'm Bree." Still not making eye contact, she shook Ms. Bradford's hand.

"Like the cheese."

"Not spelled the same way, but yeah." Bree finally

looked up as she answered. Ms. Bradford's eyes were not on her, but on the tattered pages of her book.

"Hey, have you read anything by Ntozake Shange?" Bree shook her head no. "I'm going to bring in a copy of a play by her that I think you'll enjoy. Stop by my room tomorrow and pick it up. Room 227."

"Like the television show," said Bree with a smile.

"What do you know about that show? It's before your time!" Ms. Bradford took a sip of her coffee and made a face. Bree couldn't tell if the coffee was too hot, too cold, too strong, or too weak.

"I used to watch the reruns with my mom." Bree surprised herself again. She hadn't mentioned her mother in almost a year. She'd thought about her every day, every moment. She breathed her mother's eyes, her smile, her voice. But the word "mom" had not escaped her lips since last July.

"Well, Bree, you're a real renaissance woman. Reading Hansberry, watching old black sitcoms, doing the hanging-by-yourself thing."

Has she noticed me before? "Yeah, I guess," Bree mumbled.

"I'll see you tomorrow." Ms. Bradford's heels clicked on the tiled floor as she strode away. Bree wondered if she had looked that assertive when she walked away from Keith's car this morning. She doubted it. *Renaissance woman.* Bree repeated the words in her head. She smiled, despite herself.

Chapter 5

He has to be amazing enough to make all of my coworkers jealous.

Kahlila could feel the blood pumping through her veins. There was nervousness in her stomach, but not the kind that made her sick. It was the type that let her know she was alive, and about to do something meaningful. She was getting her usual adrenaline rush that she felt whenever she was about to try something new with her students. Sitting at her desk, she organized her materials as her seniors walked into the room, loudly socializing with one another.

This was her first year teaching twelfth graders. She'd always stayed away from them, because other teachers warned her about the laziness they felt once their college applications were in. "Senior-itis," they called it. But her department head wanted more strong teachers in students' last year of high school, so Kahlila decided to give it a try. On the first day, she couldn't put her finger on exactly what was wrong with the composition of the thirty students sitting in front of her. When class ended, she walked through the hallway and saw Terrell, Alvin, and Sekou chatting in front of the lockers. Though each of them stood at least six feet tall, she still considered them her babies, as she had taught all three when they were freshmen. "Ms. Bradford," Alvin called out, "I'm heated that I didn't get you for English this year." That's when she realized there wasn't a single black or Latino boy in her senior class.

Pierce High School was one of the few public high schools in Boston that had a racial composition matching that of the city itself, which meant that while the student body was predominately white, there were a considerable number of black, Latino, and Asian students at Pierce as well. It was just the bad luck of the registrar's computer that her class was devoid of boys of color.

Still, she'd considered the year to be a success, and her students were now reading their last novel of the year, Toni Morrison's *Song of Solomon*. At this point, more than any other time, Kahlila really noticed the absence in her student population. Students, especially white boys, could not understand Guitar's rage at society, especially once the character becomes part of a group intended to inflict violence on innocent whites. Kahlila knew that her job wasn't to make them believe that Guitar was a rational person, because he indeed was not, but to help them to comprehend his feelings of rage. She got her hands on a copy of the documentary *Eyes on the Prize*, which chronicles the civil rights struggle in America, and specifically focuses on the time period when Morrison's fictional characters lived.

She had popped in the video the day before with no introduction. Students were simply left with their own thoughts as images of Emmett Till, Four Little Girls, and The Little Rock Nine flashed across the screen. Richie, one of Kahlila's favorite students, a hard rocker who never came to school without his studded belt, actually screamed when Till's mutilated body was shown in the coffin. She let the video play until the bell rang, and shouted as students walked out of the room in a daze that they would discuss it the following day.

It was now that next day, and the bell rang to begin class. She looked at the two large semicircles of desks in front of her. Thirty pairs of eyes looked back expectantly. But she knew better than to start lecturing. She wasn't going to give them all of the answers.

"I need ten of you to arrange your chairs in a circle in the middle of the room. Discuss what you watched yesterday. The only three rules—be completely honest, do not interrupt anyone while he or she is speaking, and assume that your classmates are coming from a place of good intention." In theory, Kahlila shouldn't have had to repeat those rules, as they were the class's established group norms that they'd designed during the first week of school. But in difficult conversations, the norms were always worth repeating.

No one moved. Kids avoided eye contact with Kahlila, and squirmed in their seats. But Kahlila was patient. She waited.

The first student to pull her chair into the center of the room was a black girl named Chantal, whose signature fashion statement was a pair of knockoff Burberry high-heeled boots that she somehow managed to pull off flawlessly with any outfit. "Y'all are wack," she said somewhat good-naturedly, to no one in particular. Her peers chuckled, and some of them slowly began to create the circle.

Once the ten students were situated, they still looked at her, as if expecting further instruction. "Inner circle, you're ready to go. Outer circle, jot down any observations, comments, feedback. We'll get to you in fifteen minutes."

Kahlila hoped that the class couldn't hear her heart beating. She knew what was at stake: her students' understanding of the legacy of racism was something that was just developing for most of them. An ineffective conversation could completely damage the process. She was tempted to facilitate the dialogue herself, but she knew they needed some autonomy in answering the hard questions. She sat back in her chair to listen.

"I'll start. The video pissed me off, excuse my language, Ms. Bradford. I mean, it wasn't anything I didn't know already, but seeing it like that always gets me mad," said Chantal.

"But you just seem mad all of the time. Like, you seem mad about the way things are right now, which is not the way they were during this documentary," said Isaac, a high-performing student academically who often struggled with seeing shades of gray.

"You really think things are that different in America now?" asked Chantal, looking almost amused by his naiveté.

"Well, no one's getting sprayed with hoses."

Chantal looked ready to slap Isaac upside the head, and Kahlila was about to jump in. But Ryan, an Irish hockey player from Charlestown, began to speak. "You're right, Isaac. Nobody's getting sprayed. But the people who were spraying people in those videos, they're still alive. And if they're not, their kids are. Think about how much we get from our parents. All that hate must've gotten passed down."

"Ryan's right. And the video made me mad too, Chantal. I didn't expect it to affect me like that. I mean, Toni Morrison talks about Emmett Till in the book, and Ms.

Bradford told us about it, but seeing it, seeing his body . . . my blood was boiling," said Richie the rocker.

"Imagine living during that time. Being a young black man. Knowing that you could be lynched for saying the wrong thing, or making eye contact for too long," said Tirsa, a Caribbean girl with a singsong accent who was herself just familiarizing herself with African-American history.

"I'd probably explode. Like Guitar did," said Ryan, speaking slowly, as if he were just realizing his statement to be true himself.

As students began to share their personal reactions and strong emotions to the documentary, a warm feeling began to spread through Kahlila's body. It often happened when she watched her students do something meaningful, whether it was playing a soulful saxophone solo in the school's jazz band, or giving up their seat to an elderly woman on the T, or finally having the courage to see the world through a different lens. She would get a tingling sensation all over, as well as pressure in her eyes, and it would take everything she had not to cry. Every day, she got to watch her kids become better people. There couldn't be anything more moving than that.

After fifteen minutes, Kahlila shut off the discussion of the inner circle, coolly complimenting them for following group norms. Though she was often bowled over by emotion, she rarely passed it on to her students. If they knew that she thought the things they did were amazing, they might lower their own standards. Her students never quite knew if Ms. Bradford thought they could've done it better, and their readiness to please her often made them set the bar higher than she even had. When the outer circle began to discuss what they heard from the first group, she was equally impressed with the connections they were making to Morrison's text, to today's society, and to their own biases. Students groaned when the bell rang, which was always the icing on the cake of a good lesson. "Finish the book tonight! You're going to be shocked, and most likely appalled, by the ending!" she called after them.

Kahlila had a free period next, which she was glad for. She needed time to decompress and analyze how class went. Six years into her teaching career, she was still no less reflective on her practice than she was on her first day. The work she did was important, not because students needed to love literature, but because she was equipping them with tools to do well, and to do good throughout their lives. She had to keep challenging herself to find new ways to give them those secret weapons.

She had just opened a blank document on Microsoft Word to do some journaling when her door opened. A pale green contraption on wheels rolled its way inside the classroom. It shouldn't have taken her as long as it did to realize that it was a baby carriage, but the object seemed so out of place in a school building that she processed the information slowly. Kahlila immediately stiffened. It was bad enough that she was constantly going to baby showers for the young female members of the Pierce staff. Now they actually had to bring their offspring to school to show them off? She couldn't even plaster a smile on her face for the sake of politeness.

A familiar "Hey, Ms. B." sounded from behind the carriage, causing Kahlila to curiously stand up and walk toward the door. A young woman with chubby cheeks and an hourglass figure was smiling brightly with her hands on her hips, rolling the carriage by pushing it against her thighs.

"Sparklle!" Kahlila said excitedly. A recent graduate of Pierce High School, Sparklle had been a student in her sophomore English class and was one of the best creative writers she'd ever taught. Even when Kahlila stopped being her teacher, Sparklle was a regular in her classroom after school, talking about books, boys, family, and television. Eventually, the two of them decided to start a discussion group for girls at Pierce. Kahlila had heard through the grapevine that Sparklle had a baby, but she hadn't spoken to her since she caught this bit of information.

"We came to visit you, Ms. Bradford," Sparklle said, walking around the carriage to give her a hug. Kahlila had a rule that her students couldn't call her by her first name until they graduated from college. But it felt ridiculous to hear this woman (*she's a mom, for goodness' sake!*) speaking to her with such deference.

"You don't have to call me Ms. Bradford anymore, you know." Once she said those words, she realized that it felt even stranger to give Sparklle permission to break protocol simply because she had gotten pregnant in college.

"You know I can't do that!" Sparklle laughed.

Kahlila felt somewhat relieved. At least everything didn't have to change all at once.

"Well, let's see this little one," Kahlila said in a hushed voice, and Sparklle immediately retrieved a giggly little girl the color of maple syrup from the inside of the carriage.

"This is Starr," she said, regarding her baby daughter thoughtfully. "Spelled with two r's. Starr, this is the woman who made sure I knew who I was in high school. And what I was capable of."

Before Kahlila could object, Sparklle was passing the chubby child to her, and Kahlila could do nothing but settle Starr into her hip and playfully bounce her up and down.

"How old is she?" Kahlila asked, eying Sparklle's perfectly flat stomach.

"Four months. I lost all the weight after, like, three weeks. I'm actually skinnier now than I was before.

Running around with her, running around on campus, I'm never still."

"So you're still in school?"

"Ms. Bradford! Of course I am. Who do you think you're talking to? Oops, I mean, to whom do you think you're talking?"

They both burst out laughing as they paid homage to Kahlila's obsession with grammar, and the baby giggled along with them.

"Where's Starr's father?" She knew that she could cut to the chase with Sparklle.

"In Iraq. He left a month before she was born." Sparklle avoided eye contact as she provided the details of where he was stationed and how infrequently they were able to communicate. Instead, she rummaged through her fashionable baby bag slung over one shoulder for a bottle and bib.

As if the specifics of her father's precarious situation were too much to handle, Starr began to wail at the top of her lungs. Kahlila tried repositioning her, but her screams only increased in volume. "Kids never like me," she lamented.

"Not until they're teenagers, huh?" Sparklle said with a smile, repossessing her daughter and walking to Kahlila's comfortable chair in order to feed her. Kahlila followed behind her and perched on one of the student desks as she and Sparklle continued to talk about Pierce, college, and day care.

The last time one of Kahlila's students had a baby was when she was doing the Teach for America program in Phoenix, right after college. It felt different then, because Kahlila wasn't in a place where she felt as if she should have a family herself. But as she watched Sparklle expertly feed her daughter, hold down a conversation, and check her e-mail at the same time, she felt inadequate. *This girl knows more about real life than I do.*

Eventually, Sparklle rose from the chair and announced that they had to be going. When Sparklle waved Starr's little hand good-bye and disappeared from sight, Kahlila immediately felt a burning in her eyes. From the intensity of the sting, she could guess that she was approximately seven seconds away from crying. She wasn't exactly sure why. Was it the passage of time that Sparklle represented? Was it jealousy of Kahlila's being nowhere near having a baby herself? Was it disappointment that Sparklle's life would now be ten times more difficult than if she'd waited five more years to have a child? Was it happiness that with all she had to balance, Sparklle still took the time to come and visit her?

"Are we going to the hell otherwise known as a bridal shower after school?" A voice that was perky even through the sarcasm penetrated Kahlila's near-tear moment. Looking up, a pretty blonde wearing a polo V-neck sweater with a crisp button-up shirt underneath was striding toward her desk. Madeline Ellis was a lovably bizarre coworker with whom Kahlila never would've guessed she'd become friends. On the first day that Madeline had joined the Pierce faculty, she knocked on Kahlila's door before homeroom. "Can I ask you something?" Kahlila was ready to be helpful to her new colleague, providing directions to the restroom or information about attendance procedures. "Where are the single male teachers?" When Kahlila simply looked at her sideways, Madeline continued. "I'm asking you because you're the only other person in our hallway without a wedding ring." They'd been buddies ever since.

Kahlila wasn't friends with many people in her building. The younger set incessantly discussed honeymoon destinations and diaper genies. The older crowd was more her speed, but they thought she was crazy for spending so much time at Pierce. She got tired of listening to them say what an idiot she was, working overtime for free. Until she and Madeline got close, she never thought she needed an adult companion at school. Her students were her friends. No, she wouldn't talk to them about her personal life (or lack thereof), but she did rely on them for laughs and for encouragement. Still, once she and Maddie began to hang out, she realized that she'd been functioning at Pierce with a hole in her social potential at school.

Madeline was quite a trip. Her students absolutely loved her, as she had all types of fun trivia about people in history, such as the fact that President Polk had suffered from chronic diarrhea. The interactions between her and Kahlila usually involved swapping stories about some disastrous date from the past weekend, or some fairly rude speculation about how an unattractive coworker managed to get engaged before they did.

"So for whom are we pretending to be happy today?" Kahlila asked, blinking away any evidence of tears.

"Ashley Evenwood," Madeline answered, the heels of her loafers hitting the hardwood floor.

"Do I even know her?"

"She's covering Darlene's maternity leave. She's been here since January."

"Wait a second. We're going to a bridal shower for someone who's here covering someone else's time off after we just threw *her* a baby shower?"

"Life is cruel, isn't it? It reminds me of when President Carter couldn't catch a break in the late seventies. The economy was tanking, the U.S. had to pull out of the Olympics, the Iran hostages were taken, and then he lost to Reagan at the end of it all." Noticing Kahlila's blank expression, she added, "Just when you think you can't get

any further immersed in bullshit, someone comes and
scoops another pile right on top of ya."

Kahlila was about to chime in by telling her about
Sparklle's visit, but she decided to keep it to herself.
Sometimes, if she and Madeline weren't careful, their
upbeat, sarcastic rantings about being single turned
bitter and sad. Kahlila still had another class to teach
before the end of the day, and didn't need her mood to
get any worse.

"Well, don't forget to get your gift together." Kahlila
walked over to her desk drawer and unlocked it with one
of the keys she fished from her bag. She removed one of
five gift cards to Victoria's Secret, as well as one blank
greeting card from a pile of many. She and Madeline had
started buying gift cards in bulk, because these events
came fast and furiously, and it was easier to be prepared
at all times. "What gift card are you giving her?"

"Barnes and Noble. It's what's expected of me. You're
the hot, well-dressed one. I'm the bookish half of our
pair, remember?"

"You know you're hot, Maddie. These folks just never
see you outside of your khakis and loafers. Now, what the
hell is a bride-to-be supposed to get from Barnes and
Noble?"

"She can hold on to it, and in a couple of years she can
use it to buy *Divorce for Dummies.*" Madeline's smile was
mischievous.

"You're so bad," Kahlila said, shaking her head. But at
least the stinging in her eyes was gone, and she was ready
to trudge on with her day.

Chapter 6

He must be ready for a serious,
monogamous relationship.

"Industry or nonindustry?"

"Definitely industry. She's gotta understand the work, man. If she ain't in it, she won't get it."

Darius and Rasheed were having lunch at Pastis. It was one of their favorite places to eat, because celebrities came in there all the time, and the "regular" New Yorkers who ate there were way too cool to bother people for autographs or conversation. It was the Wednesday after the "Yvonne incident," as they had termed it, and Darius had been doing some serious thinking over the past few days. Yes, he'd enjoyed the fast life, but it was time to slow down. He missed having someone to check in with, to share the events of the day, to bring to formal engagements, to wake up with on a Saturday morning and watch TV. He hadn't been in a serious relationship since Danielle, a coworker of his whom he had dated for two years, right before he entered the alternate universe of stardom. Flow Steddie had asked Darius to join him on tour, and he asked Danielle for her opinion. She thought the whole thing was impractical, and never believed that he would make it in the business. "Darius, just because you sing the hook on a couple of rap songs doesn't mean that you're gonna have a hit album yourself. You do well at Morgan Stanley and you'll regret it if you quit." He didn't hold her doubt against her, but she sure held it against him when he didn't take her advice. They didn't last a month once he started traveling. Now, two years later, she was married with a kid on the way. So even if he wanted to go back, it wasn't an option.

Darius wanted a girlfriend, and decided to pick Rasheed's brain for advice on how to go about getting one. Rasheed had been dating Toni, a local fashion designer, for the past six months, and was grateful for the time off from touring this summer, so that they could actually get to hang out together in New York for an extended period of time. Darius noticed how happy and relaxed Rasheed had been since he started dating Toni, and he longed for that same feeling of stability. Both he and his boy were very practical people, so it seemed completely sensible to them to sit at lunch with their Treos out, listing the basic requirements in a potential mate and then searching their contact lists for ideas.

"New York or L.A.?" Rasheed asked, scrolling through his cell phone and planner in one. Darius often joked that Rasheed couldn't take a dump without looking at his Treo. Not only was he on it twenty-four-seven sending messages to Toni, but he was constantly in communication with Darius's manager, publicist, and record label, as he handled Darius's day-to-day schedule.

"That's obvious. I live here. Why would I want someone on the left coast?"

"When are you gonna accept the fact that you've got money? Distance don't matter when you're paid!"

"That's true. But L.A. girls are trippy anyway. Too superficial. And most of them are coked out anyhow."

"I would define that as a gross generalization, but it's your call." Darius smiled at his friend's response. There were times that Darius wished he had moments in his everyday life videotaped, and this was one of them. He knew the world would be shocked to hear a singer's bodyguard term something a "gross generalization," because there was a stereotype that famous people and their friends were all stupid. The truth is, that was often true. But Darius had promised himself when he entered the game that he would only surround himself with people he respected, which meant people who had talent *and* intelligence.

"Singer or actress?"

"I'll be too hard on a singer. If she's not talented, I can't respect her. And all the talented beautiful singers are scooped up already. Actress—man, these New York actresses are so righteous. Just 'cause your ass is on Broadway and not in Hollywood doesn't mean you have more integrity than anybody else."

"What about a model?"

"Great idea, Rasheed. I should date a nineteen-year-old, empty-headed party girl whose entire career is based on what she looks like and what she doesn't eat."

"What's with you and the stereotypes today? You know they're not all like that."

"Name one who isn't."

Rasheed put up a "wait a second" finger and proceeded to do some more scrolling through his handheld device. After a few moments, he looked up, victory shining in his eyes. "Miko."

Miko was a model whom Darius had never even heard

of until she was cast as the "main chick" in one of his videos. Darius and Rasheed always joked that in music videos, there are video hos and there are main chicks. The main chick is the one with the storyline and the hos are the ones who shake their booties in the background. Miko had been the main chick in one of the ballads from his first album. Not only was she gorgeous, but she was an amazing kisser. He couldn't be sure, but he thought the chemistry between them was not just for the director's benefit. Still, he ended up snagging one of the video hos after the shoot and never followed up with Miko after that. When he saw her a few weeks later, she acted stand-offish, and it was clear that she was not pleased about his choice to pursue a backup dancer over her.

"She seemed cool, but she can't even stand me."

"Not true. I was having drinks with Toni the other night, and we ran into her. She asked about you. Told me to tell you hello."

"Why didn't you tell me?" Darius demanded.

"I'm telling you now! Relax."

Darius let his mind return to the two days he'd spent with Miko while they filmed the video. Though it was last winter, he still remembered a couple of the jokes she cracked on set. He'd never met a funny model before, and he hadn't met another one since.

"So, what do we know about her?"

"Her career started taking off after she did your video. Folks are calling her the new Kimora Lee Simmons, 'cause she's got the half-Asian thing going on and she's kind of sassy like her too. She's the new face for some designer bag, I can't remember."

"I didn't mean her career. What are her stats? Age, past relationships . . ."

"Oh, I got you. She's mid-twenties, although I'm sure it says something different in her portfolio. I don't know anything about who she's done in the past, bro. She's definitely not all out there, getting with everybody."

It was a decent rap sheet: she had looks, wit, and a career of her own. She did not have a bad reputation, or a lot of growing up to do. "All right. I'll give her a shout. See what's up."

"Cool. Hopefully you'll like her, and y'all can take it to the next level."

"Hopefully. Touring has been great. The lifestyle has been great. But shit, I'm tired."

"I hear you. I'm tired from being along for the ride."

Darius laughed, but it always made him nervous when Rasheed said things like that. Rasheed had his own life and career that he had put on hold when Darius made it big. He knew that eventually Rah would want to return to an ordinary life, and he wouldn't have his roll dawg anymore. But as he tried to get his priorities straight, he was glad that day wasn't today.

Chapter 7

*He cannot feel threatened by
my hanging with the girls.*

"I have bad news, ladies. The pizza is going to be late,"
Kahli announced to the twenty-five girls in her classroom. "But the good news is that because they messed
up the delivery time, the order is free!"

"Why should we be excited about that? You're the one
who's paying for it!"

Shauna always had a smart comment, and that's why
Kahlila liked her so much. "Good point. So we might as
well get started with the meeting while we wait for the
food."

Girl Talk was a group that Kahlila had started after de-
signing the concept with Sparklle four years ago. She'd
found herself devoting so much of her after-school time
to private conversations with girls whom she taught.
Sometimes girls whom she only knew from the hallway
sought her out to discuss their latest drama. These
young women were most often black or Latina, as she

was the only young teacher of color in the building who didn't have to run home after school to tend to her husband or children. So when she put an announcement in the school bulletin about starting an after-school group for young women to make connections and find support, the only girls who showed up on the first day were brown, except for an Irish girl named Kepley, to whom she had made a close connection in class. Three years later, the group composition looked pretty similar to the way it did when it began. Kepley had graduated, but there was a new white girl named Emily and an Asian girl named Giselle who never missed a meeting.

It was a struggle to fit all twenty-five desks into one circle, but they managed it. Kahlila usually let different girls lead the discussion, but it was the last day of school, and she wanted to make sure the group hit a couple of issues before the year ended. "Okay, ladies. Summertime is officially here!" Cheers, hoots, and hollers ensued. "So let's talk about how to make your summer as productive as possible." The cheers quickly turned to groans.

Kahlila gave a brief lecture about using summer months to make your profile stronger, whether with college classes, a summer job, or a meaningful travel experience. She also came prepared with a few last-minute opportunities, in case any of the girls had no plans as of yet. Going around the room and hearing what all of their plans were, she felt warmed that most of them were on the ball, and she knew that part of it was due to Girl Talk. Having a place to check in, vent, and grow was essential, but Kahlila felt like she was always justifying the existence of her group to staff members who felt like it had an "exclusionary" feel.

Nancy, a Puerto Rican girl who spoke with a slight lisp, spoke up. "What are *you* doing for the summer, Ms. Bradford?"

Kahlila was always taken aback in a school setting when she became the focus. Teenagers were usually so self-absorbed that they never turned the questioning back on her, and she preferred it that way. "Um, no big plans. Some projects around the house, several books I've been meaning to get to, that kind of thing."

"Hypocrite!" Chantal's voice was teasing. "You're telling us to make our summers count, and you're just loafing around."

"Excuse me," said Kahlila with a smile, "I already *have* a college degree, thank you very much. I already *have* my dream job. You're just trying to get there."

"You're right, Ms. Bradford," Emily chimed in with a smirk. "You already have the degree and the job. But you know what you don't have? A man!"

The room exploded into laughter and "Oh no, she didn'ts." The comment was more amusing because Emily made it, and the girls loved it whenever the "cool white girl" said anything remotely scandalous. The only thing that entertained them more was when Giselle made a spicy comment.

Kahlila waited for the room to calm down. "And if I 'had' a man, Emily, how would that change my summer?"

"It would just be better! You'd have someone to go places with, take trips with, that kind of thing."

"And you think I need a man in order to leave the house or go on vacation?"

"Don't go getting all feminist on us, Ms. Bradford," said Lisa, a keep-it-real type of senior who had graduated from Pierce a few weeks ago, but came back for the last Girl Talk meeting. "We just all agree that you're the 'ish.' And we can't figure out why you're not married, or engaged, or someone's girlfriend, when all these other wack teachers are booed up already." Heads around the circle nodded in agreement.

Kahlila searched for a response. Tried to think logically and rationally. But how could she come up with a response for Lisa, when she asked herself the same question all the time? She wasn't going to tell them about the obstacles for women of color in Boston. And she definitely wasn't going to share the details of her List. What could she say that didn't make her sound bitter? These girls looked up to her. Some of them even wanted to *be* her. If they knew how much she has struggled to find "the one," they might think that being a confident, intelligent woman was a liability.

The silence was stretching when Kahlila noticed a body in her doorway. Bree Roberts was standing in the threshold of her room, looking unsure whether to enter. Kahlila had told her the week before to stop in and pick up a copy of *For Colored Girls Who've Considered Suicide When the Rainbow Is Enuf,* and she'd never come. Kahlila began to think that it was for the best. She'd never recommended the choereopoem to a student before. The content was pretty heavy, and she wasn't sure why she offered her copy to Bree. Something about her made her seem very deep, very sad, and also very wise. But she'd never stopped by, and Kahlila had actually forgotten about her until this moment. And she was more than grateful for the interruption.

"Ladies, say hello to Bree." Some of the girls waved, others said hi, and still others whispered to one another about the new girl in the doorway. Most of them had seen her over the course of the year, and their instinct was to be suspicious of this girl who didn't speak to anyone.

"Um, hi. I just came for that book. I could come back . . ."

"No, of course not!" Kahlila was relieved that she still

had the book in her desk drawer, and quickly got up to retrieve it. "Come in."

Bree walked in slowly, stopping right outside the circle. She stood awkwardly as she waited for Kahlila to cross the room and hand her the book. As soon as it was in her hands, she was ready to bolt for the door.

"We can fit another chair in the circle if you wanted to stay and hang out for a while," invited Kahlila cheerily.

"I can't," she answered quickly, relieved that she actually had an excuse why she couldn't stay. The girls in the circle were staring at her as if she had two heads. "He'll kill me if I don't call him soon."

"Who, your father?"

"Oh no," she replied, embarrassed. Kahlila waited a few more seconds for Bree to say more, but it was clear that she was not going to elaborate.

"Someone's got his girl in check!" piped up Kiyana, a mouthy junior who only contributed to Girl Talk discussions on dating or sex. Bree looked mortified by the comment, and everyone waited eagerly to see if she'd respond.

A shrill beep startled everyone in the room. The secretary's voice came over the speaker on the wall. "Ms. Bradford?" Her voice sounded scratchy and faraway, the classic sound of a high school intercom.

"Yes!" Kahlila shouted back.

"Your pizza is here."

"Thank you!"

There was an immediate restlessness in the group. She knew that once the food came, the meeting would effactually be over. She touched Bree's arm and spoke to her softly. "Bree, just wait one second, okay?" Then more loudly, she spoke to the rest of the group. "Ladies! We will get the pizza in a moment. First, you know what time it is."

"Ms. Bradford's Final Thought," chanted the group in unison.

Kahlila always ended meetings with a summary of what they'd discussed, along with some food for further reflection. At this meeting, she'd planned to wrap up with an overview of the year and a reminder to make their summers productive. But Emily's taunting about her being single and Bree's anxiousness to call this mysterious man made her improvise a different final thought for the year.

"Ladies, you are young women, and you are at a time in your lives where romance is new, thrilling, and very important. But you can't let your desire for romance change the person who you are. Men will say things to make you think that they want a woman who will cater to their every whim. But in the end, they respect you way more when you stand up for yourself and have your own life."

"So you're saying we can't be nice to dudes, Ms. Bradford?" Kiyana probed.

"That's not what I'm saying at all. Just don't shape your lives around them. Have your own hobbies, your own friends, your own goals." Kahlila tried not to look directly at Bree while she spoke. But she hoped she got the message.

Chapter 8

Our chemistry must be instant and strong, like Folgers coffee—black.

"And they were looking at me with this pity in their eyes. Like 'Poor Ms. Bradford. We're all she has,'" whined Kahlila to Robyn and Madeline. They'd decided to celebrate the last day of school with drinks downtown. No Friendly Takeover tonight, though. They let Madeline pick the place, which meant that Robyn and Kahlila were the only brown faces in the establishment.

Madeline nodded in empathy as she listened to Kahlila's experience with her Girl Talk students. Robyn sucked her teeth and rolled her eyes. "C'mon, Kahli. You're really letting a group of teenaged girls make you feel bad? And besides, these girls worship you! I doubt they think you're pitiful in any way."

"They do worship her, Robyn. But that's why they're so concerned about her love life. If Ms. Bradford can't find the man of her dreams, then how will *they*?" Madeline earnestly pleaded as she sipped at her glass of Pinot

Grigio. As different as they were, Kahlila was often amazed by how easily Madeline "got" her.

"You two are way too dramatic." Robyn had no patience for fake problems. She dealt in the realities of an emergency room, where someone could die if you didn't think rationally and fast. Worrying whether the right guy will ever come along is a hypothetical nightmare with no purpose. Are you healthy? You getting a paycheck? Then shut up and count your blessings.

"I'm not being dramatic. I'm simply prepared to make a few minor changes in my lifestyle in order to increase my odds of finding someone."

"Do tell!" said Madeline eagerly.

Kahlila set down her drink for dramatic effect and looked back and forth between her two friends. "I'm throwing away my list."

"*The* List?" Robyn asked.

"For the summer," Kahlila hurriedly added. "As an experiment. It occurred to me that I might be a little too picky when it comes to guys—"

"No. *You?*" The sarcasm dripped from Robyn's upturned lips.

"As I was saying, it might be a good idea to take a couple of months to spend time with people without measuring them up to some preset list of standards."

"That's a great idea, Kahli." Madeline was always supportive of any new venture that might aid in the quest of a woman's finding a husband.

"I hate to be the voice of doubt. Well, actually I love it. You have the damn list memorized, I'm sure. Can you even help but measure guys against it at this point?"

"The throwing away of The List is *metaphorical*, Robyn. It's a state of mind. Of course I have the willpower to be more open-minded about the guys I date."

Robyn knew when to give in, and she didn't want to

rain on her friend's idealistic parade. "Well, then let's toast. To the last day of school for you teacher bitches, and to a summer of openness." The three ladies laughed as they raised their glasses and clinked them in the center of the table.

"Yous girls look like you need a refill." An abrasive Boston accent made Robyn, Kahlila, and Madeline look up to find a smiling, sandy-brown-haired guy standing at their table.

"My name's Joey," he said, extending his hand to Madeline first, confirming the motivation for his visit. Kahlila watched as Madeline introduced herself. From the smile on her face, she was clearly amenable to getting to know Joey. Kahlila had been turned off from the moment she heard "Yous girls." Unlike herself, Madeline didn't subscribe to a list of requirements, or at least one as extensive as Kahlila's. Madeline wanted a "good guy," who was looking to get married and have a family. He had to have a job (it didn't matter what kind), and he had to think she was amazing. Kahli firmly believed that Madeline would find happiness way before she would.

Robyn and Kahlila followed suit with the introductions, and Kahlila couldn't help but be impressed by his firm handshake. Weak grips were one of her many deal breakers. "Hey, my friends are hangin' out by the bar and we thought maybe yous girls might wanna come over. Drinks are on us."

The women strained to see Joey's friends across the room. A group of three guys, two who looked an awful lot like Joey and one whose face was chocolate brown, were laughing and looking their way. A few days before, Kahlila would have evaluated the circle of friends, made a note of what they were wearing and drinking, and then decided whether to accept the offer. But summer had begun, and she was living on the edge. "Sure. Let's go."

* * *

Keith had been having the day from hell. His boss had him on the grind all day, and when he finally had a moment to chill, he got a call from his girlfriend. Out of the blue, or at least it seemed to him, she had decided that it was over. She couldn't deal with "his craziness" anymore. He hadn't even bothered to fight back on the phone. She was probably right. They didn't really have a chance at lasting, even though he'd wanted it to last forever. They were in two different places in their lives, and he was forcing her to grow up too quickly.

He immediately called his friend Matt to figure out a game plan for the evening. "Dude, we gotta get drinks after work. My girl called me this afternoon and all of a sudden I'm single—"

"And ready to mingle?" Matt laughed on the other end of the phone.

Matt, Joey, and Colin were Keith's best buddies. The three of them worked construction for Boston's Big Dig, an architectural project that had lasted way longer and cost billions of dollars more than anyone ever expected. It was difficult for an outsider to ascertain exactly how Keith would have formed a friendship with three Irish Catholic guys from Charlestown, South Boston, and Dorchester respectively, but when Keith got to know them at the gym to which they all belonged, he found them to be the realest people he'd met in the ten years he'd been in Boston. They often got together in the evening and sat around, beers in hand, watching a Red Sox game at a dive bar and just talking about life. Keith didn't want to talk tonight, though. He wanted to forget all his problems for a few hours.

They met up at the gym, as was their routine, tossed some weights around, showered, changed, and headed to a bar within walking distance. All four were dressed in T-shirts and jeans, which was Keith's outfit of choice whenever possible. He hated those Boston black professional events where people sized you up based on what you had on, where you went to school, and what you did for a living.

The guys hadn't finished their first beer when Joey noticed three women sitting at a table about twenty-five feet from them. "Hey, Keith, whaddya think?"

Keith barely glanced over before returning his attention to his beer. "Okay, Joe, you find the only two black girls in the place and now I'm supposed to fall in love with one of them?"

Matt laughed—he was always the fastest one to do so— and patted Keith on the back. "Dude, chill out. It wouldn't hurt for you to interact with some ladies tonight, get your mind off . . . and besides, they're pretty cute."

Forcing himself to take a second look, he inventoried the table. Facing them was a perky-looking blonde with wispy bangs and a slightly upturned nose. To her right was a mahogany-colored petite woman with a serious face that revealed a dimple when she flashed a quick smile. The last one had her back to them, so all he could see was a mass of curls and slender copper-colored arms.

Colin, always the voice of reason, chimed in. "Don't push the guy. Let's just have a couple beers and relax."

As if Colin had given the exact opposite instruction, Joey immediately rose from his stool. "I'm going over to talk to them." He walked away to the sound of Matt chuckling.

As Kahlila walked toward the three men at the bar, she tried to check out the dark chocolate one without appearing too obvious. While he was dressed way too casually for her taste, there was something undeniably appealing about him. Maybe it was the chiseled bone structure. It could have also been the long, thick eyelashes that almost made it difficult to see his pupils. Perhaps it was the broad shoulders and muscular forearm that held a Corona, no lime. As she looked at him from the top of his slightly overgrown hair to the bottoms of his sneakered feet, she wondered if her underwear matched. *Why the hell am I thinking about that?* She had never in her life gone home with a man after just meeting him. But she still breathed an internal sigh of relief when she remembered that her black sheer bikini briefs did indeed match her Calvin Klein bra.

They hadn't even gotten within speaking distance when all three men rose to give the women their chairs. Kahlila immediately thought to add points onto their scores for the effort, but she had to remind herself: The List was gone for the summer. She was to keep it breezy and stop with the math problems.

After what seemed like forever, the two groups connected and Joey proceeded with the introductions, although he only remembered Madeline's name. Kahlila thought that maybe Keith (*nice name, extra points—oh, crap, never mind*) held her gaze a little longer than he did anyone else's, but she couldn't be sure.

Looking at the three other guys up close, she realized she was being hasty in her assessment that they all looked alike. While they did all share the same hair color, Colin was a tall, stocky guy with a slight potbelly; Matt had piercing green eyes and a face full of freckles; Joey was definitely the cutest, resembling a Ken doll as much as anyone Kahlila had ever seen. Colin quickly removed himself from the social situation, finding another stool way down the bar and settling in to watch the Sox. Once the gender ratio was even, Kahlila found herself seated with Keith hovering over her, and she couldn't say that she was displeased with the arrangement.

"So, what are you ladies celebrating tonight? I saw y'all over there clinking glasses," said Keith, his sooty eyelashes fanning her as he blinked.

Trying not to squirm at the word "y'all," she was about to answer when Matt, who was standing above Robyn's seat next to Kahlila, butted in. "We're celebrating too! Our man Keith here is officially on the market again."

"Oh, really?" Robyn said, uncrossing and recrossing her legs as she nudged Kahlila not so subtly.

"Ignore him," Keith instructed as he blocked Matt from Kahlila's view. "Matt's the obnoxious one in the crew."

"Quite an interesting assemblage you have here, actually." Kahlila then surprised herself by bursting into song. "One of these guys is not like the others . . ."

"Gotta love a good *Sesame Street* reference. Yeah, I get that a lot. We all hit up the same gym. Colin, Matt, and Joe work together, but they let me tag along with them to hang out."

Kahlila looked over to ask Matt where they worked, but he and Robyn were sharing a hearty laugh that seemed too precious to interrupt. Peering past them at Madeline and Joey, she saw that her friend was putting on the serious moves, as she touched his shoulder playfully and gave a coy smile.

"So, where do your boys work?" Kahlila asked, returning her attention to Keith.

"They work right down the street. They're building you and the rest of Boston's taxpayers a new highway system."

"Really? The Big Dig? I guess they'll be employed for life." She wanted to turn the focus of the conversation to him specifically, and not his friends, but she didn't want him to feel like he was being interviewed. That was how she always got herself into trouble, asking men questions and then using their answers against them. She managed to stay quiet for a full minute, until she slurped the last of her drink. "So, do you work construction as well?"

"I would love to do that. Building things—that would be my ideal job. But no, haven't managed to get to that place in my life yet."

What the hell kind of job does this man do? What place in your life do you have to get to before you can work construction? There's nothing wrong with a blue-collar man, but it sounds like this dude may not have a collar at all.

"Your glass is empty. Another one?" Keith was already signaling the bartender.

Kahlila reminded herself how many high-powered brothers thought they were too good to buy a woman a drink. *That's why The List is gone. To give guys like this a chance.* "Sure—a B-52 on the rocks, please."

"Nah. If I'm buying, you're getting a real drink. Yo, Matt! Joe!" The entire group turned to face him. "Tequila shots?"

"Hell yes!" Matt screamed back. "Hey, Colin, you want a drink?" Colin shook his head from where he sat. Kahlila guessed that if Matt was the obnoxious one, then Colin was Mr. Low Key.

"Six shots of Cuervo," Matt demanded from the pretty female bartender, who looked annoyed that Matt only seemed to have one speaking volume: loud.

"Cuervo? No way. If we're doing tequila shots, we're doing Patrón. I'm sorry." Robyn was considered the alcohol snob in Kahlila's circle of friends. If it wasn't high-end liquor, Robyn wasn't drinking it. She wasn't label conscious in any other department, but she swore that the quality of the alcohol affected her hangover the next day, and being an ER resident, she couldn't afford to be off her game.

"You heard the woman!" Matt shouted. The bartender rolled her eyes and proceeded to locate the bottle while everyone excitedly talked about alcohol: favorite drinks, drinks that made people nauseated, obscure drinks that no one knew all the ingredients of. Kahlila really didn't want a shot of tequila, especially after downing a milky beverage. But she hated to kill the festive mood. Madeline looked really excited about this Joey guy, and to be honest, Keith had her a little bit jazzed herself. Even Robyn was having more fun than usual; she'd finally found what she was looking for when she hit the town: a hilarious guy to engage in flirtatious banter and nothing more.

At last, each person was equipped with a shot glass, salt, and lime. Matt counted them off and they took the glasses to the head. Kahlila was surprised at how smoothly it went down. Maybe there was something to Robyn's theory about expensive liquor after all. She felt her body relaxing as the warmth in her stomach began to spread to the tips of her fingers and toes. It always took a while for the end of the school year to sink in, but it did at this moment. She loved her job, but the thought of nine paid weeks of vacation brought a contented grin to her face.

"You're *what*?" Madeline's voice screeched through the bar. Even the die-hard Red Sox fans turned around to see who was responsible for the outburst. Madeline rose from her stool and stood in front of Kahlila and Robyn, practically pushing Matt and Keith out of the way. "Joey's married. Can you believe that?"

Kahlila and Robyn turned to look at Joey. He had his hands in the air as if he were being held up at gunpoint. "Sweetheart, I was never comin' on to ya. I was just being friendly."

"Where the hell is your wedding ring, huh?" The left hand was the first feature on a man that Madeline noticed.

"I don't wear it at work. Jeez, hon. I'm really sorry." Joey looked at his friends for backup, but they were too busy trying not to laugh to offer any verbal support.

Madeline grabbed her purse. "Kahli and Robyn, I'll see you later. I can't waste my time socializing with deceptive men."

"Deceptive?" Joey repeated. He looked just about ready to tell her off, but Keith shot him a look and he closed his mouth.

"Do you want us to come with you?" Kahlila asked. *Please say no.*

"I'm fine. I'll catch a cab outside." She tossed one last scornful look at Joey and stormed out of the bar.

Everybody sat in silence for fifteen seconds before bursting into uncontrollable laughter.

"Dude, I really didn't know that I was leading her on. I feel wicked bad," said Joey, almost to himself.

"She's sensitive," Kahlila offered as a small token of comfort.

"Yeah, well, it's a good lesson. My wife does hate it that I don't wear my ring to work. I'd better head home." He gave Matt and Keith pounds good-bye and tried to give Keith money, which he refused. He retrieved Colin from the other end of the bar, and the two of them headed out the door.

Suddenly we're a foursome. How cozy. Kahlila was suddenly way more self-conscious than she'd been in the larger group. But the ice was quickly broken when Matt asked for their opinion about going out on the town when you're married. An interesting debate ensued, with Robyn and Matt on one side, stating that nothing should have to change, and Kahlila and Keith on the other, saying that the ring needed to be worn at all times and the partying curbed.

Matt looked over at his debate partner and gave her a friendly nudge. "Robyn, just so you know, I'm not married, and I think you're hot."

"Why, thank you, Matt, but you don't have a chance in hell."

Matt, completely unfazed, quickly rebounded with "Why not? Do you not love the taste of smooth, creamy vanilla?"

"Good one," returned Robyn with a chuckle. "I have a boyfriend."

"And what type of ice cream is he?"

Robyn put her finger to the corner of her mouth as she thought. "More of a mocha latte."

"Where is he tonight?"

"He's in Philly."

"Doing what?" Matt seemed to be enjoying the back and forth.

Kahlila couldn't tell if he was legitimately interested in her friend, or if he was just flirting for sport. "He lives there. He's a college professor."

"Whoa, Keith, we're dealing with some high-class women here."

"So I hear," Keith said, shooting Kahlila a quick glance.

Robyn took a look at her watch and grimaced. "I don't know how high-class we are, but I do know that I'll be no good at work tomorrow if I don't get out of here."

"What do you do for work?" Matt asked, obviously disappointed that Robyn was calling it an evening.

"She saves lives," Kahlila interjected. Robyn rolled her eyes. "Robyn's a resident in the emergency room at Beth Israel."

"No shit?" Matt looked impressed beyond words, and Kahlila knew that he had in fact been interested.

"Yup. It's been great meeting you guys." She stood up from her stool and shook Keith's hand first. When she went to shake Matt's, he held on to hers and swung her arm playfully. "Oh, hell no. I'm not third-wheelin' it with these two. I'll walk you out."

As Kahlila watched this interaction play out, she became more and more anxious about what was happening. In a matter of seconds, she would be at a bar alone with a man she'd just met. She wasn't worried about her safety. There were cabs right outside. But did he even want to be left alone with her? What would they talk about? Still, there was no way that she wanted to leave with Robyn. And Keith wasn't protesting the situation either. She managed a weak wave to Robyn and Matt as they headed toward the door. Although Robyn did have to work in the morning, she knew that Robyn wouldn't have gone if she didn't want Kahli and Keith to spend some solo time. She trusted her friend's instincts, so she tried to relax as Keith sat down on the stool that Robyn had just deserted.

Still desperate to find out more of Keith's vital statistics, she racked her brain trying to figure out how to get answers without asking questions. "You haven't asked me what I do," she said pointedly.

"I don't care about that shit."

Kahlila usually hated it when guys swore unnecessarily, but on Keith it sounded appealingly rugged. And while she was tempted to feel frustrated by his refusal to touch the topic of profession, she had to admit that it was a somewhat refreshing change from the Derek Andersons of the world.

Keith ordered them each a tall glass of water. "Gotta stay hydrated after a tequila shot, or we'll be paying the price later on."

"Good point. We should get beers too, to wash down

the water," Kahlila suggested with a devilish smile. *I'm cabbing it home. School is out. Why not?*

"Okay, player!" He looked at her as if he were seeing her through a new lens, and suddenly the conversation was off and running.

An hour later, Keith and Kahlila were playing a game of Q&A. Not Kahlila's usual form of the game, but a version with questions that were a lot less heavy. "Are you a coffee drinker?" she asked.

"The only way to get through the morning. I don't drink it for the taste, so I make the instant kind. Black and strong."

"How appropriate," she said, looking from his bulky shoulder down to his forearm, surprising herself by the boldness of her fliratation.

"Favorite book?" he asked, right before taking a huge swig of water. Kahli couldn't stop herself from giving him points for asking that question. Lately, the guys she'd been meeting would have sooner asked her, "Favorite stock option?"

"*Their Eyes Were Watching God.* You?"

"I only read nonfiction. Barack Obama's autobiography was pretty good. I just finished it. Favorite way to spend a Saturday?"

"Go to Pilates class, head to the Barnes and Noble next door to my gym, get a caramel Frappuccino from the café, then find a seat by the window to read *US Weekly.*"

"Don't tell me you read that tabloid crap."

"I just did tell you. And I'm not ashamed of being a celebrity whore." She grinned as his eyes got wider. "It just means that I devour celebrity gossip."

"Why? Who cares about those people?"

"I don't *care* about them. But their lifestyles are fascinating. The money, the clothes, the parties, the travel . . ." Keith was still looking at her as if she were crazy, so she decided to change the subject. "And what about you? What's your ideal Saturday?"

"Any Saturday that I'm not working is a good Saturday. And by the way, those Pilates classes are working out really well for you."

Kahlila was definitely crushing on this guy, hard. She loved everything he said, the clear, deep voice with which he said it, and the way he looked at her while he was saying it. It was pushing closing time and they had finished their second glass of water. She definitely didn't need any more alcohol, and she could feel the night coming to an end. The nerves that had disappeared an hour before now returned, as she anticipated how they would say good-bye.

A faithful reader of *He's Just Not That Into You* (she believed that the book required rereading every few months, just to keep all of the lessons fresh), Kahli no longer pursued men. As eager as she was to find love, she knew that being aggressive wasn't the answer. If the guy didn't put out effort, then things ended there. But as she felt her time with Keith wrapping up, she feared that if she didn't make a move, then she might never see him again. And after declaring her new spontaneous attitude to her friends, and then his coming out of nowhere—it could all be a sign. She pushed herself to the next level of directness. "So, what do you want to happen here? With us." She could feel her heart pounding.

"What do I *want*? Or what would be *best*?"

Kahlila couldn't decide which answer she wanted to hear, so she sat there with a fairly conflicted expression on her face.

Keith was drawn to this girl, yes. But this morning, he

had been committed to someone else. He needed time to clear his head. "What would be *best* would be if we ended our encounter on a high note, which is what this is right now." He spoke slowly, methodically, and when he finished, a silence hung in the air, despite the drunken Sox fans loudly talking all around them.

Suddenly he was asking the bartender to close his tab, and Kahlila felt helpless to stop what was happening. *Is this it? Is he really going to leave without asking for my number?* She was still in denial as he signed the bill. "You ready?" he asked. She nodded and followed him out the door in a daze.

Don't pursue a guy who doesn't want you back. But he does want me. He's just being too practical. From her many conversations with her best guy friend, J.T., she knew about guys' obsession with timing. For men, the right stage in life outweighs the right woman. If they're not ready to be in a relationship, they wouldn't make Halle Berry their girlfriend. *Something is telling Keith that this isn't the right time for us to have met.*

Outside, the air was still warm. They faced each other on the sidewalk. He was much taller than she was, probably around six-two. She imagined for a moment what it would be like if he were her man. The looks of admiration on the faces of her Girl Talk kids when he came to pick her up from school. He held out his arms and enfolded her in his chest for a hug. He smelled like a combination of Irish Spring soap and baby powder. If he hadn't held her for so long, it would have been easier to end it right there. Her heart was quickening as she got into the cab parked in front of them. He closed the door and waved once she was inside.

Keith jogged to the cab parked in front of hers and stepped inside. Kahlila replayed the feeling of his arms around her one more time. "Hold on," she said suddenly. "I'm getting out. Sorry." She didn't even look at the driver as she flung open the door.

As soon as Keith's cab began to pull off, he began to wonder if he was too hasty in his decision to cut the connection with Kahlila. He hadn't even fully processed an answer when he heard a banging on the trunk of the taxi. After a "What the . . ." from the cabbie, he stopped the car at the same time that Keith turned and saw her. Kahlila stood in the dark, her eyes squinting to block the summer wind, her hair swirling around her head.

Keith opened the cab door and scooted over, still somewhat in shock. They looked at each other briefly before staring out of their respective windows.

"Am I still going to the same place?" the cabdriver shouted to the backseat.

"Yeah," said Keith softly.

They drove in silence for the rest of the ride.

Chapter 9

He has to recognize that honesty is everything.

Keith lived on the first floor of a renovated triple-decker, nestled among gorgeous Victorian homes in an area that most people considered "risky." Boston was carved into very distinct neighborhoods by race and class, and Keith's was brown and struggling, despite the fantastic architecture and proximity to downtown. Even in the face of the crazy situation in which she found herself, Kahlila couldn't help but wonder the logistical questions: *Does he own this place? It's pretty big for just one person.* She quickly realized that these were not the concerns she should be having. *Why am I even here? Is it safe for me to be at this guy's apartment?* They still hadn't exchanged a single word by the time Keith walked through his apartment into his bedroom. His room was pretty large, with a queen bed in the center and a pretty sophisticated office space in the corner. She rested her purse on the glass desk on which his laptop rested and nervously swung her arms by her sides.

The tequila, Kahlúa, Baileys, Courvoisier, and Corona were starting to mix in her stomach and her head. The room was spinning, with Keith standing in the center of it. He was the only object that seemed fixated in one position.

She walked (*am I stumbling?*) toward him, an oak tree in a windstorm. She grabbed each arm, feeling his muscles tense underneath her palms. Angling her face upward, she closed her eyes and found his lips. They were smooth and firm and she brushed them with hers. Eager to make more pressing contact, she leaned into him. Losing her balance, she teetered, giving him a firm head butt. Keith stepped back, gently taking hold of her waist. "Kahli. You're drunk."

"No, I'm not!" The high-pitched whine that Kahli heard didn't even sound like her own voice. "I'm just . . . tired." She glanced at his hastily made bed. It couldn't have looked more inviting if it were encased in satin. She threw herself into it like a child would do to an open fire hydrant on a humid Boston summer day, and sighed contentedly at the relief she felt. Keith shook his head and began to walk out of the room.

"Noooo," Kahli groaned. "Come back."

He knew he shouldn't, but her eyes were pleading. *I'll sleep here, but I won't even take off my clothes.* By the time he closed the door, turned off the light, and returned to his bed, Kahlila was already sleeping. Keith couldn't help but smile at her slightly open mouth and heavy breathing. He decided that he could take the risk of removing his shirt, which he was glad for because the apartment was hot and he hadn't gotten around to buying an air conditioner. Settling into bed as far away from the sleeping beauty as possible, he had no time to consider how crazy his evening was before he was asleep himself.

The first thing Kahlila saw when she opened her eyes was his bare brown back. She scanned the deep crease in its center. She was so tempted to trace the line with her finger, but in the light of morning, it hit her. She did not know this man. Hadn't even learned his last name. She withdrew her hand from the vicinity of his body.

The sound of the front door opening and closing made Keith sit up with a start. She hadn't even known he was awake. Footsteps were clearly headed in their direction. He turned to her almost frantically. The look in Keith's eyes told Kahlila that trouble was on its way, and it was not a burglar. Her first instinct was to flee, but it was clearly too late for that. Bolting out of the window was only reserved for the movies, never to be actually done in real life. In her panic, she could think of no better place to hide than under the covers. She hastily pulled the sheet over her. Just as soon as her head was covered, she could hear the creak of the door being thrown open.

"Keith, we need to talk." The female's voice was aggressive, determined. There was nothing Kahlila wanted less than a confrontation with the woman behind that voice.

"I thought you were sleeping at Lisa's house," he said too quickly.

"I did. Why are you acting all weird?" Footsteps nearing. "What do you have in bed with . . . oh no, you didn't, Keith. Is that Traci?"

"Nah," Keith replied in a barely audible tone.

"You can't even wait twenty-four hours to bring some random girl into the house?" Without waiting for him to respond, she exited as quickly as she had entered, and slammed the door behind her. Ten seconds later, they heard the front door slam as well.

Kahlila didn't want to come out from under the covers. She didn't want to see his face or have a discussion about what had just occurred. She wanted to freeze time, the way Evie used to on her favorite childhood show, *Out of This World*, and unfreeze it when she was miles away from Keith's bedroom. This was her fault. *She* had followed him back to his place. He hadn't invited her. She couldn't even be angry with him. He didn't try to take advantage of her, and he didn't tell her any lies. She never asked whether his girlfriend lived with him. She never asked the reason why they were having problems. She was too busy being impressed with his little simile comparing himself to instant coffee.

Kahlila finally peeled back the sheet. Keith was already out of bed, pulling his T-shirt over his head. She forced herself not to take note of his well-defined chest muscles, or the faint hair that grew over it. Kahlila was the only woman she knew who liked hairy chests. There was something very manly about them. Men who shaved their chests were not even to be considered. It was number 103 on The List.

"I'm sorry," was all that he said.

"No, *I'm* sorry," she said, looking down at her body and realizing she had slept in her shoes. "You said you wanted to leave things at the bar, and I forced the issue."

"I didn't really *want* to leave things there, though, and you felt that."

"Okay, this conversation is no longer appropriate. I need to get out of here." She quickly got out of bed and walked to retrieve her purse, taking a long look at the desk to see if she missed any telling photographs of him and his girlfriend. None.

"How are you going to get home?"

Damn. She hadn't considered the fact that they took a cab to his house. "I'll take the bus. Or walk. I live in the South End. It's not far."

"It's too far to walk. Let me drive you."

Why does he still have to be so freaking considerate? "Why are you thinking about me and *my* needs? Do you even care that she saw you with another woman in your bed? What about *her* feelings?" Keith gave her a look of almost amusement, which revved her up even more. "Actually, maybe she's used to catching you in bed with other women. Who the hell is Traci?"

Keith sat down on the edge of his bed, shaking his head. "Look. Do you want a ride or not?"

"I'm all set." Like the faceless woman of five minutes before, she walked out of his bedroom and slammed the door behind her. For a moment, she feared that his girl might be waiting outside for her, but when she stepped into the glaring sunlight, the street was clear.

There had been a moment the night before when Keith and Kahlila held each other's gaze and smiled half smiles. In that moment, Kahli had thought, *This guy gets me.* Now, in this moment, she doubted her own intuition completely. Just hours ago, she had felt on top of the world. Now she was second-guessing every decision she had ever made about men.

Chapter 10

To: robyn.parks@partners.org,
desiree@desireethomas.com,
madeline.ellis@boston.k12.ma.us,
jt_steinway@steinwayfoundation.org
From: kahlila.bradford@boston.k12.ma.us
Time: Thursday, June 22, 2006, 12:05 p.m.
Subject: the night from hell
Message:
ladies (and jt),

the next time i say some crap about becoming
somebody i'm not, just smack me. what was i thinking, throwing my list away, trying to be spontaneous? total disaster.

desiree and j.t., to catch you up: madeline,
robyn, and i went to a bar last night to celebrate the
last day of school. i'd decided to throw the infamous List away for the summer and try to be more
open-minded about guys. perfectly timed, this
group of men invites us to hang out with them for a
few drinks. i meet this cutie named keith, and we
just totally click right away. i feel so comfortable

with him that we stay at the bar talking, just the two of us, after everybody else leaves.

okay, now for the part that no one was witness to: at the end of the evening, i decided to be bolder than usual and suggested that we keep in touch. he said he'd rather leave things where they are. in other words, i got totally dissed. he walked me outside and put me in a cab. folks, i got out of my cab to chase his cab down and climb in with him. i know your mouths are open right now. that sounds absolutely nothing like the kahli you guys know and love.

so suddenly we're in a taxi, going back to his place. i'm totally drunk. we get to the apartment, i'm stumbling around, trying to be sexy, probably looking pretty gross. i end up passed out on his bed. in the middle of the night, though, i feel him edging closer to me. so i edge closer too, and suddenly we're spooning. moment of silence for the spoon position—sigh.

the next morning, i'm actually feeling pretty good again. he respected me enough not to take advantage, we cuddled, and who knows where things might go in the future? then the front door opens, and this woman storms into the bedroom. mind you, i have no idea what she looks like because i'm now hiding under the covers. but she sees me under there and is none too happy. not to mention, her voice sounds familiar, which means i probably have met her somewhere on the boston scene in the past. as soon as she leaves, i book it out of there on foot and walk home. it took me an hour in the blazing sun.

i've hit a new low, everyone. i was feeling pretty bad near the end of school. tired of being lonely, wondering if i rely too much on my job for fulfillment, unsure whether i'll ever find the right guy in the face

of all of my pickiness. so i made a conscious decision to try to think outside the box, and i immediately made a connection, only to have it blow up in
my face.

thanks for listening. just had to vent. i can't believe i sent this from my work account—hopefully
my principal won't hack into my e-mail and fire
me for being a dumb ass. then i'd be lonely *and*
unemployed.

talk soon,
kahli

To: kahlila.bradford@boston.k12.ma.us
From: madeline.ellis@boston.k12.ma.us
Date and Time: Thursday, June 22, 2006, 1:14 p.m.
Subject: !!!!!
Message:
   Oh my goodness, Kahli. I am sooo sorry that it
turned out that way. I'm not surprised, though.
Those guys were total jerks. I still can't believe that
Joe was totally hitting on me, and then mentioned
being married like it was no big deal. Snakes travel
in packs. Look at Nixon. Those stupid friends of
Keith might as well have been Kissinger and Deep
Throat. Consider yourself lucky that you exposed
Keith for the slime that he is before you got in even
deeper.
   I was so bummed after our evening that I went
online when I got home and joined match.com,
eharmony.com, and about 3 other free dating sites.
I didn't sleep last night, choosing photos to upload,
constructing my profile, and surfing for guys. Kahli,
I've already had tons of guys contact me in the few
hours that I've been a member. They actually seem

normal, *and* they're single. Or at least they say they are. It's better than pretending not to be and then suddenly blurting it out like a total jerk.

You should totally join! I know you claim to know all the single black guys in Boston (which would explain why you didn't know Keith—he wasn't single!), but you could look for people who live outside the city, or for white guys who are interested in dating women of all ethnic groups. That's the thing, Kahli. They have to write all this stuff about themselves in their profiles, so there's no guessing what kind of person they are, or if they're interested. I can't believe I waited this long to join the online bandwagon. Get on board! You'll feel better!
Maddie

To: kahlila.bradford@boston.k12.ma.us
From: robyn.parks@partners.org
Date and Time: Thursday, June 22, 2006, 1:58 p.m.
Subject: Keep it movin'.
Message:

Girl, thank you so much for your message. I came in this morning feeling so tired from our night out. Had a splitting headache. As soon as I punch in, a guy gets wheeled into the ER with a bullet in his head. Guess he was a lot worse off than me. Anyway, spent the whole morning dealing with that craziness. He's actually gonna pull through, looks like. Point is, I needed some entertainment after that experience, and you really gave it to me. What were you thinking, following the dude home? You're lucky he didn't turn out to be an ax murderer! We knew NOTHING about those guys. Don't ever be that stupid again. That said, what a story! Wow. All I can really say is that you tend to be so quick in rushing to judgment.

You either swear off a guy in the first 3 minutes you meet him, or think he's your soul mate in a matter of 3 hours. Remain skeptical without being cynical. You *will* meet the right guy, Kahli. And I'll keep being your wing woman until you do. —R

To: kahlila.bradford@boston.k12.ma.us
From: jt_steinway@steinwayfoundation.org
Date and Time: Thursday, June 22, 2006, 3:23 p.m.
Subject: Re: the night from hell
Message:

Jeez, Kal. I didn't know it had gotten that rough for you. I just don't get it. You're hot, you're driven, you're kind. You've gotta be crazy if you think that someone isn't gonna recognize it. What really sucks about last night is that you didn't even get to have any sex, which I know you're long overdue for.

I hope this one bad experience doesn't mean that you're resurrecting The List. That thing is bad news. It's the reason why I never bother to try to hook you up with anybody. Isn't "no professional athletes" number 32 or something? Well, those are the only guys I know.

Things with me have been okay. Leaving pro-ball hasn't changed my social life much one way or the other. Marisol is still dating me, so I guess she really did like me for me all these years. Although I *am* still rich, so who knows? ☺ I have to get another surgery on my knee soon. In the meantime, I'm just working with my foundation. We're starting up basketball camp in a couple of weeks, so things are busy. You've gotta come to Jersey sometime this summer and check it out.

Hang in there,
JT

To: kahlila@boston.k12.ma.us
From: desiree@desireethomas.com
Date and Time: Thursday, June 22, 2006, 4:05 p.m.
Subject: a modest proposal
Message:

    damn it, i miss everything living in new york. i would have loved to see this keith character who had you running after a cab in the middle of the street. that might have to end up in my next book. it's quite a visual.

    i have a suggestion, and hear me out before you say no. come to new york. just for the summer. our tenant downstairs moved out, and we wanted to do some work to the apartment before we rent it again, so you can use it for july and august. you can get a change of scenery, meet some new people, and keep me company! now that you and robyn both live in boston, i miss my friends so much. i love my husband, but he's not so good at the girl talk. you'd actually be doing me a favor by coming. i vowed to take the summer off from any writing projects, and you can be my companion in leisure.

    what do you think?
des

To: desiree@desireethomas.com
From: kahlila.bradford@boston.k12.ma.us
Date and Time: Thursday, June 22, 2006, 4:44 p.m.
Subject: regarding your not so modest proposal
Message:
des,

    after e-mailing my four closest friends, here were my options for rebounding from The Incident:

(1) join a singles network online, deleting every message with any incorrect spelling, turning up my nose at every picture where the guy isn't perfect looking, and falling in love with some guy's profile who never writes me back.
(2) keep hitting the boston scene with robyn, hoping that one day there will be a guy whom i'd never noticed at the 1,273 events i'd attended before, but is apparently the one.
(3) screw finding love and just have good sex with professional athletes.
(4) come to new york.
see ya in harlem.

love,
kahli

Chapter 11

He has to want to be a father someday.

Kahlila felt her nerves relax when she exited the Triborough Bridge at 125th Street. Something about driving in New York City always calmed her. While most people would say that New York drivers were absolutely insane, Kahlila maintained that they were far superior to the folks behind the wheel in her hometown. Bostonians drove like maniacs with no actual skill. New Yorkers were excellent at negotiating sharp turns and tight squeezes. And whenever Kahlila visited Desiree in Harlem, she felt herself acquiring the necessary survival tactics to navigate the streets successfully. She wasn't on 125th for five minutes before she swerved around a bus that was slowing her progress to an unacceptable crawl.

While Kahlila tried to take minivacations to the Big Apple whenever possible, she still couldn't believe that she was spending two months there with only a few days' notice. But from the morning that she left Keith's house, she knew that she needed some time away from her life.

She had entered her condo in the South End after her sweaty walk of shame, and the emptiness of it was deafening. Without the distraction of student essays to read or a kid's volleyball game to attend, she could barely function. Summer had never been that bad. She'd always enjoyed her time off, and planned vacations to Trinidad to see her mom, or even England to spend time with her father. But this summer she hadn't scheduled anything, not because she didn't want to go, but because she didn't have the energy. Wasn't lethargy a sign of depression? She'd never thought of herself as depressed. But as she buried her face in her pillow that morning and sobbed for hours straight, she knew that her life was incomplete. And this summer, she was determined to complete it, in the company of the person who, aside from her mom, probably knew her better than anyone else.

Desiree and Kahlila had been roommates their freshman year of college, along with Robyn, and had been the best of friends ever since. Desiree began her writing career as a novelist, but once her first book was made into a movie, she decided that she wanted to give screenwriting a try as well. Soon, she was writing the script adaptations of her own books, and was being offered staff positions on some of the hottest television shows around. Desiree declined the offers, as her husband's business was in New York, and neither one of them particularly liked Los Angeles. Still, the success that she'd experienced just by doing what she loved was outstanding, and it made Kahlila enormously happy that she, Desiree, and Robyn were all pursuing their passions.

Her heartbeat quickened as she took a left onto Lenox and a right onto 122nd Street. The only available parking spot on the street was directly in front of Desiree and Jason's brownstone. Foreshadowing? She had to think so.

She had not even turned off her engine after parallel parking when Desiree opened the front door and came skipping down the steps. Even with her windows up and the air conditioner blasting, Desiree's excited squeal was perfectly audible. Kahlila quickly got out of the car and ran to meet her best friend on the sidewalk. Just as they were about to hug, Kahlila stopped short. Something was weird. Desiree's face looked gorgeous as usual: smooth café au lait complexion with a natural pink glow in her cheeks, exquisitely arched eyebrows, and full red lips. But her body—while her arms were still as toned as they always were, her chest was much fuller. In addition, Desiree always had a six-pack that rivaled Janet Jackson's, and while her stomach was still flat, it looked . . . different somehow.

"Oh my goodness. Are you—" Kahlila stared at Desiree's midsection.

"Yes! Three months," Desiree laughed.

Kahlila had no time to react, as Desiree's husband, Jason, suddenly emerged from the brownstone wearing a grin from ear to ear. "Did you tell her?" he asked his wife.

"She knew. I told you she would!" Desiree shouted back, still giggling.

In a split second, Kahlila's whole perception of the summer that stretched in front of her was changed. On the drive down, she'd envisioned getting drinks with her best friend at swanky locations, adopting Desiree's psychotic gym routine, and shopping for designer clothes on Fifth Avenue. Suddenly, Kahlila's mental picture of the next few months involved picking out baby furniture at IKEA.

She didn't have another moment to indulge in self-pity,

because Desiree was grabbing her hand and dragging her inside while Jason began to unload her car.

"Shouldn't we help him?" Kahlila asked as she trailed Desiree upstairs.

"Girl, he has it under control. Let's go see your new digs." Kahlila couldn't help but catch a bit of Desiree's excitement as they reached the second landing. Desiree threw the door open in dramatic fashion, revealing a freshly painted apartment with gorgeous hardwood floors, a modern kitchen with stainless steel appliances, and a few key pieces of furniture. Kahlila was speechless, touching the plush couch softly before peeking into a bedroom equipped with a day bed and a pinewood dresser.

"Surprise!" exclaimed Desiree, joining Kahlila in the doorway. "We're actually going to move down here in September. It's bigger than the apartment upstairs, so we're going to make the third floor the gym, the office, that kind of thing."

Guilt punched Kahlila in the gut. Desiree and Jason were putting their moving plans on hold to entertain her this summer, and she was actually annoyed that they were expecting their first child together. "Wow. I'm so overwhelmed. I didn't even say congratulations yet!"

"That's true!" Desiree laughed, and they hugged, rocking from side to side until Jason's voice sounded from the living room.

"Kahli, didn't Des tell you that you only needed to bring clothes?"

"Yeah. That's all I brought."

"Are you serious? There are ten suitcases in that car!"

Since college, Kahlila had definitely become the most fashion obsessed of the crew. She'd had bohemian taste during her school years, wearing long flowing skirts and even going so far as to put a flower in her hair on sunny days. When she returned to Boston, the cosmopolitan chic influence of the city merged with her free-spirited taste, and suddenly her personal style was the talk of Pierce High School. She expertly mixed designer labels (bought mostly from T.J. Maxx and secondhand stores on Boston's exclusive Newbury Street) with cheap items that people just assumed to be expensive.

Jason set down the suitcase, garment bag, and duffel that he had somehow balanced on one arm and did a few stretches to relieve the pain. "What are you going to do with your car? It's a hassle to move it around for street cleaning."

"I'm going to drive it to J.T.'s house in Jersey sometime over the next few days and leave it there for the summer."

"You mean J.T.'s estate," Jason corrected with a smile, and headed back downstairs to retrieve another load.

J.T. and Kahlila had been close friends since high school, where they'd both attended a private school right outside Boston. J.T. went to Franklin University first, and Kahlila followed suit the next year. A basketball phenom, J.T. had played for the New Jersey Nets for six years after college, but repeated injuries finally ended his career last season. His Franklin education served him well, and he had invested his money wisely. One of his investments was Jason's gym in Secaucus, New Jersey. Jason had already experienced a great deal of success even before J.T. came on as a partner, but they'd done extraordinarily well in recent years, making Jay's Gym a franchise. The facilities were state-of-the-art, and the NBA theme that they incorporated into the layout didn't hurt either.

It was strange for Kahlila that a relationship between people she'd introduced to one another was flourishing without her, and it even made her a little bit sad. She knew that she wasn't as up on things in J.T.'s life as Desiree and Jason were, because she was all the way in Boston. At the same time, she knew that Desiree felt the same way about her increased closeness with Robyn since she'd moved north for her residency. Kahlila looked forward to reconnecting with her friends over the next few months, although her mind was still preoccupied by the unexpected piece of news she'd received upon arrival.

"Des, are you sure it was a good idea for me to come this summer? You're pregnant, for goodness' sake! Shouldn't you be . . . nesting or something?"

"Are you kidding me? This will be the last summer where I'll be able to be a good host. Girl, I look great right now. My stomach is still flat, my boobs are huge, and my hair is growing like weeds. We've gotta hit the town and take advantage of it."

"So you've been feeling okay?"

"Actually, I've been feeling like a piece of shit roasting in the sun. But first trimester is virtually over, and a new day is here." Jason returned to the living room, dropped Kahlila's bags, and wiped the sweat from his brow with his T-shirt. "Right, baby? It's a new day."

Jason walked behind her, slipped his arms around her waist, and nuzzled his face in her neck. Desiree continued talking about her first few months of pregnancy as if her husband's touch were more natural than air itself. Kahlila watched the way he rubbed her tummy, and she said a silent prayer that one day a man might adore her half as much.

"I hope it's a boy," Desiree was saying. "It'll be nice to have one of each." Though this was Desiree's first child, Jason already had an eight-year-old daughter. They had achieved blended family bliss, where Desiree embraced Nailah as if she were her own, and considered Nailah's mother, Monique, to be one of her closest friends. "Although Jason will probably have the poor kid lifting weights before he's potty trained."

"Shit, I'll do that if it's a girl too!"

"The baby's gonna be beautiful, that's for sure," Kahlila said, eyeing Desiree's model-like face and Jason's bald head and green eyes. He'd worn cornrows for a long time, earning him a lot of comparisons to "that guy in the *Barbershop* movies," but when his hair started receding, he decided to beat nature to the punch and shave it all off.

Desiree and Jason exchanged modest smiles, as if it had never occurred to them how good-looking they actually were. "So I hope you packed something dressy in those ten suitcases of yours," Desiree said, examining the plethora of luggage scattered around the room.

"Why? Where are we going?"

"There's a fund-raiser tomorrow night in the Hamptons."

"The Hamptons?" Kahlila repeated incredulously. The closest she'd ever been to the Hamptons was a Hampton Inn. "For what?"

"For a bunch of bougie-ass celebrities to feel good about themselves, that's for what," Jason chimed in as he went to make the last run to Kahlila's car.

"Celebrities?" Kahlila could feel her eyes widening.

"You see how he talks about these types of events? This is why we never go. So I'm excited to have you around this summer, girl."

"I'm excited to be here." And as she looked around her sunny apartment bursting with life in so many ways, she really meant it.

Chapter 12

His confidence should
be smooth, not cocky.

Darius looked on as an R&B crooner who'd recently emerged on the scene sang his heart out in front of a grand piano, and he couldn't help but feel a twinge of jealousy. *They can invite me to give money to their fund-raiser, but they ask someone else to perform.* He stood with his arms folded as people whispered words of admiration for the young talent. This newcomer, also in his late twenties, was getting the kind of critical acclaim on his debut album that Darius had not experienced. They'd dubbed the singer the "male Alicia Keys," labeling him a prodigy whose piano skills were matched only by his songwriting and exceptional vocal range. Meanwhile, Darius's album reviews focused on the stellar packaging: the brilliant use of samples, the cleverly worded cameo spots by various rappers on Flow Steddie's label, and the obvious appeal of Darius himself, whose good looks garnered him female fans of all ages.

Darius actually played two instruments, the piano and guitar, but Flow had advised him against utilizing those talents on the album. "People know you as the dude with the dope voice who sings the hooks on my tracks. You want to give them an extension of that sound." Flow's advice had paid off, as record sales hit the roof almost immediately. But at the same time, he felt pigeonholed as the R&B guy in Flow's hip-hop world. He was a songwriter, but only one of his original songs was used on the final cut of his album. And even though women of all ages did find him attractive, he realized that the majority of his music fans were younger than he was, and he often heard himself on the same playlists as Chris Brown and Mario. For his sophomore project, he longed to branch out in order to be taken more seriously by a mature audience. Even more importantly, he wanted to write all of his own songs this time. He wasn't just a singer; he was a musician. And he wasn't sure how many people actually knew that.

The singer's ballad ended to thunderous applause. Darius put on a smile and clapped enthusiastically. He knew that he had absolutely nothing to complain about. After all, he'd won Best New Artist at the BET Awards just days before (but only because the R&B crooner's album hadn't been out long enough to compete against him in that category). And when he returned from Los Angeles, he went on a first date with Miko that went amazingly well. They had a three-hour dinner that flew by with talk about their goals, their mutual friends, and their mutual attraction for one another. As soon as Miko uncrossed her long legs to run to the restroom, Darius sent Rasheed a text: Perfect choice. Miko's the girl.

The crowd began to fan out through the tent, and Darius looked around for someone to talk to. He hadn't brought Rasheed this evening, and he was already bored.

It looked obnoxious for people to bring their bodyguards to private events such as this one, where everybody was somebody. But Darius would have wanted him to come just as a friend. He and Rasheed were both business majors at NYU, and remained tight after graduation. When Darius decided to make the move to a full-time music career, he asked Rasheed to come onto his team as a personal assistant of sorts. "That sounds like a bitch-ass job, dude." Luckily, with Rasheed's size, people assumed him to serve solely as the bodyguard, but in reality he handled so many aspects of his career that Darius's manager often felt left with nothing to do. Tonight, however, Rasheed was enjoying his night off with Toni, most likely eating at some trendy place downtown.

"Oh my goodness. Are you Darius Wilson?" Two girls, one white and one black, had suddenly appeared in front of him.

"Last time I checked," he answered with a generous smile.

The girls looked at each other and squealed. Darius laughed out loud at their textbook response. He guessed them to be about thirteen.

"Can we please take a picture with you?"

"It would be my pleasure, ladies."

The white girl ran off in her way-too-high heels to find someone with a camera. Her friend was left in the company of a celebrity with not a single thing to say. He decided to initiate the conversation. "So, what's your name?"

"Leigh. What's yours?" Darius raised his eyebrows amusedly. "Oh my goodness, I can't believe I just asked you that. I'm a little bit nervous. I love your album so much. My friends and I have a dance routine to 'Party Till You See the Sun.'"

Darius knew that he should be flattered, but hearing

this adolescent talking about how much she loved his song only served to fan the flames of doubt that had been swirling in his head for quite some time. "So, what are you and your friend doing at this fund-raiser?"

"My dad is one of the organizers, and Jen is just my friend from school." As soon as her name was said, Jen was back with what looked to be the camera of a professional photographer. It was huge, with a zoom lens and a gigantic flash attachment. But Jen handled it like a pro, taking a shot of him and Leigh, and then passing the camera to Leigh so Jen could get her moment to shine. The two of them happily floated off without another word as soon as the photo was taken.

On the other side of the tent, Darius caught a glimpse of Desiree Thomas, whom he heard was going to be in attendance when his publicist read him highlights of the guest list. Though they'd met a few times before, he still couldn't believe that someone as beautiful as she was had a career that was completely unrelated to her appearance. A darker-haired, slightly less booty-licious Beyoncé, she disappointed many men whenever she flashed her ring finger, which was outfitted with an elaborate diamond configuration that screamed, "I'm married, suckas!" But that didn't matter, because Darius's interest in talking to Desiree tonight was completely professional.

"So, what happens now?" Kahlila asked between mouthfuls of crab-stuffed mushroom caps.

"Well, we mingled on the lawn, drank champagne . . . well, *some* of us drank champagne"—she patted her stomach ruefully—"listened to a couple of speakers talk about the charity organization, and enjoyed a musical guest.

The rest of the evening is eating these hors d'oeuvres and, well, mingling some more."

"Fine with me," Kahlila said, popping a California roll into her mouth. She had never been to the Hamptons, but it was exactly as she had pictured it. Quaint, classy, and cultured, the place was too special even for normal green street signs. Names of roads were painted on white posts planted in the ground. People walked the streets in tennis skirts, and shopped at boutiques after leisurely lunches of lobster sandwiches and sparkling water. She and Desiree had driven up early in the day to make time for a bit of sightseeing and people watching, and Kahlila fell in love immediately.

Desiree had a contact in East Hampton who left the key under the mat for them to shower and change before the event. Kahlila was shocked by the modern architecture of a house that seemed to sit in the middle of the woods. She was equally shocked by the fact that someone would leave a key under a mat to a house that was clearly worth a few million dollars. She contemplated these wonders as she slipped into a pair of gold silky pants that she had bought from the BCBG outlet store in Wrentham, Massachusetts, with a beaded top that she'd bought from around the way. Following her usual rule of mixing coupon couture with high-quality-looking cheapies, she donned a pair of metallic Manolo Blahniks that she borrowed from Desiree and fabulous chandelier earrings that she got on sale at Claire's Accessories for three dollars. She figured that the outfit was flashy enough without too much makeup, especially since she didn't really know how to apply anything beyond lip gloss and mascara. Desiree was rocking a V-necked black wraparound dress that perfectly accentuated her cleavage while making her waist look smaller. When Kahlila asked her if she'd be okay in her three-inch-heeled Jimmy Choos, Desiree snapped, "I'm pregnant, not handicapped."

As Kahlila looked around the tent, she decided that she and Desiree were definitely holding their own in the company of Hollywood elite. In fact, she noticed an extremely handsome man headed in their direction. When he got closer, she realized that he was more than handsome. He was famous. And he was touching Desiree's arm.

Desiree turned around and smiled broadly when she saw Darius Wilson standing in front of her. Kahlila watched as they hugged as if they'd known each other forever. *I just saw this guy on TV a couple of days ago, and now he's hugging my best friend.*

He turned to Kahlila and extended his hand. "Hi. I'm Darius."

"Kahlila. Nice to meet you," she answered, taking his hand and appreciating his firm grip. Something about his introduction impressed her. Maybe it was that he didn't wait for Desiree to initiate it. Or that he only used his first name, which seemed less pretentious than if he were to have used his full name. His kind smile made her want to add that she loved his music, but she couldn't bring herself to lie. *Besides, people probably say that to him all the time.*

"Kahli, Darius contributed a song to the soundtrack of *A Hot Day in Harlem.* The song works so well in the scene in the movie where—"

"Don't tell me," Darius laughed. "To be honest, I haven't seen it yet."

"That's right, you *did* miss the premiere. Where were you?"

"I was in L.A. at the BET Awards."

"Oh my goodness! I didn't even congratulate you on your win. I am such an idiot."

"No worries. It was great. But I'm exhausted, from prepartying, to postpartying . . ."

"I'll bet. And I'm sure it all seems tame compared to the VMAs."

"Absolutely. That's gonna be bananas. Are you going?"

"To the MTV Awards? They don't invite writers to those kinds of events. Besides, my husband would never go."

Kahlila suddenly felt as if the latest issue of *US Weekly* was unfolding in front of her eyes. The headline: ATTENDING A FUND-RAISER IN EAST HAMPTON, DESIREE THOMAS, WRITER OF THE NEW FILM *A HOT DAY IN HARLEM*, CONGRATULATES R&B SINGER DARIUS WILSON ON HIS RECENT BEST NEW ARTIST WIN AT THE BET AWARDS.

As much as she loved reading the glossy pages of those magazines, she still had a long-standing rule (number 33 on her List, right after no professional athletes): no celebrities. She believed that she'd watched enough hours of *Entertainment Tonight* and *Extra* to support her theory that she was way too substantive and stable for someone famous. She also had the secondhand experience of Desiree's many brushes with stars to support her claim. Still, Desiree never spoke disparagingly about Darius Wilson; in fact, she'd never mentioned him at all.

As if he could feel Kahlila's attention on him, Darius again turned to face her. "Do you work in the city as well?"

Another example of total politeness. He could have asked whether she worked in the industry, but instead he left it open. Darius seemed to possess an awareness that there was life outside of his own. "No, actually. I work in Boston. I'm just in the city for the summer."

"Kahlila's a teacher," Desiree said proudly.

"Oh, really? What grade level?"

"High school."

"What subject?"

Is he serious? Some of my dates don't ask this many follow-up questions. "English."

"My high school English teacher was the person who got me writing poetry, which then got me writing songs. So I'm a big fan of English teachers," he said with a wink.

Kahlila was immediately smitten, so much so that she couldn't respond. Her mind was already in her classroom in September, excitedly reporting to her classes that Darius Wilson told her that he was a big fan of hers. She wanted to ask to take a picture with him so that she could show the kids at Girl Talk, but the normalcy with which he was interacting with them made her feel as if it would be uncool to bust out her digital camera from her purse.

Darius had her captivated so quickly that she was already making excuses in her mind for why her rule shouldn't count. *Most of the rules on The List were designed in response to guys who didn't live up to a certain standard. The "no celebrities" rule was put on there because of Desiree's reports about how trifling they can be. Her select experiences are no reason to swear off a whole category of people. Besides, I'm not supposed to be adhering to The List anyway. Just because my first effort at being carefree ended in disaster doesn't mean that I can't follow through with my vow to disregard The List for the summer.*

He saved her from coming up with something appropriate to say by refocusing on Desiree. "Hey, Desiree, speaking of writing, I was hoping to get your expert opinion about a literary opportunity that was presented to me recently."

Desiree was listening to Darius, but she was also picking up Kahlila's dazed smile and starry eyes. "How about we get together for dinner later in the week?"

"Sounds good."

"You don't mind if Kahlila and Jason come, do you?" She smiled graciously.

"Jason's your husband, right? Of course I don't mind. Besides, you know we'd be on Page Six if we had dinner just the two of us anyway."

"Good point. So we'll make it look like a double date instead," Desiree countered, ignoring the darts that Kahlila was shooting with her eyes.

"So, are you ready to be linked to me in the rumor mill?" Darius asked Kahlila with a smirk.

"I've been linked to worse," Kahlila shot back. The three of them shared a laugh, and Kahlila took that moment to remind herself exactly how much, in a matter of days, her summer had improved.

Chapter 13

He must be willing to have
difficult conversations for the
good of the relationship.

"Yo, Bree, you got any pineapple juice?" Ty, a twenty-
two-year-old who lived with his mom in the house at the
end of the street, held a CD case in one hand and a
bottle of Hennessey in the other.

Bree began to feel anxious. She hadn't planned to
have people in Keith's house. But she had been sitting
on her porch earlier that afternoon reading *Prep*, when
Ty walked up the steps and sat down next to her on the
other white plastic patio chair that was too dirty and
beaten up for any passerby to steal.

"What you reading?" he asked, slouching down in his
seat until he was practically reclined.

Bree held up the book as a response.

"What's it about?"

"A girl at a boarding school who doesn't fit in." She

returned her eyes to the novel, half hoping he'd go away, but also wishing that the conversation would continue. She hadn't seen Ty this close before, and had never noticed how white and straight his teeth were. She loved perfect smiles. She actually had one herself, but utilized it so rarely that she tended to forget it existed.

"Is that what you were, before you moved to the Bury? A boarding school reject?"

"No." She didn't look up from her pages, but felt his stare warming her cheeks.

"You miss your girl Lisa?" His eyes didn't move from her face.

Lisa was Bree's only friend in Boston. Though the two girls attended different high schools, they lived only two houses apart. Lisa was so friendly that Bree couldn't long resist her invitations to watch movies and listen to music. Unfortunately, she had left town a few days before to visit her grandmother down South for the entire summer.

"Not really," she lied.

"Anyone ever tell you that you're really dope, even though you have an attitude problem?"

"I've heard people mention it before," she retorted, her mouth curling despite herself.

"Oh, the girl got jokes!" Ty took the Celtics cap from his head and covered his face with it as his shoulders bounced up and down in silent laughter. "So, what are you doing tonight? Where's your boy?"

"Working." She found herself adding, "Late," and then kicking herself for doing so.

"So, you wanna chill with a few of us from the block?"

"Where?"

"At my crib."

You mean your mom's crib. "I'm not going to your house when I barely know you."

Ty was prepared with a plan B. "We'll come to you, then."

Now, two hours later, three guys and two girls were sitting in her living room watching videos and eating Bree's sour cream and onion chips. She had actually been having a good time until Ty stepped out and returned with a bottle of brown alcohol.

"I don't have any pineapple juice," she announced, hoping no one would look in the fridge and see that she was lying.

"No thing. We'll just hit it straight."

Bree opened her mouth to object, but no sound came out. Something about them reminded her of the kids she used to know when her family lived in New Haven. Back when her family was intact and life was virtually perfect. And Ty—he wasn't the most impressive person on paper, but at least he would never criticize her for wearing a miniskirt, or judge her for how messed up her life had become. To be fair, her ex-boyfriend Stanley, the only guy her own age who managed to keep her interest, would have never passed judgment on anything she did. But he did something even worse when her mother died: he felt sorry for her. And that was an emotion she just couldn't take.

She decided to just go with the flow. Keith wouldn't be home for hours and she had plenty of time to clean up after her visitors. Besides, she wasn't going to drink anything, and if they were planning on doing anything else, they'd have to do it outside. An old Keith Sweat video came on VH-1 Soul, and everyone started singing along. She couldn't remember the last time she'd felt like she was part of a group. She was suddenly more relaxed, and graciously brought a stack of plastic cups into the living room.

* * *

Keith was in a great mood. The assignment he'd been given had been handed over to a summer associate, which meant that his evening was suddenly free. He thought that he might grab Bree so they could get some food at Merengue, a Dominican restaurant down the street that they absolutely loved. But as he approached his front steps, he was assaulted by a thick layer of marijuana smoke. At the sight of Ty, the local high school dropout who lived off his mom's disability check, along with one of Ty's identityless sidekicks, Keith's blood immediately began to simmer.

"Get the fuck off my porch." His voice was even as he climbed the steps and stood directly over his two unwanted guests.

"Watch who you're talking to like that." Ty looked Keith in his eye as he put out the blunt in an ashtray he'd brought over from his mother's house.

"Don't let the suit and tie fool you, son. Stay away from this house, *and* from Bree, and we won't have any problems."

"You act like I'm bothering her," Ty said with a smile, motioning for his boy to stand up. "She's having fun inside," he called over his shoulder as he headed down the steps.

Keith steeled himself for what he might see when he walked into his house. Throwing open the door, he met the surprised stares of two girls who looked to be about Bree's age, and one guy who looked several years older. They were sprawled on the couch, holding cups that were presumably filled with Hennessey, considering the near-empty bottle on the coffee table. Bree was sitting in the recliner, her arms folded, staring past her guests and at the wall behind them. When she looked over and saw Keith's clenched jaw, her eyes filled with fear.

"Party's over, y'all," one of the girls said matter-of-factly.

All three of them rose simultaneously, leaving their cups and bottle behind as they walked past Keith and headed outside, where it wasn't yet dark.

Keith slammed the door behind them and stared at Bree. *What am I going to do with this girl?*

Keith was ten years old when Bree was born. Their parents, Celia and Stu, were high school sweethearts. Celia worked at the same bank for fifteen years, and Stu was a firefighter in New Haven. They weren't rich, but they were comfortable, and their house was full of laughter and smiles. Celia had tried to have another child after Keith for years, and had given up hope when she found herself pregnant with Bree. Keith adored his father while Bree was a mommy's girl. Spending much of his time after school at the fire station, Keith vowed to be just like his dad when he grew up. But when Stu died in a four-alarm fire from smoke inhalation when Keith was thirteen, Celia made him promise not to take on a job where one's life was in danger. Heartbroken at the loss of his father, he resisted the pull of the New Haven streets by keeping his nose in his books and graduating with honors from high school. Bree was just eight when Keith left home for college at Boston University. In the years that followed, Celia focused all of her energy on Bree, putting her daughter's emotional nature to good use through community theater. She had been on her way to pick up Bree from play practice when her front tire blew out on I-95 and the car wheeled into the guardrail. Celia died instantly and suddenly Bree was left with indescribable pain and guilt, and no one in New Haven to take care of her.

Keith had just graduated from law school the month before, and had taken a position with the most prestigious firm in Boston. But they were patient as he traveled frequently to Connecticut to establish legal guardianship of his younger sister. He and Bree hadn't lived in the same house in ten years, and they had a lot of adjusting to do. Getting reacquainted while Bree was still reeling from suddenly being orphaned had not been easy, and was still a constant struggle. And lately, Keith was thinking that he just might not be qualified for the role of caretaker. Walking in on his sister's weed-and-liquor party didn't ease his doubts.

"It got out of hand. I didn't drink. Or smoke," Bree said pleadingly to her brother, wincing in anticipation for the yelling that he was most likely about to do.

But Keith was tired. He didn't have any energy to yell, to lecture, or to punish. "Bree, I don't know how to do this. You've only been out of school a few days and you're getting into trouble. I don't know how to stop you from making these thugs and hood rats your friends. I just bought this house right before Mom . . . right before you moved in. Do we need to move? It's not the best neighborhood, I know, but the price was—"

"I won't talk to them again. I promise." Bree felt terrible. Keith didn't ask to have this kind of responsibility. She'd come into his life and messed up his whole routine. He thought that this year would be one where he could focus on his new job at Channing, Triton, and Brown, putting away cash to buy an engagement ring for his girlfriend, Traci. But instead, the little free time he had was spent making sure that his little sister was okay. Traci felt slighted, and not too happy, that Keith suddenly had another woman in his life who took priority over her. So she had ended the relationship last month, which Bree was happy about, because she never thought that Traci was good enough for her brother. But Keith never understood Bree's perspective, and had been moping around ever since, except for the night he'd met Kahlila and brought her home, a topic that they'd never revisited after Bree stormed out of the house that morning.

Keith sighed. He knew that Bree wasn't a bad kid. And it fell on him to maximize her potential. "Okay. No more chilllin' in the house all day. I'm getting you a job."

Bree knew better than to argue. Up to this point, Keith had entrusted her to find her own summer employment, and it hadn't gone so well. She'd had her heart set on working at a public library, so she could spend all of her time reading. Turned out there were other book nerds who had the same idea, and got on the ball a lot earlier than she had. So she'd been rattling around the house, devouring novels and sleeping a lot.

"Okay. And I'm sorry for letting people disrespect your house."

"You mean *our* house. And you're forgiven."

Chapter 14

There must be elements of his personality that are not obvious right away.

"Do you want to sit across from Darius, or next to him?" Desiree, Jason, and Kahlila had just arrived at an upscale eatery on Houston Street. Darius hadn't yet arrived and the girls were strategizing the best seating arrangement.

"Um, how about we sit on one side, and he and Jason can sit across from us?" Kahlila suggested.

"Perfect." Desiree pointed her husband to his assigned seat as he rolled his eyes.

"So, let me get this straight. You two talked to this guy for five minutes and now Kahli has a crush on him? Just because he's famous?" Jason was already reading the menu even as he posed the question.

"Of course not! It was how cool and modest he was, even though—"

"Even though he's famous." Jason finished Kahlila's sentence with a smirk.

Kahlila was about to argue back when Desiree murmured a soft "Here he comes."

When Kahlila saw Darius walking toward their table, she was glad that she took Desiree's advice to dress casually. Kahlila wasn't big on dressing down. But in New York, she noticed that everyone lived in jeans, and even T-shirts. The style was in the details, like the beaded shoes or oversized sunglasses. So heeding Desiree's opinion, she'd slicked her hair back into a ponytail and thrown on a pair of Joe's Jeans with a white undershirt that she'd bought in a three-pack from the boys' section of Target. Around her neck was a copper necklace with a cameo hanging from it. She nervously twirled the necklace around her finger as he approached, wearing jeans and a light blue T-shirt with brown writing that read *Trust me. I'm a doctor.* She'd actually seen the shirt before at Urban Outfitters and was surprised that he shopped at regular stores. In her mind, she had imagined a stylist bringing him his clothes on a silver platter every day.

Desiree and Jason both stood up to greet him, and Kahlila was unsure whether she should do the same. As she quickly rose from her seat, her chair tipped backward and clattered to the floor. Suddenly Kahlila had the attention of every person in the entire restaurant. Darius quickly walked around to her side of the table and righted the chair. "Good to see you again . . . Kahlila, right?"

She could only nod in response, humiliated and humbled all at the same time. She composed herself while Desiree introduced Darius to Jason, and everyone finally settled into their seats.

Kahlila decided that she would not embarrass herself anymore this evening, and the best way to ensure this would be not to talk unless spoken to. Darius initiated a conversation with Jason about his job, and soon they were in animated discussion about working out and personal trainers. Desiree tried to engage her in a conversation while the guys were talking, but Kahlila was preoccupied. There was too much to concentrate on at once. Darius was so good-looking that he was distracting. From head to toe, he was absolutely flawless. His hair was cut low with a slight natural wave. And if Kahlila's skin was copper, his was golden. His facial features didn't stand out individually, but they came together to make a perfect portrait. His body was lean, but his T-shirt revealed arms that were more cut up than paper dolls. When the waitress came and Darius ordered a gourmet cheeseburger with fries, she knew that he really must be serious about working out, because he clearly wasn't watching his diet.

"So, Desiree, how did you and Jason meet?" Darius asked as he handed his menu to the waitress. Kahlila thought that it was really considerate to show interest in Jason and Desiree's relationship, just in case Jason had any suspicion about Darius's intentions toward his wife.

Desiree and Jason looked at each other and laughed. "Funny story, actually. I'd been suffering from writer's block and my second novel was due to the publisher in a matter of months. So I met Jason and got this brilliant idea to use him for material for the new book. I was planning to play all these head games with him to see how he'd react."

Darius smiled, revealing dimples so deep that they were more like small vertical lines in his cheeks. Kahlila marveled at how white his teeth were. *He must have them professionally done.* "So, did the plan work?"

"Hell no!" Jason said, kicking his wife playfully under the table. "I was on to her scheme immediately. Fell in love with her anyway, though."

Kahlila couldn't hold in a wistful sigh. She'd heard the

story a million times, and even witnessed their saga herself all those years ago. But it never failed to stimulate her romantic-idealist bone when she watched Jason and Desiree interact with each other.

"Glad it worked out for you guys. I've thought a lot about writer's block, and I actually don't believe in it," said Darius.

"Trust me. I lived through it. It's real," said Desiree, sipping her seltzer water.

"Don't get me wrong, I believe that you were unable write anything for a period of time. I just mean that I don't believe it's something that needs to be fought. So-called writer's block is just the time an artist needs to gather his . . . or her creative thoughts. It's like the work is incubating in your head while you're supposedly stuck."

No, this man doesn't have the nerve to look good and be deep at the same time. Kahlila noticed that Jason was watching her gaze admiringly at Darius, and he amusedly shook his head at her, subtly enough that no one else saw.

"I'll go a few months without composing any songs. Then the floodgates will open and suddenly it's just nonstop writing," Darius continued.

"I didn't know you were a songwriter. Did you write all the songs on your album?" Desiree asked.

"Definitely not. I'd like to think my lyrics are a little more substantial than 'Party till you see the sun/In the dark it's way more fun.'"

Kahlila laughed, and Darius looked in her direction as if he'd forgotten she was there. *Okay, you're clearly being too quiet. You don't want him to think you're a wallflower.* But with her head spinning the way it was, she could not think of a single thing to say.

Desiree swooped in to save her. "So, Darius, what is this literary opportunity that you wanted to talk to me about?"

"Right. Well, I was approached by a major book publisher about writing an autobiography," he said, taking a swig of his draft beer.

"An autobiography?" Kahlila repeated. *Oh, great. First I'm a mute. Now I'm a parrot.*

"Well, more of a memoir, I guess. Is there even a difference between the two?"

Kahlila was about to launch into teacher-mode, explaining the subtle distinction between the genres, but she stopped herself. Instead she shrugged, trying to look nonchalant. Playing it cool was not her strong point. People tended to know exactly how she felt all of the time. When a student asked a question in class that wasn't the brightest, she had to force herself not to raise an eyebrow. If she wasn't enjoying herself on a date, she had to command herself not to look bored out of her mind. And if she actually *was* digging someone's company, it was impossible to fight the stars in her eyes. She knew that Keith had seen those starry eyes last month at the bar, in Boston, and that Darius was probably seeing them now. Although he was probably so used to adoring fans that he wouldn't even notice.

"So, what's your life story, Darius? Must be interesting, if they want to pay you for it," Jason said.

"It's nothing too special, really. I think they're just looking for a feel-good road-to-stardom story. I grew up in Detroit, and Mom held it down for me and my three sisters working as a teacher's aide. She even paid for all of us to take instrument lessons, even though we were getting by on, like, negative funds. I focused on music through high school, and got a scholarship to NYU. But once I got to the city, I saw folks in the music scene struggling to make ends meet, and decided that wasn't for me. I was trying to get paid, and buy my mom a house. Being the oldest, and the only boy . . . you know how it goes. Feeling responsible, all that. Anyway, I majored in business and got a job as a trader after graduation. But I felt this void that I couldn't shake. So I started performing my music at tiny venues, getting a little bit of a following while I was still putting in serious hours at my day job. I had made an underground CD on my own that was getting some buzz. One day, Flow Steddie rolled into the spot I was performing at, and asked me after my first set if I wanted to sing the hook on his new single. I guess the rest is history."

Somewhere between instrument lessons and wanting to buy his mom a house, Kahlila had moved from crushing on Darius to being absolutely taken. The stars in her eyes had become planets, and she could barely see straight. Remembering how secretive Keith had been about his life when they met in that Boston bar, she couldn't believe how open Darius was being with virtual strangers, when his status in the public eye gave him way more of a reason to be closed off.

The waitress arrived at the table, somehow carrying all four plates at once. She placed Desiree's food in front of her first, and in a matter of seconds, Desiree's hand was over her mouth and she was running to the back of the restaurant.

Jason slowly stood up, only looking mildly surprised. "Uh-oh. Looks like her sensitivity to smells hasn't completely gone away yet. I hope she made it to the bathroom," he murmured as he left the table and followed in his wife's direction.

"She pregnant?" Darius asked, looking slightly confused.

"Yeah."

"Wow. Kids. I can't even imagine being at that point," he said.

"Me either. I can picture marriage, but not the parenting part." *Nice going. The first words out of your mouth are that you're looking for a husband. Way to get a guy interested.*

"I'm surprised, being that you teach kids every day," he said through a mouthful of fries.

"I teach teenagers," she corrected. "Small children scare me." Darius laughed, a rich, playful laugh that made Kahlila relax a little. "They *do!* They move so quickly, and you can't talk to them rationally."

"Well, I was the oldest in my family, so I have logged a lot of hours in my life watching little kids. So I guess they don't scare me as much. I can actually see myself as a dad more easily than I can see myself as a husband." Seeing the uncomfortable look on Kahlila's face, he quickly added, "That doesn't mean I'm trying to have a bunch of kids without getting married. I just know what being a parent looks like more than I'm familiar with what being a husband is like, if that makes sense."

Kahlila tried to focus on what he was saying, but she was distracted by the running commentary in her head. *You are having a conversation about marriage and kids with a person who was just on national TV the other day winning an award in front of thousands of screaming fans.*

"I'm diggin' your necklace," she heard him say. "My mom collects cameos. My grandmother left her one when she died, and she's been into them ever since."

"Really? I really like them too. Old-fashioned jewelry is my favorite."

"Mom has a couple of pieces that have cameos of black women on them. You ever seen those?"

"Never. I would love to get a ring with one, though. Do you know where she bought them?"

"I can find out for you."

Jason and Desiree returned to the table. "Hey, guys, we're gonna have to reschedule. I need to head home.

I'm not trusting my stomach to sit through this meal,"
Desiree said apologetically.

"Not a problem. I hope you feel better," Darius said,
standing up to shake Jason's hand before they left.

"Kahli, I'm trusting you to stay and prevent Darius
from feeling as if he wasted his evening, okay?" She and
Jason were both wearing the most obvious smiles that
Kahlila had ever seen. They turned away before she
could answer.

The awkwardness descended on their table the
moment they were alone. Kahlila couldn't help but remember that this was the second time in a single week
that she had been left by one of her best friends to enjoy
the company of a gorgeous man. While she should have
been grateful for the opportunity, she was fearful that
this encounter would end up just as disappointingly as
the last. Still, she couldn't keep up this insecure, quiet
persona that she'd adopted over the course of the
evening. If this dinner with Darius was going to be successful at all, she had to be herself.

"So, I know you planned this dinner in order to get an
expert opinion, but do you mind if I put in my two
cents?" Kahlila was suddenly using her teacher voice,
which was a great deal more direct and confident than
the one she'd been using since he sat down.

"By all means."

She wouldn't expect a singer to use the expression "by
all means," and she liked it. "Don't take the book deal."

"No?"

"Writing one so early implies that the most interesting
part of your story has already happened. You're what,
twenty-eight?"

"Twenty-nine. But you'll probably read in magazines
that I'm twenty-five. My publicist is always trying to take
a few years off."

"Either way, you're young. Why write your life story when you're still on the ride?"

"I could always write another one ten years from now," Darius suggested.

"True. But in my opinion, memoirs should be written during a time of reflection. Like Bill Clinton—he waited until he was out of office to write his. You're still in the middle of it all." In the middle of Kahlila's advice, she had finally forgotten that she was speaking to a celebrity, and began to counsel him as she would anybody. Giving advice was something that she felt very comfortable doing. She was constantly approached by kids at school wondering which classes to take, which college they should choose, which girl they should ask to the prom.

"You have an excellent point there, Ms. . . . I don't know your last name."

"Bradford."

"Ms. Bradford. I thought you said you weren't an expert."

Kahlila felt her cheeks get warm. "It's not to say that your story shouldn't be told right now or anything. You should actually be visiting high schools, telling kids about your life."

"You're always a teacher first, aren't you?" Darius's tone was kind, but Kahlila couldn't help but feel self-conscious by his comment. She'd had relationships end in the past because men thought that she was unable to step out of teacher-mode. Getting slapped with lectures that sounded something like, "Your constantly being late to pick me up is unacceptable. What are you going to do to work on this problem?" guys quickly ran in the other direction. Tonight, she hadn't even been talking to Darius for a full meal and he already recognized that she couldn't separate Kahlila from Ms. Bradford.

"I try not to be," she said apologetically.

"It's not a bad thing. Tell me about some of your students," Darius said, sitting back comfortably in his chair.

The conversation was suddenly flowing like water with absolutely no effort. She had him cracking up with stories from school, like the class the year before that had a silent-but-deadly farter, or the time she got flowers delivered at school from a guy she was dating and there were so many misspellings in the card that she made it into a grammar lesson. Before they knew it, an hour had passed since the food had been cleared from the table.

Darius glanced at his watch. "I actually gotta run. Early morning appointment tomorrow."

"Photo shoot? Interview?" Kahlila couldn't resist asking.

He smiled bashfully. "Dentist."

Kahlila, emboldened due to a B-52 after dinner, countered with, "I can't see why you need a dentist appointment. Your smile is absolutely perfect."

"Well, thank you. So is yours.'"

Kahlila knew this was a lie. Her teeth were straight, yes, but her smile actually shifted slightly to the left. Most people thought this was cute, but she absolutely hated it. Instead of responding, she stood up and led the way out of the restaurant, feeling diners' eyes on them as they exited. She felt the urge to walk straighter, knowing that people were probably wondering who she was and why she got to have dinner with a platinum-selling performer. When they reached outside, Darius held up his arm and a cab immediately stopped. Kahlila had never seen a black man hail a taxi that quickly, and she wondered if the driver somehow recognized him in the dark. Darius stepped back to let Kahlila get inside, and her mind again involuntarily flashed back to the night that she had met Keith. It was only a quick flash, but she felt her stomach turn. She tried to regain her composure quickly enough to give Darius a final crooked smile.

"It was great talking to you. Sorry Desiree didn't get to give her input."

"Not a problem. Yo, maybe she can hit me up on e-mail with some feedback?"

"I'm sure she can. Does she have your info?"

"She does. All right, Kahlila, take care now."

Though she was still wearing the plastered smile on her face, Kahlila felt a bit crushed. Here he was, putting her in a cab without getting her phone number or even giving her a hug good-bye. *I should have known better than to think he'd be interested.* She sank into the backseat of the cab and gave a halfhearted wave. He shut the door and the driver quickly pulled off into the busy downtown traffic.

As she replayed the conversation in her head on the cab ride to Harlem, she realized how much she was enamored by Darius Wilson. He didn't just meet all of the requirements on her List. With the exception of number 33, he *was* The List. And while she knew that she'd made a pact with herself to forget about her requirements this summer, why did she need to do that when the perfect guy had just been sitting across from her? *Maybe it's not that he's not interested. He's probably just accustomed to aggressive women.* That's when she decided that if he wasn't going to push the envelope beyond a friendly dinner, then she would just have to take matters into her own hands. Surely the rules of *He's Just Not That Into You* only pertained to regular people, not to recording artists. And just as quickly as she'd remembered the trouble that being aggressive had gotten her into with Keith, she conveniently forgot.

Chapter 15

He must be appreciative when I go out of my way to do something for him.

While Kahlila could think of nothing but Darius Wilson after their dinner together, Darius did not think about Kahlila again until he got an e-mail from her several days later.

He had enjoyed his meal with Desiree's friend from Boston. Kahlila seemed like a really cool girl, once she loosened up. And she definitely looked good. But one unfortunate consequence of his career was that he was no longer blown away by attractive women. Most women who had the confidence to step to him were beautiful, so seeing nice-looking women was an everyday occurrence. It required much more to get him interested, and now that his mind was occupied by Miko, he really wasn't thinking twice about a girl who didn't even live in New York.

Darius did like that Kahlila refused to humor him, and instead gave her honest opinion about the book deal. Most girls would have told him that his life was so fascinating, just because they thought he wanted to hear it. And he realized when he listened to her break down the reasoning behind her advice that she was right. He'd called his manager the next day and told him that he was passing on the project, even before he received an e-mail from Desiree echoing Kahlila's sentiments.

But while he felt the impact of Kahlila's sound words, he failed to feel any real attraction to her. Between wearing a necklace that looked like it came from his mom's jewelry box, and hearing about her life as a schoolteacher, Kahlila lost a lot of the sexiness factor even as she earned points for being interesting. And one thing that Miko did not lack was sex appeal.

It was Friday night, and they were getting ready to head to the private party of a record label exec who had a renovated loft in the East Village. He sat on Miko's couch, a sectional made of the softest white leather, waiting for her to finish getting dressed. As she walked into the living room, strutting as if she were on the catwalk, Darius whistled and nodded approvingly. Miko liked to dress by theme, and tonight was obviously an Asian-inspired motif. Her hair piled into a huge bun at the very top of her head, she wore a tight minikimono with the highest heels Darius had ever seen. She stood six feet tall with the shoes on, which meant that she would be a full two inches taller than he was. But in the post–Russell/Kimora society in which they functioned, it was almost seen as a status symbol to have a girl who was taller. It either meant that she was a model, or that you were just so fly, it didn't even matter that you were short.

"You like?" She gave a couple of rapid turns in front of him.

"Definitely. Loving the dress."

"My mom bought it in Beijing for, like, ten dollars. They were trying to get her to pay fifty at first, but you know she was like, 'Please. Just because I'm a black woman in China doesn't mean I don't know whassup.'" She laughed a high giggly laugh that people might have thought was fake if they didn't know her.

Darius always enjoyed hearing Miko tell stories about her family. Her mom, a down-home sister from Kentucky, had somehow married a second-generation Chinese American businessman from New Jersey. Her mother sounded like quite a trip, choosing to name her daughter Miko to pay homage to her Asian culture. "But the name sounds Japanese!" Miko's father had protested. "Stop sweatin' the specifics," her mother shot back. She named her next child Labelle, after Patti. "See, honey?" she said to her husband. "This one is in honor of her African-American roots. And even though Patti is from Philly and I'm from Louisville, I'm not trippin'!" Somehow, Miko's parents were still going strong in Teaneck while their older daughter made quite an exciting and fast-paced living, and Labelle (known to most as Belle) worked as her sister's personal assistant. Belle was the only part of Miko that Darius did not enjoy. Though it was Belle's job to keep Miko on schedule, she tended to hang around even when Miko was off the clock. It didn't help that the sisters lived together in a Lower Manhattan high-rise apartment. Luckily, Belle was visiting her parents in New Jersey this weekend, which meant they would actually be going to the party as a couple and not a threesome.

"Oh, shit, D!" Miko looked down at her dress, dismayed.

"What?"

"I wore this dress to Quincy Jones's house in L.A., like, six months ago. And don't think I'm being a diva, 'cause I usually don't care about wearing the same thing twice, if the events are on different coasts and there weren't any pictures taken. But there are gonna be a whole mess of people at this party who were at Quincy's house that day." She had already returned to her bedroom before she even finished the explanation.

"So you and Quincy are on a first name basis, huh? Why not just call him Q?" he shouted teasingly. He wasn't about to protest her outfit change. A bit of a clotheshorse himself, he couldn't judge Miko's anticipated fashion faux pas. Besides, this was their first major public appearance together, and it wouldn't hurt for her to have on a stunner that she'd never worn before.

"Shut up, D!" her voice floated through the cracked door. He was only slightly disappointed that she didn't leave the door open while she changed. Though he and Miko had been spending considerable time together over the past few weeks, he still hadn't gotten more than some steamy kisses and a few cheap feels. But it was somewhat refreshing for a woman to dictate the pace, and it built a curiosity that only served to make Miko more appealing. He practically knew what she looked like naked already, being that she was in her underwear for half of the video that she shot with him. While it had been almost a year since then, he could still visualize her long, lean legs, impossibly small waist, and a chest that was bigger than that of any other high-fashion model he'd ever met.

His eyes scanned the living room absentmindedly, looking at the way she and Belle had chosen to design the apartment. The only photograph that hung on the wall was a poster-sized framed shot of the sisters. Darius knew that it had to have been taken by a professional photographer, because the portrait managed to make Belle look almost as stunning as Miko, which was a far cry from her real life appearance. Belle and Miko were a classic case of sisters who strongly resembled one another, but one was a showstopper and the other funny looking. Miko's exotic features worked in her favor, whereas Belle's face was a caricature of her older sister's: eyes that were spaced to alienlike dimensions, a nose that looked as if she'd had work done on it, even though she hadn't, and cheekbones that came out of nowhere on an otherwise flat face. She was also six inches shorter than her glamazon sibling.

Darius felt the vibration of his Treo and fished it from the pocket of his True Religion jeans. Anticipating a text message from Rasheed, his manager, Lamont, or a woman who hadn't yet gotten the hint to take a hike, he was surprised to see that the message was coming from his e-mail account, which was linked to his phone. *Who's sending me e-mail on a Friday night?* Looking at the name Kahlila Bradford, he knew it sounded familiar, but it wasn't until he began to read the message that he remembered her from dinner earlier in the week. He was horrible with names, and meeting so many people on a daily basis, he mentally disposed of those whom he didn't need to remember. Still, her face easily recalled itself in his memory as he scanned the lines:

darius,

it was really great having dinner with you the other night. thanks for paying, by the way. desiree and jason plan to return the favor (although if it doesn't happen soon, you'll be stuck eating at friendly's or some other child-accommodating establishment).

i was thinking about the idea of telling your "rise to stardom" story to kids, and decided to do a little research (this is what teachers do in the summer when they don't have papers to grade). below is a list of local high schools that i'm sure would love to have you come speak to their students. i nar-

rowed the list by choosing schools with a significant portion of the student body qualifying for free
or reduced lunch. they also had to be showing im-
provement in some area, like test scores, school
climate, etc. figured you could come as a reward
for their progress. anyway, not so sure how these
things work, but thought maybe your manager or
whoever could try to arrange a couple of speaking
gigs when the school year starts.

anyway, take care and if you ever want to hang
out again, to talk shop or otherwise, my contact info
is below.
—kahli

*Well, that was really thoughtful of her. I don't know if I'll
have time to be visiting schools at the same time that I'm recording an album, but it was a nice idea.* He hit REPLY to shoot
back a quick thank-you, but Miko chose that same
moment to emerge from her boudoir in what must have
been a biker-chick-inspired ensemble. Darius took one
look at the leather shorts, studded belt, and wild hair,
and he quickly returned his Treo to his pocket. *I can
write her back later.* Right now, he had an appearance to
make with one of the hottest women in the industry. Her
outfit looked like she was planning on putting a hurting
on someone later, and he sent up a silent prayer that he
would be the beneficiary.

Chapter 16

To: krystal_clear@hotmail.com
From: cheesy_bree@hotmail.com
Time: Friday, June 30, 2006, 12:37 p.m.
Subject: Miss you!!!
Message:
Hey, Krys,

I just tried to call you but your cell phone is "temporarily out of service." Girl, you still letting your bill go unpaid. How do you spend all those hours working at Forever 21 and still get your phone turned off?

Anyway, how is everything going in the Haven? I can't believe it's been four months since I've been down there to visit. Keith promised that I can still spend a week in August with you, like we planned, but I wouldn't be surprised if he changed his mind after the trouble I got into the other day.

So the latest news is that Keith is making me take a job at his law firm. Yuck! Filing papers and getting coffee all day for the same people that he complains about all the damn time. It does pay ten dollars an hour, which is more than I ever made, so I guess it's not all bad. I start Monday.

So I know I'm just asking to be miserable, but what's the update with Stanley? We talked on IM about a month ago, but I haven't heard from him since.

TTYL-

Bree

To: cheesy_bree@hotmail.com
From: krystal_clear@hotmail.com
Time: Friday, June 30, 2006, 2:06 p.m.
Subject: Re: Miss you!!!
Message:

b—you know i be forgetting to pay that damn bill. it ain't about the money. it's just my bad memory. anyhow, the phone is back on so i'll holla at you after 9:00 (off peak, girl!). but to answer your question about stanley, yeah, you probly don't wanna know. he's been kickin' it with this chick who lives around his way. her name's tenisha—she says she spells her name "ten" because she's a dime. that should tell you the kind of girl she is—straight chickenhead. you know i had to call stanley on it when i heard he was chillin with her. he was like, well, your girl was the one who didn't wanna stay together when she moved. i was like, you know it wasn't that simple. he was like, whatever. but then i told him that you might be visiting this summer and he got all interested like, seriously? how long is she gonna be here? i was like, what are you gonna do with tenisha when bree's here? and he said they weren't that serious and he didn't owe her any explanation.

i really do think that if you moved back here, you

guys would be together and happy like y'all used to be. and we can talk about this more on the phone, but i've been talking to my mom and we both think that you should come back to new haven and live with us. you know how much my mom loves you, and she's worried that keith is too stressed out with his job and everything. and i told her that you weren't happy up in boston, so she thinks you should come back for your senior year. she says she's willing to talk to your brother herself. all right—i'm about to go to work and spend my paycheck on an outfit from my store. tatyana is having a party this weekend and i need something cute to wear. and by the way, you are so lucky—ten dollars an hour? that's hot! call you later.

To: krystal_clear@hotmail.com
From: cheesy_bree@hotmail.com
Time: Friday, June 30, 2006, 4:18 p.m.
Subject: Re: Miss you!!!
Message:

You're gonna kill me when I tell you this. So as soon as I read that e-mail from you, I called Stanley. I know! I just couldn't help it. It was like, as soon as I saw that he had another girl in the picture, I had to speak to him. Not even to give him attitude or anything, just to see if we still had that . . . spark we used to have.

So I happened to catch him on his break (he's a counselor this summer at the basketball camp he used to go to—how cute is that?). He sounded so surprised to hear from me, and I can tell he was excited. He asked me right away, "So Krys told you about Tenisha?" I was like, "No, who's Tenisha?" He just laughed and told me to stop frontin, cuz there was no way you hadn't told me. He was really honest about it and said that she'd liked him for a while and he just decided to give it a chance. He said he likes her, but it's not how it was with us. That sounds like a line, doesn't it? It didn't sound like one when he said it. We talked a lot about college stuff. He's getting recruited by UCLA, so he might be in Cali for school. He kept hyping up the West Coast, saying it would be good for me since I'm an actress. I was like, "Okay, I'm not an actress first of all." But it was still sweet that he wanted me out there with him.

I can't wait to see you guys in a month. As for me moving back there, I would love that soooooo much. But I gotta be really careful bringing something up like that with my brother. He feels like I'm his responsibility and all that BS. And after that incident the other day when I had those people in the house, he said some stuff about wanting us to be a family, and wanting to try harder. His feelings would be hurt if I told him I wanted to leave. He might not even let me come visit if I ask him now. I'll work on him slowly.
Bree

To: cheesy_bree@hotmail.com
From: krystal_clear@hotmail.com
Time: Sunday, July 2, 2006, 7:46 p.m.
Subject: Re: Miss you!!!
Message:
my phone is off again, and i had to tell you real quick. stanley came into forever 21 at the mall today. at first i was like, oh no, he isn't shopping for tenisha in my store, but then i realized he was there to see me. girl, all he wanted to do was talk

about you. he said how happy he is that y'all have started talking again. he even got out his ipod to play me that darius wilson song you like so much, "love complex." he said you put him on to it and now he listens to it all the time cuz it's all about you two and what y'all have been through. he really does love you, b. it really hurt him after your mom died and you didn't want to deal with anybody. he even brought it up today—he was like, i just wanted to be there for her. i didn't care if she was moving to antartica (how do you spell that shit?). i would've stayed with her. anyway, i just had to tell you that—oh, and the most important part . . . he told tenisha he doesn't want to hang with her anymore. yes, girl. y'all have been talking again for what, three days, and he's already all about you.

To: krystal_clear@hotmail.com
From: cheesy_bree@hotmail.com
Time: Sunday, July 2, 2006, 10:01 p.m.
Subject: Re: Miss you!!!
Message:
I can't stop smiling. ☺

Chapter 17

He must stand up for his beliefs.

The offices of World Urban Music were alive with activity on a Monday afternoon. Though it was the day before the Fourth of July, everyone was back from lunch on time, trying to sign artists and sell records. It was one of the few places where Darius could still walk in the door and get absolutely no reaction. Virtually all of the top hip-hop and R&B artists were signed to World Urban, so stars walked in and out of their doors hourly.

Lamont had called that morning to see if they should meet ahead of time and arrive at the meeting together. But Darius wanted to be alone with his thoughts. He knew that he wanted to put some ideas on the table at this meeting that would not be popular. And while it made sense to have his manager fully informed and on board, he didn't want anyone trying to change his mind before he even got to make his case.

But as he stood in the lobby listening to the telephones, the no-nonsense voices, and the click of heels as people strode the floor with urgency, he began to get nervous. As friendly as everyone was at the label, it was clear that this was a business. The priority was packaging successful artists to maximize sales. And while artistic integrity was something that everyone spoke about, Darius wasn't so sure whether it was real talk or just lip service.

Tammy, the front receptionist, greeted him with a warm smile. "How you doing, Darius? You're right on time. Folks are in the conference room. We're just waiting on Flow."

"You didn't have to tell me that," Darius said with a wink. "Flow's always the last one to get here." He gave her one more appreciative look up and down and strode down the hall. It was customary for all of the celebs to flirt with Tammy. She was gorgeous, friendly, and very knowledgeable about the music industry. She knew so much about it that she knew better than to mix business with pleasure. She was aware of exactly how many groupies each artist dealt with, how much money each artist wasted, and how easily replaceable she was at World Urban. So she was content to accept the winks and keep it moving.

The conference room's glass walls allowed for Darius to see the players before walking through the door. Lamont was his manager, and had been serving in that role since Darius was performing at Open Mics to listless crowds. Lamont was the one who had used the few connections he had at the time to get Flow Steddie to come see Darius perform. So while he wasn't as high powered as a lot of the managers in the business, Darius felt a strong loyalty to him. Leslie was the straight-shooting VP of World Urban. Sean was in marketing, and there was another young-looking woman whom Darius assumed to be someone's secretary. He inhaled and exhaled deeply before pushing open the door and stepping inside.

Everyone stood, and he greeted the men with elaborate handshake-hugs that seemed unnecessary, especially since he'd seen Lamont just two days before. He and Leslie touched cheeks before she introduced him to her assistant, a plain girl whose name he forgot before he even took his seat.

With his usual impeccable timing, Flow Steddie entered just as everyone settled back into their chairs positioned around a long conference table. In his customary dramatic fashion, he'd pushed open both glass doors instead of one. Darius almost expected women in cowrie-shell-covered bras to drop flower petals at his feet. Everyone rose from their seats all over again to greet Flow, because no one would dare consider being too nonchalant with World Urban's biggest moneymaker. In the past year alone, he'd had a number one album, produced three successful artists under his own label (which was distributed by World Urban), and had more press coverage than the president of the United States (or at least that's what he said in his lyrics).

Flow Steddie was not famous because of his looks. He did not have the conventional physical appeal of Common, or the eccentric intrigue of André 3000, or even the aggressive facial features of a Jay-Z. He was the type of guy who, before the record deal, one would pass on the street and not even register. He was an average height with an average build, and a face that frankly matched the rest of him. Medium brown complexion with medium-sized eyes, nose, and mouth, he only became a recognizable presence once he created a fashion-forward look that many others had been recently imitating. King of the layers, he would wear a collared polo with a button-up shirt, sweater vest, and leather jacket. He might even sport a pair of sunglasses on his face, and another pair on top of his head. Flow Steddie was over the top in terms of his dress, as well as his personality, which was larger than life in comparison to his forgettable face. And the business meeting took on new life as soon as he'd entered the conference room.

"Let's get down to business, y'all. Money to make, money to make!" He turned his seat around so that he could sit on it backward, his legs straddling either side and his chin resting on the rectangular back of the chair.

"Okay, so I think we all agree that we plan to start recording next month for a March or April release date, yes?" Leslie immediately took control of the meeting.

All heads nodded around the table. Darius felt himself getting anxious. Trying to organize his thoughts in his head in advance of speaking, he cleared his throat so that his voice would be loud and clear when he addressed the group.

After more discussion about timelines and budget, Sean, the marketing guru, asked, "So, what are we thinking about in terms of the look and sound of this album?"

Darius opened his mouth to deliver his opinion. *Well, I know the last album killed it in terms of sales, but I was looking to take a different direction that I think will be just as successful. I'm trying to write my own stuff, have more of an acoustic sound, play instruments, make some grown-folks music. Things are too crowded right now with Chris Brown, Ne-Yo, all these newcomers. I want to sound my age and show my talent.*

The first full word of his prepared spiel hadn't exited his lips when Flow pounded his fist on the table: "MOTS! That's all I gotta say."

Leslie, a serious businesswoman to the core, had little time for Flow's odd language and obnoxious antics. "What does MOTS mean, Flow." Her statement was less of a question than a sigh with words in it.

"More of the same, baby! First album was a hit. Second album just needs to build off it. Sicker beats, bigger guest spots, crazier videos. There it is." Flow put his hands in the air as if he'd just sunk a three-pointer from half court.

"Darius. Thoughts." Leslie always minimized her words, as if she were only allowed a certain quotient per day.

"That's one way to go," he began, trying his best to sound casual and confident all at once. "I was thinking about something different. More throwback R&B. You know, harking back to Marvin and Curtis and Stevie."

Sean nodded. "I see what you're talking about. But a dude on Sony's label already has that market on lock."

"That piano-playing dude who wears the suits all the time? He ain't got nothing on lock," Flow said dismissively.

"Exactly!" Darius agreed excitedly. "I think my sound is different. But I do want to follow his lead by writing all my own music for this project."

"Hold up, hold up. We got hit-makers all lined up already. You saying you don't want Swiss and Jermaine on your album? Tim? Shit, you don't want *me*?"

"It's not that extreme. An album always needs great producers, and I'm gonna need hot beats on the dance tracks. But I'm looking to do something more stripped down for most of the songs. And I definitely want to do all my own lyrics this time. I don't think anyone in this room can say that the lyrics on the first joint were tight." Darius was becoming more confident with every word he spoke. People around the table were sitting up straight, and they seemed to be really listening to what he had to say. *Why am I surprised? I'm the artist! They're supposed to listen to me.*

"The lyrics didn't matter 'cause your voice is the shit and the music behind you was ridiculous." Flow was beginning to get an edge in his voice, and Darius knew that he was probably annoyed that this wasn't discussed with him privately before the meeting. But Flow was too over-powering in a one-on-one situation. Darius wanted the backing of his manager as well as the larger label.

Unfortunately, he didn't seem to be getting that support. "Flow's right," chimed in Lamont. "The demographic buying your music is about the club bangers and the ballads that use the right samples."

What the hell? This dude is my manager and he's not even feeling my vision. He's been starstruck by Flow since the day they met. "I wanna *change* my demographic! I'm damn near thirty years old. Why am I catering to what sixteen-year-olds want?"

There was a prolonged moment of silence, not because Darius had said anything profound in anyone's eyes, but because he'd said something so stupid. "Darius, you know the buying power of teenagers today. You can't just say that you want to cut off that market." Leslie looked at him reproachfully.

"All right, let's hear D out a little bit more," Flow announced, visibly proud of his open-mindedness. "What you trying to sing about on this album?"

"Relationship stuff, obviously. Gotta have that. I'm just not trying to have every song be about the club or the bedroom," Darius said, trying to keep his voice even.

"What—you talking about that song about Hennessey? It didn't even make the final cut of the last album!"

Darius opened his mouth to respond, but closed it again. What was left to say? He would have to find a different way to make them hear him. If he couldn't create a sophomore project that reflected who he was, then he wondered if he'd have the strength to get up and walk away from the luxury of the label.

Flow must have seen the turmoil in his face, because he tried to offer a compromise. "Look, you're my boy. I trust your talent. I have no problem with you writing the lyrics to your joints this time. But we need the big production—the heavy bass, the samples, all that. The videos have to be huge, and the songs gotta match the videos."

"You can have a big video for an acoustic song." Darius had gotten some of his fire back in light of this minor victory.

"In this industry, with the state of music as it is right now, there's only room for one person making songs with just a voice and a piano. You missed the boat, dawg." Sean pushed his chair a few inches back from the table, as if he were done taking in any additional information.

Before Darius had a chance to do what he really wanted, which was to punch Sean in the jaw, Leslie was closing her folder on the table and rising to her feet. "So, Darius, Flow, I'll trust that you guys will find a happy medium that makes you both happy and creates great sales for World Urban, yes? Fantastic."

Fan-freaking-tastic. Neither Darius nor Flow said another word as the meeting came to a close.

Chapter 18

He has to know how
to have a good time.

She'd read the e-mail so many times that she had it memorized:

Hey, Kahlila,
   Thank you for taking the time out of your summer (busy or otherwise) to do that research. I will definitely pass the info along to my people, and hopefully we can fit it in as I work on the new album. Anyway, I know it's short notice but I'm headed to an early Fourth of July party at Marquee tonight. If you and your friends want to come, I can put you on the list. It should be a good time, and I want you to enjoy your summer in New York.
Take care,
Darius

Kahlila's heart began to race when she saw Darius Wilson's name in her in-box. When she read the message, she thought she might lose her mind. *He's inviting me to a party! Are there going to be other famous people there? What should I wear? Is he asking me to be polite, or is he interested?* Kahlila had to talk to someone immediately. Remembering that Desiree was at a doctor's appointment, she quickly dialed Robyn's number. Her phone went straight to voice mail. *Damn. She must be at work.*

Her next option was Madeline, and she eagerly waited to give her the scoop as the phone rang. "Hey, Kahli!" her coworker answered excitedly. "How's New York? I miss ya!"

"New York is amazing. Guess where I'm going tonight?" Kahlila felt as if she were about to burst with the news.

"Where?"

"To a party . . . with Darius Wilson!" Kahlila exclaimed, hoping that her dramatic pause had its intended effect.

"Um, should I know who that is?"

"*What!* You're kidding, right?"

"Is he famous? I'm really bad with famous people. What movie was he in?"

"Madeline, he's a singer. You don't know that song— 'Party Till You See the Sun?'"

"That sounds kind of familiar. How does it go?"

As Kahlila halfheartedly sang the tune for her friend, she felt herself deflate. It was no fun chatting with someone who couldn't even appreciate the significance of the e-mail she'd just received. Of course, once she filled Madeline in on the entire story, she got lots of enthusiasm in return. Madeline even looked online while they were on the phone, and she was overwhelmed by the amount of information available about this rising star. "I can't believe I'd never heard of him," she said in wonderment.

"*I* can," retorted Kahlila. While Madeline claimed not

to be good with "famous people," she knew that the real issue was that Darius had not earned enough crossover appeal with his first album. It was a hit on the R&B charts, and his songs were played every five minutes on the black radio stations, but unless Madeline was at Kahlila's house for dinner, that music never entered her sphere. And even Kahlila hadn't purchased Darius's music. She heard him enough when driving in her car, and while his voice was incredible, the songs didn't match his vocal talent.

"So, do you think Beyoncé will be at the party?" Madeline asked excitedly. Everyone who knew Kahlila remotely well was aware of her obsession with Beyoncé. She was a bigger fan than any of her students were: taping all of Beyoncé's TV performances, seeing her in concert multiple times, singing her hits at karaoke bars whenever possible, and doing a pretty good husky-voiced imitation of the sultry pop star.

"Madeline, don't be silly." For some reason, she felt herself being condescending to her friend, even though she'd entertained the same thought as soon as she'd read the e-mail. "It's not like all of the celebrities hang out together every night. And even if she were there, it's not a big deal."

"Whatever, Kahli! You would lose your mind if you met Beyoncé."

"We are losing focus here. The issue at hand is whether Darius was just inviting me to be nice, or whether I might actually have a chance with this guy."

"Either way, you have to look absolutely fabulous tonight. I take it you're bringing that amazing friend of yours—the gorgeous one with the unbelievable career?"

"Desiree. Yes."

"Okay, so you two definitely have the potential to be the most beautiful, accomplished women in the room."

Madeline always insisted on going overboard with her compliments. Kahlila and her other girlfriends never spoke about one another this way. Of course, they all had immense admiration and respect for one another; they wouldn't be friends otherwise. It seemed redundant, and a bit fake, to be so heavy handed with such effusive praise.

Kahlila always responded to these moments with a humorous deference. "Yeah, we'll be the hottest chicks there. Unless Beyoncé shows up, of course!"

And even Madeline knew better than to convincingly argue that Kahlila was in some way superior to Beyoncé, so they proceeded to strategize the correct attire for the all too important evening.

Kahlila could feel a buzz in her stomach as she and Desiree approached the club at 11:30 that evening. They'd spent the day at a "Pre-Fourth" cookout in the Bronx with Jason's daughter, Nailah, and her mom, Monique. It always boggled Kahlila how beautifully blended Jason's "two families" were: Desiree and Jason spent most of their holidays with Monique, her husband, Andre, and their son, Elijah. In light of Desiree's pregnancy, the majority of the conversation revolved around babies, but Kahlila was so excited to see Darius that evening that they could have been talking about poopy diapers for hours and she wouldn't have minded.

An exhausted Desiree had insisted on taking a nap when they got home, and Kahlila was worried that they might be late for the party. But Desiree patiently explained to her that even midnight was early for New York. Boston dictated that you arrive at the club by eleven if you wanted to get your money's worth before the place shut down promptly at two. New York, however, allowed for all-night partying, and Kahlila hadn't yet adjusted to this line of thinking. There was a line that stretched about thirty people long outside, and the heavy bass of a reggae song penetrated the walls and traveled down the sidewalk. Kahlila walked toward the end of the line, and Desiree hit her arm.

"What the hell are you doing?"

She motioned for Kahlila to follow her and she confidently strutted up to the woman standing at the door with a clipboard in hand. Kahlila's nervousness increased, because with a female holding the all-powerful guest list, they couldn't even flirt their way in the door.

"We're on Darius Wilson's list," Desiree said, daring her to disagree. "Kahlila Bradford plus one?" she added before the girl could even ask a question.

She scrolled the typed columns with her finger and looked up at the two women doubtfully, as if she couldn't fully understand how *they* had made Darius's acquaintance. Still, she tapped the seven-foot-tall bouncer and he unhooked the velvet rope to let them through. No one in the line protested. It was the natural pecking order of the New York scene. In fact, if there were no list, then no one would even want to be at that establishment. Exclusivity made getting in so much more appealing.

Kahlila tried to look nonchalant as they were escorted to the VIP section by another bouncer who was slightly less tall but equally intimidating. They completely bypassed the first floor and walked up a set of stairs, meeting a closed door at the landing. It opened to reveal a completely different deejay with a much more attractive crowd than the one downstairs. Although, at second glance, Kahlila wasn't sure if they looked better in actuality, or if their private digs simply cast them in a more flattering light. Long-legged women were lounging in long leather booths as men in an assortment of ensembles—

T-shirts, jeans, sunglasses, suits, blazers, vests, baseball caps, and ties—poured champagne and nodded to the music. Kahlila wished there was a restroom to turn into before she took one step farther, but she had to settle for looking down at her outfit to assess her visual status. Wearing black cuffed shorts that were shorter-than-short and black stiletto sandals with rhinestones across the toe (shorts from Theory and shoes from Bakers), she hoped that her legs looked nearly as long as those of the model chicks in the room. She knew they were shiny enough, as Desiree had urged her to coat them twice with baby oil gel. "My thighs look like they belong in a rotisserie," Kahlila complained. "Shut up. They look hot," Desiree snapped back.

"Glad you guys made it," shouted a familiar voice over the music. Kahlila looked up from her glossy limbs to meet the dimpled smile of Darius Wilson. He extended one arm for a hug and Kahlila hoped he couldn't feel the excitement in her body as his hand slid smoothly around her waist and landed on the small of her back. It only slightly took away from the moment when he gave Desiree the exact same hug. "Y'all are looking fly, as usual." Again, the group compliment only detracted in the smallest way from his flattering words.

"Thanks. So, whose party is this?" Desiree asked, peering past him.

"You know, I'm not even sure. Diddy's supposed to be here, though. Kelis and Nas are over there in the corner. I haven't seen anybody else, but it's still really early," he said, checking his watch. Desiree flashed Kahlila an "I told you so" look, but she was too starstruck to notice.

"Okay. Who are you here with?" Desiree bluntly asked.

"I'm meeting some folks. They weren't ready to leave when I was, but I had to get out of the house. Rough day." He pushed up the sleeve of his crisp button-down shirt.

Before Kahlila could chime in with an inquiry, he was leading the way to his booth, which was in fact empty. *How long has he been sitting here by himself?*

Without having to exert any effort at all, suddenly she was sitting with a glass of champagne in hand, listening to great music (she was an eternal fan of hip-hop from the nineties and apparently so was the deejay), and having an animated conversation with Darius about whether there has been a single rapper who had come out since the year 2000 with any degree of serious talent.

"I think Eminem was the last one, and even he came out in, like, '99," Kahlila said assertively. As she sipped the champagne, she forgot how much she hated the taste of it. The liquid comfortably slid down her throat, tickling her insides with tiny bubbles, and making *her* bubbly as a consequence.

"How you gonna play my boy Flow like that?" Darius protested.

"You know what? You're right. I did forget about Flow Steddie. Love his album, although it's hard to tell if I love it for the rhymes or the beats. Either way, he's definitely talented. *Maybe* even a musical genius. But that might be overstating." Kahlila loved talking about music with guys. She considered herself an archivist of excellent hip-hop, and often shocked men by reciting every line of a Tribe Called Quest, Black Sheep, or Nice and Smooth hit. When it came to sports, she was absolutely clueless, but her musical knowledge usually made up for it.

When Kahlila had been dating her last serious boyfriend, Eugene, their favorite pastime was debating the merits of various rappers: Tupac vs. Biggie, Nas vs. Jay, Lauryn vs. M.C. Lyte, Common vs. The Roots. She'd wanted to call him when Jay-Z's *Black Album* dropped because she loved it so much and she knew he'd appreciate it. But that's not the kind of call one can make to an ex after he's gotten married to someone else.

"Wow," said Kahlila, touching Darius's arm. "Nas is one of my favorite rappers, and he's sitting ten feet away. Crazy." Darius just smiled as Kahlila shook her head in disbelief. Desiree had gotten up to say hello to someone who looked an awful lot like Lenny Kravitz, although Kahlila couldn't be sure from where she was sitting. She couldn't wait to call Madeline tomorrow. Lenny Kravitz was definitely someone she'd heard of.

Darius leaned in so he wouldn't have to talk as loudly, and Kahlila could feel the warm air from his mouth hitting her ear. "It's funny, because before I hooked up with Flow, I wasn't really all that into hip-hop. I mean, I knew the hits just like everybody else did. But it wasn't what I was rocking in my stereo at home."

"Really? What were you listening to?"

"I'm more of a Teddy Pendergrass type. Early Levert."

"Funny, I wouldn't have guessed that one."

"Why? Because of my overproduced under-original first album?"

Kahlila didn't know how to respond. Darius was talking to her, but it looked like his mind had traveled off to a place that made him pretty angry. Just as quickly as he went there, he returned. "My bad. I just had a really wack meeting with my label today."

"What happened?"

He looked skeptical as to whether he should answer the question, but finally shrugged and rolled his eyes. "Long story short, they love my sound the way it is now. I want to switch up the program. I mean, what did *you* think of my first album? Be honest."

The champagne running through Kahlila's system helped her to respond without hesitation. "If I'm being completely honest, I have to admit that I've only heard the radio releases. I'm not a contemporary R&B fan really. I'm more into the neosoul thing."

"As are a lot of people our age! That's exactly what I was trying explain to folks today. They weren't trying to hear me. At a meeting about *my* album, I felt like no one was interested in my input."

Kahlila racked her brain to think of a comforting word or a solid piece of advice, but she was stumped. Her mind was still processing the fact that he was confiding in her, and she simply could not move to the next step of having something intelligent to say.

Luckily, he saved her from having to contribute a thought. "Enough complaining. I hate being a whiner, especially when I've been blessed with as much as I have. Let's talk about you. Have I said how hot those shorts are yet?"

It's official. He wasn't just inviting me to be courteous. He actually likes me! "No, you haven't," she tossed back.

"Well, you're wearing them well."

The fact that she finally had confirmation that Darius found her attractive somehow gave her the confidence to respond to his earlier concerns. "Hey, I know I'm no record label exec or anything, but I'm gonna buy your first album tomorrow. And I'm going to *really* listen to it. Objectively."

"And you'll tell me what you truly think?"

Kahlila nodded earnestly as Darius extended his arm to shake on the deal. As she held his hand, which was strong and warm around her own, she watched a huge smile take control of his face. But it seemed like his eyes were lighting up not because of their agreement, but because someone had just walked in behind Kahlila.

Kahlila was grateful for picking up on this detail, because it made the entrance of one of the most breathtaking women she'd ever seen a little less painful. It all happened so quickly. One moment she was holding hands with Darius Wilson, and the next she was being introduced to his girlfriend, Miko (*models only need a first name, apparently*). As Darius's hands were replaced by the soft, manicured fingers of this five-foot-ten inch stunner's polite touch, Kahlila tried to keep her smile plastered on her face. But she felt her mouth twitching, the way it did when she had to pose for a picture too long. She wasn't sure exactly what she said in order to make a graceful exit (*was it even graceful at all?*), but she felt her mouth relax into a frown as soon as she turned her back to the happy couple.

She walked as quickly as she could in her three-inch heels to Desiree's side, smiling politely at Lenny Kravitz (*Oh my goodness—it's really him!*) and perching on the couch next to her. "Des, I feel like such an idiot. He has a girlfriend."

"Who?"

Kahlila gave a vigorous chin nod toward Darius's booth, and Desiree half stood up to get a better look. "Figures. They love to date those model chicks," Desiree said matter-of-factly. "It's probably not serious. They'll be broken up in a few weeks."

Kahlila stared at the exotic beauty now sitting in Darius's lap, successfully taking his mind off the stresses of the day. Even if Desiree were right, Kahlila knew that she'd been crazy to think that she had a chance with him.

The rest of the night was spent trying to pretend she wasn't sulking. In theory, it should not have been that difficult. She was surrounded by the same people she read about in tabloid magazines every Saturday. The deejay was playing songs that she hadn't danced to since college. Men and women alike kept coming up to her with comments about her well-toned legs. It should have been the best club night of all time. But every other minute, she was stealing glances at Darius. Miko had eventually gotten up from his lap and seemed to be talking like old friends to every single person in the establishment. Darius was still sitting down, absentmindedly pressing buttons on his Treo. *I would be so much more attentive than she is, if I were his girl.*

Kahlila reached inside her purse to reapply her lip gloss and saw that the screen of her cell phone was lit up. She flipped open the phone and felt her heart beat faster at the sight of a text message from a New York number that she didn't recognize:

> I'm going to keep you to that promise. Will call you tomorrow to hear your feedback on the album. Something tells me to trust your opinion.—D

She smiled and returned the cell to her bag. This time, when she looked over at her crush, he was grinning back at her. *Game back on.*

Chapter 19

*He cannot be scared to seek a
woman's opinion to solve problems.*

"Miko, come over here. The girl in this magazine has
your Marc Jacobs pants on."

*Is she serious? We're chilling, trying to have some one-on-one
time, and she wants Miko to get up and go look at a magazine?*

Darius had no patience for Belle. She was superficial
and super annoying. Her whole life seemed to revolve
around her sister, and she fully enjoyed all the perks
that came with Miko's success. While she couldn't fit
into many of Miko's clothes due to their significant
height difference, she engaged in a great deal of sisterly
sharing by joining Miko at every party, on every vacation, and seemingly on almost every date with Darius.
Today, he and Miko had decided to forgo a Fourth of
July party in the Hamptons to cook out on her balcony.
It was the perfect afternoon until Belle got home and
insisted that Darius make her a burger.

Miko jumped up from the couch on which she was

cuddled with her man and trotted over to the kitchen, where her sibling was toasting Pop-Tarts and reading *Vogue*. Darius made no effort to hide his frustration, sighing loudly and folding his arms. He was an anti-entourage person. While he did have Rasheed with him most of the time, it was as much business as it was friendship. He needed his boy when he was on tour, doing promotional events, or even hitting the clubs. The crowds could be ridiculous if he tried to handle them on his own. But he wasn't one of those singers who always traveled with the same ten guys everywhere he went. One night, he might spend an evening partying with Flow and his crew. On another day, he might reconnect with some of his old friends from Wall Street. If he was feeling like he needed to be reminded where he came from, he might fly in one of his high school homies from Detroit. Still, he was always grateful for the time he had by himself, and relished those days in his apartment with his piano.

Miko, on the other hand, was a person who believed that the more people she brought with her on any occasion, the more fun she would have. Ninety percent of the time, she went out with an army of five girls from her modeling agency. They were all tall, skinny, long-haired, and impeccably dressed. While they got a great deal of attention individually, they couldn't be stopped as a team, scoring free drinks, meals, and more wherever they went. Sometimes people raised an eyebrow at the much shorter, much less attractive seventh wheel with them, but Miko always insisted on bringing Belle along. And if Belle was aware that she did not have the same assets as the rest of the girls, she sure didn't let her insecurity show. She was the cattiest, most arrogant one of them all. In the few weeks that Darius had been dating Miko, he'd already seen Belle watching *Mean*

Girls three times. She could recite the lines the way that guys used to be able to quote the movie *Friday* back in the nineties.

Darius hadn't yet complained to Miko about Belle's constant presence during their intended private time. It was her sister, after all, and he couldn't imagine that he would score many points for insulting her flesh and blood. So he'd been biting his tongue, hoping that his aloofness to Belle would make her want to hang around them less. So far, this plan had been a complete failure.

"I do have those pants. But mine are beige."

"So are hers!"

"No, hers are, like, mustardy."

"Yeah, that's true. Yours fit way better too."

"I know that model. She's so damn thin, and she thinks she's fat. Those pants would look way better if she actually had an ass for them to hug."

Darius turned up the volume on the TV so that he could tune out the fashion-obsessed chatter. Belle was actually the least of his problems, and his mind quickly traveled back to his label meeting the day before. He and Flow had been instructed to "work something out" for this next album, and he had no idea whether that was actually possible. He was finished with compromising when it came to his music.

The first time around, Darius had been in a different place. The newfound glitz had him starry-eyed during the entire making and promotion of his last album. He was so mesmerized by the lights that he almost forgot how much he disliked his own music. With the money, travel, women, and general hype, it was difficult to argue that his sacrifice wasn't worth it. But somewhere along the way, Darius stopped being so impressed with the lifestyle. Awards shows looked better on TV. Expensive champagne tasted just as nasty as the cheap kind. So this time, all he had was his music to become excited again.

He had been so far inside his own head that he hadn't noticed Belle's retreating to her bedroom. Miko returned to the living room and flopped down next to him on the couch. "So, you've seemed pretty quiet this week. What's going on?"

Darius was glad that Miko was perceptive enough to notice that something was wrong. He took it as a good omen for their going forward. Without hesitation, he broke down the details of his meeting the day before. She listened intently and didn't interrupt once. Just the act of listening made him even more attracted to her. He remembered what a good listener Kahlila had been the night before, but here was his girlfriend with the same gift in a more appealing package.

"Darius, I totally know what you're going through. It's like when I go on a photo shoot and I know how I want to be portrayed, but the photographer has a different idea. And he wants me in something sluttier, or doing a pose that's more suggestive or whatever."

Actually that doesn't sound like the same thing at all. "Uh, what's the connection?"

"The connection is that in the end, Darius, when I see the finished product, I'm always happy with the way the shot came out. I have to remember my audience. Readers of *FHM* don't wanna see me looking like the Mona Lisa or whatever."

Darius tried to mentally craft his response before saying a word, afraid that he might sound rude if he didn't rehearse it first. "Okay, baby, I see what you're saying. But music is a little bit different. I'm at a point where I'd rather sell fewer records to an audience that's more like me than go platinum because a bunch of kids with no taste cop my al—"

"Miko! Come here. They're doing a special on top New York models on the E Channel!" Belle's bellow cut him off midsentence.

Miko looked at Darius apologetically. "I'm just gonna go look for a second. She's lonely, I think. And she's been feeling left out since we started dating, you know?"

As soon as Miko departed his company, he felt a vibration coming from the back pocket of his jeans. It surprised him how excited he was to see that it was a message from Kahlila. As his eyes scanned her lengthy message, he was shocked at how true to her word she had indeed been. She had done a song-by-song review of his entire first album. His eyes zoomed in on certain sentences as he did a preliminary scan of her words.

"Why I Didn't Call"—The riffs on this track are amazing, but the instrumentation almost covers up what your voice is doing.

"Sweatin' You"—Flow Steddie did a great job with the sample on this song, and his little rap at the end is really clever. But it almost seems like you're doing a guest spot on his record, and not the other way around.

"Headache and Heartbreak"—This is a pretty standard contemporary ballad. Kind of reminds me of the stuff out by folks these days that I don't hate, but is so overplayed on black radio that I'm just sick of it.

Bonus Track—I can't believe this song doesn't even have a name, because it's unbelievable. I was just about to eject the CD when the soft notes came through the speaker and I was totally hooked. There's no info about the track in the liner notes, but it is definitely the best song on the album. Great lyrics—the play on the word "complex," love it. And the entire melodic line was made for your voice. Starts off slow, builds up, and takes you home. Brilliant. This is what your entire next album should sound like.

While Darius couldn't help but stiffen a little at the blunt criticism of his album, her final paragraph erased any discomfort that he might have had about her honesty. She'd unknowingly chosen the only song on the album that he wrote as the one she liked best. She said that "Love Complex" should be the model for every song on his next project. Yes. Yes. He'd finally been validated.

He immediately scrolled his phone for her number and then felt his heartbeat quickening with each ring.

"Hello?" Kahlila's voice was a bit unsure, and he wondered if she knew who was calling her. She would have had to save his number after the text he sent her last night.

"Hey, Kahlila, it's Darius.'"

A pause. "Oh! Hi. Did you get my e-mail?"

"I just did. And I wanted to thank you for your honest, thorough feedback."

"It wasn't too much? I've been accused of being a little too direct sometimes."

"Oh, it stung, no doubt. But you said everything that I knew was true."

He noticed a movement out of the corner of his eye, and saw that Miko was returning from Belle's room. "Hold on a sec," he instructed Kahlila.

Putting the phone down, he said softly to Miko, "The show over?"

"No, but I figured you were bored out here by yourself."

"I'm straight. Go finish watching it with Belle."

There was no way he was hanging up the phone

before he got to tell Kahlila about "Love Complex," until he got to talk more about the sound he was going for on the second album, and until he got a better sense of who this girl was who managed to make him feel so hopeful with a few simple sentences.

Chapter 20

*He has to have his own place,
preferably a nice one.*

This can't really be my life. Had Kahlila just hung up the phone from an hour-long conversation with Darius Wilson? The man was a professional singer but was asking for her "expert" opinion. Even Darius had seemed shocked by how much Kahlila was able to contribute with her musical assessment of his album, and had to inquire exactly how Kahlila had gotten to be such an astute listener.

Kahlila wasn't a great singer, but had always been selected to be in music groups in high school because of her ability to keep others on pitch. She had a keen ear for harmony, but not a particularly special voice. The music director's instructions would always be for Kahlila to sing out, but not enough that she could be distinguished from anyone else. Once she got to college, she advanced to the area of songwriting when Robyn's boyfriend, Lloyd, a pianist/vocalist himself, began to share his music with her. She was an English major and considered to be a connoisseur of words, so he consulted her about the poetry of his lyrics. However, once it was revealed that Desiree was in fact the real poet of the crew, she was consulted less. Still, it had been enough of a crash course to acquaint her with the necessary ingredients to producing a successful song.

It looked like her experience up to this point with music had paid off, because the conversation ended with Darius's asking her to listen to some unfinished tracks that he'd been working on. Tomorrow, she would be at his apartment. What should she wear? What would they talk about? She needed a consultation.

As she dialed Desiree's home number, she could hear the footsteps on her ceiling as her friend walked to answer the ringing phone. It was probably her imagination, but the footsteps seemed like they carried a bit of extra weight. When Desiree answered, Kahlila summoned her downstairs. Despite Desiree's bun in the oven, she made it down in the blink of an eye. The two of them sat in the living room, where Kahlila filled her in on the e-mail she'd sent Darius, the follow-up conversation, and the anticipated home visit tomorrow.

Desiree let out a tired sigh. "Are you sure you want to do this, Kahli?"

"Do what? Go to his place?"

"No. Are you sure you want to be *that* girl." She gave Kahlila a knowing look.

Casting her eyes downward, Kahlila didn't ask for further information. She knew exactly what Desiree was referring to. Kahlila herself had been wary to make a connection to Darius by reviewing his music because she didn't want to fall into her typical role once more. She often ended up as the female friend of guys, the one with whom they opened up about something that they couldn't share with the girls they wanted romantically.

Two years ago, she'd met a surgeon who was an aspiring novelist in his free time. When she told him on their first date that she'd edited Desiree's writing in the early years, he started sending her all of his short stories to read. They spent endless hours in coffee shops, peering at his laptop and sharing their favorite books. She thought that the two of them were really connecting, until he proposed to a nurse at his hospital whom he'd been dating all along but who had never read a single word of his writing. After that disappointment, she added number 172 to The List: he has to show a clear interest in *me*, not my abilities.

Just last year, she'd met a young high school principal at a professional development workshop. They exchanged information and began having long conversations by phone about the challenges of working in schools. Kahlila was quickly smitten and thought that she'd found the ideal guy for her. Unfortunately, the principal didn't want to pursue someone in his field, because he thought it might get "too competitive." When she ran into him a few months ago, he was dating a flight attendant. Rule number 310 got added at that time: as hypocritical as it sounds, he can't have his own list of whom he can and cannot date.

Desiree's voice cut through Kahlila's unpleasant flashbacks. "Kahlila, you know the routine. You go out of your way to prove your usefulness to these guys. They soak up the feedback and the mental stimulation. Then you're left all wrung out to dry when they form relationships with way less interesting women. What was that doctor's name again who married the chick—"

"Right, right. I know. I could argue with you and say that this situation is different, but it's really not."

"Exactly! Darius is already with that model. And it's wrong to stereotype, but I'll do it anyway. Something tells me that she's not the best person to discuss the future of his musical career with."

Kahlila couldn't help but feel hopeful at the thought that the beautiful girl she'd seen at the club wasn't able to provide something that *she* could. "Well, I'll just have to treat it as a possible friendship. Not get ahead of myself."

Desiree looked at her friend as if she were completely out of her mind. "Girl, getting ahead of yourself is what you do. You can't help it. Since you've hung up the phone, you've probably already thought about him thanking you at the Grammys or something."

Kahlila had to laugh, because Desiree knew her better than anybody. "So I should call him back and cancel?"

"Why would I tell you to do that? You wouldn't listen to me anyway." Desiree pushed herself up from the couch as if she were way more pregnant than she actually was. "Let's look in the closet and find what you're wearing tomorrow."

Kahlila obediently followed Desiree down the hall, smiling as she imagined Darius onstage looking into her eyes as she sat in the front row. *Shows how much Desiree knows. My fantasy wasn't the Grammys. It was just a regular ol' concert.*

Kahlila reached aboveground after riding the subway to Greenwich Village, hoping that her BCBG fragrance hadn't been completely obliterated by the assortment of bodies and odors on the sweltering train. As she walked down the street, she put on her oversized sunglasses (bought from Forever 21, but resembling Gucci from afar) and tried to plan a few topics of conversation in advance, just in case there were any awkward silent moments during her time with Darius.

After walking an entire block, she realized she'd been traveling in the wrong direction. As Kahlila doubled back, she looked down at the outfit that Desiree had selected for her, and hoped that it was special enough: dark blue Seven Jeans, an oversized white button-up shirt, beaded sandals, and a four-inch-wide brown leather braided belt around her waist with a large turquoise buckle.

At last she reached a building that had a lot fewer floors than she thought it would have. It was easy to miss from the outside: simple and brick with a revolving glass door. But when she stepped inside, the marble lobby and cherry-wood furniture told a different story. A doorman in a navy blue uniform smiled brightly. "Good afternoon. Are you Kahlila?"

Kahlila smiled in surprise. "Um, yes. How'd you know?"

The doorman, a ruddy-cheeked man in his mid-forties, chuckled as he picked up the phone at his desk. "Darius told me to expect a good-looking gal to be arriving around three. You're right on time," he said, glancing at his watch. "And you're definitely good-looking!" He laughed a big belly laugh, motioning with his head to proceed to the elevator and putting the desk phone to his ear. She opened her mouth to ask for the apartment number, and he held up four fingers in the air before she got a word out. As she walked away, she could hear him telling Darius that she had arrived.

As she stepped in the elevator and hit the button for the fourth floor, she wondered if he had the entire floor to himself. But she was quickly distracted by the mirrors all around her, and she gave herself a final once-over. Desiree had convinced her to wear her hair loose, which always made her a bit self-conscious because of the uncontrollable curls. So she rearranged some of them before the *ding* of the elevator door signaled her to get out. *Relax, Kahli. He thinks you're good-looking. Or at least that's what he told his doorman.*

As Kahlila expected, there was only one door when she stepped off the elevator. The doorbell was incorporated into a treble clef design, but she didn't get to ring it, as Darius opened the door immediately. She tried not to look surprised by his ensemble: Pistons jersey, mesh basketball shorts, and plastic Umbro flip-flops. "Hey, Kahlila," he said with a generous smile. "Come on in. I dress like a scrub when I don't have to be anywhere," he added somewhat randomly, making Kahlila think that she didn't mask her surprise very well after all.

Disappointed that he made no motion toward her for a hug, she tried to look as pleasant as possible as she stepped into the apartment, which was flooded with light from a wall that was almost entirely window. She stood in the foyer and had an open view to the living room, dining room, and kitchen. Kahlila eyed the scene in fragments: hardwood floors, wall-mounted television, black grand piano, granite countertops, Soul Train Music Award on the dining room table. Her self-guided tour was interrupted by the sight of a man on the couch in front of the TV. When she caught his eye, he stood up, revealing his larger-than-life stature and eyes that crinkled when he smiled.

"Kahlila, this is my boy Rasheed," Darius offered from the doorway.

Plastering on a grin, Kahlila walked over to him and extended her hand. As much as she wanted to be annoyed that suddenly there was a third wheel in her afternoon plans, she liked him from the moment he pulled her in for a hug. "Any friend of Darius is cool with me," he said, enveloping her with his sturdy arms.

Darius joined them at the couch. "I figured since I already had you coming by, Kahlila, I might as well invite

Rah, whose opinion I trust more than anything. That way y'all can listen to some of these new joints at the same time. Give me some collective feedback."

"So we heading to the studio, man?" Rasheed asked, stretching his arms over his head. Kahlila was surprised that they didn't touch the ceiling.

"Yeah," Darius responded, already walking out of the living room, past the dining room, and down the hall. Kahlila assumed she was supposed to follow, which she did. On her walk, she realized that she hadn't said a word since she'd arrived.

"Your place is really great," she shouted feebly.

Darius didn't respond. "It's a great investment," Rasheed said as he walked behind her.

She was about to ask him what he did for a living, but Darius turned into a room up ahead and her focus moved away from Rasheed as quickly as it had shifted toward him. Walking into the "studio," Kahlila gasped at the array of technology in front of her. Again, absorbing her environment in small pieces, she caught glimpses of various objects: a keyboard hooked up to a flat-screen monitor, a microphone and headphones, stacks of stereo-looking black boxes with electronic displays, a laptop connected to speakers, and a soundboard, which Kahlila only recognized from watching BET specials where producers sat in front of the vast array of switches, saying things like "That's hot. That's real hot."

There were three swivel chairs in the room, and Kahlila wondered if this was coincidental. Rasheed sat down in one while Darius walked over to the laptop and began pulling up files.

Kahlila always joked with herself that whenever she tried to picture a situation ahead of time, it was always dramatically different from the reality. She'd gone to sleep the night before imagining Darius singing to her as they shared a love seat. The fantasy couldn't have been further from what was actually happening. She tried to focus on the situation at hand as she was given a pair of headphones.

"I'm gonna start y'all with the one I'm most excited about. Actually, I shouldn't even have said that 'cause I already biased you," Darius said as he surfed the contents of his computer.

"Dawg, you know I'm gonna keep it real with you no matter what," Rasheed answered, adjusting his headphones so they fit more comfortably. Both he and Darius looked at Kahlila expectantly. She nodded earnestly, as if to say that she ascribed to the same tenet of honesty. But realistically, she didn't know what she would do if she didn't like the song. Being truthful in that case would not help her mission to bond with Darius in a way that went beyond the music.

Luckily, her fear only lasted for the few silent seconds before the song began to play. The only instrumentation was a piano, but the scales and chords made a rich, supportive sound for the beautiful tenor voice layered on top.

No son to carry on my name
One of many high prices of fame
Whatever it takes to get to the top
Is what I do, the ride never stops

I got a hunger for life's spoils
But when you're hot, the pot could boil
What might spill is the essence of you
Can't let that happen, gotta be true

(chorus)
Gotta make my life real by speaking my mind
Real meaning is what I'm on a quest to find

Make it real, make it count, make a legacy
Can't just live life on the path that's easy

After a lengthy instrumental solo, the music eventually faded out. Kahlila's gaze, which had been fixated on an imperfect spot on his polished floor, moved up to Darius's anxious face. At the sight of her grin, the tension in his face relaxed.

"I love it. The lyrics are brought out even more by the minor key of the song. It's really haunting," Kahlila said.

"Yeah? I still gotta add the bridge, and maybe another verse. What you think, Rah?"

Rasheed rose from his swivel chair and gave Darius a pound before settling back into his seat. "Yo, for real, I don't even know if someone outside the industry can fully feel what it is you're saying. No disrespect at all, Kahlila, but the lyrics are so personal, in terms of the choices you have to make about your music, your lifestyle. It's just so on point."

"Thank you. Seriously, thank you." Darius was nodding and clapping his hands slowly, as if he had just attended a concert himself.

"So, Rasheed, I take it you work in the music business?" Kahlila was curious about his comment regarding the exclusivity of the song's lyrics. He was clearly a member of the insiders' club to which he referred.

"I work for Darius. It's less the music business than the business of trying to keep this dude on schedule and out of any drama when he goes out."

"So . . . you're his bodyguard?"

Rasheed and Darius chuckled. "Yeah, I guess that's what it looks like to the majority of folks," Rasheed admitted. "There's more to it than that, though."

"Seriously, this dude is my manager. I mean, I have a

manager, but Rasheed does the day-to-day stuff. He's the person I trust," Darius clarified.

"So, what did you do before this?" Kahlila knew she was being nosy, but once she started asking people questions, she couldn't stop until she felt that there was nothing left to learn.

"I was actually managing people's money, doing financial planning. I never so much as bounced at a nightclub before Darius got his deal."

"Do you miss your old life?" Kahlila didn't know why she asked that question. Perhaps it was the lyrics of the song that made her question whether either of them was actually happy. Or maybe it was the way that Rasheed seemed proud of the fact that he had never aspired to the fast life before it fell into his lap.

After a quick flash in his eyes, he abruptly changed the subject. "So, D, what are we talking about for instruments?"

Darius was too absorbed in the development of his song to notice that the conversation had shifted focus. "I think we need to keep the instruments at a minimum, but still get that big sound."

"So, that was you playing the piano?" Kahlila asked.

"Yeah. I'm rusty, though."

"It sounded amazing," she said, noting that she had a little too much adoration in her voice. Clearing her throat, she added, "But I can picture a drumbeat coming in midway."

"True, true. What kind of drum?" Darius asked.

Kahlila nervously widened her eyes, realizing that she'd reached as far as she could in her bag of musical tricks. She had no idea what the difference was between a snare and a high hat, and she figured that saying nothing was better than saying the wrong thing. Luckily, Darius wasn't expecting an answer, instead scooting over to his synthesizer and playing around with various drum sounds.

While Darius was preoccupied, Rasheed decided to turn around the line of questioning. "So, what is it that *you* do, Kahlila?"

"I'm a teacher in Boston. High school English."

"That's tight. My boy from high school lives up in Boston."

"What's his name? I probably know him."

"Dedric Jones."

"Yup, we went on a date once."

Rasheed started laughing and even Darius looked up curiously from the keyboard in front of him. "Wow. Is Boston that small, or are you that . . . out there?"

Kahlila smiled. "Yes, the city is tiny. And as for my being 'out there,'" she said, doing finger quotes around Rasheed's term, "I go on a lot of first dates that don't lead to second ones."

"Damn, girl, what do you do to those brothers?" Darius asked.

Pondering how exactly to answer the question, she decided to go with the short answer. "I'm picky."

"So, how'd they even get the first date?"

"They usually don't expose their flaws right away," she said with hesitation, regretting that this subject ever came up.

Rasheed, on the other hand, was loving the discussion. "So, what was my boy's flaw?"

Cheap, arrogant as hell, and wore too much cologne. "It was a long time ago. I don't even remember, honestly."

"Rah, didn't I meet Dedric that time we went to Miami for spring break in college? He was a cocky bastard," Darius chimed in.

Kahlila felt herself smiling.

"Yo, D, look at your girl. Trying to front like she didn't

remember. She knows good and well she didn't like his conceited ass!" The three of them laughed for a while longer before refocusing on "Make My Life Real." Kahlila looked out of the window at the unobstructed view of the city's skyline and sighed with satisfaction. Though she believed Darius and Rasheed that there were consequences to fame, she found herself wishing that she could abandon her own life for something more than ordinary.

Chapter 21

He has to expose me to things
I've never seen before.

Darius couldn't help but feel annoyed at the fact that Miko didn't ask to come to the studio this morning. It was a big day; he was bringing in the instrumentalists to complete recording of "Make My Life Real." They were using the private studio of a producer named Bill Notes, who had worked with Darius on "Love Complex," the only song from his first album that he really loved. Darius had called Bill to arrange a session that he was paying for out of his own pocket. He knew that Flow wouldn't like the song's acoustic feel, and he wanted to get it made before Flow even heard it.

He knew in the back of his mind that it was for the best that Miko didn't come. Kahlila was already on board to take the trip, and it might have been an awkward car ride with just him and the two women. Rasheed had made plans to hang with his girl that day, so it would have fallen on Darius to entertain both ladies. Something told him they wouldn't have very much to talk about on their own.

Kahlila met him in the lobby of his apartment at 10:30 a.m. (Miko was still lying in his bed upstairs), and they took the car service to Bill's house on Long Island. They spent the ride listening to songs that Kahlila had downloaded onto her new iPod (setting up her Nano was her summer project). Her musical taste was just as eclectic as his, and she was having a ball playing deejay and seeing his reaction to her random assortment of tunes.

Darius really enjoyed spending time with Kahlila. Since he'd invited her to his apartment just one week before, they had hung out on two more occasions. She came to his place again to hear the completed lyrics of "Make My Life Real," and he went to Harlem once to have dinner with Kahlila, Desiree, and Jason. He gathered a lot of creative energy during their time together. She was exactly his target audience: late twenties and discriminating in her musical selection. He also found himself being more thoughtful in his responses to her questions than he had been in a long time. Countless interviews asking the same things had worn him down to clichéd answers, but when Kahlila asked a familiar question, he opened up and realized things that he had never thought about before.

After a sequence of Outkast, Fiona Apple, and Gnarls Barkley, Kahlila decided to save her battery and turn off her iPod for a little while. They sat quietly in the backseat for a few minutes, watching the scenery change from granite to green as they departed Manhattan and entered the suburbs. Suddenly shifting to face him, she asked, "So, what is it like? To be famous."

It was one of those questions that he received all the time: from journalists, from his friends back home, from the girls in the club desperate to have something to talk about. His usual answer consisted of something like "The lifestyle is fun, but what's more important is that I have an audience for my music." This answer was completely true, but he never pushed his thinking beyond that.

Perhaps it was midday clarity of mind, but he heard himself saying a lot more when he answered Kahlila. "Honestly, I don't feel famous. Flow—he's famous. Your girl Beyoncé is famous. I'm on the outskirts. People recognize me, yeah. Sometimes I'm driving and my song comes on the radio, or I'm in my living room and my video comes on TV. That's a feeling not many people have experienced. But fame, that's something different to me. It's not even something I want."

"So, what *do* you want?" asked Kahlila as she curled up into the seat, bringing her knees into her body.

Darius caught himself staring at her legs, which were covered by a pair of jeans. But he had a sudden flashback of her shimmery thighs on display at Marquee, and it took a second for him to concentrate. "I want to use the notoriety that I have to make better music than I have been doing." He spoke slowly, coming to this realization only as he said the words.

"You really weren't happy with your first album, were you?"

"I think I'm just now beginning to realize exactly how unhappy," he confessed.

"Well, you have another chance with this next project, right? That's the whole point of what we're doing today," Kahlila said cheerily, trying to brighten the mood.

"That's the plan, but it's made more difficult by being on Flow's label. He wants a sound that I'm not feeling at all."

"Flow is a friend of yours. So, in an ideal world, you'd want to make the music you want while staying on his label?"

"In an ideal world, yes. But I think it's impossible."

"No, you don't," she corrected, hitting his arm. "You wouldn't be making this song on your own to bring back to him if you didn't think there was a chance he'd change his mind."

Darius smiled. "You're right. I guess I wouldn't." He settled deeper into his seat and returned his gaze to the window. It was nice to be riding in a car with a down-to-earth person who didn't want to talk about the hottest clubs, clothes, or cars. He'd meant it when he said that he didn't feel famous, but he also knew that he was closer to famous than most people would ever get. It was important to him that his core stayed the same; he'd promised his mom that he would never get "big-headed." This was why he hadn't made an effort to be-friend any celebrities other than Flow. He didn't want to get lost in the smoke and mirrors of the music game, which was becoming more and more linked to the Holly-wood hustle. It was all too superficial for him. There was no merit based on talent. There was no substantive use of celebrity to make any change in the world. He'd rather just chill in New York, write songs, go on tour, and go back to his apartment when it was all said and done.

They finally reached the sprawling estate of Bill Notes, and Kahlila was reminded of the fact that there was plenty of money to be had in the music industry. The artists were in the spotlight, but the people behind the scenes were living large as well. She almost expected a butler to open the door, but Bill greeted them himself. Once she saw his face, she thought he looked familiar, most likely due to all of the magazines she read and awards shows she watched. He was a thirty-something, ponytail-wearing white guy with a lean face and body. His attire, a Notorious B.I.G. T-shirt, jeans, and Nikes, did not match his physical appearance whatsoever. "Good to see you, D," he said to Darius as they gave pounds and pats on the back.

"You too, man. This is my friend Kahlila," he said, putting his hand lightly on her back. Kahlila could barely concentrate on smiling and saying hello to Bill. *Darius just called me his friend. A few weeks ago, I didn't even know him. Now I'm at a producer's house while we record a single. And his hand is on my back.*

Once they entered the ultramodern single-level house, Bill insisted that Darius go to the piano and play the song for him. Kahlila had only heard the recording of the song before, with a keyboard playing the chords. This time, the richness of the music was enhanced by the grand piano and the live voice floating above it. She watched Darius's fingers dig into the keys, and she traveled off to a fantasy involving his fingers on her. Guiltily, she shook the image out of her mind.

When the song finished, Bill nodded his head approvingly. "Cool. Musicians will be over in a couple of hours. Let's order lunch and get in the studio. Lay down the vocals." He was already walking out of the living room as he spoke, and they followed him down a set of winding stairs to a finished basement. After a quick tour of the private theater, bar, and lounge, they entered the recording studio.

Kahlila settled into a chair and watched attentively. She still could not believe that she was getting to see the creation of this song in person. Wanting to be helpful, she offered to order the lunch. But Bill waved off the suggestion, instead using his intercom to ask the housekeeper to order it. *I knew he had a butler.*

The next several hours flew by as Bill and Darius first played with the melodic line of the song, and then introduced live instruments to complete the arrangement.

When Darius was in the sound booth, Kahlila flashed him huge smiles every time he made eye contact with her. She sensed that he was unsure about going behind Flow's back to make the song, and even more worried about whether Flow would appreciate the finished product. Convinced that she was invited to be a cheerleader, she fulfilled her duties as best as possible.

Once Darius finished the vocals, he had more time to talk with Kahlila while Bill worked with the other musicians. He munched on his chicken salad sandwich as he watched Bill in a trying moment with the violinist. Kahlila was removing her pointy stilettos and rubbing her feet.

"Why did you wear those fancy shoes to come hang in a studio all day?" Darius asked, noting that her toenails were painted a faint champagne color.

"I had to wear high heels because my jeans drag on the ground when I put on flats. Designers make pants way too long. They cater to the type of women *you* date," she teased pointedly.

"I date *a* model. One. It's not like I have a model fetish or anything," he corrected. He found himself a bit embarrassed to be discussing his personal life. It sounded so typical for a singer to be dating a model. He felt like he was just falling into a celebrity trend. "Nice toes," he tossed out as an attempt to divert the conversation.

"They may look pretty, but they're actually powerful weapons," Kahlila said. To prove her statement true, she picked up her size-9 shoe by its skinny heel using her big toe and the toe next to it. Then she flung the shoe out of the studio area and into the lounge.

Darius cracked up laughing, almost choking on his sandwich. "You're crazy."

"Don't be jealous that your toes aren't as strong as mine," she challenged. Bill had offered her a glass of wine with the sandwich she'd eaten an hour before, and it was becoming clear that the alcohol had raised her silliness level.

"What? Check this out." He kicked off his Pumas, pulled off his right sock, sniffed it and made a face before dropping it to the floor. Kahlila shook her head in fake dismay as he grabbed the heel of her other shoe with his foot and threw it twice as far as she did.

"No fair! I only used two toes. You used four of them, making your foot into a claw." Kahlila hated losing at anything, even mindless games with no consequence.

"You sound like you're commentating on ESPN. Relax, loser," he said with a wink before returning to check on Bill.

The wink from Darius appeased Kahlila and sent her off into her own imagination for several minutes afterward.

After a long day of arranging, spontaneous composing, and multiple takes, Darius, Kahlila, and Bill sat back and listened to the initial recording of "Make My Life Real." There was more production work to be done, but it sounded phenomenal, even in the rawest form.

After the number of times the song had played that day, Kahlila could have recited the words backward. Thinking about the lyrics, she realized how she and Darius were opposite sides of a coin. He felt the need to stay grounded with ordinary things in order to make his life meaningful, and meanwhile Kahlila's life was consumed by the mundane. She wanted a taste of a more exciting life to give hers substance. *Maybe we can balance each other out. That way we can both be happy.*

Chapter 22

He has to remember my birthday.

"Surprise!" Bree walked into the cafeteria at Channing, Triton, and Brown to meet about thirty smiling white faces, as well as the smirking brown countenance of her brother. Christine, Keith's boss, was holding a fancy cake with chocolate-covered strawberries on it. *Happy Birthday, Bree!* it read across the top in perfect cursive.

Speechless, Bree put her hands up to her cheeks and felt how warm they had become. She hadn't even known that anyone at the firm realized her seventeenth birthday was today. The day had already exceeded her expectations when she received a message on her cell phone from Stanley, who got the boys in his basketball camp to sing her "Happy Birthday." As an added bonus, she and Keith had plans to go to Merengue for dinner that evening, but that was all she'd expected as far as celebrations were concerned. Yet here were all of these extremely busy lawyers singing off-key and urging her to

blow out the single sparkler in the center of her flawlessly decorated cake.

In the three weeks that Bree had been working as an
assistant to the secretaries on the twenty-sixth floor of
the firm's downtown office building, she'd made herself
comfortable in the fabric of the multimillion-dollar op-
eration that employed her brother, and now her. On her
first day, she had arrived at work wearing a long face,
clearly having been forced by Keith to take the job. But
Keith's secretary, who absolutely adored him, vowed to
take Bree under her wing. By lunchtime, Bree was out of
her shell, enjoying the company of these older women
who were the backbone of the entire firm, yet still had
time to share funny stories and show Bree the ropes.

Once Bree's beautiful smile came out the first time,
there was no end to her sunny influence in the office. In
her year of mourning, Bree had almost forgotten that
she was a natural comedian. But she soon had the secretaries in stitches, doing impressions of their bosses and
of her ultraserious big brother. She was also the most
ambitious high school intern they'd ever had. Not only
was she extremely efficient with her clerical tasks, but
she'd taken on projects such as creating a huge photo
collage of all one hundred employees, organizing little
trivia contests about people's personal lives outside of
work, and championing her biggest success, the bake-
off. After eating delicious homemade muffins from two
different secretaries, she decided to put up flyers adver-
tising a Monday morning bake-off, and even got one of
the partners at the firm to volunteer a pair of Red Sox
tickets as the prize. Bree was shocked when not only the
secretaries entered their best cakes and cookies, but the
attorneys did also. The winner was actually a male
summer associate entering his last year of law school

whose mother had taught him how to make a mean strawberry shortcake when he was just ten years old.

Bree had an important realization over her first few weeks of the job: if she stayed busy, then she had no time to be sad. High school gave her too much opportunity to retreat into her private thoughts. As the teacher droned on, she simply escaped to another place. But Channing, Triton, and Brown had her swamped with lunch orders to juggle, memos to proofread, and files to organize. There was no time to wonder what Stanley and Krystal were doing in New Haven, or to remember how much her parents had loved the summertime.

One of the ongoing sources of tension between Bree and her brother was that Bree resented Keith's stoic exterior in response to their mother's passing. In the year since her death, Keith still hadn't shed a single tear, and it made Bree mad as hell, although she'd never articulated this feeling out loud. But seeing what he did every day, how he buried himself in briefs and depositions, made it easier for her to understand how he had managed to distance himself from his feelings. And it also made her feel good to see what a star her brother was at the firm. Everyone raved about his being the strongest associate in his class (they still referred to people in terms of the year they began working at Channing). One day she walked into a meeting where Keith was doing a presentation. She was so impressed, because he was exactly himself. He didn't take the scruff out of his voice. He didn't smile unnecessarily. He just broke down the facts—no wasted words.

Once Bree blew out the candle of her cake, her brother did have a big smile and a hug for her, which earned a collective "awww" from the women in the room. As soon as Bree sliced the cake as thinly as she possibly could so that everyone could have a piece, the room began to clear. While the firm prided itself on spirit and collegiality, folks had tons of work to do. So people took their cake to-go, and patted Bree on the back on their way out. She didn't mind. It was a nice thought, and it really made her feel like part of the team.

She was about to return to her cubicle when one of the associates in Keith's class tapped her on the shoulder. Bree didn't know her name, although she'd seen her many times. The woman was wearing the type of soft expression usually reserved for regarding babies and panda bears. "Bree?" she said in a sugary voice. "I'm Janice."

"Hi."

"I just wanted to say happy birthday, sweetie. You've been such a breath of fresh air in this office, you just have no idea. You are so cute, with your adorable outfits. Good looks must just run in your family, huh? And you've really been helping out the secretaries a lot, I hear. They keep this place running, you know. Seriously, great job."

Bree felt herself standing straighter, so pleased that people were noticing her efforts.

"And I had no idea before today about everything you've been dealing with in your life," Janice continued. "You'd never know from the way you come in every day with that huge smile of yours."

"I'm sorry?"

"Christine sent out an e-mail about your birthday, just giving us background about you and what a great guy Keith is for taking you in and getting you this job. . . ." Janice's smile was fixed, oblivious of the marked change in Bree's demeanor.

"Taking me in? I'm his sister. Not an abandoned puppy he found on the side of the road," Bree said coldly, through a set of slanted eyes.

"Of course you're not," Janie continued, unfazed. "But most of us had no idea what had been going on with him over the past year. It makes his performance at work even more impressive. Anyway, you had a lot of fans at your birthday party today, young lady." She touched Bree's arm before walking out of the cafeteria.

Bree could feel the tremble in her lips before the first tear fell. Here Bree thought that all the lawyers came to her party because they'd noticed the hard work she'd been putting in. Instead, she was a charity case. Rushing into the hallway, she found refuge in a bathroom stall until she could compose herself enough to pretend her seventeenth birthday was more than everything she'd hoped it would be.

At five o'clock, Bree was finally able to stop pretending. Keith had made an effort to get out of work early, and the two of them both exhaled loud sighs of relief when they stepped into the late afternoon sunshine after being cooped in their overly air-conditioned space for eight hours. They had been running late that morning, so they drove downtown, instead of taking the T. When they reached the car in a nearby garage, Keith threw her the keys. Bree caught them clumsily.

Bree had gotten her permit last month and Keith had been forcing her behind the wheel as much as possible. His unspoken fear was that Bree would be petrified to drive after their mother's accident. So far, Bree had seemed eager to learn. So they continued with their unspoken policy of not mentioning the crash . . . ever.

For a person who'd only recently begun lessons, Bree was surprisingly comfortable in the driver's seat. Keith found himself not having to give much feedback, and he was surprised at how normal it felt for his little sister to be driving him home. He let her focus on reversing out of the parking space before he began any conversation. "So, you're really making a bunch of friends at the office, huh? I'm impressed."

"I don't know if you can call people friends who are twenty years older than me."

"Well, they're throwing you birthday parties. That has to count for something."

"I'm stuck there twelve hours a day and my mother's dead. It's a pity party, not a birthday party."

Keith didn't know where to start. First off, Bree was not at work twelve hours a day. That was only true if she waited for him at the end of the day, and most of the time she didn't. Second, it wasn't just *her* mother who was dead. He'd lost his anchor as well. And finally, where was all of this coming from? He'd convinced himself that they'd reached some type of turn in the road. For the past three weeks, Bree had been upbeat and happy.

"So, what did I miss today?"

Suddenly, Bree was angrily describing a conversation with Janice, a coworker who had always been jealous of Keith and the praise that he got from the partners. Bree could never remain that angry without crying, however, and suddenly she was blubbering, trying to wipe her nose and steer through rush-hour Big Dig traffic all at the same time. Keith wasn't sure whether to focus on the pain of her talk with Janice, or to concentrate on getting them home in one piece. But all at once it seemed as if Bree was getting herself together with no help from him. Expertly navigating the construction detours of Boston, she began to talk herself out of her sadness.

"You know what? Whatever. I do a lot in that office. And most of the people in the lounge today were people I've spoken to before. They would have come even if Christine didn't put our business on blast for the whole firm."

"You're absolutely right, Bree."

They drove in silence for the rest of the way, with the exception of Keith's driving reminders. "Don't turn so wide." "Give the person in front of you some space." "Check your blind spot."

Keith began to think that disaster was averted when

Bree smoothly pulled up to their house with dry eyes and a small smile. He was sorting a few items in his briefcase as Bree stepped out of the car and almost hit the infamous mother-mooching Ty on his bike with the car door.

"Whoa. Watch yourself, little Ma."

"Sorry," Bree mumbled.

"Yo, check you out! You driving the whip?" Since Keith had caught Ty smoking on the porch, he and Bree hadn't had another conversation. Keith had become somewhat of a "helicopter guardian," hovering over her at all times. But as tempted as Keith was to reveal himself at this moment, he decided to wait in the car and see how Bree handled herself.

Bree nodded and slammed the car door shut. She had begun walking away from Ty when he grabbed her hand. "So, whassup? Where you been hiding?"

"Ty, I don't really want to talk to you." She shook her hand loose.

"Your brother has you shook like that? Relax. He ain't gonna do nothing to you."

"It's not Keith. I'm deciding for myself. There's no need for us to have any more conversations. Take care of yourself."

Ty walked away in a bit of a daze. He had been thinking that Bree was avoiding him because her brother told her to. He'd had no idea that Bree was in the driver's seat.

"Hey, Bree." She turned around and saw her brother climbing out of the car, wearing a rare smile. "Love ya."

"Ditto. Hate Janice, though."

"Yeah, she's a bitch."

"A superbitch."

"A colosso-bitch." They laughed. "Happy birthday, sis."

"Thanks."

Chapter 23

He has to enjoy himself in a variety of social settings.

"Should I be jealous?" Miko asked playfully, her lips wearing a faint smirk beneath her red lipstick.

"Of Kahli? No. Unless you want to be my musical director instead of my girlfriend." He was buttoning up a striped shirt in front of his full-length bedroom mirror.

"So, what exactly makes her an expert in music?" she asked, her forehead wrinkled in skepticism.

"She just has an ear for what sounds good." He picked up the bottle of cologne from his dresser and pumped out two quick bursts.

"And I don't?" Miko was officially pouting.

Darius sighed. Miko's favorite group of all time was the Pussycat Dolls. Not exactly the height of musical innovation. He didn't know why she was choosing this evening to feel threatened by Kahlila. Just the other day they had all been at the same lounge, and Miko proclaimed her to be "plain" and "boring." Darius knew better than to disagree. Kahlila was less of a liability in his girlfriend's mind because she wasn't a model, actress, or singer. Miko couldn't imagine herself being overthrown by a regular girl. And despite how much fun he'd been having getting to know Kahlila, he felt no inclination to take things any further with her. Sometimes, he thought he could see some amount of romantic interest on Kahlila's part, but he just as quickly scolded himself for thinking that she wanted to be more than friends. *Kahli's probably one of the few girls who wouldn't be automatically interested in me just because I have some money and access.*

"You have a body for what feels good." He smiled, flopping onto the bed and pinning her down by the arms for a passionate kiss.

She giggled, wrapping her long legs around his waist, and began unbuttoning the shirt he'd just put on. The loud ring of the phone startled them both. He fumbled for the phone on his bedside table as he continued to kiss Miko's neck.

"Mm-hmm," he said gruffly into the receiver.

"Kahlila's here. Should I send her up?" said a doorman's voice that he didn't recognize.

"No!" he almost shouted, sitting up straight. "I mean, I'll be down in a few minutes. Thanks." He hung up the phone, avoiding the stern eye contact of his girlfriend.

"So, where are you two going exactly?" Her voice was chipped, like a fallen icicle after a snowstorm.

"Her friends are going to see a friend of theirs perform in a jazz band, and they had an extra ticket," he said, adjusting his shirt and grabbing his wallet. He didn't bother telling her that he and Kahli were going to get something to eat first.

"Doesn't this girl know anybody in the city other than you?" She found the remote control under his pillow and turned on the wall-mounted flat-screen television.

"Not everyone can be as popular as you are, sweetheart," he teased.

"People are going to start thinking you two are a couple, not us," she muttered.

"You and I are together all the time. No one would think that," he answered, searching the room for his house key.

"Well, it's not like you've confirmed to anybody that I'm actually your girlfriend." Miko's voice had become more assertive.

"Confirmed to who? The media? Everybody who matters knows I'm with you." He matched her aggressive tone, and she didn't bother to respond.

They'd had similar exchanges over the past few weeks, where Miko was ready to do an interview about what a great couple they were, and Darius wanted to be more private about their relationship. It wasn't like people weren't spotting them all over New York anyway. Why should he have to make a statement about it? He couldn't help but be wary of the publicity gain that Miko could gain from officially being with him, especially since he had never dated anyone in the industry before.

As he watched her nestle under the covers to watch TV, he began to feel guilty about going out. Suddenly, a night cuddled up with Miko seemed very appealing.

"You're staying in tonight?" he asked, debating how rude it would be to tell Kahlila he wasn't coming after all.

"Of course not! The girls are going to Tenjune around twelve thirty. I'm going to take a nap before I get ready. Do you want me to come back here afterward?"

"Why bother? I'll be fast asleep," he said, knowing that Miko never left the club before 4:00 a.m.

"I'll find a creative way to wake you up," she purred, giving him an air kiss before he exited the room.

"In that case, see you later tonight," he shouted back,

walking out of the apartment and letting the door shut behind him.

Any remorse he was feeling about leaving Miko in the house was quickly dissolved once he heard the first notes of the sultry jazz singer at B Sharp, a local hot spot for live music that had greatly benefited from Harlem's gentrification, attracting a young professional set. The vocalist was working the stage and the microphone, but her throaty tone was almost upstaged by the band playing behind her. Jason and Desiree were friends with Nicole McKie, a musical prodigy who had moved to Harlem when she was just eighteen and had become one of the most noted saxophone players in the country since then. For fun, she decided to sit in with the band at the same lounge where she had gotten her start five years before. Desiree, Jason, Kahlila, and Darius had the best seats in the house at a round table to the right of the stage.

While he was listening to the phenomenal mix of jazz standards and neosoul favorites, his mind traveled to his last tour, where he had been informed that there was no need for him to have a live band. "Why bother? Most of your songs are based off of samples anyhow. They'll just take up space, which you need for your dancers," said his tour manager. In retrospect, there were so many times when Darius should have stood up for himself and for his image. Now it was going to be twice as hard to be the musician he wanted to be.

Suddenly everyone around him was clapping and he realized that the band had taken a break. Desiree and Jason were sitting as close as they could be on one side of the table, and Darius tried to ignore the feeling that this was some type of double date. They'd all hung out before, but never in public, and never all dressed up.

Even Jason, who hated wearing anything other than T-shirts and running pants, donned freshly creased slacks for the occasion.

"So, what did you think, Darius?" Desiree asked.

"The whole band was tight, but your girl Nicole is pretty special. I'd heard about her before, but I've never seen her play. I thought people were just hyping her up with the whole 'Britney Spears of jazz' thing, but she's the real deal. How do you two know her?"

"She used to live in our brownstone when she first moved to New York," said Jason, sipping on seltzer water. Darius had noticed that Jason never drank. He wasn't sure if Jason was supporting Desiree through her pregnancy, or whether he was just a fitness nut. He looked over at Kahlila, relieved that she was sipping on one of those milky, alcoholic drinks that she liked so much. He didn't want to be the only one partaking at the table.

Even though he was enjoying himself, he couldn't get Miko's words out of his head. *Maybe I have been spending too much time with Kahlila.* Since they'd met, he hadn't called his buddies from Morgan Stanley, or any of his friends from Detroit. Flow Steddie was on vacation in Turks and Caicos, a trip that Darius turned down so that he could work on music while Flow was away. He had only spoken to his mom and sisters a couple of times, and even Rasheed had taken the opportunity to increase his own quality time with his girlfriend. The last few weeks were a series of alternating experiences of hanging with Kahlila, and going to various fashion shows, movie premieres, and birthday parties with Miko. When he thought about all of the people vying for his time and attention (including acquaintances from NYU who wanted to elevate to friend status now that he was somebody, producers who wanted to set up sessions in the studio for his new album, and his manager, who has been pressuring him to become the face of some hot new clothing designer), he wondered if putting so much time into a friendship with someone he'd just met was a good idea. *After all, she'll be headed back to Boston at the end of the summer. What's the point?*

I don't want to go back to Boston. Since Kahlila had accompanied Darius to record "Make My Life Real" at Bill's studio, they'd spoken by phone or e-mail at least once a day. She looked forward to seeing his golden brown skin across from her at Starbucks, or next to her at his keyboard. On days that she wasn't spending with him, she was spending time with her best friend, reminiscing about old times, reading anxiously about pregnancy and childbirth, shopping for furniture for the baby's room. She couldn't believe that she was actually dreading those chores when she had originally learned that Desiree was expecting. Every moment of her first month in New York had been precious, even those quiet days that she spent reading on a bench in Central Park, or shopping for finds on 125th Street.

When she imagined returning to her life in September, she thought about the routine from which she rarely strayed each day. Get to work early, make the necessary copies at the temperamental Xerox machine, spend the next six hours teaching five sections of English and meeting with individual students during her free periods, stay until six o'clock highlighting novels and grading papers, head to the gym for strength training or Pilates, pick up or cook a meager dinner, watch a television show, catch up with Madeline, Robyn, or Desiree on the phone, and pass out exhausted. Weekends were extra gym classes, high school sporting events, shopping as stress relief, and usually one bad date. *I just can't go back.*

She was lost in her own thoughts as Darius chatted with Desiree and Jason between sets. The band came out from backstage during their conversation, and the crowd applauded them as the musicians made their way through the crowd, mingling and ordering drinks. Nicole, a fresh-faced girl with long blond hair and a cheeky smile, made a beeline for their table. After hugging Desiree and Jason, she shook hands with Kahlila, who was meeting her for the first time. When Darius stood up to greet her, all of the color drained from her face.

"Nicole, you were doing your thing up there. I can't wait for the next set," Darius said with a generous smile.

"Oh my goodness. You're Darius Wilson. Oh my goodness!" She turned to Desiree and Jason. "You didn't tell me that he was coming." She turned back to Darius, her cheeks now flushed. "I love your voice. Your singing voice, I mean. Um, your speaking voice is great too, but you really do have an amazing sound. I don't think enough people notice it with all the heavy production on your songs."

Darius and Kahlila looked at each other in clear surprise. She had hit on exactly what he was trying to change about his music. He shouldn't have been shocked, being that she was a certified musical genius, composing scores for entire orchestras. But her almost ditzy initial impression threw him off. "Thanks. Hopefully I'll be resolving that problem on my next album."

"Well, if you have any room for a saxophone on one of your tracks, give me a call. I've never done any R&B before, but I'd love to work with you."

"Definitely! I'll get your info from Desiree." He shot Kahlila another surprised look before Nicole asked him to come meet her bandmates. He followed her through the cramped space of tables and chairs as they made their way to the bar.

The band's percussionist had been readjusting his drum set as Nicole was talking to them. Once she and Darius left, he climbed down from the stage and sat in the now-empty seat next to Kahlila.

"Did I hear you say that your name is Kahlila? Are you from Boston?" He had naturally curled lashes and a dimple in his chin that Kahlila wanted to put her finger inside.

"Um, yeah," she responded. Confused, she knew that she'd never met this person before. She would have remembered such an adorable face.

"You teach at Pierce High School?"

"Yeah, I do!" she answered more excitedly.

"My sister was in your class a few years back. She talked about you all the time. Sparklle?"

Kahlila put her hand up to her mouth in shock. All at once, she remembered Sparklle's bragging about her older brother who'd graduated from Berklee School of Music and was making his way in New York City. "I love Sparklle! She just came to visit me in June."

"So, you met my little niece, huh?" He smiled wide at the thought of baby Starr. Even though he was Sparklle's older brother, he was still about five years younger than she was. Younger men were completely off-limits. It was one of the initial items on her List. She hadn't thought about The List much over the past few weeks, because she was focused on a man who had almost every quality on it. The List tended to surface whenever she encountered someone new, and from the quickness with which it entered her mind at this moment, she knew that her vow to abandon it was not so successful.

"I did. I can't believe we ran into each other here," she

said, still shaking her head at the small worldness of
Boston, and that it had followed her to Manhattan.

"So . . . you dating Darius Wilson?" he asked, nodding
in the direction of Darius and Nicole, who were talking
animatedly with the horn players at the bar.

"Oh! No. He has a girlfriend," she quickly said, somewhat anxious that Darius might think she was telling
people that they were an item.

"Well, that's good. From what I've seen of the recording industry, you don't want to mess with those cats," he
said softly, leaning in closer.

"Darius is a great guy. He's not the typical artist," she
heard herself saying.

"Whatever. You would know better than I do. But seriously, don't believe the hype. What you do every day with
your students, it's way more important than any of this.
Sparklle said you held it down for a lot of girls at Pierce.
You're a role model. These dudes who just sample other
people's music and make flashy videos—they're just
trying to get paid."

Jason, who had been taking in the conversation,
flashed Kahlila a "listen to what he's saying" look.
Though she was offended by his implication that Darius
just made music for the money, she did appreciate his
sentiments about her work in Boston. "Thank you. For
valuing my job so much. I was just sitting here dreading
the start of school in September," she confessed.

He rose from the chair, noticing that his bandmates
were heading back to the stage. "You still have plenty of
vacation left. Have fun, but don't get caught up in the
lights and shit. Music is a beautiful thing, but all the
bling and bottles is for the birds. I'll tell Sparklle I saw
you," he said, turning his back before she could respond.

Kahlila was indeed grateful for the reminder that she
actually did love being a teacher. But she could have

done without the warning about Darius. When he returned to the table, she was satisfied to see that he didn't have on a single piece of jewelry other than an understated watch. *Bling is for the birds. But Darius is better than all that.*

Chapter 24

He cannot have any lingering past relationships.

When the name "Traci" appeared on the screen of Keith's cell phone, he felt his body seize. The last time they'd spoken, she'd ended the relationship, calling him when he was at work and coldly informing him that it was over, when he'd been just days away from purchasing an engagement ring that he couldn't afford, but was going to buy anyway. *Why is she calling me six weeks later?*

Tempted though he was to let it go to voice mail, his curiosity won over his appearing too busy to answer the phone. After all, it was a Saturday morning. She knew he never slept past nine. She knew a lot of things about him that very few others did: his reaction when he got the call about his mother's fatal accident was probably the most significant. Everyone except Traci thought that he'd never cried. Most of the other secrets had to do with his turn-ons and turn-offs. Traci became the woman he wanted to spend the rest of his life with because she had way more of the former, and because she didn't go running when she saw him completely lose it after that phone call.

"Hello?"

"Keith; it's me."

He could hear the tension in her voice. He thought for a moment about pretending not to know who "me" was, but he decided against it. "What's up."

"Is this a bad time?" Her words were rushed, falling out of her mouth in one quick breath.

"It's cool. What's up?" he repeated.

"Are you free for dinner tonight?"

"Why?"

"I just want to talk to you."

He briefly considered pretending to have plans, but again went with honesty. "Yeah. I'm free."

"Great. How about we meet at seven—at our favorite place?"

"What place is that?" he asked, finally giving in to his urge to be difficult.

"Keith . . ." She didn't have to finish the sentence.

He never did well with hurting people's feelings. "I was just kidding. I'll see you at seven," he said, and flipped his cell phone shut.

He purposely got there at 7:10, because he was never late, and he wanted Traci to feel like she didn't know him anymore. He actually arrived at 6:56, so he waited the extra fourteen minutes in the car. At 6:59, he saw her rushing into Vintage, her hair blowing back as it met the extreme air-conditioning of the restaurant upon her opening the door. Surprisingly, he felt nothing at the sight of her. But he knew better than to consider himself cured. Watching someone from a fifty-foot distance is different from sitting across from the person, hearing her voice, watching the lips move that you kissed thousands of times.

The sound of his cell phone startled him, and he fished it out of his jacket pocket in time to see that Bree was calling him. Guiltily, he turned down the volume and returned the phone to his pocket. He couldn't talk to Bree now. She would be so angry to hear where he was at the moment.

His sister never liked Traci. Bree and her mom used to come to visit Keith in Boston, and she would glare at Traci from across the table. Whenever Keith would ask why, she would always give the same response: "She's not *about* anything."

Keith, however, never understood Bree's claim. He found Traci to be down-to-earth, intelligent, and extremely attractive. They'd first met when he was working as the assistant director at a juvenile detention center and she visited the facility to write a story for a local newspaper. She was a textbook journalist: taking copious notes, asking probing questions, and absorbing everything with sharp eyes. Keith had noticed her, mainly because of her pouty maroon-painted lips and legs that stretched forever in a black pencil skirt that was professional and sexy at the same time. He wasn't interviewed for the story, so he was surprised to see an e-mail from her the following day. She said that she couldn't help but notice the way he worked with the boys in the center, and that she'd love to take him to dinner sometime. It was the last time that Traci had to make the move in the relationship. Keith was enamored from the moment they met at the restaurant, which he now sat outside of. They'd shared a good laugh, as Traci had picked the restaurant because she thought it was near his house. However, she'd confused Roxbury with West Roxbury, two neighborhoods that couldn't be more different demographically. "I was wondering why you sounded so skeptical when I said I knew a fabulous new restaurant in your hood!" she giggled.

Taking a deep breath, he decided to face the music and see what this reunion was all about. When he'd stepped inside the doors, he was glad to feel the overzealous air-conditioning hit his face, because he tended to get hot when he was nervous. He eyed Traci before the hostess could intervene, and as he approached the table, she stood up to greet him. Her smooth legs were encased in a pair of jeans, much to his relief, and she had a cardigan over what looked to be a skimpy top. It was too cold in the restaurant for her to be flaunting what she had. She smiled a warm smile that relaxed him before he went in for the hug. He didn't pull her in too closely, and he decided against the kiss on the cheek. But he could smell her perfume, an assortment of oils that she mixed herself. He stepped away before the scent could create any nostalgia. They sat down to the candlelit booth without having said a word.

"You look good," she said, still smiling and looking directly into his eyes.

"You too," he answered, looking down at the drink menu.

He wanted to get right to it. He was dying to know why they were there, but he knew that he should let her bring it up in her own time. They didn't even have glasses of water as yet. He prepared himself for the prolonged pretense of small talk.

Sure enough, she launched into the superficial conversation immediately. "How's work at the firm?"

"Hectic, as usual. I might actually go in later tonight while it's quiet and get some research done." It was a lie, but he thought that giving the evening a time-crunched feel might move her to the point more quickly.

She looked taken aback, and seemed grateful for the interruption of the waiter's taking their drink orders. Keith allowed her to go first, curious as to whether she would order alcohol. Sure enough, she ordered wine, which tended to get her more tipsy than a glass of bourbon would. He knew that he should keep his head on straight and drink water, but he had no idea where their discussion was headed. He got a Dark and Stormy instead.

"How's work for you?" he asked, still perusing the menu though he knew exactly what he wanted to eat.

"It's great. I'm actually on the entertainment beat now. I cover celebrity news, local concerts, openings of new clubs, that kind of thing. There are a lot of perks." She seemed excited to be talking about something cheerful.

"Oh yeah? What kind of perks?"

"I already know all the club owners in the city, so my girls and I get in places for free. And I've met a lot of famous people in just a few weeks." She paused, waiting for him to ask for names. When he didn't bite, she continued, "Bono, Matt Damon, Leonardo DiCaprio."

"So they only let you meet male celebrities?" He smirked.

She laughed, embarrassed, and hit his arm, which was resting on the table. Their drinks arrived and they each had a sip before resuming the conversation. Keith had forgotten how much he liked Dark and Stormys. He only had them at this specific restaurant, and he hadn't eaten there since she broke it off with him. *Was it really only a month ago? Feels like years.*

"So, how's Bree?"

Keith couldn't tell if she really wanted to know, or if

it was an obligatory inquiry. "She's good. She's actually working at Channing this summer with me."

"How cute! Do they love her over there?"

"Of course. She can be pretty charming when she wants to." He smiled, thinking of his little sister strutting through his office, taking charge.

"She never quite wanted to be so charming with me," Traci said wryly, to which Keith had no response.

"Anyhow, she's visiting friends in New Haven for a week. I promised her some time there, and she misses them a lot."

"So she's out of town now?" Traci said brightly, a hint of excitement in her voice.

"Yeah, she left yesterday."

The rest of the meal went in this way, with Traci seeming eager to learn the details of Keith's life as it stood, almost hopeful that there were no new players in it. Keith answered her questions guardedly, and posed none of his own regarding Traci's personal life. He figured that the bomb had to be dropping soon, and it exploded right after the dinner plates were cleared.

"Keith, I was having dinner with my family last week. And you know my dad loves his Black Label. So he was on his fourth scotch or so, and he let it slip that you had asked him for permission . . . to propose." She said the last word softly, so that Keith barely heard it, but deciphered from context clues.

He smiled and shook his head slightly, surprised but not surprised all at once. He'd always wondered if Traci had any idea how close he was to popping the question. On one hand, he thought that if she'd known, she might have been more patient about his trying to balance her, work, and Bree. Another part of him said that she absolutely knew that he wanted to marry her, and she figured that if she was going to let him go, she should do it before he made an ass of himself.

"I had no idea," he heard her saying as his mind ran a mile a minute. "I thought that you weren't serious about me, and that I wasn't in your plan as you were reprioritizing your life. Why didn't you say anything?" she pleaded.

"I thought proposals were supposed to be a surprise," he said coolly, remembering his plan to get down on his knee during the Fourth of July fireworks on the Esplanade.

"You're right. You're right," she repeated softly, almost to herself. "I fucked up."

Keith blinked in surprise. It was such a guy thing to say, both in sentiment and in language.

"You don't have to say anything," she plowed on. "I just had to make sure you knew that I didn't end things with you because my feelings had changed. It was because I thought *yours* had. We used to always talk about our future plans, and suddenly it was all about Bree, her report card, her bad moods—"

"Do you realize how ridiculous you sound right now?" He lowered his voice before continuing. "Our mother *died*. I thought you understood that, since you were sitting right there when I found out."

"Keith, stop. Stop. What I said came out wrong. All I was trying to say—" She grabbed his hand and leaned into the table. "All I was trying to say was that our breakup was a misunderstanding. I didn't know I still had a place in your new life."

"It was the same life, Traci. With new responsibilities." His voice had an edge, but he didn't remove his hand from hers.

"I understand that now, honey." She searched his face for a hint of forgiveness, but his jaw was set and his gaze steely. Giving his hand a final squeeze, she placed her hands in her lap and stared down at them. "Look, like I said, you don't have to say anything. Just consider what I told you. Let's just share a cheesecake like we always do, and change the subject." Taking matters into her own hands, she signaled the waiter and ordered dessert.

Keith was fairly quiet as they waited for the oversized slice of cheesecake to arrive, and Traci filled the space by telling a pretty amusing story about an article for her new beat. She had to cover the opening of a bar downtown, and happened to go on Lovely Lesbian night. For a reporter who was supposed to have an eye for detail, she took a full hour to figure out why she was getting so many compliments.

By the time the plate arrived, Keith was smiling. They cheerily dug into the dessert, and Traci pushed the strawberries his way, as she always did. It was comfortable, their routine. Keith watched people smile at them as they passed the table. They were a great couple on paper: both good-looking and career-minded. Neither liked the club scene (or at least Traci hadn't until this new entertainment beat), both loved cheesecake (but only he liked strawberries). It all came together to make a package that Keith had been ready to seal forever. But he'd since let that fantasy go, and here she was suggesting that it might not be a faded dream after all. As she headed to the restroom, he struggled over what to do with that information.

"All set?" she asked upon her return.

"Yeah, as soon as he brings the check."

"I paid it just now," she said with a smile. "I knew you wouldn't let me treat if he brought the bill to the table."

"Very sneaky," he said as he rose from the booth.

She walked ahead of him and he couldn't help but look at her hips as she moved. She had the most efficient yet seductive walk that he'd ever seen. It was quick, but had a switch that made him want to fall farther behind to get the view.

When they reached the parking lot, she turned to face him. They stood in front of her car, a white Acura that Keith had never seen dirty. He opened his mouth to make a comment about her sparkling automobile, and she grabbed his arms and rose on her toes to kiss him. He kissed her back. It felt nice, but it had a quality that told him they'd already lived through the best part of what they could have been. He remembered the only other person he'd kissed in the last two years. With Kahli, there was a feeling of possibility and unknown. In this moment with Traci, there was a feeling of closure.

She stepped away with a hopeful look in her eye. "Soooo . . ."

"I'll call you," he said, breaking eye contact to open her car door. She climbed inside and looked up at him standing over her. He let his eyes linger on her face for an extra moment, knowing that he was not going to make that phone call.

Closing the car door, he walked away.

Chapter 25

He has to give thoughtful gifts.

"Surprise!" a chorus of voices chanted in unison as Kahlila flipped on the light in Desiree's apartment. She blinked in shock at the faces smiling back at her: Jason, Robyn, Lloyd, Madeline, and J.T. Then she turned behind her to glare at Desiree, who was clearly behind this plan to get everyone together. Her birthday wasn't until the following week, and she'd had plans to head into Jersey to visit J.T. and eat a good meal. Instead, all of her closest friends had made the trip to Harlem, and she hadn't suspected a thing.

"I can't believe you fell for the 'Come see this new piece of furniture in my apartment' trick," Desiree said as she walked over to her stereo and hit the power button.

"You guys really got me," Kahlila admitted, hugging her guests and looking around at the impressive spread of hors d'oeuvres and beverages set up around the living room. She was also relieved not to see a pile of gifts stacked in a corner. A few years back, all of her friends had agreed to stop buying presents for Christmas and birthdays. They preferred to spend money having good dinners and taking nice vacations, and it seemed like every month, someone was getting another year older.

Everyone quickly settled into couches and chairs, balancing plates on their knees as they animatedly caught up with one another and sipped drinks made by a heavy-handed J.T., who always said that he would have been a bartender if not for his basketball talent. Desiree milled about the room, refilling plates and contentedly drinking a cranberry juice and seltzer water. Kahlila enjoyed watching everyone interact: Robyn was excitedly rubbing Desiree's still flat stomach, as this was the first time they were seeing each other in months. Jason and Lloyd watched their mates amusedly, bonding in the way that husbands and boyfriends of best friends have to.

Madeline was definitely a surprise guest, as she was a work friend whereas the others were from high school or college. She was meeting J.T. for the first time, and was clearly enamored. J.T. had been dating Marisol, a sexy Latina whom he had met at Jason's gym, for five years. Considering J.T.'s severe case of marriage-phobia, he surely was not interested in trading in Marisol, who seemed perfectly comfortable in their committed state of nonunion, for Madeline, who would walk down the aisle with someone tomorrow if she could. Kahlila saw how annoyed J.T. looked by her peppy assault of questions. "So, what was Kahli like in high school? Do you miss playing basketball? Do you like living in New Jersey? How often do you visit your family in Boston? How tall are you?" She didn't seem to notice that he wasn't getting to answer most of them.

"So, how does it feel to turn twenty-nine, Kal?" J.T.

asked above the din of conversation, eager to escape his one-on-one time with Madeline.

Considering this question for a moment, she sat down on an arm of the living room sofa. "Well, it has a depressing sound to it. Like I'm trying to hang on, but thirty is just around the corner."

"And what's so awful about thirty?" Lloyd asked, who'd passed that threshold a few years earlier. Jason, who had also left his twenties a while back, nodded his head in agreement.

"Nothing is awful about it, if you've accomplished everything you should have in your twenties," Kahlila answered.

"Exactly," echoed Madeline. "If, at your thirtieth mark, you have some type of prospect for settling down and beginning the next stage of life, then you can feel more at peace."

J.T. laughed. "You make it sound like thirty is the step before entering the pearly gates. Who says you're behind schedule if you're not married or engaged by then?"

"Madeline says so," Kahlila retorted with a smile. "I wasn't even just thinking about romantic prospects. You have to look at where you are careerwise. Robyn, you finished medical school and are kicking ass in your residency. Desiree, you've written four novels, three screenplays, been published in a zillion major magazines—"

"And what? That's somehow more meaningful than what you and Madeline do?" Desiree challenged.

"I'm not saying that I don't love what I do. Or that what I do isn't important. But where is the growth? Teaching high school is like that movie *Groundhog Day*. Every school year is the same thing with different kids sitting in front of you. I hear myself making the same jokes, using the same lesson plans, eating the same peanut butter and jelly sandwich every day for lunch."

"Sounds like you just need to do better grocery shopping," J.T. said in an effort to make Kahlila smile.

"J.T., you don't get what I'm saying at all. You lived a fast-paced, whirlwind life in the NBA for five years. Now you decide your own schedule. Every day is different if you want it to be," said Kahlila in an almost whine.

"But Kahlila, you love Pierce High School. And the different students every year are exactly what make teaching new and fresh. Plus, it's not like you aren't constantly revising your curriculum," Madeline argued.

"I know, Maddie. But I just look at the lifestyles that other people get to have, and sometimes theirs look so much better," Kahlila confessed.

"Girl, everybody feels that way. When I'm looking at some old lady's hemorrhoids, I sure do hate that Lloyd is holding some intellectual conversation in his office with some undergrad who probably wants to rip his clothes off," Robyn muttered.

"Honey, I never knew you felt like that," Lloyd said, getting up from the couch and going to massage his girlfriend's shoulders.

"Okay, this is a birthday party, not a therapy session. Who's ready for karaoke?" J.T. bellowed, finally succeeding in getting laughter from his audience.

Kahlila, Robyn, and Desiree had just finished a rousing rendition of Destiny's Child's "Say My Name" on the rented karoke machine when the doorbell rang. Doing a quick survey of the room, Kahlila couldn't imagine who else would be invited, other than Marisol, who was visiting family in Puerto Rico.

Desiree and Jason exchanged a knowing glance before she jogged over to the intercom and pressed the buzzer. Everyone was still hooting and hollering from the girls' pseudosexy performance when Darius opened the door to the apartment. "Looks like I found the party," he said with a smile.

Kahlila thought her cheeks might crack as he walked in and began giving handshakes. But her face went neutral again when Miko entered behind him, wearing an expression that revealed her annoyance to be there.

Darius gave a quick glance over his shoulder and announced, "This is Miko, everybody," before asking Desiree where the bathroom was and heading down the hallway. He placed his hand on Kahlila's shoulder for a moment as he walked by.

Suddenly the jovial mood was replaced by clunky quiet and half smiles.

"So what does everybody do? For a living?" Miko broke the silence, possibly creating more awkwardness with the question than there was before. She stood in the center of the living room with her hands on her hips, wearing skinny jeans and a silk blouse with only two buttons fastened.

Kahlila, feeling that she had some responsibility as the birthday girl to keep things comfortable, took the lead. "Desiree's a writer, Jason owns two gyms, Madeline's a teacher like me, Lloyd is a college professor, and Robyn's a doctor."

Kahlila felt a degree of pride going around the room, loving that her friends were so accomplished and fulfilled. She knew that part of the reason why she often questioned the significance of her life thus far was that she had such a high degree of success around her.

Miko had no reaction whatsoever to the laundry list of admirable professions. "What do *you* do?" she said, pointing to J.T., who'd been mixing drinks at the breakfast bar in the kitchen.

"I'm retired," he retorted, handing her an apple cranberry martini.

"You look familiar," she said as she peered over the
rim of her glass.

"He played for the Nets," Jason said in a monotone,
eager for the conversation to be over.

"Honey, come here!" she called over her shoulder to
Darius, who had just emerged from the bathroom. "He
plays basketball," she explained, pointing to J.T.

"Used to," J.T. corrected.

Darius smiled, walked over to him, and gave him an
enthusiastic handshake. "Kahlila's talked about her boy
J.T. before, but I didn't realize it was *you*, man."

"Kahlila isn't about all that name dropping stuff. She's
super down-to-earth. That's a hard-to-find quality these
days," he said pointedly, tossing a skeptical glance at
Miko. "Besides, it's not like I'm Justin Timberlake or anything. Now *that's* a famous JT."

"Yo, you heard his new album, man?" Darius asked as
he surveyed the bottles of alcohol.

"It's out already?"

"Nah. But I copped a listen a few weeks back. Shit's
tight."

"I'm surprised you like Justin Timberlake," Desiree
commented, standing up so that Miko could have a seat.

"I try to listen to a little of everything. My favorite
music is R&B and soul from our parents' generation, but
I'll listen to a country music song if the lyrics are good,"
Darius said, finally deciding on scotch, straight up.

Lloyd, a master pianist who prided himself on his eclectic musical taste, jumped right into the conversation, and
soon he and Darius were talking about artists whom no
one else in the room had even heard of. They exchanged
information so that they could hit up the Philadelphia
jazz scene whenever Darius traveled there next.

Kahlila was glad that J.T. thought to make Miko a drink, because her martini seemed to be the only thing that she was enjoying about this get-together. When Robyn asked her a question about how her weekend had been going so far, Miko made it a point to mention that they were just stopping by on their way to another event. Robyn rolled her eyes and returned to a conversation with Madeline, perfectly content to leave Miko sitting in silence.

After about a half hour, Darius stood to leave. Miko eagerly popped out of her seat, smiling for the first time that evening. "We gotta run to a get-together downtown," he said, looking genuinely sorry to leave. He walked around the room, saying good-bye to each person, kissing the women on the cheek. When he bent down to hug Kahlila, who was sitting down, he whispered in her ear, "I left something for you in the bathroom." She almost wanted to laugh, as the statement sounded so absurd. But she kept her face neutral and nodded. Miko gave a cute wave from her position at the front door, and everyone halfheartedly waved back.

When the door slammed behind them, J.T. counted down from five with his fingers. When the last finger folded into his fist, everyone began chattering at the same time. Kahlila left them all buzzing as she almost ran to the bathroom to see what Darius had left. She returned a few seconds later, opening a tiny jewelry case and dropping her jaw when she saw what it held inside.

"Wait a second. Did Darius leave that for you?" Desiree asked, peering over Kahlila's shoulder.

Kahlila nodded, still speechless. She was staring at a gold oval-shaped ring with a cameo of a brown-colored woman on it. Kahlila had never again mentioned her interest in cameo jewelry after that first time they ate dinner together. Desiree grabbed the box from her hand and began passing it around the room.

"Oh my gosh, Kahli. He so loves you," Madeline swooned, taking the ring from its box and trying it on.

"Let's slow down with the L word. Folks with money don't think about buying gifts the way the rest of us do," Lloyd said.

"Not necessarily true," piped in J.T. "When I was playing ball, I never bought a girl a piece of jewelry until Marisol. And even she only got earrings the first year."

"See?" asked Madeline, vindicated. "He so loves her."

"And if it didn't mean anything, why did he sneak her the gift? He clearly didn't want that airhead girl to see what he got Kahli," Robyn added. Kahlila was surprised that Robyn, the biggest cynic of the group, was entertaining the idea that Darius might have feelings for her.

Kahlila could feel her heart beating as her friends considered that she might have a shot at romance with someone who could make turning twenty-nine feel like the beginning of something exciting. Retrieving the ring from Madeline, she slipped it onto her fourth finger and smiled. *Perfect fit.*

Chapter 26

He cannot allow himself
to be manipulated.

Darius didn't have an appointment with his trainer, but he decided to hit the gym anyway. He did some of his best thinking when he worked out, and he welcomed the trip to Chelsea Piers, where he sweated alongside many notable New Yorkers at an exclusive fitness center. As he warmed up on the treadmill, he processed the events of the last few days.

The past week had been a whirlwind, and Darius was eager to clear his head. Once "Make My Life Real" was mastered, he changed his mind at the last minute about playing the song for Flow. He realized that even if Flow liked it, he could still say that it had no appeal to a mainstream audience. Darius needed to do something to prove that his song, and other songs like it, could sell big.

He called Marc Johnson, the founder and editor of an online black music magazine. Darius had done one of his first major interviews with him more than a year ago, and they'd gotten along well. They agreed to meet for lunch, and Darius laid his cards on the table. He was looking to change his image on his next album and hoped that Marc would have his back as he made the transition.

"D, I think it's a great call. The market is saturated with people who have your sound. You gotta make yourself distinct, especially considering that you're on the older end of the spectrum," Marc said, swigging his lemonade as if it were a pint of Guinness.

Darius wasn't offended. He knew that he was competing for sales with teenagers who wore baseball caps to awards shows and back-flipped across the stage during their encores. He reached into his backpack and pulled out a CD in a clear case. "Make My Life Real" was written with a black Sharpie on the disc itself.

"Exactly. Yo, this is a new track I did with Bill Notes. Flow hasn't heard it yet." He paused, looking at the people eating around him. "If you want to give it to your boy at HOT 97, I wouldn't have a problem with it. The deejay who also has the show on satellite radio."

Marc's eyes widened. "Dude, are you saying you *want* the song to get leaked?"

"I didn't say anything. But you do what you like. Got me?" They both smiled and finished eating their lunch.

Darius's plan worked like a charm. The song was played during the morning show on HOT 97 two days later, and continued to play throughout the day. His Treo was flooded with texts that the song had moved to all of the major urban and even some adult contemporary stations by the following afternoon. When he looked online, he found that it was readily available, and that folks were blowing up message boards with praise for the song. "Ne-Yo Meets Coldplay," said one anonymous reviewer.

Suddenly, people who doubted his probability of success were eating their words. Lamont, his manager, called him acting as if they had been on the same page all along. "I'm not sure how the song got out there, D, but it all worked out for the best. The market has been tested, and when Flow gets back from vacation, he should definitely see things the same way we do," he said excitedly.

Darius just rolled his eyes. *Damn Johnny-come-lately. He's lucky I didn't find another manager.*

Still, Darius was thrilled by the positive response and was looking to celebrate. Miko was in Paris doing a show, and they were struggling to catch one another with the time difference. So he went to dinner with Rasheed, his girlfriend, Toni, and Kahlila. He knew that Miko would not be happy if she knew that Kahlila was filling in for her, but he only felt it right to invite her. After all, she'd been there when the song was created.

He hadn't seen her since her birthday party the previous weekend, and when she met them at the restaurant, she wiggled her fingers excitedly, flashing the gold ring on her right hand. Darius had surprised himself when he called his mom and asked where he could find a black cameo. When he called the designer and she told him that the only jewelry type she had in stock was a ring, he hesitated for a moment. Buying a woman a ring was a lot different from a bracelet or a necklace. But he decided to go for it. Though he wasn't the most thoughtful gift giver, he was eager to do something extra special for Kahlila. Maybe it was the fact that she hadn't even mentioned her birthday, and he knew that she wouldn't expect anything from him. The selflessness of her friendship with him was something that really hit him hard. He hadn't made a new friend since his first number-one single. He'd definitely met countless acquaintances, industry connections, and romantic interests. But no one he really felt had no agenda beyond spending time and talking about good music.

The four of them had so much fun at dinner that they decided to extend the evening by driving to Atlantic City. Darius said he was feeling like the week was lucky, and it proved to be true when they all sat down at the same blackjack table. They drove back to the city at three in the morning, with considerably more money in their pockets than when they'd arrived.

So even though he was running on little sleep, Darius felt energized as he increased his speed on the treadmill to a run. There was only one more hurdle to overcome: hearing Flow's reaction to the leaked song. He should have arrived back in New York late last night, and Darius was anxiously awaiting his review.

After a long cardio session followed by the bench press, free weights, and machines, Darius finally ran out of steam. He realized that he was relishing his time away from his Treo, because he knew that there would most likely be a message from Flow when he picked it up. As much as he was anticipating the call, there was an element of dread as well.

In the locker room, he gave in to his curiosity and fished in his bag for his Treo before doing anything else. Sure enough, he had a text message from Flow Steddie:

> You sneaky mo-fucka. That story about someone else leaking your song is BS. Gotta give you props for getting heard, tho. The song is tight and mad headz is feelin it. So when do we start recording the next album?

Darius grinned, dropping his phone back into the book bag and swinging it over his shoulder. He would shower when he got home. He just wanted to be outside in the sunlight, enjoying the first day that he felt like he was really in control of his career.

Darius walked into his apartment building, his body shocked by the blast of air against his skin, still sweaty from his workout.

"Hey, lover boy," Harry, his daytime doorman, called to him jovially. He was waving a magazine in the air.

"What's up, Big H?" Darius asked as he walked closer. He could now see that it was a celebrity tabloid. "What you reading that garbage for?"

Harry laughed. "Rhonda in 3D left it for you. You, my friend, are the star of this magazine you call garbage." He handed its glossy pages to a surprised Darius, whose shock only grew when he saw his own face, or the side of it, pressed against Miko's as they engaged in a passionate lip-lock. The caption below read R&B HOTTIE DARIUS WILSON AT P.M. LOUNGE IN NEW YORK CITY WITH GIRLFRIEND MIKO, A MODEL WHO HAS REPORTEDLY BEEN DATING THE SINGER FOR OVER A MONTH. "'Darius was tired of playing the field and found everything he was looking for in Miko. She's gorgeous and fun. They have a great time together,' says a source close to the couple."

"Can I keep this?" Darius asked through clenched teeth.

"Of course," Harry chuckled. "I'm not hanging it on my wall, man."

He'd never been in *US Weekly* before, nor had he wanted to. It took him a second to remember when the picture was taken. The night of Kahlila's birthday soiree, Miko had been unusually affectionate at the party they attended afterward. As she kissed him in the middle of the club, he felt a flash go off, and saw Belle's mischievous smile behind a digital camera. He hadn't thought about it since.

Now, during a week when he wanted all of the focus to be on his music, he'd just gotten thrown into the pot of typical celebrity gossip by being photographed kissing a model. Miko, on the other hand, had gotten exactly what she wanted all along: a publicity boost perfectly timed with Darius's reemergence onto the airwaves.

The first thing he did when he reached his apartment was to take a long shower. It was another place where he did some good thinking, and he wanted to think long and hard before he said or did something that he might regret. When he stepped out of the steamy bathroom with his towel around his waist, he picked up his phone and called Miko, grateful for her international cell phone service. No answer. Leaving a long message on her voice mail, he hung up feeling a lot better than he had a half hour before.

The next call he made was to Kahlila. She didn't answer either, so he prepared himself to talk after the beep. "Kahli. It's me. Just calling to see what you been up to. I heard from Flow, and it looks like I have the green light to start writing for this next album. I'm home tonight working on some stuff if you wanna holler. I . . . have some other things to catch you up on too. Later."

He stared at the magazine, which was strewn on his dining room table. He finally picked it up, walked over to his wastebasket in the kitchen, and dropped it inside.

Chapter 27

He must be a good listener.

That's it. I may have three fewer inches on Miko, but I have her beat in every other category. Okay. I'm not as pretty either. Or as confident. But Darius needs someone intelligent. He needs a partner, not a trophy.

Kahlila had reached her breaking point. Every night after she would leave Darius's company, she would dissect their interactions: replaying conversations and smiles, analyzing their significance. Just now, after coming out of a doctor's appointment with Desiree, she listened to a message from him that sounded like a boyfriend checking in with his girl. She'd reached the conclusion that Darius was interested in her. It was just easy to be distracted by someone taller . . . and sexier. But as put together as Miko was, Kahlila was sure enough that she had a chance. And tonight, she was going for broke.

For someone who was not her boyfriend, Darius was excellent about communication. She knew where he was at any given time of the day; right now he was at his apartment working on a song. Since Miko was walking on somebody's runway in Europe, Kahlila knew she wouldn't be there. It was the perfect time to show up and lay her feelings bare.

When she stepped out of her apartment and onto 122nd Street, she had a moment when she considered walking to his place. That way, she could use the time to collect her thoughts and plan exactly what she was going to say. But she hadn't taken two steps before she realized that she was considering walking one hundred blocks. *He might be done with his entire album by the time I get there!*

Her strategy changed and suddenly she wanted to get there as soon as possible. Afraid that if it took her too long to reach her destination, she might lose her nerve, she hailed a taxi as soon as she hit Lenox Avenue and found herself in front of Darius's apartment building in record time.

She felt nauseated as she neared the door and wanted to take a moment to settle herself. The problem with fancy apartments, though, is the quality service. Harry, her favorite doorman, immediately swung open the glass door upon sight of her. "Hey, Kahli!" he said jovially.

See, I even know his doorman! It's like we're already a couple. "Hi, Harry. How are you?" She heard her voice sound light and cheery, surprised that it wasn't shaking like a leaf.

"I'm great. Is he expecting ya?" Harry asked with a grin, his ruddy cheeks puffing out like Santa Claus's.

"Uh, no," Kahlila admitted bashfully. Harry's question conveyed to her the rudeness of showing up to someone's house unannounced, and she quickly wanted to exit to rethink her plan. It was too late, though, as Harry was already on the phone telling Darius that she was downstairs.

"Go on up, hon," Harry said, and all at once there

were no more impediments in the way of her announcing her feelings to the guy of her dreams.

Was it the elevator making her stomach drop? As she stepped out of it and she still felt her insides flip-flopping, she knew that it wasn't. Darius stood in his doorway with a delicious smile that made her want to kiss him right then and there. *One step at a time.*

"Hey, you," he said as she neared him, taking her waist with one arm to pull her in for a hug. She could smell the detergent from his T-shirt and hoped that he couldn't feel her heart beating.

"Sorry to come by without calling." Darius shrugged his shoulders in response, as if to say it was no big deal. "I just need to talk to you."

"Sounds serious," Darius said, wrinkling his forehead in concern.

"More urgent than serious." They were now both standing in his gorgeous living room. Even with no advanced notice of a visitor, the place was still spotless, with the exception of a few sheets of paper lying around his piano. "Have a seat."

"You're telling me to sit down in my own house?" Darius laughed.

Embarrassed, Kahlila looked at the floor. *This is already not going so well.* "Sit. Stand. Whatever you want. I'm just gonna talk for a second."

"Okay," Darius said warily, staring at her strangely as he perched on the arm of his suede love seat.

"Okay." Kahlila took a deep breath and exhaled slowly, just as she did when trying a particularly hard move in Pilates class. Only this was ten times more difficult. "I have this list. I've been keeping it for years. It's a sheet of requirements for guys whom I date. I guess it's not really a sheet. More like a packet. And I guess it's not really a list of requirements for guys I date. It's a list of requirements for the ideal guy that I would *like* to date.

"Anyway, at the beginning of the summer, I decided to throw my list away, because my friends thought, and I guess I thought too, that it was keeping me from evaluating people as individuals. Basically, I was writing guys off too quickly just because they didn't fulfill requirement number fifty-five or whatever."

"There are fifty-five requirements?" Darius asked in disbelief.

"Um, there are way more than that. But some are necessities, and then others are listed in the negotiables section. Okay. So I tried to forget about The List, and then I met you. And it was like I had met the physical embodiment of my list. You have everything I was looking for—the must-haves and the negotiables too! Well, except for one thing, which was that he shouldn't be a celebrity, but I realized that I had no basis for putting that on The List in the first place, so . . ." She felt herself rambling and trailed off.

Kahlila wanted to steal a glance at him to see his reaction, but couldn't move her gaze from his white socks. "I don't know what your list is, but I know you have one. Everyone does. People just don't often write it down. But I've been getting a vibe over the past month that I might be at least some of what you're looking for. And I'm not trying to bust up what you have with Miko . . . okay, maybe I am. But I think you're amazing. And I think we'd be amazing. Together."

Silence. Kahlila slowly brought her eyes upward to meet his. He was looking at her blankly. The same expression as when he watched mindless television or cleaned the kitchen sink. *Did he even hear anything I just said?* "I'm finished."

He nodded. *Okay, so he does hear me.* But while he acknowledged her confession by moving his head up and down slowly, his mouth didn't open. His gaze moved past her. Her emotions hung suspended in anticipation.

She was so conscious of the silence in the room that she began to hear every distant noise: a car speeding by outside, the drip from his kitchen sink, her own deep breaths. After several prolonged moments of torture, a voice suddenly broke the quiet. Unfortunately, it was her own. The sound of her thoughts rattling in her brain was overpowering. *Just leave. Get out of here with a shred of dignity. Don't wait for him to politely let you down.*

She stepped out of her body and watched herself listlessly walk out of the apartment, with not a word of protest from the man for whom she'd just confessed her infatuation.

The "Later, Kahli" from Harry in the lobby sounded as if it were coming through a tunnel.

She was lying on her bed, staring at the bedroom ceiling, when she heard the vibration of her cell phone on the nightstand. *Text message from Darius,* read the screen. As she flipped open the phone, her eyes widened at the words. There's a car outside your door. It'll bring you back over here. We need to talk.

Six hours after she'd done it the first time, she was again riding in the backseat of a car, preparing to face the unknown at Darius's apartment. She tried to clear her mind completely in order to prevent herself from imagining what might happen when she got there, only to be totally wrong.

Harry was no longer working the door, but the new guy told her to go right up. When she reached the fourth floor, Darius was standing in his doorway. From the smile on his face, she began to feel immediately

hopeful. Then she scolded herself for jumping to con-
clusions. He motioned for her to follow him into the
living room. He sat on his piano bench, facing away from
the keys, and she assumed his former position on the
arm of the love seat.

"You got me thinking about lists," he began, suddenly
looking as serious as Kahlila had ever seen him. "I'd
been keeping one too. I never wrote it down, but I
rapped about it to Rasheed a lot. My girl should be in
the industry, she should live in New York, she should be
this and that."

Kahlila's eyes were a bit pleading, as if she were begging him to save her from rejection and humiliation.

"Lists are bullshit, Kahli. Everything I thought I
wanted in a person, I had in Miko. But she wasn't my
soul mate. Not even close. So, what makes you think that
I'm the one for you? Just because I have everything on
your list?"

Kahli fumbled for an answer, clearly flustered, seeing
this as the moment that might decide her future with
Darius. "Because I just feel it. Don't you?"

Darius gave her a big grin. "Definitely. I'm just giving
you a hard time because you looked so damn scared that
I was gonna play the hell out of you." Kahlila's mouth
opened in shock. "Do you still like me now?" he laughed.

"Not really!" she said, punching him in the arm.

"I'm sorry. But seriously, Kahli, you are everything on
the list that I didn't even know I had been keeping. And
when I started thinking about that, I just began writing
this song, and I wanted you to hear it."

He slid his legs underneath the piano bench and effortlessly played a few rich, major chords that almost sounded
as if they didn't need any words to make the song complete. But once his soulful, almost churchlike voice

descended over the piano keys, it was as if he breathed life
into a piece that was struggling to be whole.

Can I whisper twenty somethings in your ear?
Can I sing you the reasons why I need you here?
Can I scream out soft what you mean to me?
Can I dream to myself what we can be?

Number one—your legs are long and lean.
Number two—you always say what you mean.
Number three is that you mean what you say.
And number four is your smile that takes my breath
  away.

Number five—you check me when I'm acting funny.
Number six—you make a gray sky seem sunny.
Number seven is your bronze silky skin in the night.
Number eight—when I'm lost, you always shine the
  light.

We're just twenty-somethings in the hunt to find
Peace of mind, and a love so sublime.
Amazing walked up when I was turned the other way.
Forgive me for taking so long to finally say . . .

Kahlila never found out what he took so long to say. As
he'd sung the lyrics, she had joined him at the piano.
Now, she grabbed both of his hands from the keys and
turned him toward her. Once they were mere inches
apart, she moved her hands to the back of his head and
kissed him. The moment their lips connected jolted
Kahlila back to the last time she'd taken the initiative to
kiss someone, an incident that resulted in a head butt
and a huge disappointment the following morning. She
was shocked by the vividness of the memory, and was

almost tempted to pull away from Darius, out of fear that the sequence of events might be as disastrous as they had been with Keith.

Darius, sensing her hesitation, placed his hands on her waist, pushing up her shirt slightly so that his fingers touched her bare skin. Sliding one hand to the small of her back, he pulled her even closer, eliminating any thought in Kahlila's mind that she was wrong to have crossed the line. She gave herself over completely to being with the man she thought she would never get, but knew she deserved all along. Their kisses were so intense that the force sent Kahlila back against the piano keys, sending a wave of dissonant sound through the room. Both of their eyes popped open in surprise, and they exchanged a smile before Darius returned his focus to the bronze skin of Kahlila's face, neck, and shoulders.

As she raised her arms over her head so that he could pull off the shirt she was wearing, Kahlila could not believe that she was sharing this experience with Darius Wilson. *It feels so easy and natural with us. This is what a first encounter should be like. Not an awkward cab ride, or a drunken kiss, or an angry girlfriend.* Realizing that she was ruining the magic of the moment with flashbacks of her one-night-stand-gone-wrong, she opened her eyes one more time to sneak a peek at the man embracing her. His muscles flexed as he hoisted her on top of the sleek baby grand. Kahlila had one last glimpse of the keys' black and white pattern before she blocked out everything except the touch of Darius's hands on her body. *This is why that awful night in Boston happened. It led me to something better than I could have ever imagined.*

Chapter 28

He has to have a support system.

It was Keith's first night grabbing drinks with Colin, Matt, and Joey in quite a while. Work had been nuts for him and even worse for his three buddies, who were still reeling from a tragic accident that had occurred in one of the Big Dig tunnels weeks before. They were so depressed that no one felt like laughing over a pitcher of beer. But Keith finally got everyone together after an evening gym session.

Using his dinner with Traci as a springboard for conversation, the guys seemed appreciative of having something other than work to think about.

"So, you're really not gonna call her?"

"I don't think so, no," Keith said solemnly, staring into his Guinness Stout.

"It doesn't make sense, man. You were ready to marry the girl two months ago," Matt prodded as he signaled the waitress for a refill.

"I know. But when I was sitting across from her, I kept

thinking about my sister telling me that Traci wasn't *about* anything. I never understood what she meant before, but it started to make sense as I listened to her. She was just going on and on about her new job at the paper, and all the perks it got her. And I just kept spacing out, wondering, 'Did I only think I loved this girl because she was pretty and we had a good time together?'"

"Dude, as the representative of married people at this table, I gotta tell ya. That's kind of all you need," Joey advised.

"Sure Joe, it's important that you enjoy the person's company. But you have to have each other's backs too. Traci didn't even care about Bree. And that was a major problem."

"Hey. If she doesn't love your flesh and blood, screw her." Colin's blunt comment took his friends by surprise, as he was usually the listener and rarely the vocal member of the group.

"Exactly, Colin," Keith chuckled, downing his last gulp of beer.

"How *is* Bree doing, anyhow?" Matt asked.

"She's in New Haven right now, having a good time. *Too* good of a time, really. There's some guy there who calls my house every damn day, and I'm sure she's seeing him quite a bit," Keith said between clenched teeth.

Matt laughed at Keith's sternness. "Come on, man. The girl is almost eighteen. She's gonna have a boyfriend."

"She just turned seventeen. And I don't know anything about this kid, except that his name is Stanley."

"Stanley? How bad can he be with such a nerdy name?" Joey said, hitting Keith on the arm.

Keith gave in and cracked a smile. "I'm just worried, because she's been dropping hints about wanting to be in Connecticut for her senior year. And there's no way I'm letting her do that."

"Wow, big brother. You're tough."

"Damn straight," Keith agreed as he got up and walked to the bathroom.

When Keith returned, he could tell from his friends' hushed, serious tones that talk had turned back to their job.

"We're working our assess off. And all anybody sees on TV is corruption and greed," Joey said, unusually frustrated.

Keith took his seat and tried to interrupt with light-hearted conversation. "No shop talk tonight, guys. Shut it off."

Matt seemed relieved for the command. "So, Keith, you never ran into that girl again?"

"What girl?" He knew exactly whom Matt was talking about.

"You guys remember that girl, Kahli, right? From the night when Joey made an ass of himself?"

They all cracked up laughing as they impersonated Joey's look of confusion when Madeline had exploded on him at the bar.

"Nope. Never saw her again," answered Keith once the table got quiet.

"So, how did you two end things exactly?" Matt inquired.

Keith hesitated. He hadn't shared the details of the later part of the night with the crew. A very private person, he couldn't bring himself to describe the moment when his sister came barging into his room as Kahli hid under the covers. "We just went our separate ways. I'd just broken up with Traci that same day, and I wasn't trying to get into something else."

"But now you're over Traci. So why don't you try to find her?" Matt suggested.

"How would he do that?" asked Colin.

"Dude—you can Google anybody these days," Joey chimed in.

Keith shook his head at their enthusiasm. "I don't even know her last name. Shit, I'm not even sure how she spells Kahli."

"Well, that sucks. 'Cause she was hot, and she seemed fun."

"Matt, you were just trying to get with her friend. That's the only reason you want Keith to find her!" said Joey, pointing at Matt in mock accusation.

An animated argument ensued, and Keith tuned them out as he remembered his hours with Kahli. He *had* felt a connection with her right away. *It's Boston—I'm bound to run into her again sometime. I can explain the situation, and maybe she'll understand. If it's meant to be, she'll turn up.* He smiled to himself at the thought of seeing her again.

Chapter 29

*He has to leave me with good
enough memories to hold me
over until I see him again.*

"It was unbelievable. I felt like I was in a music video.
It was like slow motion or something. Like I could step
outside myself and say, 'Hey, look at that girl getting her
neck kissed by Darius Wilson.'"

Kahlila was dreamily recounting the story to Desiree
the next morning as they sat on stools at the breakfast
bar while Jason made pancakes.

"Wow," Desiree said, her eyebrows arched in appreciation. "So, is that all you did? Kiss?"

"Not exactly," Kahlila answered tentatively, shooting
a look at Jason, whose back was toward them as he
dropped a pat of butter on the skillet.

"I could leave," Jason said, not turning to face them.
"But then you wouldn't have any breakfast."

"You're right, honey," Desiree said, grabbing Kahlila's

arm and pulling her to her feet. "*We'll* leave. Call us when it's done, okay?"

They ran into the bedroom, giggling like preteens as they collapsed onto the bed to talk further. "So, what exactly does 'not exactly' mean?" Desiree asked.

"We didn't do it," Kahlila said, getting back up from the bed to shut the door. "But girl, he had me losing it. He sat me on the top of his grand piano, took off my clothes . . . let's just say he was very giving."

"Are you serious?" Desiree's voice was low but carried an implied squeal of delight. Thinking about it some more, she added, "That sounds like it would be really awkward positioning."

"You would think so! But it was so smooth. I was anything but uncomfortable up there."

"Hmm, I wonder how many times he's done that before," Desiree mused, and from the shocked and hurt look on her friend's face, it was clear that Kahlila hadn't yet considered that idea. "I'm sorry," she hastily added. "That was stupid of me to say."

"Actually, it was stupid of me not to think of it. He probably lays some girl on his piano every weekend," Kahlila muttered, her mood now completely changed.

"You don't know that, and neither do I. The man wrote you a song, for goodness' sake. That has to mean something," Desiree said encouragingly.

Kahlila mustered a smile, but her mind was still on the notion that Darius was simply going through the motions of her being special.

Desiree tapped her friend's arm. "Come on. Let's eat some breakfast." They reentered the kitchen to the smell of butter and syrup as Jason placed the last plate on an already set table.

"I was just about to call you ladies," he said. "Y'all done gossiping?"

"All done," his wife answered, rubbing her tummy.

"So, Kahli, tell me why you like this guy so much," Jason said as he poured her a cup of coffee.

"You met him. He's great, right?"

"He seemed cool. But I've known you for a few years now, and you've *not* liked a lot of cool dudes."

"They were missing things on my list," she replied through a mouthful of pancake.

"Is being rich and famous on your list?" Jason asked, pouring the syrup on his pancake stack.

"Jason, stop." Desiree gave him a scolding look.

"Neither one of those things is on The List, as a matter of fact. So you think that's why I'm into him?" Kahlila asked defensively.

"I'm only going on what I hear you say. 'I kissed Darius Wilson!' 'He wrote me a song!' 'What would people in Boston say?'"

"I can't help that the guy I'm into has a hit album," Kahlila said, surprising herself at how smug the sentence sounded.

Jason gave her a look that made her feel as if he could see her inner thoughts. "Kahli. Listen to yourself. You sound all caught up for the wrong reasons."

"Am I supposed to be sad that an amazingly successful, talented man wrote me a song and kissed me? You've been around for five years now, and have seen how rare it is that I meet someone special. So yes, I'm caught up. But not for the wrong reasons. I need you to be happy for me."

Kahila gave him her signature doe eyes. That combined with a reprimanding glare from his wife quickly changed his tune. "Sorry, Kahli. You won't hear me say another negative thing. I just want the best for you and I don't want you to sell yourself short." He plopped down on the stool next to her.

"Baby, that is so sweet!" Desiree got up from her chair, straddled her husband, and began planting playful kisses all over his face.

"*Hello!*" Kahlila screamed. "I'm sitting right here."

"Sorry, hon. This pregnancy has my hormones all crazy. Hearing all that talk about you and Darius on the piano has me kind of . . . well, you know."

"Okay, guys. I'm leaving. It's been real."

Kahlila took her plate of pancakes and headed downstairs to her apartment, the sound of the happy couple laughing behind her. She was simultaneously annoyed by their affection and wishful that perhaps she and Darius were headed in that same direction.

Chapter 30

He has to be an easy travel companion.

"Awwwwww, shit. This is the hotness right here!" Flow Steddie hopped out of his seat and began doing an exaggerated two-step in the middle of the recording studio. "You feelin' this, Kal? You feelin' it?" He reached out and grabbed Kahlila's hand, pulling her away from the complicated-looking soundboard to join him in his silly dance. She laughed and gave a "help me" look to Darius, who was separated from them by a panel of glass as he sang an improv verse into the recording booth microphone.

The last three weeks felt like a dream. After the evening where Kahlila was serenaded at Darius's apartment, things took off like an overfueled rocket ship. The next day, he called her midafternoon and put any fears that she might have had to rest. "I know I'm just getting out of something with Miko, but I promise you I'm ready to do this."

Kahlila couldn't believe it. She hadn't been in a

relationship since Eugene, which had ended for the final time three years ago with a level-headed, drama-free conversation about their living too far apart from one another. Eugene was perfect in so many ways, but Kahlila never felt the spark that she knew she was supposed to feel. They met in the Teach For America program in Arizona, and one day they simply moved from being friends to being a couple. She never chose him; he simply landed in her lap. Because that relationship came so easily, Kahlila thought that it wouldn't be so hard to find a similar guy, who lived in the same city that she did, and who sent more of a shockwave down her spine than Eugene did. She never expected to spend the next thirty-six months searching for a suitable replacement. *How was it easier to get Darius Wilson to be my boyfriend than it was to find an ordinary guy in Boston?*

Darius came to pick her up the following hour and they headed to HOT 97, where he was doing an interview. His "leaked" single had generated a lot of buzz, and he wanted to do some press.

"So, I see you have a pretty girl waiting for you to finish this interview, D!" the deejay said thirty seconds into their conversation. Everybody at the station started laughing as Kahlila's face burned with embarrassment. Darius had made it very clear when he was dating Miko that he didn't like people butting into his personal life. She hoped this didn't get their newfound status off to the wrong start.

"How you gonna call me out like that, dude?" Darius chuckled and winked at Kahlila. "But I do have a very pretty girl sitting here with me, yes."

"So, what's the deal? Listeners wanna know."

"I'm a private person, but I will say that this woman right here is special. Very special."

"Okay, okay! Ladies, sounds like D might be off the market. You're gonna get some angry callers today."

Kahlila spent the next several days with Darius at his apartment in front of his piano, writing songs. They would wake up and Darius would immediately go into the studio while Kahlila made breakfast. Though she wasn't the best cook, she prided herself on her crispy bacon, sugary French toast, and cheesy omelets. Robyn always told her, "Every woman who can't cook for shit knows how to make some eggs," but Darius didn't seem to care. He would come into the kitchen from the studio, eager to talk about an idea that popped into his head after listening to half-finished songs through his headphones. Most of the time, they didn't even sit at the table. Instead, they stood by the stove, eating food right out of the frying pan. The rest of the day would be spent sitting at the piano, jotting lyrics in notebooks, and recording in the studio. Kahlila tried to give Darius space, offering to head back to Desiree's house. He said he wanted her there, and insisted that she stay. They even went to Victoria's Secret and bought underwear for her so she wouldn't have to leave (he wore a baseball cap pulled very low on that outing). Still, she tried to give him creative time to himself by reading books and watching movies. But she was never by herself more than an hour before he came in, excited to share what he was working on.

Kahlila only waited until the second night that she stayed at his place to sleep with him. In her mind, she had planned for him to set the stage with music (his own, of course) and candlelight as she wore some type of ball gown or cocktail dress and they slow-danced in his living room. However, the real-life version was a lot more mundane. She was lounging in a pair of Darius's running pants and an NYU sweatshirt. Darius had just finished cooking dinner, which consisted of a pot of red beans and rice. One thing that they realized they had in common was an appreciation for food. Not gourmet food, or exotic food, but food. Period. He handed her a bowl and a spoon as she sat on the couch watching *Grey's Anatomy* on DVD. He was wearing a funny little smile that made Kahlila ask what was so funny. "I was just remembering the first time that I thought I might like you."

"When was that?" she asked through a mouthful of rice.

"That day at the studio when we were throwing the shoes across the room with our toes," he said, laughing at the thought of it.

"Babe, this is just like the scene in *The Sound of Music* when Maria and the captain confess when they first fell for each other!" she exclaimed, swallowing a huge forkful of food.

"I've never seen *The Sound of Music.* Is that the one where the chick flies with an umbrella?" he asked, flopping down next to her on the couch.

"No, you dork. That's *Mary Poppins.* We're renting *The Sound of Music* tomorrow. It's a classic! I can't believe you—" In the midst of her lecture, Darius took the bowl from her hand, placed it on the coffee table in front of them, and began kissing her deeply. She only had two seconds of worry that her breath smelled like red beans before she was caught in the moment and no longer cared. Their first sexual encounter was right then and there, on the living room couch, with *Grey's Anatomy*, season 1, episode 5 playing in the background. Darius assumed the driver's seat, making sure that Kahlila was comfortable and satisfied for the entire ride. He replaced all of her nervous energy with confident sexuality as he whispered to her how hot and sweet she was.

"Like cocoa?" she giggled.

"Way tastier than cocoa," he said, before he stopped talking in order to use his tongue for other purposes.

Grey's Anatomy had moved to another episode by the time Darius jogged to his bedroom to grab a condom. During her few seconds alone, she smiled to herself, replaying his words over again. *Hot and sweet.* Suddenly, her mind was back at the Boston bar with Keith, listening to him describe how he liked his coffee. *Black and strong.* As soon as Darius returned wearing his Sean John boxer briefs and a flirtatious smile, she was back in the moment at hand. And in every subsequent encounter, she thought of no one but the gorgeous man sharing her bed, or bathtub, or bearskin rug. Darius was adventurous and attentive, which served them well as a couple.

Though she was ecstatic that "Twenty Somethings" was most likely going on the album, she had to admit that her favorite song so far was the one he wrote for Miko:

> *Come to my concert on a Saturday night,*
> *You stand by the stage and catch the spotlight.*
> *But when the lights go down and it's just me and you*
> *You prove over and over that your love ain't true.*

Flow Steddie contributed a rap verse to the upbeat track, and "When the Lights Go Down" was a sure radio hit. It was clearly a diss song; the public was going to love it. Kahlila had to convince him to take the line out about Miko's "ugly-ass sis," but the song still had enough bite to have people talking.

Now they were in Los Angeles to work with a few West Coast producers recording some of the songs that they had written during their days of confinement in Darius's apartment. Kahlila had been to Southern California several times when she lived in Phoenix five years before, but she never knew the L.A. that she was being exposed to this time around: private parties, expensive rented cars, exclusive boutiques. When she got tired of hanging out at the hotel or sitting in on studio sessions, Kahlila would take their BMV convertible and head to Rodeo Drive. Though she only had enough money to pay for parking, she thoroughly enjoyed the window shopping. As she perused the top designer labels, she thought about how she could duplicate the look for much less when she returned to the East Coast.

Her only splurge during the trip was a pair of Gucci sunglasses. When she'd met Flow Steddie for the first time once they arrived at the airport, he said to her, "Hot sunglasses. Those Gucci?"

"Um, no."

"Who makes them?"

"I'm . . . not sure," she said, quickly taking them off and stuffing them in her purse.

Darius laughed at her when she requested a trip to buy brand-name shades. At the cash register, he handed the saleswoman his Platinum American Express card. Kahlila had to fight tooth and nail to pay for them herself. She already felt funny flying to L.A., staying in a five-star hotel, and eating gourmet meals on his dime. In Boston, she couldn't even get a guy to pay for dinner. She cringed, remembering the time a date took her to play pool, and then asked her for her half of the bill. "You owe me six dollars and twenty-five cents," he had announced with his hand extended. She knew that Darius obviously had more money than that cheap date ever would, but it still felt strange to take his spending for granted.

One of her biggest pleasures during their stay in L.A. was their time at the gym. The hotel staffed a private trainer named Leon, and she and Darius began working out together. After their first session, Leon was impressed by how much weight Kahlila was able to lift. "You must work out all the time," he guessed.

"Yeah. I do strength training a couple of times a week. It's the only way I can keep any weight on me," she said as she did a set of lunges with twenty-pound dumbbells in her hands.

"Most women would kill to have that problem," Leon said. "What other workouts do you do?"

"I've been doing Pilates for years. The instructor at my gym is phenomenal."

"Yo, people sleep on Pilates. It'll strengthen your core real quick. Darius, you should give it a try. Add something different to your workout."

Darius had been at the bench press, and sat up straight after his last rep. "Yeah, right. Isn't that like yoga?"

"No, they're really different. And what's wrong with yoga, anyway?" Kahlila asked, setting down the dumbbells and putting her hands on her hips.

"Nothing, if you're a girl."

"You know Russell Simmons is a yoga addict," Leon chimed in.

"Shit, if I had Russell Simmons's money, I wouldn't care if anyone caught me doing girly exercises either. But as things stand right now, you will not be catching me in anybody's yoga or Pilates class."

That evening, Kahlila took advantage of the concierge service at the hotel to get the Winsor Pilates DVD and two yoga mats delivered to their suite. "You're doing this workout with me."

"Or else?" he taunted.

"Or else you don't get any tonight," she responded as she pushed aside the coffee table in the living room.

One hour and several fits of hysterical laughter later, Darius had to eat humble pie. "I gotta admit, that shit is hard. I've always had an appreciation for your body, but I have a new appreciation for how you got it that way."

Darius was more than rewarded for his compliment.

Kahlila fully enjoyed the recreational portion of their trip. But she also realized that Darius's lifestyle wasn't all fun and games. When she read the magazines and saw the perks that famous artists enjoyed, she hadn't realized that these folks were real musicians. The fame was incidental. Most people had no idea how many hours were required in the studio to produce five good minutes of music. And they also didn't know what a high it was to make that music. By the end of the week they'd spent there, she was hooked. On all of it. The beats, the cars, and the cast of characters made her feel like she was sitting on top of the world.

On their ride to the airport, she took in her last few minutes of Rollerbladers, bleached blond hair, and palm trees. It all looked rosy through the lenses of her new sunglasses.

"You ready to leave this trippy place and head back to reality? We got the VMAs in a few days."

"Honey, going to the MTV Awards is not reality for me."

"Well, it is now."

She didn't respond, as she was too busy thinking about how she would deal with going back to Boston in two short weeks. *Don't worry about that until you get there. Savor this moment.* She sat back in the leather seat and enjoyed the ride.

Chapter 31

He can't be too private about his feelings.

Kahlila sat in a chair in the middle of a high-end salon, a team of beauty experts staring at her as a surgeon might regard a patient who requires an extremely risky procedure. Their brows were furrowed as they circled the subject. It could have been their hypercritical facial expressions, or it could have been the extremely bright lights surrounding the mirror in front of her. Either way, she had never felt more unattractive.

"She has good skin," one of the black-aproned women commented.

"It's oily, though," another added.

"Hair's nice," one offered.

"She'll need more of it," said the one male in the group, who was obviously the king bee, as he wore no apron and appeared to be the most fabulous. "And we're not doing her hair anyway. They're sending her to Keira for that."

"What's she wearing?" asked yet a fourth woman.

"D&G," piped up a woman who was apparently Kahlila's stylist for the day. Rebecca had spent the earlier part of the morning with her, trying on dresses. This should have been one of the most enjoyable activities of her life. She loved shopping with a passion, and here she was trying on dresses she could never afford. But it was all done with such haste and efficiency that there was no time to linger in the moment. She also very quickly realized that she had no say in the matter. "I really like this one," she'd said softly as she emerged from the dressing room in a long, sparkly number.

"Nope. My friend at Roberto Cavalli told me Beyoncé's wearing something similar."

It was then and there, at the mention of her favorite superstar in the entire world, that she realized that she needed to keep her mouth shut and let the professionals do what they did. She was in way over her head, and needed all the help she could get in order to make it through this evening without a serious blunder.

After she finished "consulting" with the makeup artists, Rebecca ushered her into the car and they joined the stop-and-go traffic of the city. "We'll go back and do your face after your hair is done. You'll get dressed over there as well," she said, typing furiously on her Black-Berry while they were stopped at a red light.

As much as Kahlila was put off by her stylist's all-business personality, she was a little saddened when she learned that Rebecca wasn't going to be joining her while she got her hair done. "I'll pick you up here when you're finished. Keira will call me."

Kahlila walked into the salon, which was considerably less fancy than their previous stop, but still very chic. The receptionist smiled at her and stepped from behind the desk. "Kahli? Welcome to Right Hair. I'll take you to Keira's chair."

Kahlila couldn't tell if she was being given the VIP treatment, or if this was the way they handled all of their customers.

Keira was a petite, brown-skinned woman about her age. She wore her hair in a bun with bangs that fell right above her eyebrows. The bangs were light brown, and the rest of her hair was black. Somehow, it worked. "Hey, girl. I'll be doing your hair this afternoon. This all you?" she said, touching Kahlila's hair curiously.

"Um, yeah."

"You go, girl. This is gonna be easy."

"They said that I might need extensions, or a weave or something?"

"Who said that? You don't need anything extra. How about we just flatiron it? Make it superstraight and sleek."

Kahlila never wore her hair straight. It took hours to blow-dry on her own, and besides, curly hair was her signature. It had been the same since college: Kahli—curly and wild, Desiree—long and straight, Robyn—short and sassy. But she liked the idea of wearing it differently today. After all, the entire experience was outside of her realm of reality. Why not be someone else?

"Sounds good to me."

Kahlila got her hair washed by Keira's assistant, and got it blown dry by a second assistant. When she sat back in Keira's chair, she noticed a small framed picture of two adorable children.

"Who are these cuties?" she asked.

"Those are my boys. Jalen is six and Trey is two," she said, removing the flatiron from its oven.

"Wow—you're in such great shape, I would never guess you had two kids. Do you work out?"

"Girl, can you believe it? I have never been to the gym. I lost my baby weight within a month both times."

"Lucky! So, where does Jalen go to school?"

This launched a long conversation about public vs. private education, cultural differences around disciplining children, and saving money for college tuition. Before Kahlila knew it, her hair was completely transformed.

Keira was putting a slight bump on the ends when she asked, "So, you're just a regular person, huh?"

From the tone of her voice, Kahlila could tell that the statement was intended to be a compliment.

"I know that sounds strange," Keira continued. "But I do a lot of people's hair—I won't name names. Anyway, none of them ask about my kids or my life. They either bitch about their weave being too loose or too tight, spend the entire time name-dropping (if they're new to the industry), or talk on their cell phones even when they're getting their hair washed. Girl, I've done Miko's hair before . . ." She looked around to see if anyone was listening. "She was so . . . empty. That's the only way I can describe her. Sweet girl, just . . . empty."

"Do you have any advice for me tonight?"

"Play the back, girl. You're gonna look fierce, but it ain't about you. Smile. Look at him like he's God. Don't flirt with anybody. Don't look starstruck when you meet people. Just shake their hands like they're Joe Schmoe."

"Do you think I'll meet Beyoncé?"

"Of course you will! I'm sure y'all are going to her birthday party at 40/40. She's a really nice person. Why don't you just ask Darius what the plan is for after the show?"

"I don't want to seem like I care more about the stars than about him."

"Girl, you're smart. You're gonna do just fine in this business."

* * *

Three hours later, she barely recognized herself. Areas had been waxed where she didn't even know that she had hair. She had on such a thick layer of makeup that the dark circles under her eyes that appeared when she needed sleep were a distant memory. Her hair, which usually hit her shoulder blades when she wore it in its naturally curly state, was now down her back and felt unusually heavy. She felt like she had caterpillars on her eyelids, but she was simply adjusting to the false lashes. Her dress was a long copper gown that fit her like a second skin, and almost gave off a nude look if one glanced quickly enough.

She received several raised eyebrows in the lobby of Darius's building as she waited for him to come downstairs. She couldn't tell if the looks were ones of admiration or bewilderment. *What if the look is over-the-top? Do I look like a complete idiot?*

A middle-aged woman in a business suit did a double take as she headed to the elevators. "Where ya headed?" she asked cordially.

"The VMAs?" Kahlila answered with that questioning lilt that her students used when they were unsure of themselves.

"Oh, with Darius? I'm his neighbor, Rhonda." She shook Kahlila's hand. "You look absolutely fabulous. Do you model?"

Kahlila laughed. "God, no. But thanks for the compliment. I was feeling a little bit . . . insecure about my look."

"And why in the world would you feel insecure?" Darius's voice said in her ear.

Kahlila turned, surprised that he'd managed to sneak up on them. As soon as she locked eyes with him, she was at ease. The entire day of being poked and prodded was all worth it for the look on his face.

Darius had thought Kahlila was cute the first time he met her. When he got to know her better, he elevated his opinion to pretty. Once he saw her minimally clothed, he modified the adjective to sexy. But seeing her all glammed up for the VMAs was a shock. He didn't even have an appropriate word to describe her. "You're . . . damn," he stuttered as they walked to the stretch Navigator parked outside.

"You too," she said, surveying his gray suit and white shirt, sans tie.

"Decided to keep it simple," he said, adjusting the sleeve of his Brooks Brothers jacket. He gave a head nod to the driver and motioned that he didn't need to open the door for them. When they stepped into the enormous vehicle, Rasheed was already comfortable, drinking a Starbucks iced coffee. There was champagne on ice directly to his right, but he never drank when he was working. Wearing a suit as well, he would have looked very similar to Darius if they weren't such dramatically different sizes. "Looking dapper, Rah," Kahlila said, giving him a kiss on the cheek.

He pulled away to get a better look at her, and gave a long whistle. "Sweetie, you're making us look average."

Darius was quiet on the drive through crawling Midtown traffic. He didn't want to drink until the after parties. He had red carpet interviews to do, he was presenting an award, and he was up for Best New Artist. There was no room for error. He looked at Kahlila as she chatted animatedly with Rasheed about who was performing at the show. She was excited, obviously. When Darius told Bianca, his publicist, that he would be bringing Kahlila, she was none too pleased. Already livid that he had broken up with Miko before the VMAs, she was not interested in a no-name girlfriend hanging on his arm. There was no good press in that. She insisted that he do the red carpet alone. He was ready to argue it, but Kahlila said she didn't care. "I'd probably be so nervous anyway that I'd throw up on camera or something," she said good-naturedly. She would hang out with Rasheed while he and Bianca talked to the press.

He was secretly relieved that Kahlila didn't care about appearing with him on camera. In his industry, he always had to be concerned that women were interested in him for the wrong reasons. Miko was obviously more into the publicity that he could bring her than anything else. But so far, Kahlila had passed every test. She refused to let him buy her things when they went shopping, she never seemed overly excited by being in the presence of celebrities, and so far none of their business had leaked to any magazines or Internet sites.

When they pulled up as close as they could to the already fan-mobbed Radio City Music Hall, Rasheed stepped out of the SUV first.

Darius looked at Kahlila, whose eyes were bright with excitement. "Just wait in here for, like, five minutes. Rasheed will come back for you once I hook up with Bianca. I'm performing early in the show, so I won't be sitting with you until afterward."

"Okay. Are you wearing the suit to perform?"

"Nah, just to present. My clothes are already here."

"Good luck, sweetheart," she said, softly kissing him on the lips.

"It's whatever. If I win, I win."

"I meant good luck performing the new song. It's going to be fantastic."

He loved that she knew what the most important part

of the evening was. This night was huge, not because he was up for an award, but because he was showcasing his new image for the first time. He kissed her again before he hopped out of the car, waving to the people whose screaming increased tenfold once they laid eyes on him.

Darius had gotten through the first few requirements of the evening without a hitch. He had a few witty live interviews on the red carpet, smiled for the hundreds of cameras, and headed inside the venue to present the second award of the night. His copresenter was a bubbly teen actress who delivered her lines perfectly and set him up well for the corny joke he had to deliver before reading the nominees. Once that was over, he headed backstage for a quick change before going back out to perform. Rasheed was waiting outside his dressing room, socializing with the other bodyguards and personal assistants whom he'd gotten to know on the award show circuit over the past year.

When Darius emerged, Rasheed fished into the breast pocket of his suit. "Kahlila told me to give you this before you went out there," he said, handing Darius a folded note.

"We're passing notes now?" Darius asked amusedly.

"I think you're supposed to check if you like her and give it back to me," Rasheed laughed.

Darius unfolded the note. *I'm so happy that you get to show them who you really are tonight. Have fun.—Your biggest fan*

Instead of handing the note back to his boy, he refolded it and placed it in the pocket of his jeans. "Rah, for real—this girl is really the shit. Seriously."

"You gonna tell a brother what the note said?"

A production assistant wearing a headset and a crazed

expression rushed toward them. "Darius, you've gotta get in place before we get back from commercial. Come with me."

He and Rasheed followed the anxious worker to the stage. Once they reached the end of the curtains, Rasheed gave him a pound. "This is big, dawg. Do good."

"No doubt. Yo, if it comes off right, and I win tonight, I might do something crazy."

"Crazy like what?" Rasheed asked with a raised eyebrow. But Darius just laughed and walked onto the stage in a simple white T-shirt, black blazer and jeans, sat down on a stool, and began tuning the guitar that was just handed to him.

"I can't believe I'm watching this crap when I have a case I need to read," Keith mumbled. He was sitting on his living room couch with his sister, eating popcorn that she'd made in order to entice him to sit with her longer.

"As soon as Darius Wilson performs, we can change the channel. He's supposed to be up after the commercial break," Bree said, sitting up straighter in anticipation.

Keith was only halfheartedly protesting. He'd missed his sister so much during her week in Connecticut that he would happily watch anything she wanted. When she had returned two weeks before, she had been so quiet and sullen that Keith felt as if all the progress they'd made during the summer had been lost. It was great to see her smiling.

"It's back on!" Bree announced, turning up the volume with the remote control.

Darius Wilson sat on a dimly lit stage with a small band behind him, strumming a guitar and singing about not losing your head in the lights of fame. It was an odd sight, considering his usual performances, which involved scantily clad backup dancers and hyped-up choreography. But once Keith got over the simplicity of the presentation, he had to admit that the music sounded good. "Yo, Bree, lemme borrow your iPod so I can get some of his tracks."

"Told you," Bree retorted in a singsong voice, her eyes never straying from the television.

"And the award for Best New Artist goes to . . . Darius Wilson!" His hit song, "Party Till You See the Sun," began to play as the cameras followed him from backstage to center stage. His smile was from ear to ear as he practically jogged to accept the award.

"This is great. This feels unbelievable. I wanna thank MTV for letting me play my new joint tonight, even though I'm winning this award for music that is very different from what I just now sang for all of you. I wanna thank the fans—" He had to pause because the screams were deafening. "And hopefully you will continue to support my projects as I mature as an artist. My family and friends, much love to all of you. My label, especially Flow Steddie—I wouldn't be here without you. Finally, I want to thank someone who just came into my life very recently, but has made it so much better in a short period of time. She's a teacher, y'all. That's the job that needs to be winning awards, not mine." Polite applause from the audience. "Kahli, I hope we continue to make good music together for a long time."

Before Keith or Bree had a chance to react to the name they'd just heard, MTV's cameras had Kahlila in a close shot. She looked surprised and overwhelmed, but still picture perfect, as she realized that she was on national television. "Oh my goodness!" Bree screamed, jumping up from the couch and running toward the television. "That's Ms. Bradford!"

"You know her?" Keith managed to ask. If it weren't shocking enough that the girl who'd slept in his bed was on TV, now his sister knew her too?

"She teaches at Pierce! I can't believe this. I cannot believe this. I'm so jealous. Darius Wilson is Ms. Bradford's boyfriend. This is crazy! I gotta call Krystal." She ran toward her bedroom, leaving Keith's mind to spin in disbelief at the turn of events that had occurred without his having to leave his living room couch.

Chapter 32

He has to look good on the beach.

The week following the VMAs was a whirlwind. Every magazine, radio station, and daytime talk show wanted an interview with MTV's Best New Artist. Instead, Darius turned them all down, focusing on shooting the video for "Make My Life Real." He didn't believe in doing too much press when there wasn't yet a new album on sale. The single wasn't even hitting stores for another ten days. It made no sense to be overexposed so early in the promotion game.

More meaningful to him than the attention he was getting from the press were the phone calls he was getting from artists in the music industry, and even Hollywood actors. They all raved about the song, praising the lyrics for hitting on the difficulty of keeping it real while living the life. He kept getting asked over and over again why he didn't write the songs on his first album. These same questions were getting asked of Flow Steddie, who had by now completely come over to Darius's way of thinking. Darius was finally an artist in control of his music, his image, and his future.

Kahlila's week had a similar busy quality, as her cell phone didn't stop ringing with calls from acquaintances back home who had seen her on TV. Most were simply calling to share their excitement and to relate the exact story of the moment the camera panned to Kahlila and they started screaming in surprise. But others were calling with specific requests: concert tickets, VIP club access, and all types of other perks over which Kahlila had no access, and which she wouldn't grant them even if she did. The most outrageous call came from a girl she'd gone to college with and hadn't seen since. She wanted to know if Darius could sing at her wedding the following week. Kahlila, who'd always prided herself on being polite, tried to hold back the laughter as she stated that Darius had other plans.

Darius watched her navigate all of the phone calls and favors with a close eye. Kahlila had flown under the radar for the entire summer, and the VMAs was her coming-out party. He wondered if she would somehow change now that she had been given a sliver of the spotlight. The first real test came on the first day of shooting for the "Make My Life Real" video. Kahlila was sitting on a stool near the cameras, eating a Granny Smith apple, when the director suggested that she make a cameo appearance in the opening scene. "People will recognize her from the VMAs. It'll be tight," he said assertively, as if the decision had already been made. "Go get into wardrobe," he instructed, with a wave of his hand.

Kahlila looked around for Darius, but he wasn't yet on set. Instead of listening to the director and going to wardrobe, she instead went straight to Darius's dressing room and walked inside. The makeup artist was patting his face with a circular duster, and Kahlila stifled a giggle.

"See, that's why you should knock, baby. You don't need to see me getting powder on my face," he said with a smile.

"Just to take the shine off," the cosmetologist said in a motherly tone.

"What's up, baby?" he asked, closing his eyes and pulling in his lips.

"Your director wants me to make a cameo in the video and I don't want to," she said, her arms folded.

"So just tell him that," Darius said, standing up and examining himself in the mirror.

"He didn't really give me the chance. Can't you tell him when you go out there?" she asked in an almost whine.

Darius shook his head good-naturedly, finding Kahlila's reluctance sweet. He could just imagine what Miko's reaction would have been had a director given her an unexpected part in a video. To be fair, he knew that modeling was Miko's profession and therefore it was a little different. Still, it was nice to be reminded that Kahlila was simply there to support him, not to find any success of her own.

Meanwhile, Kahlila was relieved that Darius seemed to have no interest in pushing the idea. Her reason for not wanting to be in front of the camera was one completely unrelated to her boyfriend's feelings. It was the fact that whether she had a wonderful summer or not, she was still a high school teacher. *How would it look for my students to see me strutting through some music video? It's bad enough they saw me in a revealing dress on national TV. I have to go back to work and make sure my professionalism isn't compromised.*

Over the last few weeks, Kahlila had found herself thinking about her students more and more. It was a natural process that occurred every August, but the feeling took her by surprise this year. Even with the trip to Los

Angeles, the music awards, and her increasing closeness with Darius, her mind often wandered to the first novel that she was teaching her sophomores, the college essay unit that she designed for her seniors, or the first Girl Talk meeting of the fall. When having dinner with Darius, she'd be tempted to interject a Pierce story: Madeline's obsession with historical trivia, the school's dismally bad football team, or the lunch lady's prize-winning banana bread. But it never seemed to fit in with the climate of the conversation, which consisted solely of talk about the new album: timelines, tour schedules, video concepts, collaboration ideas, and marketing techniques. It wasn't that Kahlila didn't get to contribute during these discussions. In fact, Darius loved her input on these topics. But she never steered the dialogue toward things that were important to her. *It's really my fault for focusing on his stuff the entire summer. I can't expect to flip it now.*

As much of a fairy tale as the past month had been, she was getting excited to return to Boston and dig into her work. She and Darius hadn't had much discussion about how their relationship would change once she left New York. Instead, they simply spent every moment together in anticipation of her leaving. And once the video was wrapped, he announced his Labor Day surprise: before Kahlila started back to school, they were going to Martha's Vineyard for the long weekend. He'd remembered Kahlila's saying that it was a favorite vacation spot of hers when she was younger, and he wanted to get away someplace where they would have some degree of privacy.

Kahlila was thrilled at the thoughtfulness of the gesture, although her excitement got taken down a few notches when she learned that it was a group excursion. Flow Steddie, Rasheed, Lamont, and their girlfriends were going to be joining them. He assured her that with the huge house they rented, there would still be plenty of one-on-one time. But a few signs pointed otherwise: they only rented one huge SUV for all eight of them, and they went grocery shopping as soon as they hit the island so they could cook all their meals at the house as a group. Still, Kahlila smiled through it. She liked all of the guys on the trip, and had spent time with Toni as well, so she was sure they would get along.

Over the next twenty-four hours, Kahlila was growing doubtful that this weekend had been a good idea. Somehow, the group dynamic, with Flow Steddie's leadership, created a vibe that Kahlila could not relate to whatsoever. She felt as if she had nothing in common with anyone in the house. Even Darius seemed different, somehow. For her, the vineyard was a place where she could relax completely. She loved the quaint shops, New England beaches, and the abundance of black families who made the Vineyard their yearly holiday. For her fellow travelers, they behaved as if they'd landed on Mars when the ferry docked in Vineyard Haven. Every aspect of the island was constantly being compared to the Hamptons, and the one spot in Oak Bluffs that played hip-hop was apparently too "bootleg" for them. Admittedly, it didn't feature bottle service or a VIP section, but drinks were strong and the deejay was actually good. Kahlila was relieved that she hadn't seen anyone she knew from Boston at the bar, because she would have been embarrassed by how uppity everyone was behaving.

The next morning, they had decided to spend the day at the beach, but Kahlila didn't understand exactly why they were all there. The girls, though wearing bikinis, were in full makeup and jewelry, reclined under umbrellas, shrieking if sand blew their way, or God forbid, if a ray of sunlight hit their faces. The guys were treating the beach like it was a backyard cookout. Rocking T-shirts, jean shorts, and Tims, they lounged in chairs with Coronas in the armrests, blasting a stereo.

Kahlila looked longingly at the group of people her age playing touch football down the beach. While she thought it would be rude to join them, she decided to go on her own into the water. When she returned, a group of girls were taking pictures with Darius and Flow while Flow's girlfriend, Rhonda, seethed from a few feet away. Beckoning Kahli over, she said softly, "Girl, let's go over there and break that shit up." But before Kahli could even answer, Darius was calling her name and waving for her to join them. Grabbing a towel and wrapping it around her torso, she trotted over to the group. Darius stood up and pulled her into him for a hug. "I'm soaking wet, honey," she said apologetically as the four girls watching uttered "awwws" and "that's so sweet" in sugary tones that gave away their disingenuous nature. Darius ignored them, instead staring at his girlfriend and kissing her forehead. Over his shoulder, Kahlila could see Rhonda trying to make eye contact with Flow.

The prettiest of the girls smiled at Kahlila once Darius released her from his arms. "Kahli, you must have been trippin when Darius thanked you on MTV."

How the hell does she know my name?

Rasheed and Darius exchanged amused glances. Kahlila wasn't yet used to groupies. Darius had done an admirable job shielding her from them up to this point. Not many club outings, no concerts. So she hadn't yet met the chicks who cooed at the girlfriends and then slept with the star when the girl's back was turned. But Kahlila looked like she was onto their strategy. "It was surprising, yes," she answered dryly, after which point an uncomfortable silence settled in.

"I'm going to take a walk," Kahlila said at last. The

girls' eyes brightened as Kahlila dropped her towel on Darius's chair and left the group.

Rasheed knew exactly how Kahlila felt. It was so much easier to just walk away from the foolishness. Being in New York for the summer had served as a reminder of how much Rasheed missed his old steelo, working in the city, making his own hours. The lifestyle of being Darius's constant companion was exhausting. He couldn't make plans without checking his friend's schedule. He couldn't check his e-mail without sifting through messages from fans who'd somehow gotten his contact information, begging him to put them in touch with his boy. And most importantly, he couldn't go forward with his own financial planning career, because there simply wasn't time.

The day before Rasheed had met Kahlila for the first time at Darius's apartment, he had actually decided to give his friend notice that he needed to hire a new personal assistant. He wanted his life back. But then he heard the music that Darius had been working on, and he knew the uphill battle he would have trying to change his image in the middle of the game. *I'll give my boy one more album. Then I'm doing my own thing.*

On the beach, he saw Darius squint in displeasure as he watched Kahlila heading to the shore. He wondered if Kahlila was cut out to be a celebrity girlfriend. Darius liked her so much because she was so outside of the industry. *But if you want to make it work with someone as big as D, you gotta have a little fight in you. You have to be willing to stare those bitches down, and sometimes you have to drag your man away, just like Flow's girl is doing right now.* Flow's exit left Darius alone to entertain four women who seemed willing to do anything just for a few more minutes with him.

"So, what are y'all ladies getting into later?" he heard Darius ask.

"Yo, D!" Rasheed called, taking a swig of his Corona.

"Whassup?" he called back.

Rasheed took off his sunglasses and gave D The Look. Since Rasheed had begun working for Darius, they'd learned to communicate without speaking. So much of their time was spent in loud arenas that they had to rely on facial expressions. They each had a few signature looks, from Rasheed's "Let's get out of here," to Darius's "I need to go to the bathroom." But the look Rasheed was giving right at this moment was "Cut that shit out," and in case Darius didn't get the message, he added an almost imperceptible nod in Kahlila's direction, who by now was just a tiny bronze figure in the distance.

Darius did indeed cut it out, and by the ride back to their rented house in Oak Bluffs, all were in good spirits. Once they reached their three-story, five-bedroom rental, Kahlila jumped in the shower and decided to stay upstairs and do some reading afterward. She could hear everyone else laughing and talking in the living room downstairs, and she closed the door to get some quiet. Her eyes skimmed over her tattered copy of *Their Eyes Were Watching God*, which she taught every year to her tenth graders. She was determined to make it more appealing to her male students this time around, and her mind was spinning with potential lesson plans when Darius swung open the door.

"Why don't you come downstairs?" He sat down on the bed hard, bouncing it up and down. "We're about to play a game."

"What game?" Kahlila asked, not looking up from Janie and Tea Cake's love story.

"Twister."

She wrinkled her brow in disapproval. Kahlila loved

games, but only ones that required some type of mental skill. Word games were the best, with Scrabble being her all-time favorite. *Twister? Having Flow Steddie's knee in my armpit is not my idea of fun.* "I'm all set. I need to do some work for school on Wednesday."

Darius didn't respond, sitting on the bed a few moments longer before rising and heading toward the door. Once in the hallway, he suddenly turned back and stood over Kahlila with a frustrated expression. "Would it hurt you to act like my girl sometimes?"

"What are you talking about?" She finally closed the book, but not before marking her page.

"Today when those hoes were in my face, you didn't even hug me back when I put my arms around you."

"I was wet and wrapped in a towel! And why do they have to be hoes, anyway?"

"Yeah, Kahli. Stick up for them. Meanwhile they're trying to take your man. You left me there with them!"

"So you were tempted?"

They both noticed that downstairs had gotten quiet. Clearly their argument had the entire house's attention.

"It's not about being tempted," he responded more softly. "When chicks are throwing it in your face, you need to feel like there's a reason not to do it."

"I can't believe this. You're telling me all this two days before I go back to Boston?"

"I'm not telling you that I don't think I can be faithful. I'm just saying that as we do this, you need to be where I am—mentally."

"And where is that, Darius?"

"Ready to make this work with you. Ready to give things up." He sat back down next to her, rubbing her back as a peace offering.

"Give things up?" she repeated.

"Obviously, there's going to be a lot of travel necessary

in order for us to spend time together. You'll need to be away from Boston on a lot of weekends."

Kahlila knew what his words were true, but they still bothered her. *Why do I have to be the one leaving town every weekend? Why can't he come visit me?*

As if he could hear her thoughts, Darius shouted toward the open bedroom door. "Rasheed, tell her how it's gonna be when the album drops!"

Prolonged silence. Then, "Don't get me into this, dawg."

"Fuck it, *I'll* tell her. Shit is bananas, Kahli! My girl will let you know. You gotta jump on the bus or get left. On dogs." Flow's voice sounded like it was getting closer, as if he was walking up the stairs as he spoke.

"Flow, mind your damn business. Get back down here. Ain't nobody ask for your opinion," Rhonda scolded.

Darius just smiled and walked over to close and lock the door. When he joined Kahlila on the bed, he circled his arms around her waist so that she was curled into his body.

"We gotta get creative once you go home. You have a webcam?"

Kahlila laughed. She was still learning all of the features on her iPod.

"Okay, we'll get you one."

"Seriously, what's wrong with the phone?" she asked, her mood lightening with every moment that they spent cuddling in a room by themselves.

"I can't see you over the phone, sweetheart. Nothing's wrong with the phone too, especially to text. I can't always talk, so texting is key."

"I think it costs me ten cents a text or something."

Now it was Darius's turn to laugh. "Time to get unlimited, baby. Kahlila, we can make this work. I guarantee it."

Kahlila nodded, suddenly sleepy from the hours spent

in the draining sun at the beach. There was no point in discussing it further. They'd figure it out soon enough, and besides, her mind was already preoccupied by Janie, Tea Cake, and the hundred forty students waiting to greet her on the first day of school.

Chapter 33

*He has to enjoy hearing
a good story from work.*

Kahlila always told her students that teachers are more nervous than the kids about the start of the new school year. This was never more true than today. She couldn't remember being more anxious about standing at the front of the classroom, even when she was just starting out in her career. As she pulled into her parking spot and saw the sea of teenagers ebbing and flowing in front of her, she began to feel a bit seasick.

Because she'd just gotten back from the Vineyard late the evening before, she didn't do what she usually did on the night before school started. Every year before this one, she looked through her class lists, made seating plans using her foolproof system (placing students next to someone of a different gender and race whenever possible), and planned out her lesson minute-by-minute. She hated to do an activity on the first day that she'd done in the past, especially because she often had students in her class whom she'd taught before.

But she was so exhausted, she hadn't bothered to do any of her usual prep, and therefore she knew that she was not going to be on top of her game today. She was using the same discussion topic in her tenth and twelfth grade classes as she had last year, and she hadn't even bothered to look to see what students were in her classes. Kahlila had many successful days in her teaching career where she had "winged it," but never on the first day of school. She felt her stomach rumbling as she slammed her car door. Instinctively, she walked to her trunk to take out her vintage New Kids on the Block lunch box, but she remembered that she'd been unable to pack a lunch this morning because there were no groceries whatsoever in her fridge. She could already anticipate how hungry she would be at 10:00 a.m., which was the time when she always dipped into her meal for a mid-morning snack.

A piercing squeal that could only come from an adolescent female pervaded the parking lot, but Kahlila didn't react. She was immune to certain teenaged noises that made other adults flinch. However, as she saw a brown-haired girl wearing a way-too-mini miniskirt bounding in her direction, she realized that the squeal had been intended for her.

"Oh my God! Ms. Bradford! How *are* you?" Kahlila thought the girl's cheeks might crack from the wideness of her grin.

"I'm fine, honey. How are *you*?" She often called her students affectionate names such as honey, and even boo, but she was using the term this time because she had no idea who this child was.

"You probably don't know me. I'm Michelle, and you taught a bunch of my friends last year. I'm so sad you don't teach eleventh, 'cause I would be psyched to get you for English this year."

"No, I'm teaching sophomores and seniors again," Kahlila responded with a sympathetic smile. She began walking toward the building, and Michelle was right on her heels.

She was poised to ask Michelle about her summer, when she noticed that the girl was distracted, fishing in her bag to retrieve something. Triumphant, Michelle pulled out a CD case that Kahlila quickly recognized to have Darius's face on the cover. Suddenly it clicked why she had a random girl following her to school.

"So, Ms. Bradford, I know you're gonna hear this a lot, but seriously, I am Darius Wilson's biggest fan. You can ask anybody in my grade. Alex, Jessie, Brittany, Nadia . . ."

Kahlila just smiled and nodded. *What the hell am I supposed to say?*

"Do you think that you can get this CD autographed for me? Oh my God, it would mean so much. I absolutely *love* his music. And when I saw you on MTV, I was like, oh my God. That's, like, everybody's favorite teacher at Pierce. I just started screaming, and my mom was, like, freaking out because she thought someone had died or something."

The whole time she was talking, she held the CD case in front of Kahlila's hand, which was stuffed in the pocket of her BCBG pantsuit. Even if she wanted to take the CD from Michelle, she felt frozen in her tracks. Yes, she had anticipated a little bit of buzz around the MTV appearance and subsequent press, but she never thought that students would be this . . . eager.

Kahlila opened her mouth to respond, still not sure of what she was going to say. Luckily, her guardan angel appeared in the form of Kayla Shaughnessy, one of her former students whom she absolutely adored. She stood in front of Michelle with her hands on her hips, a disapproving look in her eyes.

"Michelle, what the hell? Like Ms. Bradford is gonna be taking orders from every person at Pierce who wants his autograph. Give her a break!"

Michelle, immediately contrite, returned the CD to her shoulder bag. "Sorry, Ms. Bradford. I just thought if I caught you before the rush, y'know? But I understand. If you do it for me, you'll have to say yes to everybody."

Everybody? There will be more people like you? Kahlila managed a nod before Michelle walked away to a crowd of girls who seemed to be awaiting the story of the encounter.

"People are crazy, right?" Kayla shook her head in disbelief. "My family used to go through that all the time." Kayla's uncle was Joey McIntyre, the youngest member of New Kids on the Block. Kahlila had no idea about this fact until she happened to be telling a story in class two years ago about her childhood obsession with the Boston boy band. The following day, Kayla brought her the lunch box as a gift to a former fan. Kahlila couldn't quite remember her reaction to the gift, but it probably resembled Michelle's demeanor a little bit more than she wanted to admit.

"Thanks for the rescue, Kayla. I had absolutely no idea what to say."

"No problem. But you should definitely be prepared, Ms. Bradford. This is all anyone has been talking about these last couple of weeks. I got three IMs about it last night alone. And honestly, most of these kids don't even know much about Darius Wilson. I mean, not a ton of kids at Pierce listen to R&B. But they saw the MTV Awards and now they wanna act like they're huge fans, just because they know you. It's retarded."

"Kayla. Language." As much as her head was spinning, her teacher mode was back in effect.

"Sorry. I mean, stupid. And seriously, I don't know why they're so surprised about it. Everyone knows that you're awesome, and superstylish, and you like to travel and all that. Of course you're going to meet fabulous people, and of course they're going to be interested in you."

"Well, thank you." She had to smile at Kayla's matter-of-factness about the whole situation. She was one of those kids whom Kahlila wished was ten years older, so they could go out to dinner and dish over a glass of wine.

"I'll come visit you later on once I get my schedule. I am so scared that I'm gonna have sucky teachers my senior year," she moaned.

Kahlila was tempted to scold her for calling teachers "sucky," but she decided to let it go.

They parted ways, with Kayla staying outside to chat with friends and Kahlila entering the building, a vast series of corridors and lockers that could have been any high school in America with its textbook appearance.

She hadn't even cleared the door when she heard a boy calling, "Ms. Bradford, over here!" Kahlila turned in the direction of the voice and was practically blinded by the flash of a camera. A kid from one of her study halls two years ago whose name she could not remember was the photographer in question, tossing her a quick "Thanks!" before running off.

Paparazzi at my own school? Are you kidding me? I didn't even deal with this in New York. Though she had been heading to the cafeteria to get a cup of coffee, she made a quick decision to avoid the crowd and do without her morning caffeine. It was too early for the students to be in homeroom, and she could use the time to collect her thoughts and do some last-minute prep before class. She wondered if her students were going to expect her to talk about her summer, specifically her adventures with Darius. *Well, if so, they're in for a big disappointment.*

She walked into her classroom, grateful that the custodian had already unlocked it and aired it out, as it tended to be a bit musty after a long, humid summer. However, the open door meant that people were free to enter, and indeed she had company waiting for her. Madeline was sitting in one of the student desks, scanning her eyes over her plan book. At the sight of Kahlila, she slammed the book shut and hopped out of her seat animatedly.

"So, Kahli, how exciting is this? We never have to be at the loser singles table again!"

"Why do you say that? Oh my goodness—you met someone?"

"No . . ." Madeline looked mildly crestfallen. "We haven't spoken since the day after the VMAs, and I just figured that you would use your newfound connections to find me the perfect guy."

"I have connections?"

"Of course! Darius has to have a lawyer or someone who would be perfect for me."

"So I should basically find you the first white guy associated with my boyfriend?"

"How stereotypical of you to presume that his lawyer is white! I'm looking for a good guy, regardless of color," said Madeline assertively.

"Maddie, I met his lawyer. He *is* white. And old. And married." Kahlila didn't know whether to laugh or to bang her head on the desk in frustration. She felt used and manipulated by students and coworkers, and it wasn't even first period yet.

"So, there was no one interesting on your Vineyard vacation?" If Madeline noticed Kahlila's annoyance by her line of questioning, she sure didn't act like it.

"Maddie, I was kind of focused on spending the last few days with my boyfriend before I had to come back here. I wasn't looking for your soul mate."

Before Madeline had a chance to respond, her eleventh grade homeroom started to fill up. Of course, one of the first people to enter was the autograph-seeking Michelle from the parking lot, who cast an embarrassed smile her way. Kahlila sighed. *It's going to be a long day.*

After lunchtime, Kahlila was in brighter spirits. Her classes had gone smoothly, considering the fact that she was fairly unprepared. And though she'd heard a lot of whispering before the bell rang to begin each period, students put all of the gossip aside once she began to speak. She had her usual lunch with Madeline, who apologized for her overzealous interrogation that morning. Now, as Kahlila's last class of the day sat in front of her, she was finally beginning to sense that things were getting back to normal.

"Okay, class, I know you're being bombarded by all of your teachers today with information about what supplies you need, what the requirements are, and all of that good stuff. But we can get to that tomorrow. I want to get right into the basis of our course this year, which is analysis and discussion. I'm handing out a quote for us to explore together."

While students took one sheet and passed the pile around, a boy with a blond buzz cut and a mischievous twinkle in his eye raised his hand.

"Yes?"

"Wouldn't you rather hand out one of your boyfriend's songs for us to read?" Muffled laughter came from the other boys seated around him, who were obviously his buddies.

"What's your name, honey?" Kahlila said in her sweetest voice.

"Um, Ben."

Her eyes narrowed and she walked closer to his desk. "Ben. I don't know what you've heard about this class. But I'll make a bet that if you ask any student who has taken English with me, he or she will tell you that I do not play. This is my job. Nothing is more serious than my job. And guess what, Ben? Being a student is *your* job. Your full-time job. Not being a clown. Am I clear?" She tilted her head inquisitively.

"Yeah," he mumbled.

"I'm sorry, I'm having a hard time hearing you. But that's okay, because tomorrow I'm moving everyone's seat." Soft groans could be heard throughout the room. "And, Ben, you'll be sitting right by my desk. Sound good? Great." She proceeded with her lesson as every student sat up a little bit straighter.

Kahlila was hard at work making seating plans after school when Kayla poked her head in the doorway of her classroom. "Hey, Ms. Bradford, it's already around the whole school that you let Ben have it. I don't think anyone else is gonna be bothering you about your boyfriend." She disappeared from sight before Kahlila could respond.

Smiling, she glanced at her cell phone resting next to all of her papers. She was so tempted to call Darius and tell him about her day. But she decided to finish her work and reward herself with a phone call afterward.

Attendance was always excellent on the first day of school, and she only had one student who was absent: Bree Roberts. When Kahlila saw Bree's name on her class list, she was excited that she would get to know Bree more this year. She had been intrigued by the strikingly beautiful girl with the sad eyes and passion for books. As she thought about her again now that she was alone at her desk, it struck her that perhaps she should be worried by the fact that Bree did not show up to school. What if something happened over the summer? Kahlila sensed that while Bree loved to read stories about other people, she most likely had a story of her own. New to the school her junior year, always by herself, and very secretive about her home life, she had all the signs of someone who hadn't had things easy.

Next to Bree's name on her class list was her gender, race, homeroom number, and home phone. Kahlila found herself picking up her cell phone and dialing the digits before she even thought it through.

"Hello?" Kahlila recognized Bree's soft but clear tone from their few conversations months ago.

"Bree, this is Ms. Bradford from Pierce. How are you?"

Kahlila could hear her surprise in the silence on the other end. Eventually, "Fine."

"Where were you today, hon?"

"Um, I'm transferring back to my old school in New Haven."

"Really? It doesn't look like we have that on record yet, because you showed up on my class list."

"I have you for English this year?" Bree's voice perked up a little.

"You would have, yes. If you weren't leaving. Do you have a parent or guardian I can talk to?"

"My brother's still at work," Bree answered too quickly.

Kahlila didn't notice Bree's nervousness, as she was distracted by the revelation that Bree's guardian was an older brother. Her mind was already traveling to hypotheses about what could have happened to their parents. Refocusing, she responded, "Well, he's going to need to call the school and confirm that you're leaving us."

For the second time in their short conversation, the silence was almost a third person on the phone. Kahlila began to get suspicious. "Actually, Bree, what's your brother's work number?"

She told her. The surrender in her voice was audible.

"Okay, Bree, take care."

Bree hung up the phone without a well-wish in return. Kahlila sighed, knowing that what was intended to be a simple check-in had suddenly become complicated.

Dialing the number that Bree had mumbled the moment before, Kahlila felt herself getting jumpy. She called parents all the time, but an older brother? It was different somehow. Her uneasiness was in no way lessened when she heard a deep, slightly scratchy voice on the other end.

"Roberts."

"Um, hello, Mr. Roberts. My name is Kahlila Bradford. I'm calling from Pierce High School."

No response. *Does anyone in this family know how to carry on a conversation?*

"I was just calling because Bree wasn't in school today, and when I called—"

"Bree didn't go to school." It was more of a statement than a question, but Kahlila could tell that this was new information to him.

"No, and she said that she is transferring to her old school in Connecticut?"

"She'll be in tomorrow. I'll bring her myself." His responses were short, and borderline rude, but something about his voice made Kahlila want to extend the conversation.

"Okay. If you have any more questions, I'm in room 227. I get to school pretty early."

"And you are . . ."

Feeling like a total idiot, she tried to hide behind a

peppy response. "I'm going to be Bree's English teacher this year," she said cheerily.

"Great." Perhaps she was being neurotic, but Kahlila swore that there was some sarcasm behind his one-word answer. *Clearly this guy is having some issues with his little sister, but why the hell is he taking them out on me?*

Chapter 34

He has to put family first.

The following morning, there was no dropping Bree off on the corner. Because she couldn't be trusted to walk down the street and inside the school building, Keith was parking the car. Bree's arms were firmly folded across her chest as she trailed him to the entrance, her shuffling feet almost mocking the confident stride of her big brother. Instinctually, he straightened his tie as soon as they reached the front door. Bree was usually extremely conscious of the outfits she wore to school, but today it looked like she'd rolled out of bed and headed out the door. Keith had commented earlier that morning that she was going to look ridiculous in her pajama pants and hooded sweatshirt. "Kids wear this stuff all the time at Pierce," she'd mumbled back. He was annoyed as he scanned the hallways to realize that her statement was in fact true, with very few students dressed in the skirts or dress pants that Bree tended to wear.

Bree was mortified to see that Keith wasn't simply leaving her at the door. He stared at her, waiting for her to make a move in some direction. Whatever direction it was, he was going also. "We can't go to homeroom yet. It's too early," Bree announced, grateful for the first time that Pierce's stupid rule existed.

Keith quickly glanced at his watch. He had a report to write before his 9:00 meeting, and it was already 7:15. *Whatever. The firm gets too much of my time as it is.* "I'll wait."

Bree grabbed his arm and looked at him pleadingly. "Keith! You're really going to sit with me in the cafeteria? In a suit? Are you for real?" She noticed a couple of kids she didn't know looking in their direction, so she lowered her voice. "I promise I'm not going to leave. You can call the school later if you want. I just need you to promise me something back."

"Me?" Keith said incredulously. "Why do *I* need to promise you anything?"

"Just promise that when you get home tonight, we can talk about this transferring thing. I really want to do it, Keith. I outlined all the reasons and you should hear me out." Her hands were on her hips now, the exact same way their mom used to do when she had a serious point to make.

Keith sighed. "Fine. We'll talk tonight. But I can't promise that it'll go the way you want." He felt his face soften when a huge smile appeared on his sister's face. "Hug good-bye?" he asked teasingly.

"Hell no. Get out of here!" Bree whispered viciously, though her expression was still cheerful. Before he could follow directions, she had taken off, trotting to the cafeteria, all too eager to pull away from his clutches.

Keith knew he should get to work. His car probably had a ticket on it. There was nothing left for him to do for Bree at school. She could handle getting the work she missed from yesterday. But even as he reviewed all of these facts in his head, he watched his polished black shoes climb the nearest flight of steps. His feet did not stop until they reached the second floor, and as fate would have it, room 227 was just two doors down from where he stood.

As Kahlila would tell it later to Robyn, Desiree, and Madeline, she thought she'd fallen asleep at her desk when she saw Keith standing in the doorway of her classroom. Staring at the man she had chased after in a taxi, the man whose house she had stormed out of and never spoken to again, felt absolutely surreal. The hypothesis that she was dreaming was strengthened by his wearing an expensive suit and showing up at her school, when she never told him where she worked. Though she couldn't be sure, she might have done something absolutely foolish, like shaken her head from side to side, trying to wake herself up. To Keith, it probably looked like she was telling him to go away.

"Is this a bad time?" Keith calmly asked, as he rested an arm against the frame of the door.

Kahlila looked down at her desk. All her lesson plans for the day were carefully arranged, and a stack of paperwork for her homeroom kids lay exactly where it was supposed to be. She had to resign her theory that this encounter wasn't real and just go with it.

"Um, no. You can come in," she said, trying not to reveal her nervousness in her voice.

He strode into the room, his shoes assertively hitting the hardwood floor. Extending his hand well before he actually reached her desk, he took her own firmly in his grip and shook it as if they were meeting for the first time. "Keith Roberts," he said, looking directly into Kahlila's eyes.

She cast her gaze downward and released his hand, overpowered by the intensity of his stare. "I know who you are, Keith. What are you doing here?"

"I don't think you heard me. My last name is Roberts. You didn't know that when we met the first time." He kept his eyes focused on her until she met his gaze again. She looked flustered and confused. "Bree's my sister."

Kahlila's eyes and mouth opened so wide that Keith had to chuckle. She formed her mouth to ask a question, but she couldn't figure out which one she wanted to ask first. It took so long for her to respond that Keith helpfully added, "We spoke on the phone yesterday."

The additional information gave her a jumping-off point for her questions. "Is that when you realized that you and I had . . ." She let the question remain unfinished, but completed it a million different ways in her mind. *That you and I had met at a bar before? Had been interested in each other? Had gone back to your place and spent the night together?*

"I discovered who you were when my sister and I saw you on television a few weeks back," he answered with a smirk.

Kahlila could feel the fire in her cheeks, and hoped that they didn't look as red as they felt. "Oh," was all she could think of to say.

After an awkward moment of silence that seemed to stretch for hours, but was really only about five seconds, Keith redirected the subject. "So, you're Bree's English teacher this year?" he asked, taking a seat on the desk portion one of the chair-desk contraptions where the students sat.

"Yes, I am," Kahlila said in her most professional tone, happy that the subject matter had turned to areas where she felt confident and in control.

"English has always been my sister's best subject. She

got recommended for A.P. English this year, but she didn't want to do it," Keith said, appearing annoyed just thinking about it.

"Why not?"

"I think she was hatching this plan in her mind to go back to Connecticut and live with one of her friends while she finished high school. The more successful she appeared to be doing at Pierce, the less likely I would be to let her go, I guess." Keith had gone from sounding frustrated to sounding tired.

"You sound like you're thinking about giving in?" Kahlila probed.

"From the way you phrased your question, I can tell you don't approve."

"I don't know enough about the situation to approve or disapprove," Kahlila responded cautiously.

"You said when we met that one of your faults was coming to judgment too quickly. So you disapprove, whether you have a right to or not," Keith tossed back.

Kahlila had forgotten how much she'd told him that night at the bar once all of their friends had left them alone. What surprised her even more than how honest she had been was that he still remembered. "Okay, you got me. So tell me why you're considering it."

"Bree's had it rough. And it's hard for me to watch her unhappy day in and day out. I thought we were making some progress this summer, but when she went to New Haven to visit, she got really nostalgic and immediately dreaded starting back to school in Boston . . ." He stopped talking, realizing that he was discussing personal family issues with the wrong person.

But he'd already said enough that Kahlila was ready with a response. "Look, Bree's college application is going to be stronger without all the back and forth between schools. And can you trust that the family she'd be staying with would be on her the way they need to be about college stuff?"

Keith didn't respond. He was staring at her nails, noticing how perfectly manicured they were. Last time they saw one another, her nails were short and looked like she bit them. He wondered if her new fancy lifestyle required that she get her nails done.

"Give me some time with her. I'll see her every day in English class, and I think I can get her to join my Girl Talk group."

How is this girl trying to act professional when the two times I've seen her have been drunk at a bar and profiling on TV? "You sure you have time in your busy schedule?"

Kahlila jerked back in her seat, almost as if someone had lunged at her with a clenched fist. Things had seemed so cordial between them just a moment ago. *And why is he acting like he has a right to be angry with me? What did I do wrong?*

"I'm sorry. I shouldn't have said that. Look, Bree really likes and respects you. After I got home last night and had it out with her about cutting school, she said that the only good thing about staying at Pierce this year would be having you as a teacher."

She wasn't completely ready to move on from the sudden attack, but she knew that she should for the sake of their working relationship. "Bree and I have only spoken a few times, but I was really excited to see that I was going to have her as a student this year as well. Do you want me to talk to her after class today about this transferring issue?"

"No, lemme rap with her tonight. I'm used to persuading people in my line of work."

"I'm sorry, what do you do?"

"I'm a lawyer."

Kahlila hoped that the shock was hidden on her face,

but she doubted it. Her mind flashed back to the T-shirt and jeans he had worn the evening that they met, and his reluctance to say what he did for a living. Hadn't he even said something about working construction as a dream job? *I didn't know this guy at all.*

"So, maybe you can keep me posted on how Bree's doing? In school, I mean." He didn't look at her when asking the questions, but at the walls of her classroom, which were completely bare. She liked to start decorating the room anew each year, and since it was only the second day of school, the space was still barren. By October, the bulletin boards would have students' essays posted on them, and the walls would be plastered with photo collages of her students. She was tempted to explain this to him, but decided that he probably didn't care anyway.

"Of course, not a problem."

He stood up, and Kahlila allowed herself to really look at him from head to toe. She'd forgotten how impressive his height and build had been, and while his dark suit jacket and blue button-up shirt masked the muscles underneath, she flashed back to the sight of his bare back on that disastrous morning. He removed his wallet from his inside jacket pocket and pulled out a business card.

"E-mail is the best way to reach me," he said, handing her the white square with raised lettering. "I'm not always at my desk."

"Sure, no problem." *Did I already say that?*

"Take care, Ms. Bradford," he said with a head nod before walking out of the classroom.

She waited until the sound of his footsteps were inaudible before she read the business card still positioned between her thumb and index finger.

CHANNING, TRITON, AND BROWN
KEITH ROBERTS
ASSOCIATE

His phone and fax numbers were displayed, along with his e-mail address. Kahlila stared at the numbers and letters, trying to wrap her head around the situation. Obviously, the coincidence of his sister's being in her class was overwhelming. But she was used to crazy small-world stuff happening to her, especially in a city such as Boston, where there was only one degree of separation between any two black people who were the same age. She should have known better than to think that she wasn't connected to Keith in some way. His blue-collar vibe had thrown her off, and as she remembered, had even turned her off a little. A college degree was a must on The List. When Desiree began dating Jason five years ago, she'd decided to cross it off because Jason was such a great guy and he only had a high school diploma. The experiment didn't go so well, as every guy she dated acted intimidated by her level of education, even when they made more money than she did. So she reinstated the requirement, and only gave Keith a chance that evening because she was trying to throw The List away completely. But then she met Darius and realized that she didn't have to abandon any of her standards.

Darius. She'd almost forgotten about him in the craziness of her morning. It had only been two days since she'd last seen him, but she could already tell that the long-distance aspect of their relationship was going to be tough. She couldn't help but wonder what it would have been like if she and Keith had begun a relationship when the summer began. The trip to New York would never have occurred, and she'd now be dating someone who lived and worked a matter of minutes away from where she did.

What am I thinking? Seeing Keith today doesn't change what happened that morning his girl busted into the house. Darius has everything that Keith does and more. Feeling guilty that her imagination had wandered into a hypothetical relationship with someone else, she fished her cell phone out of her bag and sent Darius a text message: Good morning, sleepyhead. Make good music today. Miss you. She felt herself returning to a state of equilibrium as the bell rang to dismiss students from the cafeteria.

Chapter 35

*He has to have an intriguing quality
that makes people want to know more.*

Kahlila took a deep breath before entering her first
and last name in quotation marks and hitting ENTER. The
last time Kahlila had Googled herself was toward the end
of the previous school year. One of her students had told
her that her Google results were "boring." Kids at Pierce
Googled their teachers all the time, often hitting paydirt
with the younger ones by finding a MySpace page or the
Web site of their rock band. Kahlila's hits, however, consisted of a fellowship she'd won in college, several articles in local newspapers from when she won Boston
Teacher of the Year, and a link to Desiree's Web site
where Des thanked all of her close friends and family
members. It was a snooze-fest for teenagers who were
hoping to catch a glimpse of the unpolished Ms. Bradford, and it caused them to resolve in their minds that
Ms. Bradford as the bad girl was a character who simply
did not exist.

A few short months later, every student at Pierce who had previously believed that Ms. Bradford's life consisted of teaching class and going home to grade papers (which wasn't actually too far from the truth) was now salivating at the smorgasbord of gossip available to them with just a few quick keystrokes. Even her mom, who lived in the Caribbean now and was pretty far removed from American pop culture, had called her to tell her how much information she'd obtained about her own daughter online. And as the hundreds of listings appeared before Kahlila's eyes, she didn't know whether to feel intrigued or revolted. Hesitatingly at first, and then more greedily, she began to explore the many short articles about her and Darius Wilson.

Click *here* to listen to the first radio interview after Darius Wilson began dating Boston teacher Kahlila Bradford. He doesn't mention her by name, but she's obviously in the studio, and he sounds sprung as hell!

Here are some pictures of Darius Wilson on the red carpet at the VMAs. He's looking mighty fine, but where is flame Kahlila Bradford? He bigs her up like crazy when he wins Best New Artist, so why aren't they posing together beforehand?

We broke it first! Who's the mysterious "Cali" who Darius Wilson thanked on MTV? She is 29-year-old Kahlila Bradford, a high school English teacher in Boston. Sources say that they met through a mutual friend, novelist and screenwriter Desiree Thomas. They'd been seen together in New York and L.A. in the weeks before the VMAs, but her identity wasn't confirmed until his acceptance speech on national television.

Check out this excerpt from *Entertainment*

Weekly's interview with Darius Wilson after MTV's Video Music Awards:

EW: Congratulations on Best New Artist. Were you surprised by the win?

Wilson: I really was, to be honest. I hadn't been featured too much on MTV, and my videos didn't get a lot of airplay. No one other than BET really had my back until the song from *A Hot Day in Harlem* soundtrack got released.

EW: You sound a little bitter, man.

Wilson: [*laughing*] No, not at all. Better late than never. MTV has been really supportive of my new music, and they let me play whatever I wanted at the VMAs. I couldn't be happier.

EW: Is your happiness due to your Moon Man or the new woman in your life?

Wilson: [*laughing again*] Very slick transition, dude. I would have to say both.

EW: Just a month before the VMAs, a picture of you and model Miko appeared in *US Weekly*.

Wilson: Is that a question? [*chuckles*] No, things happen. That's all I can really say.

EW: I hear your girlfriend lives in Boston. Are long-distance relationships difficult?

Wilson: Sure. But when you're in this business, every relationship is long distance, even when you live in the same city. I'm constantly traveling, so whoever I'm with has to understand that.

Below is a photo of Darius Wilson and his girl on the beach in Martha's Vineyard (thanks to T-Flav for the pic!). For all the ladies who want to know the stats on the girl who snagged one of black music's most eligible bachelors, I managed to find a few fun facts for you. Kahlila Bradford is originally from Boston and still lives there as a high school teacher. She met Darius while staying in New York for the summer (lucky her!). No, her hair is not weaved out. It's natural. She's rocking that bikini too. And she graduated from Franklin University in 1999. Props to Darius for appreciating beauty *and* brains!

Kahlila's articles about her commitment to public service had been pushed to page 17, replaced by more popular articles on gossip Web sites and fan blogs. She immediately picked up her phone to call Darius. He answered on the first ring.

"What's up, baby?" He was speaking loudly, over a din of lighthearted conversation.

"Nothing much. Whatcha doin'?" Kahlila was always careful to sound casual when asking about his whereabouts. She didn't want to become the paranoid girl who gave in to her concerns about all the women he could theoretically be meeting every moment they were apart from each other.

"I'm at dinner with a bunch of folks," he said, half laughing at a comment that someone else had made in the background.

Kahlila glanced at her bedroom clock. It was 11:15 p.m. She never got used to how late people ate in the city. "Want to call me back later?"

"We're just finishing up. It's all good. Hey, I can't wait to see you tomorrow."

Kahlila smiled. World Urban Music was throwing a congratulatory party for Darius's Best New Artist win. He'd begged them to have the event on a Saturday night just so Kahlila could attend. In New York, people seemed to party harder on Tuesday nights than they did on weekends. So she was planning to pull an all-nighter to get all her students' papers graded (which was why she was procrastinating by Googling herself). She figured she could sleep on the Chinatown bus down to New York the following morning. "Me either. Random question for you—have you ever Googled our names before?"

Darius laughed, this time at her question. "Of course I have."

"How come you never told me all the stuff that was online about us?"

"I figured you'd seen it all."

"Um, no! I hadn't."

"So are you upset about it or something?"

Kahlila thought about this question. Why exactly *was* she so worked up? "I'm not upset. I just can't believe that my students are reading all that."

"All what? There's nothing scandalous on there. I was pretty impressed, actually. There weren't even any negative comments about you on my message board."

"Your what?"

"You don't read the message board on my Web site?"

"Baby, the only time I've ever visited your Web site was after the first night we met. Once I realized that I had access to you in person, reading about you on the Internet seemed like a big waste of time."

"That makes sense. I love that about you, actually. That you're not all obsessed with the craziness."

He loves that about me? That's not the same thing as saying that he loves me, is it? She was too lost in her own head to respond.

Distracted by his dinner companions, Darius didn't notice her silence. "These fools are wilin' out. I'll call you later, okay?" He hung up before she could answer.

She stared at her cluttered desk. In one intimidating stack lay her students' summer reading reports, all of which she needed to read if she was truly going to enjoy her weekend in New York. But her laptop kept catching her eye, as its bright screen listed several more sites featuring her and Darius that she hadn't yet visited. After a few indecisive moments, she finally gave in to temptation, quickly becoming absorbed in the endless links of online gossip about herself. The glare of the computer screen began to burn her eyes, and by the time she picked up a red pen to mark the first paper, she put her head down on the desk and went to sleep.

Chapter 36

He has to root for me to
advance in my career.

"Ms. Bradford, you can't stand in front of us and act like everything is the same! How can you *not* talk about him?"

Kahlila took a deep breath in and exhaled slowly. The first Girl Talk meeting of the year had so far consisted of her avoiding answers to questions about Darius WIlson. She'd spent so much effort for the past five years not bringing her relationships into the classrooms. Always believing that it was inappropriate to talk to students about boyfriends, she'd resolved that until she was married, she would never bring a man into her students' lives. But here she was, her private life displayed on national TV, and her teenagers rightfully wanting details. What could she tell them that wouldn't compromise her professionalism?

"Ladies, this is really awkward for me. I'm an adult. You girls are my babies. It doesn't feel right for me to share this kind of stuff with you."

"Why not?" Chantal protested loudly. "We talk to you about our love lives all the time."

"Not because I ask you about it," Kahlila reminded Chantal in her most authoritarian voice.

"Okay, okay. Just tell us one thing. Where was your first date?" Bree sat poised on the edge of her seat as she awaited the answer. She was surrounded by the same girls who had barely spoken to her last school year, but whom she'd begun eating lunch with for the past week that they'd been back to school.

First date? We didn't leave the house for the first four days we were together. But I can't tell them that.

"Ms. Bradford?" The secretary's distorted voice burst through the intercom. The girls moaned and sighed in frustration.

"Yes!" Kahlila shouted back.

"Mr. Howard wants to see you," she said, clicking off the intercom before Kahlila could say that she would be right there.

"Ooooooh," sang the girls, as was customary whenever anyone got called to the principal's office.

Usually, Kahlila would be annoyed to have to leave the group, but this was actually perfect timing. She put the eighteen girls into their fall planning committees before leaving the classroom and walking to the office.

Mr. Howard had been the principal at Pierce High School since the year before Kahlila was hired. He was in his mid-forties, with a receding hairline and a stern face that could change to friendly mode at the blink of an eye. She remembered sitting down for her interview in front of an intimidating hiring committee, and Mr. Howard's saving his question for last: "What's your favorite TV show?"

She had been so relieved for the easy question that she didn't think to filter the answer for her audience.

"*Sex and the City,*" she said cheerily, as five pairs of eyebrows raised in response and Mr. Howard's serious expression changing to one of amusement.

Later, once she was hired, she told Mr. Howard how humiliated she'd been by her answer. "No reason to be embarrassed. You were being honest. I ask that question of every potential teacher, and the only wrong answer is one that isn't true. I've had people tell me that they don't own televisions, or that they only watch PBS. If I can tell that you're lying, there's no way that you're gonna last a day in the classroom. Kids smell fakers a mile away."

Kahlila respected Mr. Howard as a school leader, especially over the past couple of years that she had begun to serve on the Faculty Senate and School Site Council. He was fair, thoughtful, and believed in a system of shared responsibility. If a teacher came to him with a suggestion, his most frequent answer was "Sounds great. Get to work on it and let me know if you need any help."

She tried to guess why he might want to meet with her after school, but she couldn't think of anything. The main office was in a state of calm after dismissal, and the secretary motioned for her to walk right into his smaller private space.

Knocking on the door, she was beckoned in by Mr. Howard, who was standing next to his disheveled desk wearing an unreadable expression.

She had taken two steps inside when he asked, "How was New York last weekend?"

Kahlila blinked in surprise, as she hadn't told anyone except Madeline that she was going. "Um, the trip was fine."

"This was the first time you've ever missed our opening football game of the season. We lost, of course. Anyway, I only know you were in New York because one of our student office volunteers brought this in today," he said, motioning toward a copy of *In Touch* magazine on his desk.

Kahlila could see from where she was standing that the page contained a picture of her and Darius. The bright red Diane Von Furstenburg wrap dress that she'd borrowed from Desiree made it easy for her eyes to identify. She just nodded, not knowing exactly what to say.

"Your personal life is none of my business, Kahlila. But I will say you've seemed very happy since returning to school from the summer. We here at Pierce all think you're fantastic, and know that you deserve the best. Still, I'm a little bit concerned about how this . . . relationship might impact your role here at school." He sat down in the swivel chair behind his desk and motioned for her to take a seat as well.

"Mr. Howard, I can assure you that you will see no difference in my performance. Pierce is my first priority," she said anxiously, too nervous to sit.

"Kahlila, I know that you would never allow your students' learning to suffer. I'm only bringing this up because I see your playing a larger role in the vision of this school, and I'm curious whether your summer away has you thinking about a possible relocation." He again pointed to the empty chair.

This time she obeyed, almost missing the chair completely because she was so distracted. "Relocating has not been a point of discussion at all." She wanted to add, "We're not that serious," but she didn't exactly know if that was true. This past weekend, it was clear to Kahlila that everyone in Darius's life knew exactly who she was and what she meant to him. Executives at the label went out of their way to introduce themselves, and every female who approached him made sure to acknowledge she was there and keep conversation with Darius to a reasonable amount of time. He insisted that she pose in every picture with him, and he freely hugged her and danced with her all night. Kahlila was relieved that they were simply sitting next to each other in the picture on the principal's desk.

"Well, I'll be direct, then. Mr. Adams is retiring at the end of this year, and I'm looking to hire an assistant principal who is ready to take risks and move the school forward. I've watched you mentor new teachers, lead faculty discussions about race and culture, handle discipline issues with the most challenging students. You do it all well. How do you feel about moving into administration?"

Kahlila was speechless. She knew that Mr. Howard thought her to be a strong teacher, but to be his right-hand person in leading the school? The timing seemed almost too perfect. She had been talking with Madeline recently about her frustration with creating an environment of critical thinking and risk-taking in her classroom, only to hear students complain that with the exception of just a few teachers (Madeline's being one of them), most classes failed to engage or challenge them in any meaningful way. Kahlila longed to get into other teachers' classrooms and work with them on curriculum and instruction, but she never had time because of her own busy teaching schedule.

"I realize that you're not certified to be an administrator, so the school is willing to pay for you to start your degree part-time," he continued, handing her a folder. "The course information is in there. It starts in two weeks, and it means even more constraints on your time."

She looked through the contents of the folder, half dazed.

"You might also be unwilling to leave the classroom completely, so I'm willing to let you teach a class even in your role as assistant principal," he went on, as if his strategy were to keep talking until she said yes.

This is too good to be true. A huge pay raise, a chance to really make some positive changes in the building, a free second master's degree, and an opportunity to still teach an English class? She was just opening her mouth to say yes when a high-pitched beep sounded from her bag. Hurriedly reaching into her zippered compartment to turn off her cell phone, she saw that it was a text message from Darius: "When the Lights Go Down' is #1 song on R&B charts!

Kahlila smiled at the message, almost forgetting for a moment that she was in an important meeting. Mr. Howard's voice brought her back to the task at hand. "Don't answer me now. Give it a few days and think about it." He stood up and began walking away from his desk.

Kahlila gathered her bag and newly acquired folder, and joined him at the door. "Thank you for meeting with me. I have a lot to think about," she said, resorting her possessions so that she could shake his hand.

"I'll talk to you soon," he said with a serious expression.

She had begun to leave the main office when he called her name. The secretary had gone, and the place was deserted. "Hey, if you meet Garth Brooks or James Taylor during one of your adventures, get their autographs, would ya?" Embarrassed, he hurriedly added, "For my wife."

Kahlila giggled, happy to have a funny story to bring back to her nosy young ladies at the Girl Talk meeting.

Chapter 37

To: darius@dariuswilson.com
From: kahlila.bradford@boston.k12.ma.us
Time: Wednesday, September 13, 2006, 8:32 p.m.
Subject: the perfect day
Message:
hey, babe,

   when you said you were going to get me a webcam, i didn't know that you meant a whole new computer with a webcam in it! i got home from school in time to catch the delivery guy dropping off my brand-new sony laptop. it's fantastic, and so tiny! i'm using it right now. thank you, honey.

   so today was your promo event in atlantic city with flow, i believe. you're probably in the casinos by now. hope you're not spending too much money. i'm sure that flow is going to be at the most high-rolling tables you can sit at. don't feel like you have to sit there too. okay, enough nagging from me.

   first, congratulations on your #1 single! i had no doubt it would fly up the charts, especially with the video being as good as it is. second, i have big news: the principal of my school offered

me an assistant principal job for next september!
i just have to enroll in a master's program in a
couple of weeks so i can get certified as a school
administrator.

yay!

kahli

To: kroberts@channing.com
From: kahlila.bradford@boston.k12.ma.us
Time: Wednesday, September 13, 2006, 8:56 p.m.
Subject: Bree update
Message:

Hi Keith,

Thanks for the e-mail you sent earlier this week.
It seemed like Bree was having a good first few
days at school, but it was nice to hear that confirmed. I'm glad that you two reached an understanding about her staying in Boston for senior
year. A socially disappointing decision for Bree, I'm
sure, but she already seems to be doing a lot better
in that department. We had our first Girl Talk meeting of the year today, and Bree was voted the head
of the Events committee after presenting an idea to
the group about putting on a school play. I didn't realize what an extensive background in theater she
had. You are clearly a talented family.

Academically, we've only had a short writing
piece so far, along with their summer reading
essays, and both assignments were strong. We will
be starting college essays once we finish reading
King Lear, and I expect that it might be difficult, de-
pending on what she decides to tackle as a topic.
I'll continue to keep you posted.

Take care,

Kahlila

To: kahlila.bradford@boston.k12.ma.us
From: angelabradford@gmail.com
Time: Wednesday, September 13, 2006, 9:16 p.m.
Subject: Congrats!
Message:
Hi, honey,

I got your message from earlier today. You probably don't want to know that I spent the day at the beach with my hubby. Although you did just return from Martha's Vineyard recently, so you should be happy that your mom is getting some sun and relaxation.

Congratulations on your promotion offer! I don't know why you're so surprised, considering the years of dedication you've given to that school. It's going to be a tough year, though, balancing a full-time job with an accelerated master's program. What does Darius have to say about this development? It will definitely impact how often the two of you get to see each other. But if he's as wonderful and intelligent as you say, I'm sure he'll back you 100%.

I hope you're getting enough sleep now that you're back to work. You know you get those dark circles under your eyes when you're tired. And what are you eating these days? I'm sure you're not turning on your stove, so I hope all that takeout that you order at least consists of some leafy salads. Don't forget to take your multivitamin every day either. You're rolling your eyes by now, but it's hard for me to be so far away from my baby! I have to nag from afar.

Love you,
Mom

To: kahlila.bradford@boston.k12.ma.us
From: kroberts@channing.com
Time: Wednesday, September 13, 2006, 9:21 p.m.
Subject: Re: Bree update
Message:
Hello Kahlila,

Thank you so much for helping Bree with her disappointment about not returning to New Haven, and for keeping me in the loop about what's going on. It's that classic routine when I get home from work, where I ask her how school was, and she says, "Fine," through a mouthful of dinner with her head buried in a book. She would probably have a fit if she knew we were e-mailing each other. You're the one person she does talk about regularly, mostly about your "off the hook" clothes and your "perfect" boyfriend. Are you sure you're actually teaching *King Lear*? If you listened to Bree, you'd think you were teaching a course in becoming *America's Next Top Model* (Bree makes me watch it with her when I'm home—don't laugh).

My sister does indeed have quite a talent for acting, and has been involved in theater productions for a bunch of years. The downside is that I can't always tell when she's lying to me, but the good news is that she'll probably be rich and famous one day. Then her overworked brother can quit his job at the firm and start the nonprofit he's always dreamed about.
Take care,
Keith

To: kahlila.bradford@boston.k12.ma.us
From: darius@dariuswilson.com
Time: Thursday, September 14, 2006, 4:10 a.m.
Subject: Re: perfect day

Message:

Baby,

It's four in the morning so I'm not gonna risk your wrath by calling you. Of course I didn't follow your advice about staying off the blackjack tables with Flow, so I had to sit there until I broke even. It took a while.

That's big news about the assistant principal job, huh? I'm a little surprised to hear that it's something you're interested in. You always talk about how much you love being in the classroom. Doesn't the vice principal just send kids to detention and do lunch duty? At least, that's what mine did back in Detroit. And what's the schedule for the master's program you have to do? If classes are on weekends, that's going to be a problem, no?

I'll call you at a more decent hour. Oh, glad you like the laptop. It's cute and cool, like you. ;-)

D

To: desiree@desireethomas.com
From: kahlila.bradford@boston.k12.ma.us
Time: Thursday, September 14, 2006, 5:19 p.m.
Subject: checking in
Message:

hey, des,

i'm so sad that we didn't get to really hang out during my quick ny visit. i'm the rudest friend—showing up to your house, borrowing a dress, and then disappearing for the rest of the weekend. the party was really fun. i wish you and jason had come, but i understand that you're a lot more tired than you used to be.

i've been thinking about you a lot this week, remembering how exciting things got for you after you sold the film rights to your first book. suddenly you were being featured in women's magazines, going to movie premieres, and meeting huge stars. i kept asking you, "aren't you excited?" and you tried to explain that after the initial coolness of it all, it quickly just became your job again. even more importantly, you got to see the life you'd dreamed about for what it really was, which wasn't all it had been cracked up to be.

if you would have told me a couple of months ago that i would have been appearing in gossip magazines, attending awards shows, and having a conversation with beyoncé at her birthday party, i would have told you that you were insane. but it's already starting to feel . . . normal. does that make sense? that's not necessarily a bad thing; there's no need for me to be running around behind darius all wide-eyed forever. it's just that i feel like the novelty is wearing off, and i'm becoming more aware of some of the potential road bumps that could come along in my relationship with him.

darius and i had a long conversation this morning that has me a little uncomfortable. mr. howard, my principal, offered to pay for me to go to graduate school for a degree in administration (he offered me the assistant principal job for next year!). when darius found out that the program starts in two weeks and requires me to be in class every saturday, he had a little bit of a hissy fit. not only would it mean that i wouldn't be able to travel to see him on weekends, but it meant that even if he came to boston, i wouldn't be available. he said that he'd hoped we'd be able to see each other at least every other weekend in the fall, because his

european tour starts after christmas. so i called mr.
howard and asked if i could put off starting the
coursework until january. he said that as long as i
was earning credits toward the degree by the
spring, it was fine. so, it actually all worked out, but
i still feel funny. i've never in my life made a major
decision based on a man before. this is why
eugene and i broke up; neither of us was willing to
relocate for the other person. is this what people in
relationships do, or did i just play myself? it's not
like he's my husband, or like we've discussed a
future at all.

i'm e-mailing you because i feel like you can
relate, especially considering some of the choices
you made in your career in order to accommodate
jason's needs. i wanted to get robyn's take as well,
but she's working night shifts and has been a
walking zombie lately. besides, i'm kind of scared
that she'll cuss me out if i tell her that i decided to
put off school so that i can spend weekends with
my man. she and lloyd have never compromised
any of their aspirations for one another, which is
why they've been living in different cities for the
five years they've been together! you could argue
that the level of independence they have is either healthy or harmful to the relationship—take
your pick.

anyway, call or write.

luv,
kahli

To: kahlila.bradford@boston.k12.ma.us
From: desiree@desireethomas.com
Time: Friday, September 15, 2006, 8:48 a.m.

Subject: Re: checking in
Message:
Girl,

I'm just now checking my e-mail, and I know you're in school. So I'll start with a written response and we can continue this conversation tonight. First off, I can definitely relate to the feeling that you described: reaching a point where you're taking the fabulous experiences that you have on a daily basis for granted. Obviously, the life of a writer is never as outrageous as someone in the entertainment industry, but I did have a good stint of the types of things you've been doing with Darius: parties, media, etc.

Here's a major difference between our experiences: I was thrust into that life because of my work. My man hated the lifestyle. He thought everyone was superficial and he couldn't stand having to smile for the cameras all the time. But you—you are in the life *because* of your man. So when I was ready to go back to my behind-the-scenes existence, Jason was ecstatic. But you don't get to choose whether you want to stay out of the public eye. I'm only pointing this out because right now you are already becoming disenchanted with the life you used to read about in magazines. A few months from now, the feeling will only get worse. What are you going to do then?

Part of my decision not to move to Los Angeles and do the screenwriting thing was because Jason's whole life is in New York. And I made that decision because I love Jason more than I can even stand sometimes. You asked me about your choice to put off grad school for Darius. Well, there's nothing wrong with it . . . if your feelings match the action.

Are you planning to come to New York every weekend because you can't stand being away from him? Or are you coming because you think you should? Why *wouldn't* Darius Wilson's girlfriend want to jet-set to see him as often as possible? I really like Darius, Kahli. I do. But I wonder if you're getting deeper and deeper into this relationship because you're still just sort of surprised that he's interested in you.

You mentioned your ex, Eugene. Let's keep it real: things didn't work out because you weren't in love with him. If you were, then you would have relocated when he asked you to. There was nothing keeping you in Boston. Your mom had moved, you didn't have that many years under your belt at Pierce, and you hadn't even bought your condo yet. Meanwhile, Eugene was in a Ph.D. program and couldn't come to you. You and I both know that the last time you were in love was in college, with Dave, and that you would have gone to the edge of the earth for him. (And I should also remind you that your love for Dave and your ambivalence toward Eugene were in no way based on any sort of list. It was just a feeling you had inside you, which is the only indicator you can go on). So I'm saying all this to tell you that if you find yourself making sacrifices for Darius, ask yourself if you're falling in love. If you are, follow your heart and make it work. If you're not . . . well, let's talk more this evening.

Love,
Des

Chapter 38

He has to take risks for the greater good.

Keith wasn't exactly sure how he'd gotten himself in so deep. It began with a few e-mails back and forth about his sister. Then Kahlila was asking him about his dream of starting a nonprofit. Soon he was describing his vision of an advocacy group for males ages eighteen to twenty-five. He'd spent three years after undergrad working at a detention center for boys, and the injustice that so many of them had faced was what drove him to apply to law school. The plan was always to return to public service once he stacked enough bills doing the corporate thing. But over the past year, between his family crises and his hours at the firm, he'd almost forgotten about his lofty ambitions.

Within a week, the e-mails about his work with troubled youth turned into phone calls. Then they were planning an after-school trip for Girl Talk to visit the detention center where Keith used to work. He still spent one afternoon a month there, running a Brother to Brother discussion group (it was the one space in his schedule that his secretary knew not to touch). When Kahlila heard about it, she thought that it was a perfect opportunity for a coed rap session.

He met Kahlila, his sister, and fifteen additional teenage girls in front of Pierce high school at three that afternoon. The girls were giggly and a bit awkward, knowing that they were on their way to sit down with a group of boys their own age who had gotten into some type of trouble that ended them up in a detention facility. But Keith was feeling just as uncomfortable, greeting Kahlila with a clumsy handshake and talking to her without quite looking her in the eye. He wasn't sure exactly what had him so nervous. A part of it was his worry that the event they had planned wouldn't go well. He had a lot of faith in the boys he'd been working with, but they were never completely predictable. Another source of anxiousness was being around Kahlila and Bree at the same time. Though he knew the moment he had shared with Kahlila was long past, he hoped that his sister didn't sense the attraction that he felt for her teacher.

Everything was going smoothly as the whole group hopped on the Green Line to travel to the detention center. The train was surprisingly empty, and Kahlila plopped down next to Keith in a small row of just two seats and began talking as if they were already in the midst of a conversation.

"You should call my friend J.T. He has a foundation in New Jersey that does a lot of charitable work. He would be a great contact when you were ready to get your organization started," Kahlila said, taking her brown leather messenger bag from off her shoulder and placing it at her feet.

"Yeah? Did he get a lot of grants and private funding at first?" Keith tried to position his legs so that they didn't touch hers, but there was limited space for their long limbs and her bag to share.

"Probably. But he's pretty loaded himself," she answered before yelling to the girls in front of her to lower their voices. "He used to play pro ball."

"Hold up," Keith said, twisting his body toward her. "J.T. Steinway is your boy?"

Kahlila nodded. "We have one more stop, right?"

"So hanging out with rich people is what you do on the regular, huh?" he probed, ignoring her question.

"Not at all! I know J.T. from high school. Before the money," she said, seemingly eager to avoid some type of gold-digger label.

"So is J.T. how you met Darius?" Keith knew he was being uncharacteristically nosy, but he'd wanted to know how the whole thing went down from the moment he saw her on TV.

He couldn't tell if she heard his question or not, because the train suddenly lurched to a stop and Kahlila was yelling to the girls that it was time to rock and roll.

Two hours later, the group emerged from the center wearing huge grins. But no one was happier than Keith. Any hesitation that he had felt allowing Kahlila to plan the agenda was erased in their first few minutes after bringing the boys and girls together. She had arranged for pizza to be delivered to the rec room, and they actually began with a half hour of social time before the organized discussion began. By the time Keith wheeled in the TV to begin the conversation, everyone was laughing and comfortable.

Kahlila was the one who posed the idea of using the music industry as a springboard for dialogue about the depiction of masculinity and femininity in popular culture. Keith couldn't help but wonder when she first suggested it how influenced she had been by her famous boyfriend to choose an entertainment focus. But he went along with it, and from the moment Kahlila played the first snippet of the Snoop Dogg video she had chosen, everyone was hooked.

What followed was an animated discussion about violence, "video hos," and victimization in current day hip-hop. The kids were so thoughtful and passionate about the topic that Kahlila and Keith had stepped out of the conversation and were listening as they munched on a few slices of leftover pizza. So they hadn't seen it coming when Jarrell and Jaquan suddenly stood up and got in each other's faces because of a disagreement over whether a certain rapper had lost his street cred because of his radio-friendly tracks. Their voices were steadily rising as Keith approached them, but Bree reached the two furious boys first.

"Guys," she said with a smile, stepping into the small space between them. "You have sixteen sweet ladies here joining you today. We're supposed to be having a good time. Let's not wreck it over something small. Okay?" She touched Jarrell's arm lightly and he looked at her hand, surprised to find it there.

The room was so silent that Keith could hear Kahlila's deep breaths. Jarrell's face softened and he nodded at Bree. "My bad, ladies," he mumbled, and sat back down in his seat with his arms folded. Jaquan quickly followed suit, and the train smoothly returned to its tracks.

As Keith walked ahead of the group to their aboveground

transit stop, he was almost bursting with pride in his sister. Seeing Bree diffuse that situation with absolutely no fear in her eyes reminded him of exactly how much she was like their mother: strong and nurturing.

He hadn't noticed that Kahlila had walked up and was standing next to him. "So, that was pretty great, huh?"

"Definitely," he said with a smile, suddenly almost running to stay in step with Kahlila. Looking at her feet, he saw that she was wearing three-inch heels. The only time he'd ever seen her walk was the middle of the night after several drinks, so her long stride was new to him. They reached the tracks of what old-school Bostonians still called the "trolley," and settled against the wall to wait. It was a warm day for early October, and Keith had to put his hand over his eyes to see Kahlila in the glare of the sun. They stood facing one another, not saying anything, until the train announced its arrival with a loud rumble. Quickly breaking eye contact, they focused their attention on getting all of the girls on board. Watching Kahlila climb the stairs onto the trolley car, he couldn't help but appreciate her figure and remember the feeling of her nestled against his body in the middle of the night.

They slid into a pair of seats, and Kahlila stared out of the window at Boston University's campus. She seemed lost in her own thoughts when four of the girls sitting closest to them began singing "Make My Life Real." Kahlila's cheeks were flushed with embarrassment as she turned toward them and pleaded with them to stop singing.

"Do we sound that bad, Ms. Bradford?" Emily asked in a whine.

"No, you're just . . . disrupting the other people on the train," Kahlila said brusquely, returning her gaze to the window.

"You're pretty possessive over your boyfriend's songs, huh?" Keith said with a nudge.

"They're just always trying to bring him into the conversation somehow. It's frustrating," she said softly, making sure that none of the girls were looking in their direction.

"But can you blame them? They have a direct link to their favorite singer. I know Bree sees it that way," he said, matching her quiet tone.

"I guess. But I feel weird talking about him to people. It's like I'm trying to make it more than it is or something."

"I mean, he shouted you out on TV. It has to be pretty serious."

She paused, considering his comment. "Darius and I were really tight this summer, definitely. But now that I'm back to my regular schedule, I don't feel like he really knows me. I got to see so much of his life, but he hasn't seen any of mine."

Keith was surprised, not by what she said, but that she was actually confiding in him about it. "You gotta get him to meet these kids. Once he sees how cool they are, and how great you are with them, he'll understand why you give so much of your time to your job."

"Right," she scoffed. "I should have him come sit in the back of the room while I teach a class. I'm sure the kids won't even notice he's there."

"Well, why don't you have him come perform at Pierce?"

"I couldn't ask him to do that."

"Kahli, you're not an obsessed fan. You're his girlfriend. You can ask him whatever you want."

This statement was clearly a revelation to her, as she tilted her head thoughtfully and returned her eyes to the view outside. Keith wasn't sure exactly why he was giving

Kahlila advice about how to make Darius appreciate her more. There was no question that Keith was interested in her himself. He felt like he knew her better than he really did, because of how often his sister told stories about her: jokes in class, deep conversations during Girl Talk. He also felt more ready to date someone than he had been when they first met during the summer. Traci had just broken up with him and his head had been spinning. But now he felt closure with Traci, and a new sense of peace with Bree. Even though his schedule was still hectic and stressful, he knew that he could make time for someone special. Especially someone who was so clearly "*about* something," something so similar to his own desires to make a difference in teenagers' lives.

But Kahlila didn't enter my world to make a difference in my life. She came along to make a difference in Bree's. To see his sister smiling and happy was more than he could ask for, and he decided to focus on that satisfied feeling as they all rode together back to where they'd started.

Chapter 39

He has to be flexible.

Later that evening, Kahlila and Darius sat at their desks in their respective cities, staring at their calendars. They were trying to solidify a "visitation schedule" that would take them through Thanksgiving. Because Darius had to spend a few weekends on the West Coast to do some more recording for his album, the available time to see each other was limited. As it stood, Kahlila was going to meet Darius in Miami for Columbus Day weekend, and she was going to a Halloween party with him in New York at the end of the month. He was trying to convince her to come to Los Angeles for a long weekend that she had in November, but she was resisting.

"Do you know how tired I'll be at school, trying to fit a cross-country trip in three days, including travel time?"

"I don't understand. You guys get personal days, right?"

"I only get four. I already used one last time I came

down there. My principal is looking to make sure my performance doesn't slip."

Darius didn't say anything, and Kahlila could picture his frustration on the other end of the phone.

Trying to change the subject, she launched into an animated description of her day. "You wouldn't believe how amazing my afternoon was. I took my Girl Talk group to this detention center for boys," she began, her voice picking up enthusiasm with each additional sentence. She was just at the part where Jarrell and Jaquan began to argue when she heard the sound of fingers typing on the other end of the phone. "Um, what are you doing?"

"I'm e-mailing you the link to the hotel that we're staying at on South Beach. You're going to love it. If you were happy on the beach in the Vineyard, you're gonna lose your mind at the sight of the Shore Club's pool."

Kahlila was rendered speechless for a moment, but she was never at a loss for words very long. "Were you even listening to me?"

"Of course I was," Darius retorted. "You took your girls group to meet some juvenile delinquents."

Though his voice was teasing, Kahlila was annoyed. "That's really not funny."

"Kahlila." It wasn't a full sentence, but it carried the weight of how bothered he was by the growing tension in their conversation. "Obviously, I was kidding about the boys being delinquents. I've probably had more experience in Detroit with friends of mine in the juvenile justice system than you've had at your college prep high school in Boston. Second, even though the schools aren't my passion, I listen to every story you tell me."

"Not your passion?" Kahli repeated incredulously. "Do you think ten-hour-long studio sessions are my passion? Of course they aren't. But I've become more interested in them because you've exposed me over the last couple of months." Remembering Keith's encouragement to show Darius her life in Boston, she added, "You would love Bree if you got to know her."

"Who's Bree?" he asked offhandedly.

Kahlila forced herself to take a deep breath before responding. "I've only been talking about this girl for a month. I know your publicist, your bodyguard, your manager, your tour manager, your label head, your—"

"But you spent all summer here. I haven't even been to Boston once."

"That's the point. You need to come here. It's all good to meet up in Miami and all these wonderful places, but you're not going to fully understand who I am until you see my world. And my world is here—at my school, at my condo, at my gym, at my grocery store—"

Darius laughed. "Grocery store? Don't even front like you cook meals in Boston."

Kahlila felt herself smiling, despite herself. "No. But I buy the lunch meat for my sandwiches there."

"Yeah, that's what I thought. See, I know you better than you think I do. But seriously, Kahli, I didn't realize how important it was that I visit Boston. I figured it didn't matter, since your family doesn't live there or anything. When do you want me to come?"

She hesitated. "I had this idea, but you'll probably think it's crazy."

"Tell me."

"Every year, on the morning before Thanksgiving, my school has a huge prep rally before the big football game the next day. We lose the game every year, but the pep rally is still a major event. The cheerleaders do a routine, and the band plays, that kind of thing."

"Uh-huh," he said with a get-to-the-point lilt in his voice.

"So the rally always opens with someone singing the

Star-Spangled Banner." She stopped there, figuring that he could deduce what she was asking.

He quickly picked up on her hint. "You've never heard me sing the Star-Spangled Banner. It's not a good idea to book an artist without hearing the material first."

Though Kahlila hated how difficult their long-distance relationship had become, she did love that she could still feel the warmth of Darius's smile through the phone. "I'm listening. Audition for me."

He set his phone down in front of him and began to belt out broad stripes and bright stars. His voice effortlessly hit the critical notes of the song, and Kahlila felt the goose bumps on her arms. The private concerts that he occasionally treated her to were even more special than her being publicly acknowledged on television. As she cradled the phone to her ear, she felt as if there were no one else on earth but the two of them. It occurred to her how much she loved that feeling. And she wondered if having to work so hard to block out the rest of the world was why she'd banned celebrities from her List in the first place.

Chapter 40

*He must follow through
with his promises.*

Darius felt the grit in his eyes when his alarm clock went off at 5:30 a.m. He tried to blink the dryness away, but his limited sleep that night was working against him. Flow Steddie had thrown a party the night before at Stereo to celebrate Thanksgiving two days early. Darius had laughed when Flow suggested a Thanksgiving party at the club. "Isn't Thanksgiving supposed to be time with family and turkey?" he'd asked.

"Look, my New York peoples *are* my family, turkey!" Flow shot back.

So they'd spent the evening in the company of folks whom Flow had invited via a massive text message. His guest list included label mates, video girls, producers and managers, groupies, promoters, models, actors, and strangers willing to spend five hundred dollars on bottle service. Darius was surprised by how many people were still in town two nights before Thanksgiving, but apparently everyone intended to head home the following day. He had the same game plan. First was a stop in Boston to perform at Kahlila's school. After a day and a night with his girl, he would fly to Detroit to spend a few days with his own family. Even as he drank champagne in a booth near the deejay, he could taste his mom's homemade stuffing and gravy.

Most of the evening at the club was spent networking with a couple of artists he wanted on his album. The rest of the time, he watched the majority of people have a lot more fun than he was having. Flow had recently broken up with Rhonda, and was enjoying all of the female attention coming his way. Even though Flow was sitting just a few feet away from him, Darius wasn't even getting a second look. It was pretty well known by this point that he had a girlfriend whom he didn't cheat on. But Darius found himself wishing that someone would kick a little flirtation in his direction, simply because he was so bored. When Kahlila first returned to Boston, they used to send text messages back and forth all night whenever he was at parties in the city. But after the first few weeks, she began to complain that she wasn't getting enough sleep to function at work during the day. She would call him on her lunch break and suck her teeth in disgust that he was just waking up. So even though he was dying to send a message to her saying how much he couldn't wait to see her in the morning, he looked at his watch and decided against it.

Rasheed was already at his mom's house in Virginia to celebrate the holiday. Had he been there, he would have warned Darius about drinking Patrón after two glasses of champagne. He would also have made sure that Darius left the club early enough to get some sleep before his flight to Boston. But because Darius was on his own, he settled back into his seat and started throwing back drinks, which kept appearing in his hand without his having to order them. With every sip, he retreated deeper into his thoughts about Kahlila, and how much their relationship had changed over their short time together.

Miami in October had been fantastic in some ways, and awkward in others. They spent most of the weekend lounging by the pool and relaxing in bed, neither one of them feeling any inclination to get out and explore the city. Because it was such an upscale hotel, no one looked twice in their direction. Kahlila commented on multiple occasions how nice it felt to be left alone. Darius agreed with her, but at the same time, he couldn't help but feel defensive. *She acts like it's my fault that we don't get to be around each other very much. Our limited time is just as much because of her job as it is because of mine.*

But his mood was soothed whenever he looked to his right and watched Kahlila's skin bronze in the sun. When she dove into the pool, did a leisurely backstroke through the water, and emerged several minutes later, there wasn't a single model he'd worked with who could touch her at that moment. He found himself flashing back to that image—jet-black curls clinging to her face, bright orange string biniki, glistening copper skin—over and over again in the weeks to come. It bothered him that his perception of Kahlila had become so relegated to the physical, when their relationship was predicated upon a bond that was so much deeper than that. But he was having a harder and harder time remembering what that bond was exactly.

Lately, it felt to Darius like he and Kahlila were battling for airtime, as if each person needed to be reassured that the other cared about who they were and what they did. Each story he told about recording the album or writing a song was quickly followed with a story from her about a class she taught or a field trip she planned. He wondered if his visit to Pierce High School the following day might get things back to a state of equilibrium. He was eager to prove to her that she didn't have to make him take an interest in her life. He already had a genuine curiosity about her existence in Boston.

At four o'clock in the morning, he finally got the energy to get up from the booth, give Flow a pound good-bye, and catch a cab outside. He silently congratulated himself on remembering to set his alarm, and fell asleep before another thought could enter his mind.

The ninety minutes of unconsciousness felt like ninety seconds when the loud buzzing jolted him awake. After a few shocked moments, he instinctually hit the snooze button to get a few more precious minutes of shut-eye. But the next sound to rouse him was the ring of his cell phone. He fumbled for it on his nightstand, and flipped it open without even opening his lids.

"Hello." His voice was hoarse, as if he'd been shouting at the top of his lungs for hours straight.

"Oh, good. I thought you might still be in the air. How far away are you?" Kahlila's voice was full of energy.

Darius's eyes flew open and he zoomed in on the red numbers on his digital clock: 8:30. His flight had been at 7:15. And he was still in bed.

"Shit. Shit! Baby, I am so sorry. I must've hit the Off button instead of Snooze on my alarm. I'm not sure what happened." He was suddenly on his feet, pacing back and forth in his bedroom.

"Are you telling me that you're in New York right now?" Her voice was soft, but far from calm.

"I am so sorry," he repeated. The words sounded empty even to him.

"Okay. Okay. We can figure this out. It's a half day at

school today, which means that the kids are here until noon. You'll miss the pep rally, but as long as you get here by then, you can get on the intercom or something. Wish them a happy Thanksgiving or whatever. There are flights out of New York every half hour, I'm sure. You should be able to catch something." Kahlila sounded like she was pacing the floor as well.

"Kahli, it's the day before Thanksgiving. It may not be that easy." He was saying this partly because it was true, and partly because standing up made him realize what a pounding headache he had. Rushing to the airport as he suffered from a hangover did not sound like fun.

"Darius. The whole school is expecting you. Some kid called the local news. There are cameras here. You can't not show up." The tension in her voice was audible. "Disappointing a thousand students because you're too lazy to get on a plane and get here is not an option."

Her last comment changed his mood from apologetic to angry. It was bad enough that his head felt like it was going to explode. He didn't need a lecture when he already felt guilty. "Are you worried about the kids, or are you worried about yourself? Scared that your coworkers might think that things aren't going well with your famous boyfriend?"

"Hold on."

Darius could hear her high heels clicking on the floor, as she was most likely moving to an unpopulated area of the school building.

"I can't believe you just said that to me. How dare you try to turn the tables so *I* look like the bad guy?"

Her voice was catching in her throat, and Darius realized that he had never heard Kahlila cry before.

Remorse flooded his body before she finished her first sniffle. "I'm being an asshole. Lemme call the airlines and see what I can do."

"No, it's fine," she said, her voice more composed. He could picture her on the other end of the phone, wiping her eyes. "That was a stupid idea that I had anyway. My principal is not gonna go for an all-school serenade over the intercom."

Darius sighed. "I blew it, Kahli. I feel like shit."

"I think I'm just upset because I'm not going to see my mom for Thanksgiving, and I was really looking forward to this as the highlight of my holiday." She sounded like she might cry again.

"I have an idea," said Darius, a smile appearing on his face for the first time that morning. "Lemme call you back in an hour."

"Okay. I have to go to this pep rally anyway, and figure out what to say." She took a deep breath and exhaled, hanging up without saying good-bye.

Kahlila's phone vibrated in her hand right as the Pierce Big Band was playing the school's fight song. She quickly exited the gymnasium and ran a far enough distance away so that she could hear herself talk. "Hello?"

"So there's nothing to Boston until really late tonight, which seemed like a waste since I have to go to Detroit first thing in the morning."

Kahlila felt the disappointment in her stomach.

"But here's what I did—I booked myself a flight home from New York for tomorrow, and I changed the reservation I had from Boston so that it's now in your name."

Not sure that she understood, she asked, "Say that again?"

"I guess I should back up. Would you please come with me to meet my crazy-ass family in Detroit for Thanksgiving?" There was a playful mischief in his tone that caused Kahlila to smirk despite herself.

She had plans to go to a restaurant with Keith and Bree the next evening for Thanksgiving dinner, and she had actually been looking forward to it. But this was Darius's effort at reconciliation, and she felt like she had to accept. Besides, it was a pretty big deal to meet a guy's entire family. *Maybe this relationship has more of a future than I gave it credit for.*

"So, what's your mom cooking?" She grinned at the sound of Darius laughing on the other end of the phone.

Chapter 41

*I have to feel at home around his
family, especially his mom.*

Kahlila's Thanksgivings were always quiet. When her
mom lived in Boston, they celebrated the holiday in sub-
dued fashion with an adult dinner for eight. Her grandmother, aunt, uncle, and cousins usually devoured food
before splitting into two rooms to watch football or play
board games. She had spent last year in Trinidad, where
Thanksgiving obviously wasn't celebrated, eating shrimp
roti and soaking up the autumn sun on her mom and
stepdad's patio.

Her prior Thanksgiving experiences had in no way
prepared her for Detroit with the Wilson family. After
meeting up with Darius at the airport and driving with
him in a rental car to their modest home right outside
the city, she stood in the driveway and raised her eyebrows at the volume coming from the windows. It
sounded like there were fifty people inside screaming
over one another. For a moment, her mind traveled to

the serene evening she had planned with Keith and Bree. When she canceled her dinner with them, they decided to accept an invitation from Joey and his wife to spend the day at their house with several Big Dig employees. Bree wasn't so thrilled about it, but refrained from complaining since Keith was allowing her to travel to New Haven the following day for a weekend with Krystal and Stanley, to whom she spoke on the phone every night for at least an hour. But the excited look on Darius's face brought Kahlila back to her current reality, and she flashed him a smile.

Kahlila tried to hide her shock when they walked inside and there were only six people sitting in front of her. Everyone in the kitchen burst out laughing as they entered, which made Kahlila feel as if she had interrupted some private joke. Darius went around the room kissing cheeks, as he was apparently the only male at the function. Knowing that women were generally a tougher audience, Kahlila stretched her smile extra wide. Each person looked at her warily, not moving to even shake her hand. Even the toddler sitting on her mother's lap gave her a frown. She was glad when they got through everyone and Darius suggested that they go into the den to meet his mom. *These people probably haven't heard of me before. But he told his mom I was coming, and that wasn't the first time she'd heard my name. Maybe she'll be friendlier.*

"I hope you're not sensitive to cigarette smoke," he said softly as he swung open the door to a room down the hallway from the kitchen.

She had no time to answer before she was assaulted by a white cloud of Marlboro-generated emissions. She choked a little and put her smile back on as they walked inside. Three older women, approximately the same age, size, and complexion, sat on a couch watching what looked to be a soap opera on the big-screen television in front of them. "Darius! You're standing right in front of the TV," the woman sitting in the middle barked.

Kahlila had to smile at her pronunciation of "TV." She often teased Darius about his emphasis on the first syllable of that word, as if it were spelled Teee-Vee, and this woman said it the exact same way.

Darius quickly jumped back so as not to obstruct their view. "Mom, Aunties, I wanted you all to meet Kahli."

"Of course we will, honey. We'll see y'all after you eat. Go get some food in the kitchen so I can finish watching my stories," the same woman responded with a dismissive wave of her hand.

Darius shrugged good-naturedly and walked out of the room, Kahlila following behind. Closing the door softly, Darius said, "So, that was Mom and her sisters. We're not much into formalities around here."

She didn't know how to answer, so she focused on the delicious-smelling food that permeated the house. The opportunity to eat was doubly welcomed by Kahlila: she was starving, and she was happy to use the excuse of her mouth being full as a reason not to make conversation. Another burst of laughter exploded as they reentered the kitchen, and she pretended to fully concentrate on piling her plate with salad, turkey, ham, baked macaroni and cheese, stuffing, gravy, rice, and vegetables.

Once she settled into a wooden folding chair on the opposite side of the room from Darius (no one volunteered to make room so they could sit next to each other), Kahlila realized that she hadn't need to worry about contributing to the discussion. There simply wasn't any room. She could barely keep track of where to direct her attention: Aunt Pat, who was telling an animated story about her stepfather's ex-wife who had worked some voodoo on her when she was little, or cousin Donna, who was swearing up and down that Mexicans hate black people more than white supremacists do, or little niece Zakia, who was proclaiming Ciara to be a more talented performer than Beyoncé. Kahlila shot a look at Darius to see if he'd noticed the teenager's outlandish statement, but he sent her an unspoken warning with his eyes to let it go.

She realized that the only way she could gain points in this crowd was to eat a lot of food and try her best to listen to and laugh at all of the stories that were crisscrossing one another at the speed of light. Kahlila did enjoy observing how Darius was treated by the women in his family. They alternated between ignoring him completely and overwhelming him with attention. Not once did anyone mention his career. All conversation directly addressed to him concerned his more immediate needs: "You got enough food, baby?" "You look cold, sitting over there. Want me to turn up the heat?"

Kahlila finally felt as if she'd gotten into the raucous rhythm that was his family when she was summoned into the "other" room. Cousin Donna had gone in there to check on the three elder stateswomen, and returned to announce that they wanted to see "Darius girl." *No apostrophe S,* thought Kahlila as she tried not to cringe. The kitchen crew loudly sang their "Oooooohs" as if her name had just come over the intercom to go to the principal's office. Darius simply raised an amused eyebrow as she hesitatingly raised herself from her chair, feeling self-conscious of standing among a group of sitting women. Their eyes traveled up and down her body, not with any malicious intent, but with the judging gaze that the families of princes can never turn off.

The other room was just as smoky as when she'd visited it earlier. She knew better than to cough as she entered the dense fog, and willed her lungs to accept the intense battering.

"So, you enjoying yourself, sweetheart?" Darius's mother was a short, thick woman with smooth skin the exact same golden color as her son's.

You would think her skin would be all wrinkled if she smokes like this every day. "Definitely. Thank you so much for welcoming me," Kahlila said.

"Mm-hmm. Girl, as soon as I saw you I had to send you back into that kitchen to get you something to eat. You are too skinny, and you ain't even a model, right?"

Kahlila laughed. "I'm a teacher."

"Right, right. Darius told me that. That's real nice. I worked thirty years as a teacher's aide before I retired last year." It was at this moment that Kahlila realized that Ms. Wilson's two sisters were not going to speak at all. They were simply observers of a one-on-one conversation, and would most likely give their commentary on it once she left the room.

"So, Kahlila, what do you like about my son?"

Unprepared for such a dramatic subject change, she shifted a little bit on her feet. There was an empty chair next to the couch, but she didn't dare sit down without being invited. "Oh, wow. There's so much."

"Name something."

"Okay . . ." She felt her heart beating. "He's really outgoing, and kind, and intelligent."

"What about his voice? You like that, right?"

"Of course. But when I met him, I was attracted to how down-to-earth he was more than the fact that he could sing."

"He gotta be down-to-earth coming from this family, honey. When Darius comes home, ain't no special treatment 'cause he's makin' a little money and got some little girls chasin' after him." She did an apologetic wave of the hand to express that she wasn't referring to Kahlila.

Kahlila nodded in understanding, though she

couldn't help wondering if his mom was actually direct-ing that insult at her.

"So Darius has never brought a girl back to Detroit before, even that one from his job who he was with for quite a minute. Now I'm a little bit confused. You live in Boston?"

"I do," she said, tugging on the sleeve of her sweater nervously.

"How is that gonna work? You leaving your job?"

"No, I'm not," Kahlila answered eagerly. "I'm getting a promotion at school, so I'll probably be there a little while." Thinking that his mom would be happy that she wasn't looking to crowd her son, she was surprised at the look of displeasure she received in return.

"Honey, Darius only has a few months left being able to do this whole everyday lifestyle thing. When the next album comes out, he's gonna be on another level. If y'all two get married, there's no way you can be holding down a regular job when he has to go this way and that way."

Married? Kahlila must have shown her shock all over her face, because one of the sisters chuckled.

"Don't get me wrong," his mother continued. "It's nice that you're independent. But you gotta think about what you really want, girl. 'Cause there's no room for it to be about you too, if you decide to be with Darius for real."

"What about Will and Jada?" the chuckling sister asked. "They both have careers."

"They both movie stars. It's different." Finally motion-ing for Kahlila to sit in the empty chair, Darius's mom studied her carefully. "I'm gonna be honest, child. You don't seem all that into my son. When y'all both came in here, I didn't feel any kind of vibe. But at the same time, you don't seem to be all wrapped up in the glitz and glamour either. I just can't figure you out."

A silence followed, at which point Kahlila realized that she was supposed to explain herself. "I'm sorry, Ms. Wilson, if I don't seem excited to be here. I am. It's just that this trip was a surprise, and because I hadn't planned for it, my mind is all over the place. I have so many papers to grade and things to plan at school, and I'm thinking about my own family, whom I haven't spoken to yet today—"

"Girl, lemme tell you. If you're really in this, and I know Darius really wants you to be, you're not even gonna be able to keep that job for long. You got your own dreams and goals. That's great. But something's gotta give. Okay. You can go back to the kitchen now." She picked up the remote control on the coffee table in front of the couch and turned up the volume on the Teee-Vee.

There was nothing left for Kahlila to do but get up and leave. She wished she didn't have to return to the kitchen. It was so loud that she wouldn't be able to think. And apparently, she had a lot of thinking to do.

Chapter 42

He has to make grand romantic
overtures every once in a while.

Two weeks after Thanksgiving came Pierce's production of *For Colored Girls Who'd Considered Suicide When the Rainbow Is Enuf.* Bree was playing the Lady in Blue, and she directed the play as well. Twice in the past few days she got in trouble in Kahlila's class for hiding the notated script behind her copy of *The Scarlet Letter.*

As faculty adviser for the production, Kahlila had been spending many late nights at school for dress rehearsals and sound checks. She was grateful for the distraction, as her head was spinning since her weekend in Detroit. Even though the first few hours in her boyfriend's hometown had been rocky, she'd ended up having a fantastic time. After the interrogation session with his mom in the "smoke room," she was met in the kitchen by hysterical laughter and a tall glass of "Wicked Wilson Punch," which cousin Donna said she'd earned after facing the Three Sisters. After guzzling the rum-based concoction, she'd settled back in her folding chair, taking in the sights and sounds in a completely new way. What had previously been deafening noise was now an almost musical conversation, with highs, lows, stops, and starts. The rhythm finally became clear to her, and she was able to punctuate the rests with quarter notes of her own, seamlessly blending into the family's composition.

Even Darius's mom had become less intimidating, when Kahlila earned extra points that evening for knowing all the words to the Motown hits playing on the stereo after dinner. They had even more to talk about when his mother noticed the cameo ring that Kahlila was wearing. The next morning, before Darius woke up, Kahlila helped her fix breakfast (the only meal she was good at preparing), explaining that she wanted to find a middle ground between having her own separate life and abandoning her career completely. By the end of the weekend, Ms. Wilson held her tightly in her chubby arms and said that she'd better see her again real soon.

Before the trip was even over, Kahlila felt confident in the decision that she'd talked out with Ms. Wilson, and then Darius, to leave Pierce at the end of the school year. There were plenty of schools in New York that would be happy to have her. It seemed like the logical compromise between maintaining the long-distance relationship and leaving teaching altogether. Darius was thrilled by the prospect, leaving a message for his real estate agent while they were still in Detroit that his girlfriend would be working with her to find a place to live. Kahlila couldn't help but catch his excitement. *It's not like I'm going to New York and latching on to his life. I'll still have my own job, my own apartment, and my own friends.* She even called Desiree right before she boarded the plane back to Boston, who squealed in delight that her best friend would be closer to her, Jason, and her baby boy, due in January.

That Sunday evening, after she unpacked her bags and dove into a pile of essays at her desk, her cell phone rang. Seeing Keith's name on the screen caused an odd jolt in her stomach. She hadn't thought about him since that moment in the driveway of the Wilsons' house in Detroit. Though she had successfully exorcised him from her mind for the entire weekend, she was suddenly hungry to hear about his and Bree's holiday.

They cheerfully exchanged hellos, and Keith explained, "I figured I'd check in while I waited for Bree at the train station. She should be here in a few minutes."

"I'm sure she had a great time in Connecticut."

"Yeah. Too great. I spoke to her yesterday, and apparently, she and that dude Stanley are now officially back together, whatever that means. They can't possibly talk on the phone any more than they already do."

"So I take it you don't approve?"

"I don't know the kid, so I'm not sure what to think about it."

"She's mentioned him a lot this year. Sounds like he has plans for his future, headed to the West Coast most likely to play basketball for UCLA." Kahlila pushed her essays aside to fully concentrate on the conversation.

"Well, that explains why Bree's college list has so many California schools on it," Keith muttered.

Kahlila couldn't help but smile at Keith's fatherly concern. "Why don't you have Bree invite him to Boston so you can check him out?"

"Yeah, right. And have him stay in my house?"

"Wouldn't you rather him sleeping in your living room than having Bree meet up with him at Krystal's house?"

"This is true," he admitted. "There's definitely not

much privacy at my crib . . . as you know," he laughed uncomfortably.

Kahlila was surprised at the subtle reference to her sleepover at his place back in June. Their first encounter was something about which they never spoke. But it was somehow freeing to hear him bring it up, as if they were far enough past it for it not to matter.

"Every once in a while, I think about how crazy it would have been if Bree had seen that it was you under those covers," he continued.

Kahlila tried to find her voice, but his nonchalant statement had a stronghold on her throat. It had never occurred to her that it was Bree who entered the room that summer morning. She always assumed that Keith had in fact been a player of sorts. It made it easier to dismiss him as a romantic possibility. Every time he took more than a few hours to answer an e-mail, she assumed that he was out with one of the women he was dating. When she saw him take a call on his cell and talk softly into the receiver, she imagined the girl on the other end of the phone. After all, he never spoke about his social life, so she figured that he had plenty to hide. And while all of that might still be true, she was shocked by the fact that she no longer had any proof that Keith was anything but an honest, single guy, working hard to take care of his little sister.

"Oh—here she comes, with a big old grin on her face. I'll talk to you later," he said cheerily.

"Bye," Kahlila managed to choke out, flipping her phone shut and staring at it like it had just betrayed her.

The next day at school, she couldn't bring herself to go see Mr. Howard and tell him that she was turning down the assistant principal position. Each time she took

a step in that direction, her mind flashed back to the
morning almost six months ago when Bree's dramatic
entrance into her brother's room interrupted a thought
that Keith could indeed be something special. She remembered how respectful he had been the night before,
and how he offered to drive her home the next day.
She'd been so angry that she barely let him get a word
out to explain himself.

She tried again the following day to take the trip to the
principal's office and announce her plans. On her way
down the hallway, Bree intercepted her and gave her a
huge bear hug. "Keith said that Stanley could come to
Boston for the weekend of my play! He said that it was your
idea. Thank you, thank you, thank you!" Bree skipped
away wearing a huge grin. Kahlila remembered seeing her
many times in the cafeteria or the library last school year,
and never once glimpsing a smile on her face. Something
about their brief exchange in the hall made her turn
around and head back to her classroom without talking
with Mr. Howard. She rationalized that she might as well
wait until after the play was over and done with to say anything formally.

"Thinkin' won't do me a bit of good tonight. I need to
be loved. And haven't the audacity to say 'where are
you?' and don't know who to say it to," Bree swooned
from the stage, the words smoothly flowing from her
lips. Her head was wrapped in a blue silk scarf, and a
matching sarong was slung around her waist. Her bare
feet walked the stage with the confidence of a seasoned
actor, and the vulnerability of her love-seeking character.

"She's incredible," whispered Robyn to Kahlila as they
sat mesmerized in the second row of the theater. Robyn
was excited that her time off from work coincided with

opening night for the play. Kahlila had been gushing about it for weeks, and was hoping that both Robyn and Desiree could have made it to the show. But Desiree's doctor told her that she might have little Langston a few weeks early, so she was staying close to home.

Kahlila nodded, stealing a glance at Keith and Stanley sitting side by side in the row in front of them. Their facial expressions were identical, as they listened intently to every syllable spoken by their number-one girl. Kahlila had spent a little bit of time with Stanley before the play began, and he made a good initial impression. He was a handsome kid, tall and athletic, with a quick smile and a quiet demeanor. He seemed appropriately intimidated by Keith's stern questioning, and appropriately enamored by Bree's beauty and talent. Bree made eye contact with him briefly from the stage, and her performance became even more fiery in that moment.

As the play moved to its dramatic conclusion, Kahlila wondered if she should have invited Darius after all. He'd even asked if he could attend, but she thought it might take the attention away from Bree and the rest of the cast. She also promised Bree that she would spend some time that weekend with her, Stanley, and Keith. "My brother is so much less scary when you're around. I don't want Stanley to be nervous," she'd begged.

But this would have been the perfect occasion for her to share her Boston world with Darius, as he still hadn't visited a single time. He'd carved out a few days over the holidays, but she was headed to Trinidad to spend Christmas with her mom. As it stood, their next scheduled face-to-face time was New Year's Eve in Times Square. Darius was performing on a Dick Clark–type television special with several big-name artists. Kahlila knew that his mom had been right. The new album wasn't even out yet, and he had already been thrown into another level of fame.

Kahlila was so far in her own head about Darius that she missed the moment when the entire audience collectively rose to its feet for a standing ovation. She quickly joined them, beaming as Bree stepped forward to take her bow. She spotted Madeline standing at the far end of the auditorium, flashing her the thumbs-up sign. Madeline had been so helpful over the past few days, selling tickets and handling last-minute snafus. The applause swelled and Bree's cheeks flushed at the accolades. Stanley stepped forward and handed her a bouquet of roses that he'd been hiding under his chair. She looked like she might cry when the curtain closed and separated them.

"Can I go backstage?" Stanley asked Kahlila breathlessly.

She nodded, pointing to the door that would lead him there, and he excitedly took off running.

"Oh, crap. Lloyd left me three messages during the show," Robyn said, staring at her cell phone. She walked out of the auditorium and into the school hallway to return the call.

Kahlila felt a soft tap on her shoulder and turned around to see Keith standing in front of her, so close that she had to look up to see his face. He looked just as serious as he did when he was watching his sister perform, his clenched jaw not even budging into a smile.

"Thank you so much, Kahli. For everything." His voice was low and deep, and she had to get on her toes to hear what he was saying. The last time she had been this close to his lips, she had drunkenly kissed him. Now, drunk from the success of the evening, she felt the same urge.

A scream of delight pierced through the auditorium, and suddenly a mob of people congregated near the last row of seats. Flashbulbs were illuminating every few seconds, and the buzz of the crowd increased with each passing moment. Kahlila quickly ran to the source of all the fuss, thinking that perhaps Bree had come in through the back door, and people were that excited to compliment her on her performance.

Her heart stopped as she reached the center of the chaos and saw Darius walking toward her with a bouquet of flowers in his hand.

"Bravo," he whispered in her ear, handing her the wildflowers as hundreds of pairs of eyes looked on.

"Did you see the whole show?" was all she could think to ask.

"I did. Snuck into the back once the lights went down," he said proudly.

Sneaked. She fought the temptation to correct him. "Looks like you didn't do as good of a job blending in once the show was over, huh?"

"Guess not," he laughed. "So, where's Bree? I wanna meet this girl."

Kahlila quickly glanced behind her to see if Keith was still visible, but she'd lost him in the crowd. Though she knew that it would complete Bree's night to meet Darius, she felt a pit in her stomach at the thought of introducing them in front of Keith. "Um, let's go to my classroom upstairs and I'll call her on the cell."

He followed her lead, stopping to take pictures and sign autographs. *This is exactly why I didn't ask him to come. He's taking the attention away from the people who really deserve it.* Just as quickly as she felt the annoyance at the fanfare, she felt remorseful. Just two weeks ago, she'd told his mother that she liked him because he was outgoing and kind. Here he was, showing those two qualities, and she was judging him for them.

They finally freed themselves from the throng of people, and headed up the stairs to Room 227. Kahlila unlocked the door with a key from her purse, and walked inside to flip on the light. Before she could, Darius grabbed her by the waist and kissed her. Though they were alone in a pitch-black room, she couldn't completely give herself to the moment, stiffening after a few seconds. She pulled away, flipping on the light. "It just feels weird . . . in school," she explained.

"I understand," he said, eagerly walking around the classroom and looking at the photos and student work she had posted on bulletin boards.

"So this is your magic kingdom. The place I've been hearing so much about," he teased, rejoining her at the door.

"This is it." She finally allowed herself to smile, realizing how long she'd waited for Darius to come to Boston and see her life. Here it was, all happening completely by surprise.

"Baby, you don't know how much it means to me that you're leaving this behind so we can be together."

Kahlila's smile stayed frozen on her face as she remembered that she had no excuse not to tell Mr. Howard that she was leaving. The play was over, and she was supposed to start her graduate program in a few weeks. She had to tell him tomorrow.

Darius took her hand, holding it between his two clasped palms. "Seven, seven, oh, seven. Remember that date, Kahli. You and me on the tour bus, cruising the highway, making good music together the way we did last summer. I'll be in Europe touring starting in January, so you can give your full focus to Pierce during your last semester in Boston. The album drops in March, so I'll be doing crazy promo during the spring while you finish out this school year, and then we can finally be together twenty-four-seven."

Kahlila was hearing his words, but her mind was still inside the auditorium. Appearing in front of her eyes were her amazing Girl Talk members, their proud parents, and her supportive colleagues. When the packed house burst into thunderous applause, Kahlila could not remember a time when she'd been happier: not at the Video Music Awards, not on the beach in Miami, not even sitting at Darius's piano. She wanted to explain the feeling to him, how proud she was of the community she'd created, but she didn't know where to begin. *Thinkin' won't do me a bit of good tonight. I need to be loved.* And as she circled her arms around Darius's waist for a hug, she tried to block out everything else, but the sound of feet running up the steps became more distinct. She thought she heard Bree's voice among the excited teenagers.

"Ms. Bradford! Ms. Bradford!" It sounded as if students were calling her name from every direction while the footsteps got closer.

It was impossible to ignore.

Chapter 43

He has to make me feel like a star.

On a sparkling afternoon in July, Kahlila watched the dotted lines on the highway blend into each other as the bright sun and light wind crept through the cracked windows. She looked at the smiling face of the man sitting next to her and every care that she had flew outside, into the summer breeze.

She couldn't believe that she had ever defined her life as boring. An existence where she got to live her passion every day could never just be average. She'd fooled herself into thinking that people in glossy magazines were somehow luckier than she was. In actuality, she and Darius were doing the exact same thing with their lives: engaging with interesting people every day, sharing their thoughts with an audience, doing what they were best at. Meanwhile, she had been searching to become something she wasn't.

"You good?" A firm hand squeezed her leg.

"Better than good."

As the wheels sailed along the smoothly paved freeway, she reflected on all of the changes that the last seven months had brought. The hours after the school play in December set off a series of events that completely altered Kahlila's course. She had been hugging Darius in her classroom when Bree and her Girl Talk pals burst into the room. There was more shrieking and squealing than Kahlila was able to take, so she left the room to locate Madeline, who had her digital camera. On her way down the hall, she jogged directly into Keith.

"Looks like you got some unexpected company tonight," he said with a smirk, steadying her with his hands on her arms.

"Yeah," was all she could think to respond.

"I'm glad he's getting an opportunity to see you do you. If that makes sense." Keith avoided her eyes as he spoke.

"It does."

"Listen, tell Bree that me and Stanley will be in the car, okay?" He walked past her before she could even answer, but shouted a quick "Stanley and I!" over his shoulder.

Kahlila smiled at his grammatical correction. She couldn't even remember if she had ever told him about her pronoun pet peeves. But she and Keith had engaged in so many conversations over the course of the school year thus far, she probably shared more things than she had intended.

That night, as Darius slept beside her in her tiny South End brownstone apartment for the first time, she couldn't stop tossing and turning. While she should have been replaying the moment when Darius had appeared out of nowhere with a bouquet of flowers, she couldn't erase the look of disappointment that she swore she saw in Keith's eyes during their encounter in the hallway.

She crept out of bed and into the bathroom, taking

her cordless phone with her and locking the door. Debating which friend to call, she finally decided on Robyn. She needed the toughest love and the most straightforward advice that she could get.

"Hello." Robyn's voice was raspy and annoyed.

"I woke you up?" Kahlila asked guiltily.

"It's three in the morning. I'm due at work in two hours. What the hell do you want?"

Kahlila tried to speak as quickly as possible, keeping her voice low so as not to wake her sleeping boyfriend. "Darius showed up to the play after you left. And I should have been super happy, I know, because it was so sweet of him to do. But it was like everybody else at Pierce was more excited to see him than I was. And I don't know why."

"I know why," Robyn uttered through a yawn. "You like Bree's brother."

"What?"

"Kahli, you were staring at him almost as much as you were watching the damn play. And frankly, I don't blame you. He's gorgeous, and kind, and you two just click. I saw it the first time we met him all those months ago."

"But Darius is great too," Kahlila whined in a whisper. "If you look at The List, he actually has—"

"You will not bring up that freakin' list nonsense at three o'clock in the morning," Robyn seethed. "Here's what you need to do with that list. Narrow it down."

"I can do that. To how many?" Kahlila asked eagerly.

"To one thing."

"One thing!" Kahlila repeated.

"Write down what it is you want in a single sentence. When you can do that, the answer should be easy. I'm hanging up on you now." Sure enough, the phone went dead.

Kahlila tiptoed to her living room, sat at her desk, and turned on her laptop. For the first time in six months, she opened the Word document that contained The List. Three hundred sixty-five items. One for each day of the year. One for each date disappointment (and sometimes two, three, or four). One for each fantasy that she barely believed would ever come true. Now here she was, with two amazing men in her life, having to decide what it was that was really important to her. She became dizzy as she scanned the pages. Overwhelmed, she shut down the computer and grabbed a piece of paper and a pen.

She sat in the dark for what felt like hours, reliving the special moments spent with Darius. What occurred to her after a deluge of memories was that Darius always had a costar: the Hamptons, Los Angeles, Miami, Detroit, Martha's Vineyard, an exclusive nightclub, the Video Music Awards, the studio, the piano. She couldn't deny that he was one of the most wonderful people she'd ever met. But she also couldn't give herself more credit than she deserved. Just as Jason had told her at the beginning, she was drawn in by the novelty of it all just as much as she was captivated by the man himself.

Slowly, her pen scrawled a sentence across the blank white paper. *While he is making the most of who he is, he has to let me do the same; we can't shortchange ourselves by being together.* She read over her words, grateful that she knew the rules of semicolons and was therefore able to make her sentence longer.

The man dozing in her bed was smart, thoughtful, and ambitious. But so was she. Their lifestyles made it impossible for either of them to be fully committed to their goals while being a couple. Even more significantly, Kahlila wasn't in love with Darius. She was in love with the idea of being with him. And to leave her hometown, her school, her kids—it required more than she was willing to give.

When Darius woke up several hours later, Kahlila was

already dressed and in the kitchen, sipping coffee from her favorite mug.

"Morning, baby," he mumbled groggily, joining her at the breakfast bar. "Coffee smells good."

"I think I put too many coffee grounds in it," Kahlila said, frowning at the dark brown liquid swirling in her cup. *Black and strong.* Even as she prepared herself to engage in a serious conversation with Darius, she couldn't get Keith out of her mind.

"I'll pass, then. Got any cereal?" Before she could answer, Darius was opening and closing her cabinets.

Kahlila decided that it was as good a time as any to say what was on her mind. Taking one last swig of her bitter coffee, she cleared her throat and listened to the words come from her mouth. "I decided that I'm not moving to New York."

Darius's hand froze on the box of Cinnamon Life. "You're not moving this summer?" he asked slowly. "Or you're not moving . . . ever?"

She sighed, rising from her seat to place the mug in the sink. Reluctantly, she met his eyes. "My life is here, Darius."

He shook his head quickly from side to side, as if he were attempting to shake out the confusion. "I don't understand. When did you come to this conclusion?"

Leaning against her counter for support, she braced herself to be as straightforward as possible. "Leaving Boston wasn't something I ever wanted to do. Well, actually, I guess I did want to leave when I arrived in New York for the summer. And then I met you, and it was so wonderful that there was nothing I wanted more than to extend that July and August to last forever." She watched Darius's face soften with her words, and she realized she needed to get to the tough part. "But then I came back here, and my kids were great, and I got offered the A.P. job, and I started to feel really . . . settled. The summer was amazing. Intense. Beyond my wildest dreams. I wouldn't trade it for anything. But it was a season, you know?"

"Baby, a season can turn into a lifetime," he insisted, grasping both of her hands in his.

"Not if we already filled our roles. I was the support you needed as you transitioned musically. And you—you reminded me that there are still kind, decent men out there." She squeezed his hand appreciatively, but he withdrew from her grip.

"Hold up. Are you breaking up with me?" He tilted her face toward him, as her gaze had drifted to the floor.

"I'm sorry," she almost whispered, unable to look him in the eye.

"Kahli, you don't have to do this. It's not an absolute choice: New York or nothing. We can figure something out." When she failed to respond, he finally began to come to a full understanding. "Oh, I get it. You don't *want* to work something out." His tone of voice carried surprise, hurt, and anger all at once. "What the hell? Have we been in the same relationship for the past four months? I've never been so happy as I am when I'm with you."

"Because what we are doing isn't real! We are each other's escape from our everyday lives. We guest star in the other person's existence." She wanted him to see it her way. His desire to keep her in his life made ending things so much harder.

They sat back on their stools and kept talking for another hour. Kahlila explained that at the end of the day, the partner who would make her happy would be the one who could support her in the life she already had. "And you deserve the same," she insisted.

Though Darius was despondent, he had to admit that he really didn't know Kahlila as well as he thought he did. They shared many unforgettable experiences, but the purposes they'd served for one another had run their course. Eventually, there was nothing left for Kahlila to do but drive him to the airport.

Madeline was the first person to call after Darius left Boston. At the news of their breakup, she went into borderline hysterics. "Kahlila! What were you thinking? Darius was perfect! How could you become single again just as I had my first successful match-dot-com date?"

Kahlila shook her head at her friend's overdramatization, but she couldn't help but feel a little of the anxiety that Madeline was projecting. *Did I just make a huge mistake?*

She instinctually scrolled her cell phone for Keith's number and dialed. It just made sense to call him, as she'd been going to him for months with a range of issues: fear of moving out of the classroom into administration, worry that Girl Talk wasn't the change agent that she wanted it to be for her female students, frustration that she and Darius couldn't seem to connect the way that they had in the summertime.

When she told him that she and Darius had ended their romance, Keith was surprisingly neutral. He listened to Kahlila's thought process in making her decision, and refrained from giving his opinion. What he did, however, was tell her about his relationship with Traci for the first time. He talked about their growing apart, and his realizing that they had different priorities in life. It was the first time he'd shared something that personal with her, and over their next several conversations, he began to open up even more, recalling stories about his parents and conveying his fears about taking care of Bree on his own. Their conversations had a depth that Kahlila's interactions with Darius never did.

Still, it took four months before Kahlila and Keith moved from their status of just being friends. She was scared that since he'd never actually said outright that he was interested in her, it all might be in her head and she could be brutally rejected. He was worried that since she just got out of a relationship and was busy with her master's program, she might not want to start anything new. Finally, when they went to dinner one evening with Bree in April to celebrate her acceptance to the University of Southern California, they got completely called out on their "secret" interest in one another. "Keith, when are you going to tell Ms. Bradford how you feel about her? This mess is getting ridiculous!"

That night, Keith dropped Bree at their house before driving Kahlila back to her place. "Do we want to be this obvious?" Kahlila asked apprehensively.

"Um, what *doesn't* Bree already know?" Keith countered, amused by Kahlila's concern for discretion.

They pulled into an empty space on her quiet residential street, turning to face one another once the car was in park. In an instant they were tangled together, kissing and laughing as their legs hit the gearshift and the horn honked accidentally. "We're no better than Bree and Stanley!" Kahlila chuckled.

"Shit, if Stanley is doing any worse than this with my sister . . . he's in serious trouble."

Kahlila rolled her eyes in fake exasperation and hopped out of the car, kissing him goodbye through the window as if she'd done it a million times before. While Darius felt like someone plucked out of a life that didn't belong to her, Keith felt like he'd always been there, a corner piece in her life's puzzle that she wasn't complete without.

There was pleasant chatter coming from the backseat of the SUV. Everyone was in a great mood. They were about to reach their next stop, Las Vegas, and the R&B station on satellite radio had kept them fully entertained for the past few hours. Now the sequence of songs stopped, and the smooth, baritone voice of the radio host began to speak. "Before we play our number-one song on the countdown, let's hear an interview we taped yesterday with the multiplatinum artist."

A younger, more hyped deejay took over the airwaves. "Yo, we got the man with the number-one album in the country up in the building. Darius Wilson!"

The voices behind Kahlila cracked up laughing.

"D, man, congratulations. Sophomore album is doing big things!" the deejay pressed on, unaware of the reaction he was causing on a West Coast freeway.

"Thank you. I'm excited about the new music." Darius sounded almost bored compared to his interviewer's level of animation.

"Let's talk about the title of the album. *Twenty Somethings.*"

"Yeah. It has a couple meanings. First off, there are twenty songs on the CD, as you know."

"That's a lot of tracks."

"Figured I'd give folks their money's worth. The other piece of it is just the stage of life I'm in right now. You know, twenty-something years old . . . barely." He laughed, and the sound of his familiar chuckle made Kahlila smile. "Trying to leave the fun and games behind and get serious. Focus on the next stage."

"So since you brought up getting serious . . . I've been hearing rumors about you getting serious with a certain lady."

"Let's not get into that today," Darius said lightheartedly.

"You know listeners want to get up in your biz, Darius. And it's your fault for putting your personal life out there at the VMAs last year. Clearly it's fair game to talk about. Lemme just tell you what I heard. I heard that when you were touring in Europe a couple months back, you hooked up with a chick in your band."

Kahlila felt her throat tighten. She wanted to look over to her left, but couldn't bring herself to do it.

"Is that what you heard?" Darius asked in a monotone.

"Yup. And not just any chick either. Nicole McKie, one of the best horn players of our time."

Darius took a moment to compose the response in his head before speaking. "Nicole is definitely an amazing saxophonist. She's also a terrific composer. You'll hear some stuff we worked on when the live album drops in a few months."

"So, how exactly did you convince her to leave her jazz band to go on tour with you?"

"I thought we were talking about the album!"

The hand that had been resting on Kahlila's leg now moved to turn down the volume of the radio all the way. "Are you jealous?"

"Why would I be?" She finally turned her body around so she could face him, his stern jawline clenched as he drove his SUV down the freeway. The muscles in Keith's forearm seemed more pronounced than usual, a result of his gripping the steering wheel harder than he needed to.

"I wanna hear the rest of the interview!" Bree protested from the backseat. "Ms. Bradford, you may not like him like that anymore, but I do. Sorry, Stanley," she said to her boyfriend, who was half sleeping next to her. It had been a fun-filled cross-country road trip, with Kahlila and Keith taking turns at the wheel on a two-week-long journey to drop the kids in California for prefreshman orientation. Stanley's mom had five younger children to take care of, and she was thrilled when Keith offered to transport her son to school. At times, the close confines of the car created a certain level of bickering, but they were each beginning to feel a degree of sadness, knowing that their drive would be finished in a matter of days.

"Bree, I have to say now that you've graduated, please stop calling me Ms. Bradford. It's kind of weird," Kahlila said, wrinkling her forehead.

"Fine, *Kahli*," Bree said pointedly. "Now can someone turn up the volume?"

Keith grudgingly returned the sound to an audible level, to Bree's satisfaction and Kahlila's anxiousness.

"So set up this song for us, number one on the charts this week," the deejay was saying.

"Okay, this track is one of the last ones I wrote for this project. It's about what love is supposed to feel like when you're with the right person. I like this ballad even more than "Make My Life Real," which was the first number one on the album."

"So check it out, we're gonna play it right now with no more delay. Here is 'More Than Ordinary.'"

The four of them grew silent as the guitar strummed, giving way to a simple melodic line. Darius's voice floated through the quiet.

My ordinary life becomes an extraordinary life when I remember that you are the center of my life ./ And I thank you for making me so much more than ordinary . . .

"The man does write a good song," Keith said with a begrudging smile, winking at Kahlila.

Bree's singsong voice piped up from the backseat. "Told you."

Check Out These Other
Dafina Novels

Sister Got Game
0-7582-0856-1

by Leslie Esdaile
$6.99US/**$9.99**CAN

Say Yes
0-7582-0853-7

by Donna Hill
$6.99US/**$9.99**CAN

In My Dreams
0-7582-0868-5

by Monica Jackson
$6.99US/**$9.99**CAN

True Lies
0-7582-0027-7

by Margaret Johnson-Hodge
$6.99US/**$9.99**CAN

Testimony
0-7582-0637-2

by Felicia Mason
$6.99US/**$9.99**CAN

Emotions
0-7582-0636-4

by Timmothy McCann
$6.99US/**$9.99**CAN

The Upper Room
0-7582-0889-8

by Mary Monroe
$6.99US/**$9.99**CAN

Got A Man
0-7582-0242-3

by Daaimah S. Poole
$6.99US/**$8.99**CAN

Available Wherever Books Are Sold!

Check out our website at www.kensingtonbooks.com.

Look For These Other
Dafina Novels

If I Could
0-7582-0131-1

by Donna Hill
$6.99US/$9.99CAN

Thunderland
0-7582-0247-4

by Brandon Massey
$6.99US/$9.99CAN

June In Winter
0-7582-0375-6

by Pat Phillips
$6.99US/$9.99CAN

Yo Yo Love
0-7582-0239-3

by Daaimah S. Poole
$6.99US/$9.99CAN

When Twilight Comes
0-7582-0033-1

by Gwynne Forster
$6.99US/$9.99CAN

It's A Thin Line
0-7582-0354-3

by Kimberla Lawson Roby
$6.99US/$9.99CAN

Perfect Timing
0-7582-0029-3

by Brenda Jackson
$6.99US/$9.99CAN

Never Again Once More
0-7582-0021-8

by Mary B. Morrison
$6.99US/$8.99CAN

Available Wherever Books Are Sold!

Check out our website at www.kensingtonbooks.com.

More of the Hottest
African-American Fiction from
Dafina Books